THE HEARING

Books by James Mills

NONFICTION

The Underground Empire

On the Edge

The Prosecutor

FICTION

The Hearing

Haywire

The Power

The Truth About Peter Harley

The Seventh Power

One Just Man

Report to the Commissioner

The Panic in Needle Park

JAMES MILLS

THE HEARING

WARNER BOOKS

A Time Warner Company

This book is a work of fiction. Names, characters, places, and incidents are either the product of the author's imagination or are used fictitiously, and any resemblance to actual persons, living or dead, events, or locales is entirely coincidental.

Warner Books, Inc., 1271 Avenue of the Americas, New York, NY 10020

Visit our Web site at http://warnerbooks.com

A Time Warner Company

Printed in the United States of America

First Printing: July 1998

10 9 8 7 6 5 4 3 2 1

Library of Congress Cataloging-in-Publication Data

Mills, James
The hearing / James Mills.
p. cm.
ISBN 0-446-51958-8
I. Title.
PS3563.I423H4 1998
813'.54—dc21 97-32284
CIP

To Jill

THE HEARING

1

Gus Parham felt as if he'd been pushed off a cliff. The air pressure changed, and along with it his orientation, perspective, priorities. Everything hurtled by, robbing him of breath and reason. He'd be dead in an instant.

"So what that means, Judge Parham, is she's alive. You want to meet her or not? If you want to meet her, there are certain conditions."

"Where? Where is she?"

"Certain conditions, Judge Parham."

"May I see it again?"

"Certainly."

So they watched the video again. How beautiful she

was. Eleven years old, short black hair, slender, smiling, going somewhere and happy about it. He had never seen anyone walk like that. Head, shoulders, hips, legs—everything was in that walk, as if she were headed for a brick wall and knew, just *knew*, she could go right through it.

Gus said, "What do you want?"

"Withdraw."

"But . . . How will . . ." Mumbling, babbling. He was still falling.

"I can't hear you, Judge."

"I'm sorry. I just—"

The man punched the eject button and removed the cassette.

Gus said, "I'll have to talk to my wife."

"Show her this?" He held out the cassette.

Gus took it.

The man opened his attaché case and handed Gus a manila envelope. "This too."

Gus took the envelope.

The man said, "You've got three days. Close of business Monday, we have to know."

"And if I say no?"

"Alternatives. You won't like them."

An hour later Gus sat with his wife in the kitchen of their rented house in Vienna, Virginia. It was smaller than the kitchen in their home in Montgomery. The walls were yellow and the table was round and small. They'd moved here three weeks ago when he'd been nominated for a seat on the Supreme Court. The confirmation hearing was scheduled to begin in a week. And now this. What would this do to

Michelle? Their marriage was perfect, they had never stopped loving each other.

She looked at him, worried. She could see it in his face.

"Michelle . . ."

"Gus, what is it? You look like someone died."

Alternatives. Television, newspapers, exposure, humiliation.

He put the cassette on the table, reached across for both her hands, and said, "Michelle, I love you. I will always love you. No matter what."

"What is it, Gus?" Her eyes fixed on the video. "What is that?"

Thirteen years ago, before they were married, she had said she was ending the pregnancy. He had believed her, for all those years. She had let him believe the lie—to save his feelings, out of love for him and their marriage, but a lie nevertheless. He understood, he loved her for taking all the pain on herself, but how would she react? He wasn't sure.

He stood. "Let's go in the living room."

They sat on the sofa, still holding hands. Her face was dark, sensing trouble.

"I'm afraid, Michelle, that when I say what I have to say there may not be a chance to tell you again how much I really love you."

She was staring into his eyes, scared to death.

"Tell me, Gus."

He said, "Honey, I know you didn't end the pregnancy."

Her fingers tightened around his hand, but her eyes did not leave his face. "Who . . . How do you know?"

"I'll tell you in a minute. There's something else."

Her eyes went to the video in his other hand. "What is it?"

He got up, put the video in the VCR, and came back and sat next to her with the remote in his hand.

She hugged herself and shivered.

Gus said, "Are you all right?"

"I don't feel well. I'm freezing."

"Do you want me to get you something?"

She closed her eyes and shook her head. "Let me see it."

He pressed the button.

She tilted her head forward, looking up, tentatively. The girl came on the screen, walking. Michelle didn't move. Her face didn't change. Short black hair, slender, smiling, determined. When the screen went blank and it was over, she said, "She's very pretty."

Her face was frozen. Then she smiled, a thin, false smile he had never before seen on her face. She let out a small mirthless laugh. She laughed again. She put her head on her knees and laughed and laughed and laughed. There was more pain in the laughter than there would have been in sobs. Gus touched her arm. She jumped from the sofa and ran back into the kitchen. She cleared the dishes from the table, dumped them noisily into the sink, turned on the water, and began scrubbing blindly.

He didn't know what to say, what to do.

Her hands full of soap and plates, she put her head back, took a deep breath, and released an almost inaudible shriek of pain.

Gus grabbed her and she collapsed against him, gasping for breath, sobbing. He carried her to the bedroom, laid her on the bed.

"Michelle, it's all right."

She turned onto her stomach, buried her face in the blanket, and cried like a child. Gus dropped to his knees beside the bed, laid his arm across her shoulders, squeezed her, and pressed his cheek to her hair.

Ten minutes later her breathing steadied. Thinking she had fallen asleep, Gus rose silently and went to a chair by the bed.

Her face still buried in the blanket, she said, "Where is she?"

"I don't know where she is."

She turned to face him.

"Who knows where she is?"

"The attorney who gave me the video."

"Who's he?"

"Someone who doesn't want me confirmed, doesn't want me on the Court. He works with the Freedom Federation."

"So if you don't withdraw they won't tell us where she is."

"They'll do worse than that, Michelle."

2

Gus's grandfather had made all the money, and his father took care of it. Gus thought that not having to make any himself had robbed his father of the joy of struggle and conquest, of his manhood. All he had to do was fight off the vultures, and spend, spend, spend—more money than anyone in the family could ever need for anything they could ever want. They spent wildly but quietly, observed only by others doing the same. Don't let the common people see beyond the iron gates, tinted car windows, protective expressions of grace and breeding.

Then Gus went to Harvard. Wow! Deep end of the pool, never learned to swim. Who *were* these people?

Where had they *come* from? Across the hall, a Polish boy with a twisted, half-paralyzed face who picked his nose. Upstairs, an eighty-five-pound, pop-eyed anorexic girl who played the trombone, knew the Koran by heart, and beat everyone at poker. He was outside the gates, on the other side of the tinted glass, and the sights were shattering. Where had these people *been* all his life? He loved them.

The one he loved most was called Michelle Bart. He met her his senior year. She was a freshman, eighteen, just arrived, beautiful inside and out. What would his mother say of a girl named Michelle? "Is that—is that *French*, dear?" And what could anyone make of Bart? Even more exotic, she was from Alabama. She was dark and rare. Sultry didn't begin to describe it. Her words came out rich, warm, and damp. Just listening to her made him sweat. If she breathed on something, it began to grow. She breathed on him.

He graduated, moved over to the law school. His destiny appeared to be money management. His father couldn't go on forever, and Gus had no brothers or sisters to look after the family's wealth. He and Michelle kept dating, fell in love. It was months before she went to bed with him. They were on a skiing weekend in Stowe. After dinner, at the door of her hotel room, the resistance crumbled. Nine weeks later, when she told him she was pregnant, he was stunned.

"How could you be pregnant?"

"You *know* how I got pregnant, Gus."

"I mean, you take the pill."

"Not till we got back from Stowe."

"Why not?"

"I'd never taken it. I wasn't having sex."

"You were—"

"A virgin."

Could you make love with a virgin and not know it?

"Why didn't you tell me?"

"I didn't want you to change your mind. I'd decided."

"Well, when you decided, you should have decided to take the pill."

"Don't be angry."

"I'm not angry, I'm just—what are you going to do?"

"We can get married and have the baby, or we can not get married and I'll have the baby by myself."

"Or you can—"

"I won't do that, Gus."

That night he went for a walk. He had solid ideas of how he was going to get married and under what circumstances. He didn't want the kind of marriage his parents had, the kind of family it had produced. As long as he could remember, when the bickering and battles, the accusations and counteraccusations became unbearable ("All you ever had was money!" "All you ever *wanted* was money!"), he comforted himself with the knowledge that this was only half his life, the half he'd been born into, had no control over. The next half—his own marriage, his own family—was his to pick. He'd pick his wife carefully, take all the time it took, and he'd be *sure*. He wouldn't spend the second half of his life the way he'd spent the first.

And now. Pressure. Coercion. Blackmail. Michelle wasn't blackmailing him, but something was. Circumstances. Violation of a lifetime promise. The wrong decision, and he'd spend the rest of his life regretting it.

The next day he said, "Michelle, I've made a decision. I—"

"Don't say it, Gus. I've changed my mind."

"What do you mean?"

"If you want to—if you don't want me to have the baby, I won't."

Release.

They went to a doctor and a counselor. Michelle made it clear she wanted to have the baby, but she wouldn't force him. She didn't want a forced marriage, even if he loved her. In the end, she agreed to terminate the pregnancy. "But not around here. I couldn't do it here. I'm going home."

The next day, when he called her, her roommate said she'd packed up and left. She hadn't even said goodbye. She didn't want his help.

3

Michelle saw her coming, Auntie Dana. She wasn't Michelle's aunt, she wasn't anyone's aunt, everyone just called her Auntie Dana. She was in her eighties, bald, wore a white wig, never married, a lipsticked mouth pouring forth honied venom and sweet slander. Wedding receptions like this were her natural habitat. Half of Montgomery was here. She'd have heard of the pregnancy, come laden with stones to cast.

"Michelle, you're looking perfectly radiant. How are you, my dear?"

"Pregnant, thanks. How are you?"

"I beg your pardon?"

As if she didn't know.

"I said, 'Pregnant, thanks. How are you?' "

"My goodness, I didn't even know you'd got married."

"I didn't get married. I just got pregnant."

"Is your husband here?"

"I said I'm not married, Auntie Dana. I'm just pregnant."

"But you can't be pregnant without a husband."

"I wasn't aware of that."

"Does your mother know?"

Michelle saw her mother bearing down, glaring at Michelle, guessing the worst.

"Ask her."

Skidding to a stop, her mother said, "Auntie Dana, it's really nice to see you."

"Michelle's pregnant."

"Yes, Mom, I'd meant to tell you."

"Stop it, Michelle. Excuse her, Auntie Dana. I think she's trying to be funny."

"Then she's not pregnant?"

"Oh, yes, she is pregnant. And we're all just delighted."

"Is her husband here?"

"She doesn't have a husband. The father is a very nice young man."

"Oh, I'm sure he is. Well, yes, of course he is."

Michelle left them. A waiter stopped with a tray of champagne. Michelle smiled at him and shook her head.

She'd arrived home from Cambridge a week earlier, on a Saturday, and the next day after church, sitting around the living room with the family before lunch, she'd said, "There's something I have to tell everyone."

Weeks ago she'd told them about Gus, but they'd never met him.

Nolan, her older brother, looked up from the sports section. "Getting married?"

It was supposed to be funny, but no one smiled.

She said, "This is really hard. This is the—" Her voice broke. Her mother nudged Nolan over and sat beside Michelle on the sofa. Michelle turned her face to her mother's shoulder and began to cry.

Nolan said, "What's happening?"

Her father said, "Be quiet, Nolan."

Michelle heard the men get up and knew they'd gone to the porch.

"I'm pregnant, Mom."

Her mother tightened the hug but didn't speak.

Michelle raised her head and said, "I really love him, Mom."

"I thought you did."

"But I don't want to marry him."

"Does he want to marry you?"

"I think he does—I know he loves me—but he doesn't want to be forced. I don't want to marry him like that, because he thinks he has to. I want him to marry me because he just can't *not* marry me. Do you know what I mean?"

"Yes, I do, honey."

Michelle wiped the tears.

"I've thought about it a lot, and I've prayed about it, and I know one thing for sure—I don't want to hide that I'm pregnant, lie about it, pretend that I'm not. I don't care who knows."

"I think you're right. What do you want to do?"

"I'm only twenty. Barely. Two months ago I was a teenager." She hesitated, her eyes watering. "I think I should have it adopted."

She didn't tell her mother that she'd told Gus she was ending the pregnancy.

"But I don't want to have it adopted here. I don't want to spend the next ten years, however many years, looking at every child I see in Montgomery and wondering if it's mine. I don't want that for you and Dad, either."

"Do you think you should call Gus, talk to him about it?"

"He'd think I was pressuring him—and maybe I would be. I don't want to do that. This is my decision, Mom."

A pastor at their church asked friends at a Montgomery adoption agency, who recommended an agency in Milwaukee. Six weeks before the baby's due date Michelle moved there with her mother. A month later she took out a sheet of notepaper on which she had written Gus's phone number, laid it on the table by the phone in the hotel, and picked up the receiver. She hesitated, thought about it. What would she say? "Are you still sure you don't want to marry me and have the baby?" Make him say no all over again? Torture them both? Anything she said, even the fact that she'd called, would be misunderstood. He'd be sure to think she was pushing him. He wasn't going to change his mind. It would be a painful disaster. With tears in her eyes, she set the phone down and put the paper back into the pocket in her purse.

Two days later, the birth was artificially induced. Michelle, under a general anesthetic, never experienced labor, never saw the baby, never heard it cry, never had any direct awareness of its presence outside her body.

When she awoke in the recovery room she knew she had lost more than her child, that she was less alive than she had been before the birth. The baby had been hers, it was gone, and something of herself had gone with it. Something had been amputated, and she would never have it back.

Three days later Michelle returned to Montgomery. She awoke the first morning back and began to cry. At six that evening, she'd been in bed all day, crying and talking to her mother about the baby.

"How do you think she is?"

Her mother said, "She's fine, Michelle. Of course she's fine."

"They said she was healthy. But they didn't say anything about the parents."

"She's with people who want her very much and will love her dearly."

"They make mistakes, though, sometimes, those agencies."

"No, honey. They didn't make a mistake. That little girl is with loving parents."

4

The wheels of the twin-prop Cessna touched the asphalt, and Gus looked out at the mountains and plains of northern Colombia, struggling, as he had every day since Michelle left Cambridge, to keep his mind off what might be happening to her. He was tagging along with his father on a business trip, hoping it would give the two of them time to talk to each other. They had never been close, often quarreled, and with his father approaching seventy, Gus wanted to do what he could to heal their relationship before it was too late. He didn't want to spend the rest of his life asking, Why didn't I do more to get close to my father? Why didn't

I ever tell him I loved him? Because he did love him. Sometimes he wasn't sure why, but he loved him.

As Gus turned his head to look toward the front of the passenger cabin, he heard a sharp *Pop!*, saw a window burst inward and the back of an empty seat tilt violently sideways, its headrest exploding in shredded fabric.

His father's soft, almost inaudible voice said, "Someone's firing at the plane."

The plane stopped.

A black BMW screeched to a halt out of sight beneath the left wing. In a moment, the Cessna's door opened and two soldiers entered behind a tall, slender man in his seventies wearing a beige suit and wide smile.

The man said, "Please do not be alarmed. I am afraid we have a party of hunters in the woods, where it is quite forbidden. They are after the wild boar. The security forces are seeing to them now. Shall we disembark?"

The elderly man stepped up the aisle to Gus's father.

"It is so good to see you, Stephen. I apologize for this inconvenience."

His words seemed unnaturally refined, and were it not for the other man's Latin coloring, he and Gus's father might have been brothers. His father's own regal aspect had intimidated Gus since early childhood. His speech had always been as controlled and secure as a bank vault, and his countenance, smiling or angry, was as controlled as the voice. When Gus was a child he had made innocent attempts to move in behind the face and the voice, but had never even come close. His mother, a compulsive supporter of crusades, causes, and charities, identified herself in Gus's young mind as a glitteringly dressed specter always on the move, arriving and departing, fleetingly applying pecks to the cheek.

"It's all right," Gus's father said to the slender man, looking a little gray. "Nothing to apologize for at all. May I introduce my son? Gus, this is Señor Vicaro-Garza."

Vicaro-Garza, owner of thousands of acres of cattle land as well as vast forests, had flown them to his ranch for the weekend. Gus's father sat on the board of a paper company dependent on Vicaro's timber.

Gus, still recovering from the gunfire, shook hands.

It was midafternoon and the sun was blazing. Señor Vicaro led Gus and his father up wooden steps to the top of a platform where fifty guests sat on folding wooden chairs overlooking a small bullring. Vicaro raised fighting bulls, selling them to the Mexican bullrings and hoping eventually to export them to Spain as well. Because bulls were said to inherit their physique from the father and their courage from the mother, Vicaro periodically held *tientas* at his ranch to test the courage of the female calves. Those that passed were used for breeding. The others were butchered.

Across from the platform, soldiers with automatic rifles perched on the top of the ring's wooden wall. In the BMW racing across the tarmac from the plane, an American congressman who had boarded the plane with them in Bogotá had told Gus that the gunshots shattering the plane's window had no doubt come from rebel guerrillas in the countryside around Vicaro's ranch. Vicaro had recently shifted financial support from their leader to a coca-trafficking member of the Colombian senate. The congressman, a young man in spectacles, explained that his "committee work" in Washington involved fact-finding trips to Latin America. "When it comes to what's happening in the region,

Vicaro's the oracle. Anything he doesn't know, his guests know."

The soldiers on the wall were joined by children crawling precariously along the ledge, risking a ten-foot drop into the ring. One of the children, a bully-faced boy of about fifteen who was too fat to climb to the ledge with the others, leaned against a wooden barricade about two feet in from the ring's wall. He wore a black T-shirt and expensive-looking black leather boots with pointed metal toes. The other children amused themselves by dropping things on his head—paper cups, wads of chewing gum—and he retaliated angrily by snatching at their ankles, which dangled just out of reach.

"Who's the kid?" Gus asked the congressman, who was in the seat beside him.

"Vicaro's son. Ernesto."

"He looks too young."

"Vicaro has children younger than that."

"Where's the mother?"

"Ernesto's? Who knows? The mothers of Vicaro's children are too numerous to mention. Or count. Or remember."

Vicaro waved to a man on horseback who held a metal-tipped lance resting on his right stirrup. The man smiled and waved back. A few seconds later, a wooden door swung open and a calf three feet high, its horns well formed, trotted aggressively into the ring.

The rider maneuvered the horse sideways, lowered the lance, and caught the charging calf between the shoulder blades.

Blood flowed, and the crowd cheered. For once, Gus was glad Michelle wasn't with him. She loved animals, and this would have enraged her.

As the rider backed off, preparing to receive another charge, a wad of paper struck Ernesto on the head. He made a sudden leap, grabbed an ankle, and brought its owner tumbling heavily into the ring. His fists pummeled the smaller boy.

The calf, attracted by the movement, swung toward the boys. Ernesto ducked behind the barricade, intentionally blocking the other boy's way. The calf lowered its horns and charged. As the audience gasped, the boy scrambled to his feet, raced to the gate, and slipped out. Ernesto laughed.

The rider lowered his lance, and the wooden gate swung open. Ernesto waited for the calf, blood flooding down its black flanks, to move past him on its way out of the ring. Then he pulled his leg back and with astonishing aim, strength, and cruelty drove the steel point of his boot hard into the calf's hindquarters beneath the tail.

That evening, at a cocktail party in the ranch's wood-paneled reception hall, Gus stood with a glass of Dom Pérignon, marveling at the odd collection of guests—bankers, generals, actors, cowboys, journalists, senators, and cops.

He watched as Ernesto, carrying a glass-laden silver tray, approached one of the tuxedoed bankers. The banker took a glass, smiled. The cuff on Ernesto's extended hand pulled back to reveal a gold, diamond-ringed Rolex. The white dinner jacket concealed much of his excess weight, and the polite smile covered the brutality displayed only hours ago in the bullring. He continued on his rounds, the obedient son passing drinks, speaking briefly with each of the guests.

Gus marveled. Ernesto seemed transformed in this adult atmosphere of champagne and social chatter. Maybe it was adolescence—one foot in the nursery, the other in the world. Right now the boy appeared so thoroughly at home he might himself have been the host.

"He'll run the whole show by the time he's twenty."

Gus turned to see the congressman. He said, "You think so?"

"He could just about run it now. Don't let the thuggish behavior you saw at the *tienta* fool you. He's every bit as clever as his father. And even nastier, if that's possible. The old man brags about the kid's meanness, encourages it, says he wants a tough son. When he was eight, he played the violin, loved it, good at it, and one night Vicaro grabbed it out of his hands and smashed it to splinters against the bedpost. Pushed an AK-47 at him, helped him hold it, and blew out the wall to the bathroom. True story. Kid hasn't been the same since."

Gus didn't know what to say.

"Watch him. He looks like he's passing champagne, but he's not. He's studying everything, remembering everything. An extremely ambitious, Machiavellian little bastard. He could be president of Colombia by his thirtieth birthday. What a boost that'd be for the family business."

"What is that business, exactly?"

"You name it. Timber, tobacco, airlines, hotels—if it makes money, Vicaro's hand is in it, probably up to the shoulder."

"And cocaine."

It was a breach of etiquette.

"Well . . . I suppose . . . discreet and indirect."

Gus drifted in the tide of guests, thinking of Michelle, worrying about her, longing to be with her. He'd shattered something that could never be repaired. A thousand times he had wanted to call her, to hear her voice. But how could he call her? To say what—that he worried about her, wanted to be with her, that he was sorry? By now it would be weeks or months since she had ended the pregnancy. It was done. He knew she would never forgive him. You can't smash something rare and beautiful and then stand sorrowfully over the fragments wishing them back together.

The next morning Gus and his father flew back to the family home in Connecticut. They had had time together, and Gus felt closer to his father at the end of the trip than he had at the beginning, but there remained a great distance between them that Gus despaired of ever bridging.

A year later Michelle was back in Cambridge, ordering fettucine at a table in Guido's. Gus saw her from the bar and couldn't believe it. All the times he had wanted to call her, talk to her, be with her, the times he had sat alone for hours, thinking about her, grieving over the smashed fragments of their love—and now here she was.

He steadied himself, slipped off the bar stool, and took a slow walk to the men's room, circling past her table, making sure. On the way back he stopped at the table, touched her shoulder, playfully, like it didn't matter. She turned. A microsecond of nothing at all, then an explosion in her eyes. He saw such joy there, his legs went limp.

The next day they had lunch. She'd come to Cambridge to see a friend, "and I guess I hoped maybe I'd run into you." She wasn't returning to Harvard. "I'm through with that." They didn't talk about the pregnancy. Their love was like a living miracle not even that pain could kill. Something had changed, something so big even the universe would never be the same. They knew they were going to spend the rest of their lives together, and the pain that had driven them apart had never happened. They wouldn't even talk about it. How could you talk about it? It had never happened.

They spent the next weekend in Montgomery, so he could meet her family. A red-clay, deep-country road, overhung with Spanish moss. Steam rising from the flanks of riding horses in a paddock. An antique wood-decked pickup truck. A white porch running the length of the house, with ceiling fans and wooden chairs. Her father was huge—crew-cut hair, white socks, a smile warmer than the weather, and a redneck drawl Gus could hardly understand. Two brothers, teenagers, all grins and muscles. Her tiny mother, bony, beautiful, black curly hair, never at rest, never empty-handed. Trays of drinks and food.

Did they know what had happened? They would never have approved. They were so religious. There didn't seem to be any problem Michelle's father didn't expect God to solve. "And does he?" Gus asked. "One way or another. Not always my way, but what right've I got to tell the potter how to make pots? Ain't that right? Is that right?" Had Michelle had the pregnancy ended by herself, never told her family? Their reaction to him gave no clues. Their affection seemed as genuine as it was unreserved. No, they *couldn't* know.

He sat with the family on the porch, his sweat chilling under the fans, drinking cold white wine pressed from grapes that grew on vines by the house. If this wasn't heaven, it was close enough.

The ranch had a hundred head of cattle, six Thoroughbred horses, and two springer spaniels called Touch and Go. Michelle took him for a walk down a wooded hill, past pecan trees, to a pond stocked with blue gill. "What do you think?"

"It's beautiful."

"That's not what I meant."

He looked at her.

She said, "Not just the pond. The whole—everything."

"I think your dad's great. It's all great."

She beamed. "He only wears those socks when he—"

"I love his socks."

They walked another fifty yards past the pond to a swamp with cypress trees.

"My dad shoots turkey in there. My mom marinates it in wine—what you were drinking?—and she makes pies from the pecans. In the spring—"

"It's great, Michelle." Words came to his lips, but he held them back. Then he said, "I wish I'd been born here."

She laughed. "In this hick place?"

"Yeah, in this hick place."

"You live in a palace."

She'd never seen his family's home, but she'd heard.

He said, "It's a very complicated palace."

When Gus graduated from law school, they married, moved into a two-bedroom house on the other side of Montgomery from Michelle's family's ranch, and tried to have a child. After twelve months, they saw a doctor. Gus's sperm count was normal, but an inoperable obstruction in Michelle's Fallopian tubes made pregnancy impossible. The doctor was sympathetic but firm. They would never have a child.

They left the doctor's office and drove home in silence. Gus knew what she was thinking. She'd had her chance. There wouldn't be another. He had never been sadder, had never loved her more. There were no words worth speaking.

Gus gave up the idea of managing his family's money, and eventually talked himself out of the guilt. His father would continue, and when he was too old they'd have to hire an outside professional. Gus wanted a life of law. He wanted to be a judge. His real dream was to sit on the Supreme Court, interpreting the laws of the most powerful nation on earth. He hardly dared to think that that would ever happen, but it focused his ambition.

Gus worked seven months as a Montgomery County public defender, despised it (the clients were sullen, lying, and usually guilty), but made enough of a name for himself to win an assistant's job in the U.S. Attorney's office. Michelle wasn't too sure about the job change. It made her nervous, Gus sending people to jail.

"I don't send them to jail, they send themselves to jail."

"That's not what I mean. What if they decide to, you know, do something?"

"Hurt me?"

"Or us."

"They won't, Michelle."

Anyway, it was better than if he'd been a state prosecutor, dealing with robbers and killers. People who committed federal crimes in Montgomery were mostly check forgers, bank embezzlers. Not the violent people.

5

Gus and Michelle's best friends were Carl and Esther Falco. Carl was Special Agent in Charge of the DEA's Montgomery office, and Gus often handled his cases. One day, when Gus had been in the U.S. Attorney's office about a year, Carl called him at work.

"You gotta see this, Gus."

"What is it?"

"The Gardens." A suburban development north of Montgomery. "Be quick."

"That's not a what, that's a where."

"You'll know when you get here."

"Tell me now. I'm busy."

"Not too busy for this."

He hung up.

Carl and Esther had a son named Paul who was nine and a six-year-old girl called Ali. Gus and Michelle often baby-sat for them, sometimes overnight or through weekends. The two families had dinner at each other's homes about once a week, and sometimes they went to church together, usually at the insistence of Esther.

Carl was from New York, a man of few words, and he had many of the same values as Michelle's father. "Carl has a very simple life," Esther told Michelle with a resigned smile. "All he wants to do is put traffickers in prison, and he works about twenty-five hours a day, eight days a week. I wish he was home more, but at least he's doing something that counts. Anyway, that's what I keep telling myself."

When Gus got to the Gardens he found six DEA agents and about a dozen men from the ABI, the Alabama Bureau of Investigation. Most of them were inside a barn, standing around a horse stall. The barn was stacked with large, half-opened cardboard cartons. Each carton contained twenty-four wrapped packages that looked like loaves of Wonder Bread. But they weren't bread. A false floor had been lifted to expose wooden stairs down to an underground chamber. Carl took Gus's arm. "You're not gonna believe this."

At the bottom of the stairs, six feet underground, Gus stood in an area the size of his bathroom. The walls were cardboard cartons like the ones in the barn. Straight ahead, a floodlit tunnel the agents had made by removing carton after carton reached to the far end of what appeared to be an enormous cavern. Two other tunnels extended to the walls left and right.

"It took us half an hour," Carl said, "to get to the far

walls. If the cartons are packed in here solid, there's one thousand three hundred of them. And if each one holds what the ones upstairs hold, there's over sixty thousand kilos in here."

Sixty thousand kilos of cocaine was worth $1,200,000,000 wholesale—over ten times more than had ever before been seized in the United States. Even Gus had trouble appreciating the implications. This would have to be a major—*the* major—storage and transhipment point for the entire eastern half of the United States.

But you couldn't put cocaine in prison.

"You get any flesh with this, Carl?"

"Come with me."

The agents had three men, each handcuffed in the back of a different DEA car. One of the men was so fat his belly touched the rear of the front seat. The windows were down, and Gus could smell the sweat.

"You read them their rights?"

"They slept through it."

"We know them?"

One of the men looked familiar.

"Only one."

Carl was smiling.

Gus said, "So?"

Carl showed him a Colombian driver's license. The fat guy. "Ernesto Vicaro-Garza."

Gus turned the card over, examined the reverse side, turned it back to the front. He couldn't take his eyes off it. Just a few years after Gus's summer vacation from law school, when he had watched the teenaged Ernesto Vicaro pass champagne at the ranch, Ernesto had appeared in intelligence reports as a rapidly rising figure in the cocaine industry. Only six months ago Gus had read a DEA intelligence report that spent twenty-one pages profiling the young Vicaro. He'd been a member of the Colombian senate, a diplomat, an intelligence officer. The aging father, for years a controlling power in the Latin cocaine industry, had become too enfeebled to prevent his son from seizing power. The young man's reputation for cunning, ambition, and brutality had continued to grow. A fourteen-year-old Mexican girl who lived on his ranch outside Cali, one of twelve teenagers available to him and his guests, had called him "an obese monster."

"When I told you you wouldn't believe it, I didn't just mean the coke."

Gus said, "Why'd he come?"

Carl shrugged, still smiling. "Couldn't stay away? Sixty thousand kilos. Had to have a look. Everything's new. Hasn't been here more than a month."

"How'd you find it?"

"Dumb luck. A vet came for one of the horses, smelled something funny, called a friend at the ABI who called me, and we came over together."

"Pride and greed. Get you every time. The old man'll be ashamed."

"Family breakdown," Carl said. "No respect for parental authority."

"Fills the prisons."

The TV had it that night, the papers in the morning. Biggest drug seizure in the history of the country. And Ernesto Vicaro-Garza was the biggest arrest. He and his father were legends. They controlled a Pan-American holding company that owned, among other things, a multinational corporation of banks, hotels, restaurant chains, shopping malls, soccer teams, health-care facilities, and a so-called trading conglomerate named TransInter, which turned out to have at its center one of the largest cocaine trafficking organizations on earth.

Ernesto Vicaro and his father owned virtually all the cocaine coming out of Colombia, which was just about all the cocaine in the world. DEA had run more than five covert operations over the past twenty years trying to entice the elder Vicaro into entering the States, where he could be arrested on a number of secret federal indictments. Now, finally, miraculously, sitting in the Montgomery Federal Correctional Center was his son, heir, and chief operating officer. Given his father's age and diminishing operational importance, the son was the bigger catch.

Gus's phone never stopped ringing. TV crews arrived. Newspapers. Magazines. Everyone wanted to talk to Gus. Every talk-show host from Jay Leno to Oprah wanted to fly him in for interviews.

Gus told his secretary, "Tell them I'm busy. Talk to them yourself."

Even Dave Chapman called. *Senator* Dave Chapman. They'd been friends since Harvard, when Chapman accidentally broke Gus's arm during a lunchtime game of touch football. Chapman had missed an afternoon history test, knowing it meant a failing grade, so he could stay with Gus at the hospital while they set the arm. He was two years ahead of Gus, had come to Harvard from a Denver high school where he'd been a star running back, president of the student body, editor of the school paper, and valedictorian. He was big, bright, friendly, good looking. Chapman went on to Harvard Law, followed by Gus two years later. They stayed in touch, had a meal together at least twice a month. After graduation, applying for a management job at ABC Television, Chapman was offered a spot as a correspondent. But the looks and personality that qualified him for on-camera TV also qualified him for politics, and within six months he'd left ABC and was running for the Colorado state legislature. He was elected. Four years later he was in Washington, in the Senate. People began talking about him for the Presidency.

Chapman called the day after Vicaro's arraignment.

"You're famous, Gus."

"Yeah. I oughta run for the Senate."

"It'd be great to have you here. We could clean this place up."

"You're doing all right without me."

That evening, Gus arrived home to find Michelle in the living room with Carl's daughter, Ali, on her lap. Esther had taken Paul with her to the supermarket.

Michelle was watching the TV news, a deep frown clouding her face.

"Where's this going, Gus?"

"Ernesto Vicaro's going to prison, is where *he's* going."

"They've been talking about all the people he's killed."

"He hasn't killed any U.S. prosecutors."

"He's never had to."

"Michelle, don't worry. The TV exaggerates everything. Tomorrow they'll forget all about it."

It was a week before the suppression hearing, when the defense team—six attorneys from Miami, New York, and Washington—would argue that the search warrant had been flawed, that it was improperly executed, that the cocaine had been illegally seized, that the evidence—$1.2 billion worth of cocaine—should be suppressed. Without the cocaine, there was no case. It was the quickest, easiest way for Ernesto Vicaro to win.

At 10 A.M. on Monday, John Harrington, a member of the defense team, appeared in Gus's office. He was from Washington, with a million-dollar reputation and a smile to match. "Just wanted to introduce myself."

They chatted, Harrington as warm and friendly as they come, grinning out at Gus from under thick black eyebrows. It took him less than twenty minutes of small talk, offhand as could be, to mention what a terrific job Gus had ("Used to be an assistant U.S. Attorney myself, loved the work"), and the great career advantages it offered.

Harrington said, "They asked me to run for the House, but I turned it down. Who wants the hassle?"

He never mentioned money. He didn't have to. The reputation and the smile did that, as well as the wealth, power, and political clout of his client.

When Harrington left, Gus felt sick. He knew why he'd been there. Suppression hearings were so easy to lose. There were so many technicalities, so many ways the agents could have screwed up the search. And the loss never reflected badly on the prosecutor. Lose this one, the sky's the limit. That was what Harrington meant. So easy. So profitable. It made Gus sick—sick and angry.

Two days later Gus received a brown manila envelope in the mail. Heavy, something loose inside. He tore it open and found two keys. Serrated edges on four sides, four-digit numbers on the plastic ends. Luggage locker keys.

Gus called Carl and they drove to the airport.

On the way, Gus said, "How's Esther?" Carl's wife was

a tiny blonde firecracker. A very *loving* firecracker, but a firecracker nevertheless.

"The same. 'You work all day, all night, you're the SAC, make someone else work for a change, what'll happen to your children when you get blown away, I thought this job, finally we'd have a normal life, no more up all night bang-bang,' et cetera, et cetera, et cetera. She's consistent, I'll say that for her."

"You'll say a lot more, too."

"Yeah, I love her. She says I oughta have a nice, safe nine-to-five job like you."

"Yeah, right. Nine-to-five."

"She loves Michelle. 'Look at Michelle, *she* doesn't stay up nights wondering where her husband is, dead in some alley. *She* leads a normal life. *She's* beautiful. *She's* not haggard, old before her time, bitching at her husband.' "

Gus laughed. "You're lucky, Carl."

"I know, I know. Great wife. Two terrific kids."

For five minutes, they rode in silence. Then Gus said, "So what do you think?"

"Someone wants you to find something. I just hope it's not ticking."

"I thought of that."

"Don't worry. If it was a bomb, there wouldn't be two."

The lockers were in the south concourse, side by side on the bottom row of a three-tiered stack about fifteen lockers long. Gus put a key in the one on the left, turned it, and swung the door open.

Two large black shell-back Samsonites, side by side.

He dragged one out. They stared down at it, sitting on the gray tile floor.

"So," Carl said, "the bomb squad?"

Gus laid it on its side and pressed the latch. It snapped open. He lifted the top. Inside, layers of paper-banded bundles of hundred-dollar bills.

After a moment, Gus put his hand into the suitcase, counted the layers.

"How's your arithmetic, Carl? Ten thousand per bundle, thirty bundles per layer, five layers."

"One and a half million."

"One and a half million. Well, well, well."

Gus gave the lid a touch and let it fall closed. He dragged out the second bag, opened it.

Carl said, "Another one and a half."

Gus said, "Let's check the other locker. We're on a roll."

He turned the key, swung the door open.

Carl said, "Empty."

"Not quite."

On the floor, in the center of the locker, a piece of paper. On top of the paper, precisely in the center, standing upright, two shiny brass bullets. Gus reached in, picked them up, held them in the palm of his hand.

Carl said, "Hollowpoints, .357 Magnum."

Gus stuck his other hand into the locker and removed the piece of paper the bullets had been standing on. He turned it over, and his face went hard. Carl looked, opened his mouth, but didn't speak.

The paper was a color photograph of the front lawn of Gus's house. Gus and Michelle were walking across the lawn, holding hands. They were laughing.

His eyes still on the photograph, Gus said: "Get help."

Carl jogged to a bank of pay phones at the end of the concourse. Three minutes later a Montgomery police sector car cruising the area, hearing a radioed "assist officer" code, responded with siren screaming. Five minutes after that, the airport filled with Montgomery police, crime-scene units, ABI agents, FBI, DEA. DEA agents took the suitcases into custody, the money, the photograph, the .357 hollowpoints.

Standing by Gus's car, Carl said, "Michelle?"

"I'll tell her."

"You want me to come?"

"No."

"This is for real, Gus."

"I know that. I'll call if I need anything."

"Let me send some agents with you."

"It's okay. I'll call you."

Michelle was in the kitchen, stirring something in a bowl.

"Got a minute?"

She looked up, saw his eyes. "What is it?"

She put the spoon in the sink, and they sat at the kitchen table.

"This isn't as bad as it's going to sound."

"What is it?"

"You know I told you about the lawyer who visited me? Wanted to give the impression there'd be great things in store for me if I should happen to blow the suppression hearing?"

"Yes."

Her eyes looked ready for anything.

"Well, there's been a little follow-up. Carl and I were just out at the airport looking in some luggage lockers. Someone sent me the keys."

"Go on."

"Well, one of the lockers had three million dollars in it."

She sat back, as if he'd pushed her.

"Whose money is it?"

"Who do you think? Ernesto Vicaro's, I would guess. Right?"

"What about the other locker?"

"That's the problem, Michelle. I don't want you to be alarmed. There were some bullets."

Maybe if he didn't tell her there were two. And if he left out the part about the photograph.

But he could tell from her eyes, from the tilt of her head and the slight parting of her lips, that she knew.

"How many bullets?"

"It doesn't matter."

"Two, right?"

"Yes. Two."

"Is that all?"

He walked over to the sink.

"What else, Gus? Please tell me everything and get it over with."

He sat back down.

"There was a photograph of us on the front lawn."

He leaned toward her.

"It's just intimidation, Michelle. These people never carry through their threats. If they're really going to do something, they don't warn you first. They're just bullies. When you stand up they back off. It's intimidation."

She said, "Like, what's his name, Alfredo something—like him?"

Alfredo Guzman, a Colombian informant, had gone home from a meeting with Carl and found his wife and three children stabbed to death in the living room. That night a police lieutenant in Medellin called to tell him his grandparents, an uncle, and three cousins had been shot to death.

Two weeks later Alfredo was blown away by a shotgun blast on the street outside the hotel he was hiding in.

"That was different, Michelle. He was one of them, a traitor. They've never hurt an American prosecutor."

"Not yet." Her eyes began to tear. "I'm sorry. I know you have to do this. I'm glad you're doing this. I just—it's just hard, that's all."

Gus said, "Do you want to move?"

"No! This is our home. I'm not moving."

"I'll ask Gus to send over a couple of agents. Maybe I can get some marshals. The cops'll put the house on their watch list."

"I don't want any of that, Gus."

"I know you don't. It's not your choice."

Ten days later a federal magistrate in Montgomery denied the suppression motion. Less than a month after that, Ernesto Vicaro—faced with a Continuing Criminal Enterprise charge that could give him a life sentence with no parole—accepted a plea bargain guaranteeing twenty years in prison. It was a triumph for Gus. He'd locked up the biggest cocaine dealer on earth.

For the Montgomery papers it was a case of a local boy defeating a world-class dope dealer, an army of big-city lawyers, and doing it all despite threats to himself and his wife. And the praise wasn't just local. Invitations continued to come from national talk shows. The *New York Times* ran an editorial: "A choice between a bribe or a bullet. Three million dollars or the murder of himself and his wife. And Gus Parham didn't even think it over. He called the cops. Today the man who made that threat is in prison serving 20 years, and Gus Parham is still in his office in the Montgomery federal building preparing what we hope are more cases against criminal bullies like Ernesto Vicaro-Garza."

Nineteen months after the Ernesto Vicaro case, Gus was appointed federal magistrate in Montgomery. A year later he stepped up to district court judge in the middle district of Alabama, located in Montgomery. It was the answer to a dream, not as big as his Supreme Court dream, but big enough, to see if he could be the kind of judge he knew a judge should be, to answer not to clients or complainants or police or politicians, but only to the truth and to the law. When people thought to ask about his politics, the answer was always "He doesn't have politics, he only has principles." People who tried to contradict that came up empty.

Gus had been a district court judge for less than a year when his Harvard friend Dave Chapman, then serving in the Senate, was nominated to run for President. In November, Chapman was elected.

6

Traffic slowed and Gus saw flashing red police lights in the block ahead. An accident. It was early April, a beautiful spring day. He gripped the wheel and sighed. Why did these things always happen when he was in a hurry? A murder defendant, her attorney, and the prosecutor were waiting outside his chambers, ready to work out a plea bargain to a reduced charge of manslaughter.

He didn't usually take this road. A construction detour had forced him from his regular route onto something called Bakersfield Boulevard. The name rang a bell, but he couldn't remember having been here before. And now it looked as if he might never be able to get off it.

Three minutes later the line of cars began to move. He crept forward, and as he approached the police lights, he saw a crowd.

It wasn't an accident. Some kind of disturbance. A group of protesters was waving placards. The placards said BABY KILLERS!

And then Gus remembered where he'd heard the name Bakersfield Boulevard. Twenty feet in from the street, a one-story white stucco building sat behind a metal sign reading HAMILTON-SMYTH CLINIC.

Years ago, Gus had found it in the telephone book, the only abortion clinic in Montgomery. That must be where his child had been killed. He knew a lot of people wouldn't look at it like that, that his child had been killed. He wished *he* didn't look at it like that. But he could never think of the child as simply a lifeless mass of tissue, as anything other than a child—his child—who had been killed. Killed with his approval. At his insistence. The only child that would ever occupy Michelle's womb.

It was then, when he found the name in the phone book, that he had thought of going over and looking at the clinic. It was the closest he would ever be able to get to the child. It was the only place on earth to which the child had had any physical connection. Maybe if he went he could get some sense of the child—of its presence, of its existence.

But he hadn't done it. As much as he wanted some memory or experience of the child, he didn't think he could spend the rest of his life with the picture of that clinic before his eyes. It wouldn't do anything but increase the pain.

Now he knew he'd been right. He was in a panic to escape, to get away from the clinic, the protesters, the placards.

He jammed the car into reverse, twisted in his seat, looked back. Police cars blocked his way. He tried to move forward. An ambulance filled the intersection. He put his head on the steering wheel and closed his eyes.

When he'd first found out about the clinic, he had thought that if he went there and talked to the doctor, the doctor might remember if the child had been a boy or a girl. That was crazy. How could the doctor remember? Gus had never been able to ask Michelle. Even if she knew, he could never inflict on her the pain that question would bring. His parents' siblings and most of his cousins were men, and since it was the man's genes that determined sex, Gus had decided to believe the child had been a boy. Michelle had become pregnant at the beginning of March, so the child's birthday would probably have been early December. They would have named him after his father, Stephen. Every year Gus thought about him on the fifth of December, a likely birthday. Stephen Parham, born December 5—a child Gus had never seen, but the only person he had ever loved as much as he loved Michelle.

He *knew* how strange that was, celebrating the birthday. But he told himself the boy *had* actually lived, he wasn't someone Gus just made up, so why didn't Gus have the right to celebrate his birthday? Was that *so* wrong? If he'd died one second after birth, they'd have had a funeral, remembered his birthday, every year they'd go to the cemetery with flowers.

Someone tapped on his window. A cop. A lane had been cleared. Gus wiped his eyes and eased the car forward.

For years he had quietly noted every milestone in his son's life, the days when he would have started preschool, kindergarten, first grade. He had read someplace that children who die continue to grow in heaven, and when we see them there we will see them as adults. That was crazy, but—was the boy now thirteen years old in heaven?

Was that wrong, to think like that, some kind of sickness, an obsession? He was haunted by the fact that it was he who had pressured Michelle, talked her into ending the pregnancy. He had acted not just against the child but against Michelle herself. *He* hadn't wanted a marriage like his parents', *he* hadn't wanted to marry under pressure, *he* hadn't wanted the pregnancy—so he had destroyed their child.

In Sunday school, when he was nine, Gus had heard how God told Abraham to sacrifice his only son, Isaac. At the last moment, with Abraham's knife raised, God had called it off, and Isaac lived. Now Gus knew what it was to lose a son, but for him there had been no reprieve. Stephen was dead, sacrificed by Gus on an altar of selfishness.

Gus eased the car past the protesters, now separated by a row of cops from another group that was shouting slogans back at them. It struck Gus how much alike the two groups were—nice looking, impassioned, unbending in their rage. Gus was glad that as a judge he never had to be in the middle, never had to decide which of them was right. The law was in the middle, not him.

He made it to his office, splashed water on his face in the men's room, apologized for being late, and then tried to listen to the woman tell him how she'd stabbed her husband in the throat with a pair of scissors because she'd caught him in bed with their nine-year-old daughter.

* * *

Gus was in his chambers during a lunchtime recess when his secretary told him he had a call from a Mr. Steve Borgman in Washington.

"I'll take it."

Gus had been in law school with Borgman, who now worked for a Washington law firm.

"Gus?"

"Steve, how are you?"

"Great. Michelle?"

"Very good."

"Listen, I have something to run by you. Confidential."

"Sure."

"I have a partner here knows I know you, and he's asked me to get your informal, unofficial reaction to something."

"What is it?"

"This partner has a friend called him from the White House counsel's office, mentioned confidentially that they expect Hoskins to resign before the end of the summer. They're drawing up a list of possible nominees to replace him, and—"

"Hoskins?"

"Supreme Court."

"Oh, right."

"He wondered if you'd agree to have your name on the list."

"You've made a mistake, Steve."

"No, I haven't."

"No one's gonna nominate me for the Supreme Court."

Years ago his Supreme Court dream had been buried beneath reality.

"It's not like they're offering you the job, Gus. There's

probably hundreds of people on the list. They write down everyone."

"Thanks. I'm glad you cleared that up."

"Can I say you agree? To be on the list?"

"Sure. I agree to be on the list. If it's true, I'm honored."

"But Gus, it'd be best if you didn't tell anyone. This is a long shot."

"You can say that again. No one but Michelle."

"*Supreme Court!*"

"Easy, honey. It's not gonna happen. It's like a ticket for the Florida state lottery."

So they forgot about it. Well, Gus *tried* to forget about it, but the old dream, resurrected by Borgman's phone call, wouldn't leave him alone.

Weeks later they read in the paper that Hoskins was resigning.

"So it's true," Michelle said.

Gus was silent.

The next month, Michelle read in the *New York Times* that a decision had been made, a former senator from Rhode Island. Everyone liked him. He'd been a federal judge. A couple of days later it turned out he'd written a *Law Journal* article fifteen years earlier knocking affirmative action. Now no one liked him at all.

Every day names floated across the op-ed pages, and every day political sharpshooters blew them away. Weeks went by.

Then, finally, in early summer, a winner. He was from Idaho, son of a farmer, a former judge who'd been legal counsel to a half dozen public-service groups before taking a job as professor of constitutional law at the University of

Idaho. Someone at the White House described him as "a down-to-earth man with a heart for public service and one of the top constitutional minds in the country."

Before the week was out, a *Washington Post* columnist reported that twelve years earlier the nominee had been a member of the governing council of an Episcopal church whose priest had been charged with sexually abusing a teenage boy over a period of two years. "If he didn't know about it, he should have."

Back to Idaho.

The next morning, a Sunday, Gus was washing his car when the phone rang. Steve Borgman again.

"You remember I told you I had a partner had a friend at the White House, wanted to know could they put your name on a list of possible nominees?"

"Yeah, I remember that."

"The White House friend would like to talk to you personally."

"What's his name?"

"Philip Rothman. He's chief counsel."

Rothman was in the papers almost every day. A short, chubby, balding man, he had a soft face and a reputation for bloodthirsty ruthlessness that would have shamed a shark.

"What's going on, Steve? Really."

"He'll tell you."

Half an hour later, Rothman called. Gracious, but all business. No phony charm. For the first time, it struck Gus that people really were considering him for nomination to the Supreme Court. It made his voice shake. The dream became a longing.

Rothman said, "Frankly, you weren't on our short list. But we've thrown that out, and we're looking at a few people we might not have considered that seriously before. You might say we've altered our criteria a bit."

"Sexual abuse will do that."

Gus almost bit his tongue. This was the chief White House legal counsel, and he's making jokes.

"Exactly. So the President's chief of staff, Lyle Dutweiler, and I would like to talk to you. Can you make it to Washington? Dinner tonight?"

Gus wondered if there was a chance Dave Chapman would be there. He hadn't seen him in years.

A government limousine picked Gus up at National Airport, drove him through a White House gate. The Washington heat was stifling. He was led to a small dining room with silver, crystal, and two white-jacketed Filipino waiters. Gus noticed, with a touch of disappointment, that the table was set for three.

Rothman, waiting for him, had a solemn expression constantly threatened by a smile, which he did his best to suppress. He said, "I'd like you to meet Lyle Dutweiler, the President's chief of staff."

Six hours earlier Gus had been washing his car, and here he was having dinner in the White House. Dutweiler said, "We appreciate your coming on such short notice." His eyes were like scalpels, dissecting Gus, going for the soul. He didn't want another mistake. "I was a judge once myself, and I know what your day must be like."

So why didn't they nominate Dutweiler? He have a secret? The face smiled, but the scalpels kept slicing. He was skinny, six-three. His tie was ugly, his collar too big.

Gus said, "I'm pleased to be here. Puzzled, but pleased."

Dutweiler said, "I guess this comes as a bit of a shock."

"A bit."

Dutweiler took those eyes off Gus long enough to glance at Rothman.

Rothman said, "You're relatively invulnerable. You're a hero in your state, and to some degree beyond that. People remember the Ernesto Vicaro case. The bullets and photograph."

Gus kept quiet.

"You have no published articles or speeches anyone can take apart. Your decisions on sensitive issues are pretty much down the middle. You're young, but that means there's not that much to attack."

Silence. Eyes.

Dutweiler said, "So we have a couple of questions."

"Okay."

"First question, is there anything you know that you think we may not know?"

"You mean like child-abusing priests?"

Dutweiler smiled. "That's what we mean."

"No."

"Second question. We don't want to take anything for granted. Washington's not everyone's cup of tea." He glanced at Rothman then back at Gus. "So. Do you want the nomination?"

They watched him, but neither spoke. Were these guys for real? Neither had the phony charm of rich lawyers and winning politicians. Was that the trick? Reverse charm?

"Just like that?"

"I wouldn't say 'just like that,' " Rothman said. "This meeting is the tip of a very carefully scrutinized iceberg."

"But you're—"

They stared at him, recording every twitch, watching the sweat flow from every pore. They had lab coats and clipboards.

Rothman said, "It's not exactly a fait accompli, Gus. The President's waiting to see what happens here. But—"

Dutweiler interrupted. "We have to know your response. None of us wants the President to call you, and you say no. If you're inclined to say no, tell us now."

Would he buy a used car from these guys?

He took a sip of wine. It was white, cool. Much lighter, much drier than the yellow wine Michelle's dad made. He put the glass down. "This is going very fast."

"We understand."

More silence. Waiting.

"I need to think. I'd like to discuss it with my wife."

This was a tougher decision than money-filled Samsonites versus a couple of .357 hollowpoints.

"Of course. May we take that as a tentative yes?"

"I have to think."

Rothman and Dutweiler exchanged glances. Neither had even looked at his food.

Had he blown it, failed the test? Can't make his own decisions, has to clear it with the old lady? Michelle had been raised in the red-clay heat and reality of homemade wine and wood-decked pickups. Counterfeits, vanity, things of the air—she smelled them coming. He needed to talk to Michelle.

Dutweiler's eyes suddenly fixed on the door. Rothman's head spun, and the waiters flattened themselves against the wall. Gus turned.

"Gus, how are you?"

Dave Chapman was across the room in two strides, taking Gus's hand.

"It's been too long. How is Michelle? Lyle told me you came up here on about twenty minutes' notice. That's really nice of you."

"It's good to see you, Dave."

Chapman looked heavier than the last time Gus had seen him, both physically and in spirit. The familiar exuberance was there, but it'd been lowered a couple of notches. He looked fatigued, less buoyant.

Waiters appeared with a fourth chair, a silver coffee urn, cognac, cigars.

Chapman sat down quickly, refused coffee. He was in a hurry. The room filled with silence. After a moment, he said, "Lyle? Phil? If . . ."

Lyle and Phil cleared out, and the waiters went with them.

When they were alone, Chapman said, "How are you, Gus? Really. How's Michelle?"

"Fine. Michelle's fine. Everything's ticking along really well. What about you? It's hard to tell from the media."

"You can't tell anything from the media. But it's okay. I was really happy to hear you'd agreed to come. I wanted to see you. Not just for the nomination. You have to see people you knew before you were canonized, when you were still a human being. It looked like we'd be able to have dinner, but—you can't imagine, Gus."

"I guess not."

"And in case you're wondering, it wasn't me who put your name on the list. Your name got on the list all by itself."

Gus was silent.

Chapman put his hands flat on the table, and when he glanced up, into Gus's eyes, he looked embarrassed.

"Gus, I have to be frank. I wanted to see you because there is one thing I have to say. It's sounds corny and maybe phony, but I have to say it."

"You're not going to say anything phony, Dave."

"Gus, you're *supposed* to be on this Court. I just know that. Some critical cases are approaching the Court, and they'll change more than law. They're going to change our culture, they're going to change what our country *is.* Shaping the Court that will shape our country is one of the most important things I'll do as President. I want you on the Court, Gus. Remember the dinners we used to have, our conversations?"

"I remember."

"You still believe all that?"

Gus smiled. "I'm not sure I would still want to support everything I said then. I was twenty."

"You know what I mean, Gus."

"Yes, Dave, I still believe all that. Everything I said. Especially about the courts. The country's changed direction."

"When the earlier candidates had to be withdrawn, Gus, it was because I'd relied too heavily on the opinions of other people. I know a lot *about* them, but I didn't *know* them. With you I have my own experiences and opinions. I *know* you, Gus. I want you on the Court."

"I don't know what to say, Dave."

"I don't want you to say anything. I want you to think about it. Because if you accept, there won't be any backing out. Not by me, anyway. You will not be withdrawn no matter what anyone says or threatens. This is it, Gus. You're the one."

Chapman stood and put out his hand. "Give my love to Michelle."

Gus took the hand.

Holding it, squeezing hard, Chapman said, "I am asking you personally, alone, between the two of us, to accept the nomination. For the country."

Chapman released Gus's hand, turned, and walked out.

Dutweiler entered, followed by Rothman.

"Interesting conversation?"

"Yes."

Dutweiler said, "Do you have anything you want to tell us?"

"I have to talk to my wife."

"You mean you didn't say yes? The President asked you to be on the Supreme Court and you told them you'd *think* about it? Is that what you said? You really *said* that?"

"Not exactly, Michelle. I wanted to discuss it with you. Some wives, they'd be happy about that."

"I *am* happy. I just can't imagine it. 'Supreme Court? Well, I don't know. Let me run it by the wife.' "

They were spending the night at her parents' place, sitting on the porch in the twilight. Her mother and father were at a movie.

Gus said, "I'm only thirty-eight, Michelle. This is for life. We'd have to move to Washington. You want to live in Washington?"

"I don't know. I've never been there."

"It's like Jupiter, only less hospitable."

"You like being a judge. You can't be any more of a judge than on the Supreme Court."

"That's me, Michelle. That's not you. You'd miss this

ranch. *I'd* miss this ranch. Not to sound corny, but this is where I first found out I'm alive. I'm not sure what would happen if we went to Washington."

They were side by side, bodies touching, on a wooden swing suspended by chains from the ceiling. He gave the floor a light kick with his foot, and the swing rocked gently in the breeze from the ceiling fan. A porch swing. A ceiling fan. This was the nineties in the United States of America? They were going to leave this, go to Washington? People *killed* themselves in Washington. White House people.

He had dreamed about the Supreme Court. But it'd been *his* dream, it wasn't *her* dream, it wasn't *their* dream.

"Look at it this way, Gus. If we don't go, will you ever have peace? Will we ever have peace? Will we ever stop wondering?"

Finally, it was the peace thing that made up his mind. Michelle was right. He had to know. They had to know. If they hated it, he could always resign.

7

Gus and Michelle rented a small two-story brick bungalow in Vienna, Virginia, a forty-minute drive from Washington. An accountant lived across the lawn on one side, a young attorney on the other, and an engineer with the Department of the Interior across the street. At night it was so quiet you could hear neighbors cough and tree leaves rustling in the breeze. Michelle liked that. It made her feel secure.

And then, two weeks after the nomination, had come the video.

John Harrington, the attorney who had been in Montgomery for the Vicaro case, had invited Gus to his Washington office and, with more curiosity than caution, Gus had gone. He'd watched the video, taken it home, showed it to Michelle. Lying on the bed, recovering from the shock of seeing her daughter for the first time, she'd said, "Where did he get it?"

"Harrington said the girl's father, the adoptive father, sent the video to the adoptive mother two years ago. They're separated and he took the girl. He wanted to prove to his wife that the girl was safe and happy, so he sent the video."

"Where did he take her? Where is she now?"

"Harrington said he didn't know. He didn't want to tell me anything. He just wanted to show me what he had so I'd withdraw from the nomination."

"Who are they?"

She sat up, and Gus moved next to her on the edge of the bed. He said, "The parents? I don't know."

"Is she all right?"

"She looks all right on the video. That's all I know. I think it's all anyone knows."

"What are we going to do?"

His desire, his principles, his heart, everything most important to him said, *Fight.* But prudence, reality, responsibility, his obligation to Michelle and their daughter, his love for Michelle and their daughter, said something else, and that was what he told Michelle.

"I'll have to withdraw. We'll go back to Montgomery."

"And just drop it? Just like that? You can't do that, Gus, not after seeing that video. We have to know how she is, where she is, is she all right, is she safe."

"I—"

"We don't even know if the man's looking after her. Where is he living, what's he doing?"

"Michelle—"

"If you withdraw and we go back and pretend nothing happened, we'll never know, we'll spend the rest of our lives just—we couldn't do that, Gus, we . . ."

"What do you want to do?"

"Why do you have to withdraw? Can't the White House find her? Can't they make Harrington say where he got the video? Why do you have to withdraw just because they've got a video of our daughter? That's not a crime, you haven't done anything wrong."

"It doesn't have to be a crime. They've got more than the video."

"What do they have?"

He went to his briefcase and took out the manila envelope Harrington had given him.

"They have copies of our interviews with Dr. Novatna, and your conversation with a woman at the adoption agency."

She put out a hand. "Let me see."

When she had agreed to end the pregnancy, they'd gone to see a counselor, a Dr. Novatna. Gus had told him that he wanted Michelle to have the pregnancy terminated. Michelle had agreed, but her reluctance was clear. Novatna had taken notes. The notes were full of Gus's insistence and Michelle's reluctance. Finally, Novatna had said he would schedule an appointment for the termination, but he asked Michelle, point blank, "Are you sure you want to end this pregnancy?" Michelle had hesitated. "Are you sure?" Finally, she said, "Yes. I'm sure." Novatna had said that before he proceeded he wanted to have another meeting. "Give you time to think about it a little more."

They had never gone back to Novatna. Instead, Michelle had told Gus she would have the termination in

Montgomery. That was the last he had seen of her before her return to Cambridge twelve months later.

The counselor at the adoption agency in Milwaukee had also taken notes. Michelle had confided in her. She had said it was Gus who had wanted the pregnancy ended, that he had insisted. She said she had left him and decided to "save my child."

Michelle finished reading the reports and handed them back to Gus.

Gus said, "They make me look like I forced you. I look like a monster. I *was* a monster. I'm sorry, Michelle. I was wrong. I'm sorry."

"It's all right," she said. "It didn't happen anyway."

Michelle reached for his hand.

After a minute she said, "She's very pretty."

"It's hard to believe."

"We're going to find her, Gus."

"The nomination is off." Everything in his brain said that was true. But his heart was screaming.

"Why?"

"Michelle, they'll give all this to the media. How could I be nominated now? The pro-life people won't support someone who pressured his own wife to end a pregnancy. And the pro-choice people will say that whatever I did I was uncaring and heartless. And think what it will do to the girl, and her adoptive parents. Everything will come out. The father taking her away. The girl's life—how will she react to this? It'd be all over the TV and newspapers. Maybe she doesn't even know she's adopted. What have her parents told her? Nothing good could come from this, Michelle."

"Maybe you're wrong, Gus."

Oh, if only he were wrong.

"Tell Dave Chapman. Tell Dutweiler. Ask what he can do. The White House has power, Gus. We might not be able to find her, but the White House can. If Harrington could get that tape, the White House can find out where he got it. They can find her. At least then someone can talk to her, see how she is. Then we can decide what to do. But we have to find her, Gus. We have to know."

"Michelle . . ."

She blew her nose but didn't speak. He had never felt such sorrow for anyone. She couldn't share his joy that their daughter was alive because she had never thought she was dead. All she had now that she didn't have before was the pain of thirteen years lost with the stranger on the video.

She lowered her head and began again to cry. How could Harrington do this to them? The joy of seeing their daughter, his distress at what it had done to Michelle, the impossible position they were in—everything turned to anger. "Cheap, malicious little bastards."

"So what?"

"What do you mean, 'So what?' "

"Gus, when some cheap, malicious little bastards left those bullets and photograph in the luggage locker at the airport, you *knew* what to do."

He had known what to do because that had been a threat he could overcome. This was not even a threat. This was a certain consequence. Fail to withdraw as the nominee and that video would be on TV, along with the notes of their interviews. The girl in the video would be hounded and destroyed. Michelle would be crushed.

"Michelle, I—"

"*Didn't you?*"

"Please don't shout. Of course I did."

"Well?"

"Michelle, this is different."

"This is *not* different. This is *exactly* the same. You are someone those bastards don't want. You are going to do things they don't want you to do. You believe things they don't want anyone believing. What's the difference? That time the threat was against you and your family. It's *still* against you and your family, only this time it's your *whole* family, daughter included. Gus, you can't just roll over and play dead. You will *hate* yourself if you do that. For the rest of your life you will hate yourself."

"Michelle, there isn't—"

"At least talk to Dutweiler. See what he says. Maybe he can do something."

The morning after she saw the video, Michelle woke up, and the sense of amputation that had haunted her since the birth was gone. She watched the video again and again and again. There her daughter was, before her eyes, alive and strong. Thirteen years ago the loss had filled her with sorrow, and now the rediscovery filled her with joy—and apprehension. One had been a newborn, this was a child of thirteen. Where was she, how was she, who was she? Was she happy? Who were her parents? What did her bedroom look like? Did she have brothers or sisters? Michelle felt herself becoming once again the person she had not been for the past thirteen years. Her daughter was alive, *she* was alive. She wanted desperately to see her daughter, talk to her, hold her, ask her forgiveness. She wanted to know her.

8

"You said you had a video?"

Saturday evening, and Lyle Dutweiler was in a tuxedo. When Gus and Michelle had arrived at his house they'd seen a limousine waiting at the curb.

Gus handed over the video, and Dutweiler walked across the book-lined study and slipped it into the VCR. Phil Rothman was there too, bald, chubby, amicably sinister, sitting on a sofa.

Gus said, "I'm sorry to disturb your weekend."

"Don't worry about it. You said it's important, so it's important. You want to tell me what it's about?"

Michelle said, "I think it'd be better to watch the video first."

Dutweiler nodded, smiled, and returned to his seat on the brown leather sofa next to Rothman. "Anyone want a drink? Michelle? Gus?"

"No, thanks."

Dutweiler crossed his legs, picked up his gin and tonic, and pressed the play button on the remote control.

The eleven-year-old girl came out of a house, walked toward them, smiling, in a hurry. A few yards from the camera, the picture went blank and the video ended. The whole thing didn't last more than ninety seconds.

Dutweiler said, "Beautiful girl, but I don't understand. You'll have to explain. Who is she? What's it all about? I'm in a fog."

So they told him, about Michelle's pregnancy, the proposed termination, the adoption.

Dutweiler interrupted. "Excuse me just a second, Gus."

He took three steps to his desk, pressed a button, and said, "Michael, could you come in a moment, please?"

A tuxedoed young man appeared in the doorway.

"Yes, sir?"

"Please tell Mrs. Dutweiler we won't be going this evening. And ask her if she could telephone our regrets?"

"Yes, sir."

"Thank you, Michael. That okay with you, Phil?"

Rothman nodded.

On the way back to the sofa Dutweiler withdrew the videocassette and handed it to Gus. Then he undid his black bow tie and loosened the collar. "Sorry, Gus. Please go ahead."

They showed him the documents. Dutweiler read them in silence, handed them to Rothman, waited for Rothman to read them. It was impossible to know their reaction. They were attorneys, conditioned to give nothing away.

Dutweiler said, "Where'd you get the video?"

Gus told him.

"They got lucky. They found the mother—sorry, adoptive mother—and she gave it to them, sold it, whatever. So . . ."

He smiled and shook his head. He put his elbows on the arms of the leather chair and rested his chin on his clasped hands, thinking. Then he sat up and said, "Well, the first question, Gus, is what does this do to you? And you, Michelle? Where does this leave us?"

Gus said, "If I haven't withdrawn by close of business on Monday they introduce their so-called alternatives."

"What do you think those are?"

"You could answer that better than I can."

"What's your answer?"

"Publicity. Give it all to the media."

Rothman said, "They wouldn't be that stupid."

Dutweiler said, "Phil means they might not want to look like people who would use a child to destroy a nomination. This sword has two edges. They'll just show it to opposition senators and staffers on the Judiciary Committee and hope quiet conversations with the White House will do the trick. Publicity would be a last resort. They wouldn't shrink from destroying that kid and the parents and you and Michelle if they had to, but they won't want the return fire that would bring. We could do a little destroying ourselves. My guess is if you don't withdraw I'll get a call from Harrington myself and he'll be chummy and reasonable and talk about how reluctant everyone is to drag the girl and her parents into this."

Gus said, "Then what would happen?"

Rothman said, "Then it's up to the President."

Dutweiler said, "But you haven't answered my question, Gus. What about you and Michelle? Harrington's told you to withdraw. What are you going to do?"

"We've been thinking about that all weekend."

"Well, you need to know something, Gus. We aren't exactly novices here. Harrington and his people may not want to suffer the agony this could bring them. If this goes down to the wire it'll turn nasty—it's already turned nasty—and the issue with these mud-and-blood brawls is always the same. Do the ends justify the pain? Who can inflict the most agony? How much damage is each side prepared to endure before they cut and run? When I take this to the President I have to know how much pain you're willing to tolerate. Both of you. The President's going to ask me that—he may want to ask you directly—and I have to know the answer. When he first decided to nominate you, he said he wanted you because you were a slave to the law—that was his phrase. But the decision is yours. If you want to withdraw, that's that. I wish you had more time to think about it, but all you've got is till tomorrow at five P.M."

Michelle had been leaning out of her chair, chin forward, eyes riveted on Dutweiler. When he paused for breath, she said, "We don't need till five P.M. tomorrow. We've been thinking about this since Friday. Gus is not a withdrawer and neither am I. We don't want to withdraw."

Gus said, "I agree with Michelle. We do not want to withdraw. We're in this for keeps. With one condition."

"And it is?"

"The girl and her adoptive parents. She's our daughter, and those parents have raised her. You mentioned pain. I'm not going to volunteer them for this war. They're going to have to volunteer themselves."

"What does that mean?"

"Find them. I want to talk to them, explain what's happening, have the same conversation with them I've just had with you. How much pain, if any, are they prepared to tolerate."

Rothman said, "I'm not sure if—"

Dutweiler interrupted. "What if we can't find them?"

"Harrington found them."

"They had five weeks to look."

"But they weren't the government. They didn't have your resources."

"Don't kid yourself, Gus. People like Harrington—they have extremely sophisticated investigators."

"Better than the FBI?"

"Not better but a lot less encumbered by legal restraints. They can do things we can't touch."

Michelle said, "We have to talk to our daughter and the parents."

"So it boils down to this," Dutweiler said. "If we find the girl and her adoptive parents and they say okay, you want to stick with this?"

Gus said, "That's right."

"All the way? No matter what?"

Michelle said, "All the way."

"You're not going to wait until we're in deeper than we can get out and then tell us you've changed your mind?"

"I won't do that." Gus waited, and then he said, "Will you?"

"I won't."

"The President?"

"I can't speak for the President. He does what he wants. We do not ask the President for promises."

"But you'll find them—the girl and the parents?"

Dutweiler said, "Between now and Monday evening? Two days?"

He looked at Rothman. "What do you think, Phil?"

"Forget the two days. Harrington's just babbling. The Judiciary Committee's not scheduled to vote till the end of next month. We can push them. At least two weeks. Probably three or four. Plenty of time."

Rothman stood, walked to Gus, and put out a hand, palm up. Gus put the video into the hand. Rothman's soft, chubby fingers closed around the black cassette.

"Consider them found."

Dutweiler walked downstairs to show the Parhams to the door, then returned to the study. He lowered himself onto the brown leather sofa and fixed his eyes on Rothman.

"So what do we tell the President?"

"I'd tell him we're stronger now than ever."

Dutweiler laughed. "Always looking for the bright side. If you fell off the top of the World Trade Center, Phil, you'd be celebrating when you hit the concrete."

"Look at it realistically, look at—"

"I'm *looking* at it realistically. Parham tried to talk his wife into having an abortion."

"But she *didn't* have it. Whatever anyone tries to say, there was *no* abortion."

Dutweiler sighed.

Rothman moved forward in his chair.

"On the one hand, Lyle, Parham's pro-choice because he urged his wife to abort. On the other hand, he's pro-life because he's delighted that she didn't. Something for both sides to like."

"Or hate."

"But you're missing the point. The key here is the girl. Did you *see* that girl?"

"I saw her."

"You cannot believe for one minute—not for one *minute*—that Harrington or anyone else is going to be crazy enough to come against her. It'd be like shooting Bambi."

"You think we can find her?"

"Oh, we can find her. For sure, we can find her. Lyle, Parham's an even better nominee now than before we saw the video. Thirteen years ago, in the heat and pressure of the moment, he urged his girlfriend to have an abortion—no one's gonna hate him for that. But today—well, look at the girl on the video. *Not* aborted, beautiful and full of life. He's delighted she wasn't aborted. And who wouldn't be? How can you attack him?"

"What about the others? *Someone's* going to tell the President that video makes Parham unconfirmable."

"Unconfirmable—like, for example, Clarence Thomas? Pornography, sexual harassment, pubic hairs on Coke cans, remember all that? A complete nightmare. *Much* worse than anything Parham will *ever* be accused of. And he was confirmed."

"Are you ready for another bloodbath like that?"

"I'll tell you a bloodbath I'm *not* ready for. I'm not ready to tell the President we blew it again. Politically, after two previous mistakes, we cannot afford to withdraw this nominee. I don't know why we're even discussing this. There's no choice, Lyle. And aside from the politics, you've heard the President say it a hundred times—Parham is the man.

There's no *chance* he'd withdraw him. Parham is the President's *man.* He's been nominated and he's going to stay nominated."

"So your advice is . . ."

"After every advisor who can pack into the Oval Office sees the video of that girl—I don't think there'll even be an argument. This is *not* a negative, Lyle. We just got very, very lucky."

"That's your position."

"That's my position."

"And you're gonna stick with it right up to the minute your face hits the concrete."

"I am. Definitely. Absolutely."

9

Helen Bondell loved to fight and she loved to win, but she did not like to be ugly. Not physically ugly—she was thirty-two, blonde, and just this side of gorgeous—but even the most accomplished charmers in Washington, the ones who knew what she did, could not keep the contempt from their eyes. They called her unprincipled.

In fact, her principles were so huge they blocked the horizon, so wide and towering you had to pull back to get a look at them. All Helen Bondell wanted was to *help*. She did whatever she could to get certain legislation passed, reminding herself when the blood flew that the legislation helped the people she wanted to help, people like impoverished, husbandless, jobless mothers who wouldn't be helped unless legislation imposed penalties for *not* helping them.

Her natural habitat was the battlefield, and it was covered with blood. The sword in her hand was the Freedom Federation, an alliance of public-interest groups with a zeal for "social change." A *Washington Post* reporter had asked her to define the term.

"Well," said Helen, green eyes sparkling with a charm younger lobbyists practiced in front of mirrors, "social change is whatever the Freedom Federation says it is." Helen loved to shock (those helpless mothers couldn't shock—who would care what they said?), and she had found that nothing shocked more powerfully than candor.

"In other words," the reporter said, "it's whatever *you* say it is."

"I think that's probably fair."

Her cocky willingness to thrust her head above the parapets, to invite attacks on her eccentric honesty, made good copy, which was part of the game. Sometimes it was the whole game.

She knew what was right and what was wrong, and if you agreed with her she didn't care what label you carried or who you slept with. What she hated were the people who were wrong, knew it, and didn't care.

She admired compassion and honesty. Her late husband—who'd had both, plus courage—had been blown away (literally, a bomb landed under his table) at a café in Algiers. The media said Islamic fundamentalists. She hadn't even known he was out of the country. He was an international banker—Third World investments, multinational loans, barter agreements, economic recovery projects. But while he wasn't looking—or maybe while he was—his business became mixed with politics and ended in terrorism. He'd been smart, informed, and so were his friends. She knew her husband had been doing what was right.

And so was she. People on the other side said she'd set new standards for dirty fighting. New standards. In a business whose hallmark was an absence of standards. If you won you were great. If you lost you were—well, you weren't anything, you were as close to invisible as live humans ever get.

And anyway, the standards weren't hers. She had created and cultivated a reputation for ruthlessness, knowing that the meaner she was thought to be, the nicer she could actually be. Myths were important in Washington. If you could convince people you were what you had to be, it left you free, sometimes, to be what you wanted to be.

She had just arrived in her office overlooking Pennsylvania Avenue, three blocks from the White House, and was snapping open the lid of her Gucci attaché case, a gift from her late husband.

It was 7:15 A.M.

The fax machine clicked on.

Glancing at the cover sheet creeping from the machine, she took papers from her attaché case, closed the lid and placed the case on the floor behind her desk.

She pressed a button on her phone. "Laura?"

"Good morning."

"Just wanted to know if you were here. Can you give me about ten minutes and then come in with the messages?"

"Right. Hang on. Warren just walked in."

"Oh, not *him* again."

Warren Gier had worked his way through Yale Law as

a part-time private investigator, and for the past four years had made a good living moving from one senator's payroll to the next, concealed behind various staff titles, as nasty little jobs arose that required a political predator to prowl the Washington underbrush, alert to legal snares but unencumbered by weighty moral restraints. Happily friendless, he'd been proud to learn that his enemies called him "the Ferret."

Helen said, "Hold him a second."

"Love to."

Employed at the moment by Eric Taeger, chairman of the Senate Judiciary Committee, Warren was never out of touch with Helen and the activist group leaders clustered under her Freedom Federation umbrella.

She glanced over at the pages still creeping from the fax machine and saw the familiar heading of the American Bar Association. The ABA's Standing Committee on the Federal Judiciary rated White House nominees for judicial appointments. The head of the rating committee was a close working friend of Helen's. She picked up the fax.

The White House gave the ABA the names of potential nominees for screening before the nominations were publicized. The ABA routinely passed the names to Helen's Freedom Federation. Helen then shared the names with other activists groups. If the groups disapproved of the nominee, their opposition, voiced to the ABA screening committee, some of whose members shared the political goals of the Freedom Federation, could kill the nomination on the spot.

The fax said the White House was requesting a qualification rating on a Federal District Court judge named Augustus Parham, sitting in the Middle District of Alabama in Montgomery. *Augustus* Parham? Sounded like some seventy-year-old redneck coot.

Warren walked in. "Sorry for interrupting."

"No you're not. You ever hear of Augustus Parham?"

"Why I'm here. The President's gonna nominate him for the SC."

Warren only had time for abbreviations. You had to keep up.

"I won't ask you how you know that."

Dark-haired, perpetually tanned, a good listener, Warren was a charmer, and Washington was loaded with lonely female staffers. He made it his business to woo the most vulnerable, feeding them dinners and kindness, periodically harvesting their office secrets as a shepherd shears sheep. Information was power, and power was money, excitement, and fun. No one in Washington understood that better than Warren.

Helen said, "Who is he?"

"You don't remember?"

"Warren, if I admit you know more than I do, will you tell me?"

"Five years ago, locked up some Colombian dope dealer, the media went crazy for him."

"Oh, yeah."

That Augustus Parham. Certainly. Gus Parham. How could she forget? She'd seen him on the *Today* show. Looked like they'd had to tie him to the chair, unhappy to be wasting his time but gracious about it. Guts but nice. Good looking. Like her first husband. They always ended with tire tracks up their backs, or blown to bits in cafés. She wondered what his wife would be like. Even had a brief fantasy, before a commercial dumped her back in reality. Gus Parham. Supreme Court. My, my.

She said, "So what do you think?"

Warren shook his head. "Bad news."

"Because?"

"I haven't had much time, just since lunch yesterday. Grandfather made a lot of money in tobacco and timber, father still takes care of it, lives on a forty-five-acre estate in Connecticut. Gus's personal holdings are in a blind trust. His judicial record and reputation show anti-choice, anti–affirmative action, heavy on judicial restraint, *stare decisis*, the usual coloring of your basic rich Ivy League southern white conservative right-wing fundamentalist bigot."

"That's quite a lot since lunch yesterday."

"Just the highlights. Film at eleven. You wanna call Bobbie?"

Bobbie McQuire was national director of the Reproductive Rights Alliance, one of the nation's largest feminist rights groups.

"Does she know yet?" Everyone would know. If Warren hadn't told them, Helen would do it when he left. Sam Waller of the National Defense League, Debbie Jennert of the Women's Assistance Fund, Sheila Riesman of the Social Action Center, the whole array of activist groups who lived and died by influencing legislation, appointments, nominations.

Warren grinned.

"You told her."

"Maybe."

What made Warren so secretive? No one knew him. You called, all you got was the machine. Did he have a home? Where'd he take the women?

10

"Hi, Ernie."

John Harrington had never been comfortable calling Ernesto Vicaro "Ernie." He wasn't a first-name person, and a man as fat, ugly, and evil as Ernesto Vicaro was not someone Harrington could think of as Ernie. It was hard having clients you hated. But Harrington was a product, like a right fielder, for sale to anyone with the money. Ernesto had insisted. "Call me Ernie." Sweating and wheezing. So what the hell, at $500 an hour he'd call him Ernie.

Harrington lowered his chin and looked up through his thick black eyebrows. "What can I do for you?"

Down to business, get in and get out. Prisons depressed

him. He'd never been in a prison till Vicaro. People in prison rarely had enough money for lobbyists.

"Wrong question." Vicaro smiled, tiny baby lips opening a damp red wound in the heavy flesh. "I'm gonna do something for you."

"What's that?"

Vicaro said, "Gus Parham."

Harrington wasn't surprised to hear the name, though he had no idea what might be on Vicaro's mind.

Vicaro waited, looking smug.

The interview room was like a green-walled toilet, smelling of sweat since Vicaro had oozed into the metal chair.

Vicaro didn't speak. Harrington was determined to wait him out, stink or no stink.

After half a minute, Vicaro opened his mouth and exhaled loudly, his foul breath propelling droplets of foaming spit. "I just read about him in the papers."

"Did you?"

Harrington moved his chair back. At $500 an hour he had to listen to Vicaro, but he didn't have to breathe his spit.

Harrington said, "He might be nominated for the Supreme Court." Some *Washington Post* columnist had had it three days earlier, mentioning unnamed sources on the Hill.

Harrington, a senior partner in Parks & Simes, a Washington law firm that lobbied for a half dozen international corporate clients, had had a call last week from Helen Bondell letting him know that Parham was a potential nominee. Helen's Freedom Federation was opposing the nomination—"We don't like his record"—and she obviously suspected that Harrington wouldn't be too happy with it either.

She knew that Parham's strong anti-crime views were not likely to match the goals of one of Harrington's clients, Ernesto Vicaro.

And of course she was right. Vicaro, serving time in a federal penitentiary from which he continued to direct the multinational activities of a South American conglomerate whose interests included cocaine trafficking and arms dealing, wanted changes in the American government's approach to law enforcement. He was after a relaxation of federal sentencing guidelines, a tightening of procedural controls on police and prosecutors, broader authority for federal parole board members, a far more malleable procedure by which convicted federal felons might win early release. The last two of these, which could critically influence the possibility of Vicaro's eventual freedom, were encapsulated in *Javez v. Rench*, a case challenging the federal law under which Vicaro had been sentenced.

He also wanted the decriminalization of marijuana and, eventually, cocaine. He already controlled coca plantations, processing labs, and distribution networks. Legalization would eliminate all the people Vicaro had to pay so liberally to do his illegal processing, shipping, warehousing, and retailing. Hundreds of millions of dollars in bribes to Latin American officials would no longer be necessary. Decriminalization would let Vicaro turn his expensively illegal operation into an even more profitable legal enterprise. Another R. J. Reynolds.

If the drive for legalization could ever be moved out of the legislative branch, where it had little support, into the Supreme Court (as abortion had been), Vicaro wanted justices there who would not oppose it. And the thin edge of the decriminalization wedge was almost certain to appear before the Supreme Court later that year in the form of *Hacker v. Colorado*, an appeal testing the constitutionality of a state law prohibiting the growth of small amounts of cannabis in private homes. Vicaro saw the court as evenly divided both on that case and on *Javez v. Rench*. He did *not* want Gus Parham's vote tipping the balance.

And if Vicaro, who paid Parks & Simes $20 million a year, didn't want Gus Parham on the Supreme Court, John Harrington didn't want him there either. So when Helen Bondell called, Harrington had said, "Thanks for letting me know. I'll do what I can."

At eight o'clock the following morning, Harrington had had a phone call from "Jonathan." Harrington had never met Jonathan, knew nothing about him except that he had the voice, vocabulary, and diction of an extremely genteel upper-class Englishman. Whenever Vicaro needed Harrington to know something and didn't want to send a letter or observe whatever prison procedures were necessary for making a phone call, he managed, in ways Harrington had no desire to know, to contact Jonathan. And Jonathan, for reasons Harrington also did not want to know, ever so graciously passed the message to Harrington.

"Yes, Jonathan?"

"My friend would like to see you. He says it's extremely important. Today, if at all possible."

"I don't know if I can get a flight. I'll try. If I can't make it late today, I'll be there tomorrow."

"Thank you very much. He said today. I'll see he gets the message."

So Harrington had told his assistant to clear his calendar and book him on the next flight to Chicago, nearest airport to the federal prison where Vicaro was incarcerated.

Responding now to Harrington's remark that Parham might be nominated for the Supreme Court, Vicaro said, "You are wrong, my friend. He will be nominated for nothing. And if he is, he will not be confirmed."

"You sound very certain."

"Mr. Harrington . . ." Vicaro always called him Mr. Harrington when he was serious. Harrington didn't like it—nobody liked it—when Vicaro got serious. "I'm going to tell you something, and you will know what to do with it."

Harrington didn't like the sound of that, but he said, "I'm listening."

Vicaro leaned forward, an operation requiring the labored displacement of more than 300 pounds of deadweight flesh. He looked up at Harrington and exhaled. This time Harrington did not pull back. He had a son at Princeton and a daughter at a private school in Virginia.

"Parham's a thief."

Vicaro, studying Harrington, looked like a delicately triggered bomb. Harrington didn't want to disturb the atmosphere. After ten seconds he said, "Why do you say that?"

"Because . . . I am thinking of the airport."

Harrington didn't understand. "Yes?"

"And the suitcases."

Still in the dark. "Yes?"

"There was four million dollars in the suitcases."

Oh, *that* airport, *those* suitcases. "Okay."

"You're not surprised, when I tell you that?"

"Should I be?"

"They *counted* three million, Mr. Harrington. Three million one hundred eighty-six thousand and four hundred, to be exact."

"You have a good memory."

"It was my money."

"What are you saying?"

"What am I *saying*?" Vicaro wheezed, pushing himself heavily back into an upright position. "I am *saying* that Judge Augustus Parham is a thief."

"Why is he a thief?"

"Because he *stole* eight hundred thirteen thousand and six hundred dollars. Out of the suitcases."

This was ridiculous. If Gus Parham had been after money he'd have accepted the offer Harrington made in his Montgomery office. But that had been vague promises. This was stacked cash, right before his eyes. People who had never seen four million dollars in hundred-dollar bills didn't understand. The sheer blaze of it could burn principles to a crisp.

"What makes you so sure?"

"I was there when the four million went into the suitcases. I counted it. Parham said he sent the cop—Carlos somebody—to the phone to call for help. So while the cop was gone, he scooped up a few handfuls, stuffed them into his briefcase, pockets, whatever. The *fact* is, when they counted the money at the bank, there was only three million one hundred and eighty-six thousand and four hundred dollars. Eight hundred thirteen thousand and six hundred dollars was missing. Parham took it."

"That's very interesting."

True or not, Harrington didn't care. If it was true, it'd be easier to prove. But even not true, it might be made into a credible allegation. When you wanted to destroy a nomination, credible allegations were all it took.

"That's what you call it? *Interesting?*"

"It's more than that, Ernie. But it's your word against his."

"Maybe not."

Vicaro smiled. Those little red baby lips, pulling back from tobacco-stained teeth. Harrington had never seen anything so revolting.

"Tell me your thoughts."

"I think the cop—Carlos . . ."

"Carl Falco."

"Yeah, Falco. Carlos knows."

"What makes you say that?"

"He was there, right? Maybe he got some too. They're good friends, I hear."

Harrington thought it over. Vicaro could swear out an affidavit. It wouldn't be worth anything, a convicted felon accusing the prosecutor who locked him up, but it'd be a piece of paper, a document. Carl Falco, a conspiracy between him and Gus, that was—*no one* would believe that. But Vicaro. An affidavit. Maybe. Yeah. The more he thought about it, the better it got. Handled *just* right. He'd give it to Helen Bondell. She'd know how to make the most of it.

Carl saw him on the corner across the street from the Montgomery DEA office, just standing there, doing nothing. He did not look like a man who stands on street corners doing nothing.

Carl turned right, headed for the garage where he parked his car, and heard footsteps at his back. He stopped at the corner. The steps stopped. He crossed against the light. The steps followed. Outside the garage, Carl stopped, turned, and faced the man.

"Was there something you wanted to ask me?"

The man was young, early thirties, small, tanned, nice-looking. His dark gray suit jacket fit like another layer of skin. The laced shoes were black and shiny. His smile, filled with charm, matched his friendly eyes. Carl had never seen him before, but he knew him. An attorney, good school, ambitious, sharp, fun to be with until he started chewing on your liver.

"Excuse me for following you. I wanted to talk to you, but I wasn't sure how to make the approach."

That'll be the day.

"Can I walk along with you for a minute?"

If this isn't a setup that's not his suit.

"It's a request, really. Unofficial, very informal you might say. Just something for you to know."

Carl remained silent.

"It's about the thing a few years ago at the airport? When all that money was found? The amount of money the police said they counted was substantially less than what was really in the bags, and someone thought that maybe you would be willing to help clear up the question about why that was. My client—well, I don't know how to say this. He's very wealthy, and he wanted just to let you know that if you were ever willing to help clear up that question he would be very appreciative, and if—"

Carl took a step forward and planted his right foot solidly on top of the man's left instep. As the man looked down in surprise, Carl placed his other foot on top of the other instep. Then, applying all his weight to the top of the feet, Carl put both hands on the man's chest, and pushed. The man let out a sharp cry, flailed briefly at the air, and fell stiffly backward, his feet still flat on the pavement.

Carl heard a sound like the snapping of dry Popsicle sticks. *Crack! Crack!*

He left the man in the street, recovered his car from the garage, and met Esther and the kids at McDonald's for lunch. He was starving.

"What happened?" Esther said. "You look really pleased."

"Someone had a difficult question, and I was able to give him an answer."

"That's nice."

"Yeah."

No one was sure who had designed it—Helen or a predecessor—but everyone liked the Freedom Federation's conference room. It was ostentatious, flamboyant, cocky, deliberately pompous. It mocked itself, mocked Washington, and mocked the people who met there. The walls were white, the carpet was white, the ceiling was white, the table was white, the chairs were white, the telephones were white, the pads of paper were white, the pencils were white—even Helen, when she hosted Freedom Federation meetings there, tried to wear white. Warren Gier once showed up in a white suit and white shoes. He said the room was like an albino cat. "A Siberian tiger, I think, invisible against the snow, eyes of burning phosphorus, ferocious. The perfect background for spilled blood." Helen said Warren was probably the only one who really appreciated the self-ridiculing irony of all that white. Some other Federation operatives, lacking Warren's flair, would have preferred the color of mud.

She said, "Okay. Everyone here?"

Around the oval table: herself, four other women, Warren Gier, John Harrington, and Isaac Jasper, a political consultant on loan from a lobbying group called the Institute for Social Justice.

"John, we'll start with you. I know you're busy. Thanks for coming."

Men with John Harrington's fee structure didn't usually attend the Federation's daily anti-Parham strategy sessions.

"Good to be here." He slipped several sheets of paper from his attaché case, handed them around. "Let's start with a look at this."

Warren read his copy, a smile widening across his face. "Love it."

Harrington said, "It's an affidavit from someone who says Parham stole some of the cash seized at the Montgomery Airport eight years back. Question is, what do we do with it? I asked Helen, and she suggested we discuss it here."

Becky Yankevich, a lanky young woman with glasses and short black hair who was director of the American Policy Coalition, said, "Is this true?"

Warren turned his smile on Becky. "What difference does that make?"

Harrington finally offered to deal with the matter personally, and everyone agreed. That had been his intention in the first place. The broken ankles had destroyed his resolve. It was not healthy to make insulting suggestions to men like Carl Falco. If Vicaro wanted to bring accusations of thievery and corruption against Falco, he could get out of prison and do it himself.

Helen said, "Isaac, you look particularly chirpy this morning. Anything to add?"

That was a joke. Isaac Jasper never looked chirpy. From

rumpled hair down to sagging socks, Isaac always looked as if he'd slept on someone's floor. Paula Yost called him the Unabomber, and indeed that disheveled killer and Isaac had been classmates at Harvard.

He looked up, his solemn face contorting for a moment into a grin. He had a Yasser Arafat beard—you never knew if he liked it scraggly or just couldn't be bothered to shave. "I'm a little troubled."

Isaac was a specialist in political trauma. If your campaign suffered a sudden attack, blood gushing from arteries, you called Isaac, a genius at resuscitation. Idle at the moment, he was on hold with the Parham opposition, helping out until some client dialed 911.

Helen said, "Yes?"

"I don't like the girl."

"What girl is that?"

Isaac glanced at Harrington. "I thought everyone knew."

Harrington lifted his hands and sat back.

"They do now, Isaac."

Isaac, not particularly caring if he had exposed one of Harrington's secrets—Harrington had too many secrets anyway—said, "Parham evidently has a daughter no one knows about. He thought she'd been aborted."

Helen said, "What are you thinking, Isaac?"

Isaac dragged a dirty handkerchief from his pants pocket, wiped his nose, stuck the handkerchief back. "This girl has a very bad smell. I don't mean—"

"We understand, Isaac, you're not commenting on her grooming habits."

"I know it looks good. Parham tried to have her

aborted. That has to hurt him any way they play it. But still, I hear she's, what . . ." He looked at Harrington. "Thirteen?"

Harrington nodded. "And pretty."

Isaac said, "There's a lot of power there. You could find things getting out of hand, situations developing where conventional tactics don't meet your needs. It could be volatile, unpredictable."

Warren said, "Politics is always unpredictable."

"Not when you do it right."

Helen said, "What do you think, John?"

"If she were ours, and we could control how she's used, I wouldn't be worried. But she's not. We can use her, the fact that she exists, the abortion thing, but she's not ours. If they find her, I don't know exactly what they'd do with her, but I can imagine a number of unpleasant scenarios."

Gier said, "If they find her?"

"Well, they know she exists, so of course they're looking for her."

"So are we looking for her?"

Harrington looked at Helen.

"Are we?"

Helen was silent.

Gier said, "Yeah, are we?"

Helen said, "You volunteering, Warren?"

11

Warren Gier on his way to lunch. Just walking along. What a beautiful day. Bright sun, brisk breeze, spent the night with a Justice Department secretary who lost *all* control. Next time, hit her up for the Parham files.

And now this—invited to lunch at Washington's most expensive restaurant by one of the three most powerful attorneys in town. Been thinking all morning, working it out, how to use the lunch. This is not food and fellowship. What do I have that Harrington wants? What does Harrington have that I want? Think about it. Go way out. What could I have when this lunch is over that I don't have now? Money . . . new contacts . . . what?

And what does Harrington want from me? Find the girl? Track a new lead on Parham? Helen said Harrington told her he had something on a DEA agent, Carl somebody, and the luggage-locker money. That sounded good, hot, great potential.

Nothing better than dusty, dirty long-buried secrets, things the buriers thought were safe. Only fools think safe. Nothing's safe. Not from Warren Gier. Everyone has a secret, and the destiny of every secret is discovery.

Here's the restaurant. Push open the door. Walk in.

Standing by the coat room, Carl watched the maître d'hôtel lead Warren Gier to a table. Hair longer than in the photograph, but no doubt about it, that was Warren Gier. Carl waited until Gier had picked up the menu, then walked purposefully to the table and sat down.

"How's it going, Warren?"

It had taken Carl just thirty-six hours to find out everything he needed to know about Warren Gier. Phil Rothman had told Carl that Gier, the most active investigator within John Harrington's reach, was the most likely to have found the video and documents. A ladies' man, Gier had dated a Judiciary Committee secretary named Martha Petrucina. Carl's toll analysis on Warren's office and home phones showed a series of calls to the Milwaukee home of a private investigator named Roger Budrow. A Milwaukee police detective told Carl that Budrow had been a suspect in several burglaries. The adoption agency Michelle said she used was located in Milwaukee. A burglary at the agency had occurred just fifteen days before Harrington showed Gus the video. The burglary date was two days after Gier's final call to Budrow's phone. Gier's Visa card record showed the purchase of a Delta ticket from Washington to Milwaukee the day after the burglary. So Gier must have started out digging up one of Michelle's old Montgomery girlfriends, who remembered that Michelle, pregnant, had gone to Milwaukee. Gier then went to Budrow, who found the adoption agency, and burglarized it.

Warren lowered the menu. "I'm sorry. This table's taken."

"Relax, Warren."

Gier raised a hand, signaling toward the front of the restaurant, looking for the maître d'hôtel.

"Take it easy, Warren. John couldn't come."

Carl had had Rothman's secretary call Gier's office, saying John Harrington wanted to meet him for lunch.

Gier lowered his hand. "Where's Harrington?"

Carl gave Gier his broad, charming undercover smile, the one that made traffickers think he was as crooked as they were.

"Couldn't make it. Sent me instead."

"Who are you?"

"A fortune-teller."

"Leave this table or I'll call the maître d'."

"Don't believe it? Martha Petrucina's gonna sue you for sexual harassment. How's that? Sound like your future?"

"I never met any—"

"Gonna happen, Warren. In the cards. Want more?"

"I never heard of—what's this all about?"

"Conspiracy to commit burglary. State of Wisconsin. A sure thing."

Gier's hands began to tremble.

A waiter appeared.

"Will you gentlemen have an aperitif?"

"My friend here would like a drink. Needs a drink. What'll you have, Warren?"

"A double Dewar's, please."

"Double Dewar's for my friend. I'm fine."

When the waiter had left, Gier said, "What do you want?"

"Good question. Very sensible. You're a sharp operator, Warren. Martha said you were sharp, liked you a lot, right up until the moment you grabbed her—"

"What do you want, Mr.—who the hell are you?"

"I want the girl and the adoptive parents. Names, addresses."

"I don't know what you're talking about."

"Warren, Warren, Warren. I talked to Roger Budrow. He had *so* much he wanted to tell me. Says the burglary was all your idea. That right, Warren?"

Warren glanced to his left and right.

After a minute he said, "If I tell you what you want to know, what happens?"

"My crystal ball breaks. Martha forgets, Roger forgets, I forget. Life goes on."

He loved bullying guys like Warren Gier.

"How do I know you'll keep your word?"

"You don't."

Carl grinned. Esther said he had the nastiest grin this side of Jack Nicholson.

Gier unbuttoned his jacket, took a deep breath, exhaled.

"The girl's name is Samantha." What did he have to lose? He'd been told to get dirt on Michelle, and he'd done it. No way could Carl, or anyone else, undo that. "The adoptive mother's name is Doreen Young. Husband's Larry. I only met the mother. She said she divorced Larry four years ago, got custody of the girl, but he took off, took the girl with him. Doesn't know where they are. That's it."

"Why'd she tell you this?"

He shrugged. What woman wouldn't tell things to Warren Gier?

"Your natural charm and boyish good looks was all it took?"

"Doreen Young is a woman with her eye out for what she can get."

So he'd had to pay her.

"Where's Doreen live?"

"Milwaukee."

"The video?"

"Larry sent it to her two years ago, presumably to prove the girl was safe and happy. She'd been searching for him, hired a detective. She thinks he thought if she thought the girl was okay she'd stop looking."

"That's very good, Warren. I appreciate your help. So here's what you're going to do. You're going to go get all the documents Roger stole and gave to you and you're going to bring them to me right here. Now."

"You're crazy. I can't do that. They're—"

"Warren, are you listening? I don't care where they are. I have enough faith in you to know you have them within your reach. So get them. And make sure all the names, addresses, phone numbers are still there. And bring the original video the wife gave you, not a copy. If you're not back in time to pay the check I'll have to send it to Martha's lawyer. Or the Wisconsin state prosecutor's office. Now run along. I'm a fast eater."

Carl reached for the menu and signaled the waiter.

"But there's not time to—"

Carl ignored him.

The waiter appeared.

Carl said, "How's the lobster thermidor? Good today?"

"For two, sir?"

"Just one. My friend's not eating. See you later, Warren."

Carl circled the block twice. Second time around, he stopped at the corner and wrote down the plate number of the Jeep Cherokee parked in front of the house.

He went to a pay phone, called the local DEA office, and asked them to run the plate number. Ten minutes later they called back. The Cherokee was registered to a twenty-three-year-old Caucasian male named Danny Sullivan. They'd checked him with the Wisconsin State Crime Information Center, whose computer said he'd done a three-to-five for assaulting the manager of a homosexual nightclub and was presently wanted on a warrant for manslaughter. The Cherokee's VIN number identified the previous owner as a California gun store specializing in automatic assault rifles. Carl asked the DEA dispatcher to give the Milwaukee PD the location of the Cherokee.

He left his rented Ford where it was and walked back to the house. The sky was overcast, looking like rain. Things were more complicated now. From what Warren had told him, from the presence of the Cherokee in front of the house, and from a feeling of deep unease in the pit of his stomach, Carl was sure this was no longer a simple matter of locating Samantha's adoptive parents so they could be asked how they felt about identifying Samantha as Gus Parham's biological daughter. It was going to be much more involved than that.

Carl wondered if maybe Gus was wrong to want this job so bad, go through all the crap people were willing to put him through. When they got to Washington Carl had put that question to Gus, and Gus had told him, "As soon as I accepted the nomination, the Supreme Court went from a dream to a possibility. It became something I knew I was put on earth to do. No one's going to make me withdraw. If the Senate fails to confirm me, that's that. But no one will make me withdraw."

Gus was a great lawyer, a great judge, and a great friend, but he'd never been in the street, never had his nose in the dirt. Carl thought he was like a meteorologist who'd studied all there was to study about storms, but dealt with them from the safety of his office, never experienced their violence and destruction or the hardship of those caught up in them. He was good at dealing with life, but what if life took him someplace he'd never been before?

Carl walked up the front steps to a wooden porch and pressed the bell.

The door opened on a chain. He caught a whiff of cigarette smoke. A slender face, angry and dreary, with a pile of blonde hair on top. "Yes?"

"Are you Doreen Young?"

Her dark eyes looked him over, neutral, ready to go either way.

"Yes."

"My name's Ed Parker. I'm a friend of Warren Gier. Can I come in?"

Warren had paid her. She'd be looking for more.

"Oh, sure. Hang on a second."

The door closed. He was going to tell her as little as possible, just enough to get her talking. If she knew he'd seen the video, that he was looking for Samantha, she could use it. She'd already spoken to Gier. Information was power.

Five minutes later, when the door reopened, the anger and dreariness were gone. Doreen Young was wearing makeup, a pink blouse, black slacks, and a not-now-but-maybe-later smile that had just the right mix of charm and suspicion.

They sat in a small, dim living room with the smell of cigarette smoke. Doreen wasn't smoking. A large posterlike painting of the zodiac hung over an orange couch. He glanced quickly around for photographs of Samantha. There were none.

"Who are you, Mr. Parker?"

"I represent a client who wants to locate your husband. Mr. Gier thought you might be able to help."

"How do you know Mr. Gier?"

"We're old friends." He grinned, letting her know that was gonna be it.

"Who's your client?"

"Someone who wants to find your husband. He thought that since you've also been trying to find him, you might be willing to pool resources."

"Pool resources?"

"He has funds. You have information."

She laughed, a lighthearted chuckle.

"Well, I've got information all right. Why's your client want to find my husband?"

"He wants to ask him some questions."

"About what?"

"They're personal."

"You won't tell me who your client is, you won't tell me why you want to find my husband. I'm just supposed to tell you everything I know and be happy with that? I hope I don't look that stupid."

"What do you want?"

"What do you have to give?"

"What did Mr. Gier give?"

"That's between Mr. Gier and me."

"Let's put it this way, Mrs. Young. If you provide information that helps me find your husband, I promise to tell you where he is. All the expense of finding him will have been borne by my client. You want to find him and I want to help you do that. You have nothing to lose."

"Oh, I don't have anything to lose. But there's profit in this for you and your client, so why not me too?"

"If I find your husband, I'm quite sure my client will want to disclose himself to you. He just doesn't want to do it now. What profit, if any, there might in it for you I can't say. But I know him to be a very generous man, to those who are on his side."

She leaned back in the chair and crossed her arms and legs.

"What do you want to know?"

"Anything that will help me find your husband. Where was he the last you heard from him?"

"In a bar."

Carl couldn't be sure if the touch of insolence in her smile was directed at him or at her husband.

"Where?"

"I have no idea. He called me from a bar."

"How did you know he was in a bar?"

"He's always in a bar. And from the background noise."

A sound came from another room, a door closing, maybe a closet.

"He spent a lot of time in bars?"

Her voice quickened. She wanted to end this, get rid of him.

"He works in bars. He's a pianist, plays in bars, nightclubs."

"Where was he working last?"

"I told you, I don't know. He just called."

"What did he call about?"

"The usual. 'Get off my back. Stop looking for me.' Called me names. Told me what a bitch I was. Whenever he runs out of people to hurt he calls me."

Voices came from the other room. A girl and man quarreling. Samantha? Carl's heart stopped.

"I'm afraid that's all I can tell you, Mr. Parker." She stood. "If I think of anything else I'll let you know."

"Do you have a picture of him?" She was in a hurry. Carl stayed in his chair. "I thought maybe a publicity photo, from a nightclub or something?"

The kitchen door swung open and a young man in jeans and a black T-shirt walked in, *swaggered* in.

Doreen opened a drawer in a cabinet and handed Carl a photograph. To the man, she said, "I told you to stay out of here."

The man ignored her and dropped into a chair. The T-shirt was too small for his muscles. Carl had put cuffs on hundreds of guys just like him. Fake tough, pumps iron in front of mirrors, bullies women and gays. Gutless, brainless, a wimp with biceps.

Carl grinned at him. "Hi, Danny."

The man rolled his shoulders and looked up. "How'd you know my name?"

Doreen glanced at Carl, and her eyebrows came together in a tiny frown. Before she could add her question to Danny's, the door opened again, and an obese fifteen-year-old girl stood in the doorway. Barefoot, draped in a black dress from neck to ankles, she had a shaved head and angry blue eyes, mean beyond her years.

Carl watched her, relieved she wasn't Samantha.

Doreen opened the front door. Danny glared.

"Let me know when you find the bastard."

"Absolutely."

He walked down the porch steps to the sidewalk. He'd been in a lot of living rooms with a lot of strange people, but he'd never been as uncomfortable as he'd been with Doreen and the fifteen-year-old. Danny didn't bother him—he was an open book. But the girl had filled the room with menace. He had sensed the traces of it when he was alone with Doreen, like a leftover stench, and when the girl came in, the two of them together, it turned real. He had never experienced that feeling before, not from anyone he had ever arrested or any place he had ever been. He knew how to handle guys like Danny, he was safe with them, but Doreen and the girl were different, the danger was different. What had it been like in that house for Samantha? Had the girl been there then? Where did all that evil come from?

He had to find Samantha.

It began to drizzle. Next door to Doreen's house an elderly man was on the front lawn raking leaves. But there were no leaves. And he was doing it in the rain.

Carl walked slowly past him. The man looked up and smiled. "How you doin'?"

"Not too bad," Carl said, smiling. "How're you?"

"Okay."

He stopped raking. This was a man with something to say.

Carl intensified his smile and nodded at the house. "You know them?"

"Oh, yeah. Sure do."

He gave Carl a look. Carl tried to make his smile talk. *We're on the same side. Speak to me.*

"Well, I can't exactly say I *know* them—if you mean like in a social way, so to speak."

"So you don't know them socially."

"Not at all."

"Not your kind of people."

He gave his head an exaggerated shake. *No way.*

"What kind of people are they?"

"Well, I wouldn't want to speak against them, neighbors you know, but—" He hesitated.

Carl said, "I can understand that."

"You a cop?"

"No."

"But a sort of cop, right?"

"Maybe. Yeah. A sort of."

"Somethin's wrong in that house."

Carl waited.

The man looked as if he might be about to say something. Then he glanced at the Cherokee, lifted the rake, and walked back toward his house.

Carl headed for the car, imagining what might have been on the man's mind. He wondered what it had been like for Samantha in that house, and what it was like for her now with Larry Young. How much should he tell Gus? It wouldn't help Gus and Michelle to know about that house and Doreen and the girl and Danny. He'd just tell them Larry was a pianist, plays in bars, nightclubs. That was the helpful part, the lead, what he'd come for.

As he pulled out of his parking place, he spotted a dark blue Plymouth with two men in the front seat headed the other way, toward the house. In his rearview mirror he watched the Plymouth stop next to the Cherokee.

"Milwaukee's finest," Carl said aloud. "Doing their duty. Goodbye, Danny."

12

Senator Eric Taeger sat at his desk, staring bleakly at a rain-drenched asphalt parking lot, reflecting on the past week, one of the worst of his life. Tuesday he'd seen his lawyer, who told him his wife was leaving him. Thursday he'd seen his doctor, who told him he had Parkinson's disease. Stay away from lawyers and doctors.

Not that he cared that much about his wife, but they'd been together forty-seven years. Well, together—they shared a house, but not a bedroom, they shared an abiding hatred for each other, and they shared the love of their two children. A week ago she'd moved out, told her lawyer to tell him that with both children now out of the house—his son was at West Point, his daughter had just married—she saw no reason to continue the marriage ("the agony," she called it).

He knew he was a lousy husband, had been guilty of just about everything his wife accused him of, which was everything she could suspect or imagine. If ever a man deserved to be abandoned by his wife, it was he. But what really startled him was what had happened yesterday afternoon, Friday, a day after the doctor told him he had Parkinson's disease. It had suddenly occurred to Taeger, with great certainty, that if his wife had known about the Parkinson's (there were, as yet, no symptoms evident to her) she would not have been able to leave him. She would have felt compelled—by duty, pride, the pressure of friends—to stay and look after him, to care for him as he disintegrated through debility to death. He discovered with amazement a profound relief, deep in his heart, that simply because he saw the lawyer before the doctor, she had been spared that. Somewhere far beyond his hatred for her, he had uncovered a tiny, still-warm ash of what had once been love. Incredible. Wonderful. If the disease had given him that, the disease was not all bad.

His intercom buzzed, and he heard the voice of his secretary.

"Mr. Harrington is here."

"Send him in."

Harrington stuck his head through the open door and saw Taeger bent over a stack of papers. The old man looked up, studied him for a moment, dropped his eyes back to the papers, and said impatiently, "Well, all right, John, where are we?"

Taking that as an invitation, Harrington approached the

mahogany desk. Twenty-two years earlier, Harrington had been an attorney on Taeger's Senate staff, and today Taeger remained his bread and butter. Access to Taeger, and through him to other senators and senior staffers, wasn't all he had to sell, but it was most of it. Take away Taeger and Harrington's shop looked bare.

Taeger was seventy-six years old, six-feet-six, skinny, white-haired, rich, and scary. Harrington wasn't sure who frightened him more, Eric Taeger or Ernesto Vicaro. When it came to fear, Taeger's office was not that different from the interview room where Harrington met Vicaro. Both stank, literally or figuratively, with a coldly regulated savagery. That Taeger's power was predominantly political and Vicaro's predominantly physical made little difference. The thought of those two men coming together against a common enemy—even Gus Parham—made Harrington shudder.

Taeger had earned his money from a nationwide chain of 232 automobile repair centers, and he conducted much of his Senate business out of this office on the second floor of the main center a few miles from Capitol Hill. Lobbyists said it was the only place in town you could change legislation and your brake linings in one stop. Taeger hated more people, had hurt more people, had made and destroyed more careers than anyone else Harrington could think of.

Harrington sat in a black suede chair overlooking the parking lot and heard Taeger repeat his question. "Where are we?"

Harrington said, "How long do you have?"

Taeger's praying-mantis body hunched over the desk. He'd been leading the committee's interrogation of Judge Parham, and so far the media was calling it a draw.

"About five minutes." His eyes swiveled up to catch

Harrington's gaze. "But for you I'll stretch it to ten. I've gotta be back on the Hill by three."

He smiled, although you had to have known him awhile to know that's what it was.

"You talk to the dean?"

Harrington said, "He says he wants to check her SAT scores, but it's okay. He's not happy, but he'll do it."

"He doesn't have to be happy. You tell Derek?"

Derek Seleck, a pro-Parham senator on the Judiciary Committee, had an academically mediocre daughter applying at an Ivy League university whose admissions dean owed a debt to Taeger. (Harrington didn't even want to guess what that debt might be.) Taeger had suggested to Seleck that his daughter's admission could be assured for the price of his vote. It had then been Harrington's job to tell the dean that if the girl were admitted his debt to Taeger would be forgotten.

"I thought maybe you'd want to do that."

Taeger made a note, but didn't speak.

Harrington said, "Seleck's wife plays bridge with the wives of two senators on the—"

Not lifting his head, Taeger said, "Tell me something I don't know, John."

He continued to read documents, applying his signature, making notes. "What about this Vicaro affidavit?"

At their last meeting, Harrington had told Taeger about the possibility of a Vicaro affidavit accusing Parham of stealing some of the luggage-locker money. Taeger had had a recollection of Vicaro. They'd met seven years earlier at a reception in the Colombian embassy. Taeger said Vicaro stuck in his mind because at the tender age of nineteen, between years at Florida State, he was already serving as a second secretary in the political section. A year after that he'd been elected to the Colombian senate. With a rich and influential father, he was clearly on the fast track. And now here he was doing federal time for cocaine trafficking. *Sic transit gloria mundi.* No wonder Vicaro hated Parham.

"Still working on it. It's got some major problems."

Taeger said, "I hear someone got hurt."

"Hurt?"

"Broken ankles. Young fellow from your office."

"Oh, you heard about that?"

"Too bad." Taeger's eyes swiveled up again, pinned Harrington. "Always regrettable when politics gets violent."

Was that supposed to be irony? No one knew more than Taeger about the occasionally lethal kinship between politics and violence. Fifty years earlier, when Taeger was a young politician running for the Kansas state legislature, his opponent had been arrested with a prostitute in the front seat of a car, five ounces of marijuana in the back. Charged with reckless driving, lewd behavior, and felony drug possession, the opponent had hanged himself in his jail cell the night of his arrest. Taeger won the election, and a month later the prostitute told a vice squad cop that Taeger had paid her to jump into the opponent's car, grab him around the neck, spill perfume and alcohol, and drop the marijuana. The prostitute later recanted, left the state, and no charges were filed.

Harrington, referring to what had happened to his assistant's ankles, said, "I wouldn't call that politics."

The senator had lost a son in the Vietnam War, another lesson in the violence of politics. He said, "More like police brutality?" Then he smiled, if that's what it was.

* * *

The FBI, working with the chief of security for the Sony Corporation, had identified the videocassette Warren Gier handed over as one of a batch Sony originally shipped to Singapore. Sony's Singapore wholesaler identified it as part of a consignment to Hong Kong, where it had been sold locally.

So Carl flew to Hong Kong. It was his first visit in seven years.

He had not been in his hotel five minutes when the phone rang.

"Hello?"

"Carl?"

"Who's calling?"

"Doug Cabot."

"Well, Doug Cabot. How are you?" A Honk Kong–based DEA agent. Carl wasn't surprised to hear his voice. He'd seen the surveillance around his taxi on the way in from Kai Tak Airport. The Hong Kong Narcotics Bureau had the best surveillance teams in the world, men and women on foot, bicycles, motorcycles, in cars, trucks, and taxis, weaving in and out, coming and going, here one moment, gone the next. They didn't fight the traffic, they became the traffic. They didn't watch you, they enveloped you.

"Fine. How was the flight?"

"Great."

Carl had worked with Cabot sixteen years earlier in the Chicago office and found him sly and manipulative. What did he want?

"I'm just calling because I saw a cable this morning from the Congressional Liaison Office asking for a daily update on your activities. Thought you might like to know."

"I appreciate that."

Carl felt a sudden pang of disappointment. How cheaply some people sell their loyalty. He could guess where the congressional request had come from: Senator Eric Taeger, chairman of the Judiciary Committee. Leading the stop-Parham campaign in the Senate, Taeger would naturally want to know what a pro-Parham investigator was doing in Hong Kong. And Cabot was ready and eager to curry a little favor, help him find out, look good with the senator.

"You need anything, Carl, give me a call. How're you fixed for transportation?"

That'd really make Cabot's job easy, know everywhere Carl went.

"Just fine, thanks. I'll call if I need anything."

"Do that. We're here to help."

"Of course you are."

So now Cabot had something to put in his answer to the cable. "Special Agent Falco arrived Hong Kong. HKNB surveilled him to the Kowloon Park Hotel, where Special Agent Cabot telephonically confirmed his presence."

Later on, Cabot would hit HKNB for the surveillance reports and for transcripts of Carl's telephone conversations from the hotel room. Send it off to Washington, make it sound like he did it all himself—wouldn't Cabot look like a good little boy then? Politics screws up everything, even sixteen-year-old friendships.

Carl hadn't been to bed for almost thirty hours, but it was just past midnight, perfect for what he had to do. He left the hotel, ignored the taxi rank, walked two blocks, flagged down a cab, took it through the tunnel under the harbor, and got out at the Mandarin Hotel. He gave the concierge a hundred-dollar bill and said, "I'm looking for a friend who plays piano in a bar or nightclub. Problem is I don't know which one. Where should I look?"

Wordlessly, the man fished a sheet of notepaper from under the counter and began listing names. When he'd put down eighteen, he gave the paper to Carl.

"If it's not one of these, it would have to be—"

"Low-down."

The man smiled, a tiny quiver at the corners of his mouth. "I'd try these, sir."

"Thanks very much."

By the time the sun came up and the bars and nightclubs had closed, Carl had been to eleven of the names on the list, talking to managers, flashing his DEA badge, showing his picture of Larry Young. None admitted to seeing him.

He went back to the hotel, slept four hours, and at noon set out again. Just after five that afternoon, he found a food and beverage director at a hotel in Kowloon who remembered Larry.

"We had him in our piano bar for four months, then he decided not to renew his contract. He said he had a job in London, wanted to get back to Europe for his daughter's education."

Carl showed the man a picture of Samantha, taken from the video.

"Yeah, that's her, pretty girl. Nice girl, what I saw of her. Larry didn't like bringing her to the bar."

Carl went back to his hotel, grabbed his bag, and headed for Kai Tak Airport. He reserved a seat on a Swissair flight leaving in an hour for Zurich, connecting to London. Then he found a pay phone and called Doug Cabot at the DEA office.

"Dinner tonight?"

"Love to, Carl. How was your day?"

"Can you meet me at the Mandarin bar at eight?"

"Fine. Perfect. Everything okay?"

"Terrific. I'll be around for another four days, then I'm off for Caracas."

"Caracas? What's in Caracas?"

"You won't believe it, Doug. Tell you all about it tonight."

"Great. See you then."

Give Cabot something to put in today's cable. Tomorrow he can try to explain how come he got it all wrong.

This time he didn't have to worry about surveillance. London cops couldn't follow a train through a tunnel. Trying to make ends meet on a government expense allowance of $175 a day, he asked the Heathrow cab driver, a Pakistani, to take him someplace small, cheap, and off the beaten path.

It was practically on another continent. The neighborhood was a sea of black faces, and when he walked into the entrance hall the smell of curry almost knocked him down. A desk, a stairway, six rooms upstairs.

He was in his room—no TV, no phone—trying to get the window open when the young man who'd checked him in downstairs knocked on the door.

"Telephone."

Carl said, "There isn't one."

"Downstairs. Telephone for you."

"No. That's a mistake." He hadn't told anyone where he was.

"No mistake. Telephone for you."

Carl followed him downstairs, into the cloud of curry stench. He took the phone, put it to his ear. "Hello."

"Welcome to Caracas."

Doug Cabot. Carl couldn't believe it.

"You guys are better than I thought." Flatter him.

"We have our moments."

"I'm going to bed, Doug. You should, too. It's late in Hong Kong."

At seven that evening—followed or not, he wasn't sure—Carl found himself in the large, wood-paneled office of the manager of a Mayfair gambling club. The club had a piano bar, and Carl was about to hand over a photograph of Larry Young. Dressed in a tuxedo, a deep tan, and arrogance, the manager roamed regally around the office, talking into a gold-colored, fold-open cellular telephone hardly larger than a cigarette lighter. Absently, he waved Carl to a chromium chair. Something a little too imperious in that wave kept Carl on his feet. An enormous Saint Bernard sprawled on the beige carpet.

The manager, still on the phone, wandered over to the dog, his back to Carl. The Saint Bernard, its head the size of a microwave oven, lumbered to its feet and moved next to Carl, panting.

Carl patted the dog's head and waited.

The man hung up but remained silent, his back to Carl.

Carl said, "Thanks for seeing me. I'm looking for someone they told me downstairs used to play the piano here. He—"

The phone rang. The manager raised a hand for silence, flipped open his gold cellular phone, listened, whispered, and resumed his random walk around the deep-piled carpet, mumbling into the phone.

Carl waited.

The man hung up.

Carl said, "As I was saying, his name is—"

The phone rang again. Another raised hand. More whispering and wandering. The manager hung up.

Carl said, "His name—"

The telephone rang again.

Carl said, "Excuse me—"

The man, now on the other side of the Saint Bernard, again raised a hand.

Carl had had enough. He stepped around the dog, gripped the man's wrist, and removed the phone. Then he closed the phone, slipped it into the panting mouth of the Saint Bernard, and held the jaws closed. He felt a heavy gulp. He released the jaws. The dog, licking its mouth with a tongue as big as a dishcloth, looked placidly at Carl.

The stunned manager stared incredulously at the Saint Bernard. "You gave him my telephone."

"You'll get it back."

"He swallowed the telephone."

"Forget it. We have to talk."

"He swallowed—"

The dog dropped lazily to the carpet, lay its head on its paws, and gazed contentedly up at its master.

The manager said, "Is he all right?"

"He's fine. I'm looking for a man named Larry Young who used to play piano here. Do you remember him?"

Still watching the dog, the manager said, "Yes, that's right. Larry Young." He looked up from the dog, and his eyes fixed on Carl. "Larry Young. Yes."

"Tell me about him."

"I wish he'd never left. He had a great way with the

clients. The richer they were, the more they liked him. I always thought it was the Albanian thing. Do you know him?"

"The Albanian thing?"

"He was from Albania, related to the old royal family, at least that's what he said. He said he changed his name when he went to the States. He went to Saint-Tropez for the summer. Said he wanted his daughter to see the Continent."

"Did you meet her?"

"Yes, unfortunately. A little bitch."

"Really?"

"Precocious. Very demanding. Thirteen years old and she's acting like she's his agent. Larry tried to keep her out of here, which suited me fine. Guys had started to hit on her. Very mature."

A mild explosion, followed by a stench worse than the hotel curry, filled the office. Carl and the manager turned to the Saint Bernard, whose expression had gone from dreamy to mildly concerned.

After a moment, Carl said, "I think he's about to return the phone."

The Saint Bernard rose heavily to his feet, stood uncertainly, then sat back down with the preoccupied expression of a dog having an unfamiliar internal experience.

The manager said, "Should I call the vet?"

"I don't think so. Just be patient."

13

Carl sat at the end of the crowded bar with a Heineken that cost exactly four times what he'd have had to pay in Montgomery. The place was packed, but the piano was silent.

He asked the bartender, a pretty redhead with a smile and an English accent, when the music started.

"He's just on his break. Coupla minutes."

The tables, reaching from the bar to an open terrace bordering the port, were filled with vacationers Carl guessed had come to the south of France for the sun, sex, and imagined glamour. Carl had been in Saint-Tropez long enough—about two hours—to see the yachts along the port, smell the sea air, and have his eyebrows almost singed off by a fire-eater performing in the crowd oozing through the narrow medieval streets. He saw a lot of young girls, many with men who were not so young. But he saw no one who looked like Samantha. He wasn't happy to think she might be here.

Carl smiled back and said, "What's his name?"

The bartender reached under the bar and handed Carl a black-and-white leaflet, French on one side, English on the other.

LIVE
At the Papagayo
Larry Young
11 to Dawn

The picture showed a handsome, tuxedoed young man at a piano, smiling into the camera. He was the man in the photograph Doreen had given Carl, the one he'd been displaying all over Hong Kong and London.

Carl saw a door open in the shadows at the back, and a man came in. He stood for a moment in the half-light, back bent, looking tired. Then he smoothed the front of his tuxedo jacket, took a deep breath, straightened himself, and started toward the piano. Before he entered the light, his face changed, a smile came on, and by the time he reached the piano he was beaming greetings to customers. A few nearest the piano smiled and nodded.

He played a few show tunes, some modern pop numbers, Cole Porter, even a little Bach jazz, working hard to propel the magic beyond the fans at the piano's edge. It wasn't easy. Compelling conversations—seductions and con stories, Carl guessed—resisted intrusion at the outer tables. Carl listened and watched, impressed. Larry was a fighter, throwing personality and talent against a fortress of apathy. His head was back, eyes closed, playing from the heart, or giving a good impression of it. Sweat rolling down his cheeks darkened the white collar. A professional, Carl thought, good at what he does, and he's gonna do it whether anyone listens or not. What had his relationship been with Doreen? What was it now with Samantha? What had that family been like, when it was still a family? Where was Samantha? As Carl watched Larry playing, he thought, I've found him, now how do I keep him?

Larry was on the run with his daughter. If Carl followed him back out that door the next time he took a break, Larry might make a run for it. It was dark out and Carl didn't know the streets. But if he confronted him here in the bar, Larry could still take off. An entire side of the room was open to the port.

Is he a runner? Carl wondered. Or a talker, or a fighter?

Several people had approached the piano with written song requests. Carl took a card from a stack on the bar and wrote a request of his own.

"Dear Mr. Young: I am not a cop, I am not from Doreen. I am a friend who is on your side. I have important news for you. Can we talk?"

He folded the card and asked the bartender if she had a paper clip.

"Will a pin do?"

"That'll be fine, thanks."

He pinned a 500-franc note to the card, walked over to the piano, and laid it on top of the others. He stayed until

Larry had glanced up and met his eyes. Larry smiled, said "Thanks," and kept on playing.

Carl went back to his stool, sipped his beer, and waited. People drifting in from the port, drawn by the music, filled the empty tables. Larry was winning. The seducers and con men were losing.

Larry finished a song, drank from a glass on the piano, and lifted the cards. Carl slipped off his stool and moved toward the piano. He was five steps away when Larry unpinned the 500-franc note and unfolded Carl's card. Carl watched him read it. *A runner, a talker, or a fighter?*

Larry finished reading, turned the card over, read it again. He slipped the card slowly into his jacket pocket, not looking up. Then abruptly, making a decision, he raised his eyes and found Carl.

Carl tried to get the whole message into his smile. *I'm safe, talk to me.* But he was ready to run.

Larry put the other cards into his pocket, smiled at the faces nearest the piano, and headed back toward the rear door. He wasn't hurrying, and by the time he reached the door, Carl was with him. Carl held the door, and they stepped into a narrow street between the back of the bar and a small café.

Larry said, "Who are you?"

"A friend. Can we talk?"

Standing, Larry looked smaller than he had at the piano. "Tell me who you are."

The beaming smile was gone, an act abandoned as he left the stage. His tired eyes were filled with a sadness that made Carl want to trust him.

"It's too long a story. It's not any of the things you're

thinking. You couldn't possibly guess. But I'm a friend. Believe me. Can we talk? You won't be sorry."

Larry hesitated a moment. Then he said, "I have to do something first."

Carl had expected more of an argument. This was too easy. What was it Larry had to do?

Larry said, "Wait for me in the café. I'll be back in ten minutes."

He walked down the street to the corner, made a left, and disappeared.

Carl was going to believe that? Back in ten minutes? But if Larry looked around and spotted Carl following, it would be the end of whatever fragile shred of trust he might have won. Larry was desperate, and desperate men are eager for someone to trust.

The café had a zinc bar, four tables, a bartender, and one other customer, an old man with a newspaper and a glass of something milky white.

Carl told the bartender, "Coffee, please," and sat at one of the tables.

He faced the street and looked at his watch. When the ten minutes had passed he began to curse himself. What a jerk. Conned by a piano player. "Be back in ten minutes." Sure you will, yeah, right. His brains must be softening.

He gave it another five minutes, then paid for the coffee and walked out. He took the left turn Larry had taken. Halfway up the block he saw a small illuminated sign. HOTEL. No name. He walked past on the other side of the street and looked in through the glass front. A tiny entrance hall, a desk with an old woman, stairs.

He had turned back toward the café when a figure appeared at the desk. It was Larry. Carl watched as Larry said something to the old woman, came out to the street, and headed toward the café.

Carl ran.

His empty coffee cup was still on the table. He had it to his lips when Larry came through the door.

"Sorry I took so long."

"No problem. Happy to relax for a few minutes."

Larry asked the bartender for coffee, hung his tuxedo jacket over the back of a chair and sat down. He was still sweating. "Tell me who you are."

"I represent someone in the United States who wants to talk to you. It has nothing to do with anyone else who might be looking for you. It's completely independent of that."

"Who is it?"

"Someone important. You might have heard of him. I know this sounds crazy, but what I'm saying is someone wants to talk to you and I can't tell you who it is, only that it won't hurt you and could help you a lot. I know I shouldn't expect you to believe that, but it's all I can say."

"What do you want?"

"The person I represent wants to meet you, and he sent me to find you. I've found you, and now I'm asking if you'll meet him. He's in the States. If you say yes, he'll be here to-morrow afternoon. He'll meet you anywhere you like, and you can take any precautions you like. He'll explain every-thing. There won't be any mysteries. And I can guarantee that you'll be glad you've seen him. You won't be sorry."

"How'd you find me?"

"From the video."

"The video?"

"The one you sent Doreen. I traced it back to Hong

Kong, showed pictures around, got a lead to London. Someone in London sent me here."

"That was a lot of work."

"It's important you talk to this guy. Don't even try to guess what it's about. You'll be amazed. And you'll be pleased."

Larry drank from his cup, slowly, then set it back on the saucer, right dead in the middle, thinking. "Does it have something to do with my daughter?"

"Yes. But nothing to do with disagreements with Doreen. This man does not want to get you into trouble. In fact, this man wants to talk to you specifically *because* he wants to protect you. There's something he's thinking of doing but he doesn't want to do it without consulting you first. If you say no, that'll be it. He'll go home and you can forget you ever met him. Your life will go on as if he'd never been here."

"You talked with Doreen?"

"Yes."

"How was she?"

"Nasty."

Larry smiled, not a happy smile. "How did you meet her?"

"Looking for you. All I had to go on was the video."

"Where'd you get that?"

"From someone Doreen gave it to."

"Who?"

"You don't know him."

Larry pulled an end of his bow tie and unbuttoned his collar. "What's your name?"

"Carl."

"What's your last name?"

"Let's just stay with Carl. I don't want to lie to you."

"What's going on? Really."

Carl felt sorry for him. He was a man with problems, and now he had another, something else that might hurt him, hurt his daughter.

"I've told you all I can."

"And if you're lying to me, I'm in a lot of trouble. Maybe you're from Doreen. She wants Samantha back."

"I've told you all I can tell you."

Larry nodded, took another sip of coffee, and sat there, silent, thinking. Then he shook his head and looked a lot more tired than when he'd come in through the door to the bar. He closed his eyes and sighed. It sounded like four years of desperation.

"When do you have to know?"

"Soon as you can tell me. Right now would be best."

"I can't tell you now. Come back tomorrow night. I'll see you during my first break."

"Fine."

"I have to get back."

"Larry . . ."

"Yes?"

"I just want to tell you . . ." Carl waited while Larry buttoned his collar and put on his jacket. The tie hung loose. "It's important that you believe me. If you say no, it'll be a big mistake. Meet this man. Hear what it's about. You'll be glad you did."

"See you tomorrow."

There weren't many things Carl had ever wanted to know more than he wanted to know if Samantha was in that hotel. But if he made a move to find out—talked to the old woman at the desk or came back in the morning to watch the entrance—and Larry found out, that would be the end. His instincts, rehabilitated after Larry's return to the café, told him Larry was not going to run for it. Have confidence, play it cool.

So he want back to his hotel and called Gus.

"He's here. I spoke to him, just said someone wants to talk to him. He's gonna give me an answer tomorrow night."

"Is Samantha with him?"

"I don't know."

"I'll be on the next flight."

"Why don't you wait till I'm sure Samantha's here?"

"I can't wait, Carl. I'll be on the Delta flight leaving New York tomorrow night. It arrives in Nice the next afternoon."

"I'll be there. Is Michelle coming?"

"Are you kidding?"

When Larry got back to the hotel on his 2 A.M. break he stopped outside Samantha's door and listened.

"Daddy? Is that you?"

He'd tried to be quiet, but she had ears that heard everything.

He cracked the door.

"Go back to sleep, Samantha. It's two A.M."

"I can't sleep."

So he went in and turned on the light. It was a tiny room, across the hall from his own, and she had put up posters of horses and rock stars. She slept with a stuffed bear the size of a cocker spaniel.

"What's wrong, honey?"

"Nothing. I'm just awake. Let's play cards."

Walking back to the hotel, he'd been wondering how much to tell her about Carl. She had a child's innocent wisdom, a natural discernment quick to detect frauds and swindlers. He found the cards in a bureau drawer.

"Five-card stud?"

"Yeah, great."

She smiled, sat up, and smoothed the sheet. He sat on the edge of the bed and dealt. They used to play fish and old maid, but six months ago, in London, he had taught her poker. They played for used postage stamps. When she won, she pasted her stamps in an album.

He said, "I met a man tonight."

"Who is he?"

"I don't know."

She peeked at her hole card and looked up. "Is he nice?"

"I'm not sure. He wanted to talk to me."

"What did he say?"

She had a pair of queens showing and reached into her envelope of stamps.

"He has a friend he wants me to meet."

She pulled her hand back.

"A friend he wants you to meet. So who's the friend?"

"I don't know. Someone he says I should meet, that it's important, I'll be glad if I meet him."

"But he won't tell you who the friend is?"

"No."

She laid three stamps on the bed beside the cards. Knowing she had him beat, Larry raised her another three.

She said, "Sounds fishy."

"That's what I thought."

"What's he like?"

"He seems like a nice guy. I guess I believe him."

"You believe everyone."

"That's true. Raise you another three."

"I wonder who it is."

"Yeah."

He dealt the last card.

"Maybe someone famous wants you to work for them."

"I don't think so."

"Maybe it's something really exciting."

Larry laughed. "That's what I'm afraid of."

"Don't be so pessimistic. I think you should meet him. Why not?"

She was smiling, full of confidence, adventure, and hope. He loved her enthusiasm. She did more for him than he did for her, and he wished he could change that. Sometimes she was all that kept him going, all that kept him away from the bottle.

He waited until she had won all the stamps, then said good night and kissed her cheek. She got out of bed to lock the door behind him.

In the doorway he said, "See you later."

"Good night, Daddy. I think you should see the man's friend."

He waited in the hall until he heard her snap the lock, then hurried back to the club, quickly arranged his jacket, arranged his face, and headed for the piano.

The next night Carl waited in a doorway near the corner where he could see both the entrance to Larry's hotel and the rear door of the Papagayo bar. At 10:30 he watched Larry come out of the hotel alone and walk toward the bar.

Carl moved out of the doorway's darkness and caught a glimpse of a man at the end of the street ducking into a black Peugeot 205. He stepped back into the doorway and looked into the car as it moved past him up the street. There wasn't much light, and maybe he was overcautious, but the man behind the wheel looked alarmingly like Warren Gier.

As Carl made his way through the crowds along the port to the bar's terrace entrance, he kept thinking, It couldn't be Gier. There's no way that could have been Gier. Gier could *not* have been in that car.

He took a seat at the bar and listened to Larry play. Their eyes met but neither gave a sign of recognition. At the first break, Carl walked outside and waited at the back entrance. He searched the street for a black Peugeot 205. He was certain now that the dim, fleeting profile could not have been Warren Gier.

Carl stepped up to Larry as he came out through the door. "Can I buy you a coffee?"

"I have something I have to do for a few minutes. But it's okay. I'll see your friend. How do we do it?"

"I'll pick you up tomorrow morning at eleven."

"At the café?"

"See you there. And listen, just a question."

"Yes?"

"Has anyone else contacted you in the past couple of days?"

"No. Is there someone else?"

"No, I just wondered. See you tomorrow. I'll hang around and listen to the rest of your performance."

But he didn't hang around, not for long. After half a glass of beer and ten minutes' thought, Carl went back to his hotel and called Gus. It was late afternoon in Washington, and Gus was about to leave for the airport.

Carl said, "Gier's here."

"Warren Gier?"

"The man himself."

Carl told him about the Peugeot.

Gus said, "I'm on my way."

14

You awake?"

Michelle, sleepless for more than an hour, had thought she heard an unfamiliar sound outside the house. Something scraping. They were leaving for France the next afternoon.

"Yeah."

She felt Gus turn toward her in the darkness. Knowing he was awake made her feel safer.

She decided not to mention the sound. Instead she said, "I can't get that stupid thing out of my mind."

In the *Washington Post* that morning one of the columnists had called Gus a racist. He quoted an unnamed "black community leader" in Mobile who claimed that Gus gave stiffer sentences to blacks than to whites.

"Me either."

"Is it worth it, Gus? I mean for you. It's worse for you."

"It's bad for both of us, Michelle. But, yeah, it's worth it. Nothing good comes easy. It's only lies, anyway."

"How can they say that, Gus? He *has* to know it's not true."

"Truth has nothing to do with it."

Major activist groups were holding the threat of a primary battle over the head of any southern senator who voted for Gus's confirmation. To give teeth to that threat, the opposition had to arouse anti-Gus sentiment among black voters. Middle-class concerns like privacy and affirmative action wouldn't do that, but racism would. So for the past week TV spots, newspaper ads, and certain columnists had painted Gus as a racist.

"Oh, Gus, I just—" She put a hand on his cheek. They were silent, wide awake.

Gus said, "Would it keep you awake if I took a shower?"

"No. Go ahead."

She felt him get out of bed, heard the bathroom door close, saw cracks of light around the door.

Michelle heard the shower go on—and then the scraping noise again. She went to the closed window and listened. After a minute, she heard it again, something downstairs by the garage.

"Gus?"

He didn't answer, probably couldn't hear her above the noise of the shower. She didn't want to bother him. She decided just to go downstairs and take a peek out the kitchen window.

A moment later in the kitchen, she put her face to the glass and strained to see the edge of the garage entrance. A faint light flashed for an instant from the garage into the front yard. Her heart stopped. Through the door connecting the kitchen to the garage, she heard the scraping sound, something dragging across the concrete floor. Two dozen cardboard cartons filled with Gus's papers, still unpacked since their move, had been stacked next to the car.

She didn't know what to do. If she called to Gus, he might not hear, and whoever was in the garage would escape. If she ran upstairs, Gus might not get down in time. She opened a kitchen drawer, took out the longest knife she could find, and stood at the door to the garage. She held the knife above her head, put her other hand on the doorknob, and took a deep breath. Then she threw open the door, screamed as loud as she could, stepped into the garage, and flipped the light switch.

He was young, short, overweight, stooping over a carton. He looked up, a rabbit caught in the headlights, eyes on her face, then on the knife. He ran from the garage and jumped into the passenger side of a car that roared out of the driveway in a cloud of exhaust and smoking rubber. She didn't see the driver of the car or its plate number or even the make. But she would never forget that face, burned forever into her memory, as she was sure the image of her knife was burned into his memory.

She stepped back into the kitchen and was almost knocked down by Gus, stark naked, charging in from the living room. His eyes went from Michelle to the knife.

"Who screamed? What's wrong? Put the knife down."

She dropped the knife and fell into his arms.

"Michelle, what's wrong? What happened?" She was trembling, hanging on. "It's all right, honey. It's all right."

He led her into the living room. "Tell me what happened."

"A man was in the garage. I think I scared him to death."

"Are you okay?"

She had stopped shaking. She was smiling.

"I'm fine. Just a little—I'll bet he's shaken up. Crazy lady with a big knife."

"What was he doing?"

"He was bending over a carton, like getting ready to lift it."

Gus got up and went back to the garage.

"Where are you going?"

"Count the cartons."

"Who was he, Gus?"

"Someone looking for dirt."

Michelle waited. She didn't want to see that garage again tonight.

Gus came back, carrying the knife. He dropped it in the sink. "Twenty-three. One missing."

"What's in it?"

"I don't know. I'll have to go through the others."

"Gus, I'm scared."

He put an arm around her. "Let's go to bed. I'll call Rothman tomorrow."

"We're going to France tomorrow."

"I know. Rothman can deal with your burglar friend."

Carl was at the café at ten, and spent the extra hour on countersurveillance, more disturbed than ever about the black Peugeot. He checked the surrounding streets, walked through a parking lot a block away. No black Peugeot.

As he returned to the café, he met Larry on the street. They were walking to Carl's car when Carl spotted a man fifty meters away between two parked cars, his face hidden behind a small hand-held video camera. The camera was aimed right at them.

Carl said, "Just a second. I'll be right back."

He started toward the man, who lowered the camera, jumped into one of the cars, and pulled out into the street. Carl ran, and the car, a black Peugeot 205, accelerated past him, almost knocking him down. This time, through the windshield, he had a clear view of Warren Gier behind the wheel.

Carl went back to Larry, got them both into his car, and was just turning the ignition when he heard a sudden banging on the passenger window. He swung his head, his hand moving instinctively to the Walther in his waistband. A girl's face was at the window, her knuckles beating angrily on the glass.

Larry, yanking the door open, shouted, "Samantha!"

He jumped out of the car. "What are you doing here?"

The girl said, "You shouldn't have done that! I'm going with you!"

She looked seventeen, tall, slim, pink T-shirt, white shorts, pink espadrilles. An older, long-haired, and very angry version of the girl in the video.

Larry said, "You can't go with me. I told you."

"You shouldn't have just left me."

"I didn't just leave you. I told you I was going out. You can wait in the hotel. I'll be back soon."

"Who's he?"

Carl had come around from the driver's side, standing at a distance, staying out of it. She was full of fire, tear-filled eyes flashing anger.

"He's the man I told you about. Carl, this is my daughter, Samantha."

Carl said, "Hi."

He put out his hand, smiling.

"Hi."

Her grip was firm. She took him in at a glance, a one-second study that seemed to tell her everything she needed to know for the moment. Then she looked sharply back at Larry.

"Where are you going?"

"It doesn't matter, Samantha. I'll be back later. Madame Durand will give you lunch."

"I want to go."

"You can't go."

"Why?"

"Samantha, this is something personal between Carl and me."

"I'm scared."

"Samantha, that's—"

"I saw someone following you."

"No one's following me, Samantha."

She turned to Carl, facing him straight on, and this time the eyes tried to pull him to pieces. He felt sorry for her. She was terrified at the possibility of Larry driving off and leaving her. Or maybe she'd seen Gier tracking them with his TV camera. She wasn't the only one concerned. Carl wanted to get back in the car and clear out.

"I don't want to interfere, Larry, but why not let her come? It doesn't bother me."

Samantha reached for the door handle.

"There, so I'm coming."

She climbed in the back seat, sitting straight, arms crossed.

Carl and Larry got in the front, and when Carl looked at her in the rear-view mirror she caught his eye and smiled. The fire was gone, and with it the tears and anger. What was Gus going to say when he came off the plane and saw that face?

Heading out of Saint-Tropez, Larry said, "I hope it's really okay, Samantha coming."

"Absolutely."

"Where are we going?"

"My friend's arriving at the Nice airport. We can meet him there and have lunch."

Carl had been watching Samantha in the rear-view mirror. "That sound okay, Samantha?"

She smiled. The girl in the video.

"Yes, thank you." The eyes were gentle, the aggression gone. "That would be wonderful."

Polite. Shy, even.

"He's where?"

John Harrington had walked into Helen's conference room late and nodded quickly at the three others who were already around the table. Since an earlier meeting, the one at which Isaac Jasper had mentioned conventional tactics that "don't meet your needs," several Freedom Federation members had found excuses for staying away.

Helen said, "Saint-Tropez."

"Gier's in Saint-Tropez? In *France*?"

"So is Parham's daughter. With Carl Falco. Her name's Samantha."

Harrington, shocked into silence, sat down.

Isaac slouched in one of the white chairs, elbow on knee, unshaved chin cupped in his palm. His eyes were closed.

Helen said, "Isaac, are you awake?"

The eyes opened slowly, but the chin did not come off the hand.

"Oh, yeah. Sorry. Just thinking." Now the chin lifted. "I don't want to sound like a prophet of doom, but . . ."

"Go ahead."

"You guys have had it."

Helen said, "Samantha's in France, and we've had it? You're pretty quick to throw in the towel, Isaac."

"Maybe so. But they've found her. Some innocent, pretty little thirteen-year-old goes on Larry King, Letterman, Leno—you've had it. You will *not* find fifty-one senators willing to vote against the kind of sympathy that'll produce. My opinion, maybe I'm wrong. Could be wrong. Hope I'm wrong."

Helen looked at Harrington. "John?"

"I think Isaac's a little prematurely glum. These things are never easy. The question's always the same. How bad do you want to win?"

Helen said to Isaac, "You don't think we can win?"

"I never said that. You can *always* win, if you're willing to do whatever it takes to win. What I'm saying is, what you're doing now won't win. You'll have to do something more effective."

"Like what?"

"That's not my job. That's your job. I'm just giving an

opinion. Business as usual—media, celebrities, phone banks, direct mail, press conferences—that won't do it."

Paula Yost stretched and looked wearily at the ceiling. "Kidnap the kid." She pulled her arms down and her eyes met the shocked stares. "Just kidding!"

Isaac said, "I'm not suggesting anything like that."

Helen said, "Of course not, Isaac. You may be many things, but you're not violent."

"Possibly subviolent." Harrington said it with a grin.

Helen said, "I beg your pardon?"

"Like the suggestion that Parham grabbed some of the luggage-locker money."

Helen said, "Why is that 'subviolent'?"

"It's a lie," Harrington said, "but we use it. A sort of invention. We all know he didn't take the money, but no one rejects the idea of using the accusation."

"Dishonest."

"Of course. But subviolent."

A cloud of silence fell over the white chairs.

Helen said, "What's your thinking, Isaac?"

"Are you talking about lying? If we minded lying we wouldn't be here. Let's not get philosophical."

"Is that what you meant when you suggested something more effective?"

"Helen, let's stop screwing around. This isn't Politics 101. You want to keep Parham off the Supreme Court, keep him off the Supreme Court. Do what's necessary."

After the meeting, Helen asked Isaac if he needed a lift.

He said, "Where are you going?"

"Wherever you are."

In the car, Helen said, "Isaac, you've been in this town

a long time, including places most people never go. In your opinion, as you say, what will we have to do to win?"

"I like the word subviolent. It's a nice euphemism."

"Euphemism for what?"

"There's a spectrum, Helen. What word you use just depends on how many people get hurt. It's a progression. At first, people call it politics. A smile, a handshake. Polite hypocrisy. A lie. Then gentle intimidation. A small threat. Mild blackmail. Someone gets beaten up. Suicide. Murder. People die. Before you know it, you've got bombs in subways, parking garages, department stores. Politics changes its face, changes its name. Now you call it terrorism. But it's all still politics. Getting people's approval, getting them to see things your way."

"Isaac—"

"Bombs in London, bombs in Beirut, bombs in Palestine, New York, Oklahoma—acts of war or terrorism or politics? Politics."

"Isaac, this is a Senate confirmation hearing."

"Sorry. Right. Not even a campaign. Not politics at all."

She turned her head to look at him. Warren Gier would have had a cynical smile. Isaac was just staring out the window—looking rumpled, detached, and not very happy.

Michelle was filled with longing and dread. She wanted to know everything there was to know about Samantha, but she did not want to meet the man who had raised her, cared for her, the man Samantha called Daddy. As the plane banked low over the Mediterranean and its tires screeched onto the tarmac of the Nice airport, Michelle felt fear grow into terror. Where was Samantha? Her adoptive father was waiting in the airport, but where was Samantha?

She glanced at Gus. He was pale. How would Larry Young react, meeting Samantha's biological parents? Would he see them as enemies, a threat? Maybe he wouldn't even talk to them.

Holding hands, they moved with the crowd through Passport Control, down a corridor, and reached a wide stairway to their left. She looked down the stairway and saw Carl waving up at them. She smiled and waved back, keeping her eyes on his face, not ready to see Larry.

She started down the stairs, and her knees went limp. She stumbled. Gus grabbed her arm. "You all right?"

She didn't answer. She had seen a face at the bottom of the stairs. The face was looking back, timid, trying to smile. A girl. It was like staring into a mirror.

Carl shook their hands. "Gus . . . Michelle . . ."

The face was behind him, eyes lowered. For the first time, Michelle noticed the man next to Carl.

Carl said, "How was the flight?"

"Fine."

It was the only word Gus spoke. Michelle reached for his hand. It was damp. She looked at him, tearing her eyes off the girl.

"Oh, I'm sorry," Carl said, "let me introduce Larry Young."

They shook hands.

"How do you do?"

He appeared as distressed as she was—nice looking, an uncomplicated face, simple enough to look embarrassed.

"Nice to meet you."

"And Samantha."

Michelle said, "Hi, Samantha."

Samantha put out a hand. The grip was firm, but shock and fear covered her face.

"It's wonderful to meet you, Samantha."

"Me, too." The voice was soft. She was as tall as Michelle. "I mean I'm happy to meet you." Michelle could see it in her eyes—she'd had the same reaction, her face in a mirror.

Carl said, "Baggage claim is over here."

They passed through double glass doors.

Michelle said, "I'm sorry. Is there a ladies' room?" She thought she was going to be sick.

Larry said, "Back up the stairs and turn left."

"Thanks."

She took three steps, stopped, and heard herself say, "Samantha, would you like to come with me?"

Stupid! Why would Samantha—

"Yes, sure."

When they reached the bathroom, Michelle went to a sink, splashed water on her face, held her fingers over her eyes, pressing, trying to make her head stop spinning, her thoughts come to rest. She put her hands under the tap. The florescent bulb was broken, flickering. Samantha moved next to her, looked at her in the mirror, staring.

Michelle smiled back, her face dripping. "Hi."

Samantha met her eyes in the mirror, silent.

Michelle said, "You know who I am, don't you?"

Samantha said, "You're my mother." Samantha's head was up, her eyes moist. "You look just like me."

Michelle reached for her, touched her shoulder. The water was still running, the bulb flickering.

"Samantha . . ."

The shock and fear were gone, replaced by an expression of uncertain hope.

"How did you—"

The uncertainty disappeared and a smile broke out.

Michelle hugged her. Samantha's hair smelled like sunshine.

Gus felt sorry for Larry. Suddenly he finds himself at the Nice airport with a mysterious stranger from the States and a woman who's the spitting image of his daughter. His tanned, soft, piano player's face looked bewildered, embarrassed, unfamiliar with all these strange people, uncomfortable with his ignorance of the relationships between them.

Gus said, "The first thing I want to do, Larry, is answer questions." He reached into an inside breast pocket of his jacket, withdrew a white envelope, and handed it to Larry. They were with Carl at a bar one flight up from the baggage claim area. Michelle had taken Samantha for a walk around the boutiques.

Larry's dark eyes fixed hesitantly on the envelope.

Gus said, "Open it."

Larry tore the envelope, removed six sheets of paper, and studied them for five silent minutes. Then he looked up at Gus and said, "Samantha's your daughter?" The pages were certified copies of documents attesting to the identity of Gus and Michelle and their relation to Samantha.

"Yes, Larry. I'm a federal judge in Montgomery, Alabama. I've been nominated for a seat on the Supreme Court. People who oppose the nomination have discovered that Samantha is my biological daughter. They've also discovered that thirteen years ago, when I first found out my wife Michelle was pregnant, I urged her to end the pregnancy. In fact, I've been under the impression throughout our marriage that she had done that. I only found out three weeks ago that she had the child and put her up for adoption and that that child is Samantha. Before I decide to remain as a nominee, Michelle and I want to obtain your and your wife's permission. We feel that's necessary because once the news media know about Samantha there'll be a lot of publicity and we don't want to put you through that without your permission."

Gus had rehearsed this speech a million times, and now he felt as if it had all come out in one breath.

Larry looked as if he'd turned to stone.

After about fifteen seconds Gus said, "How do you feel about that?"

"I don't know. Sitting here—I mean, meeting you, Samantha's father, I just . . . I don't know what's—what's going to happen. I just . . . love her very much."

"Nothing's going to happen that you don't want to happen."

Larry lowered his head. Gus thought he was crying. But when he looked up, his eyes were dry.

"And that's really true? You're Samantha's real father and you're going to be a judge on the Supreme Court?"

"Well, Larry, you say 'real father.' I'm her biological father, but I know that, in a sense, you're her real father. You raised her. I never saw her before today. That upsets me. It upsets me a lot—that Michelle and I lost all those precious years. But I'm not kidding myself. Biology doesn't make fathers. Time and care makes fathers."

Larry stared at Gus. Now Larry's eyes were moist, and Gus himself knew that if he said another word his own voice would break.

Larry said, "You're really going to be a Supreme Court judge? I can't believe Samantha's the daughter of a Supreme Court judge."

"She's not, yet. The nomination has to be confirmed. There's strong opposition. You and Doreen and Samantha may find yourselves under a lot of pressure. I'm not going to let you be put through that unless you agree."

"And if I do agree?"

"You'll probably find yourself hounded by reporters and by others wanting information from you about how you feel, what you think. Some will want statements critical of me."

"That doesn't sound so difficult. Samantha'll love it. She's always ready for a fight. What's Doreen say? Did she agree? She wanted money, right?"

"We haven't asked her yet."

Carl said, "I talked to her, when I was looking for you, but no one's asked her about the nomination."

"Don't bother."

"Why?"

"She won't care what you do, just as long as she gets something out of it. If you're concerned about her feelings, forget it. She's a tough lady. Something like this, she won't care one way or the other, except as a business proposition."

"So you don't mind if I proceed with the nomination?"

"No, not at all. Go for it."

Gus said, "May I ask you a question?"

"Yes."

"Does Samantha know she's adopted?"

"Yes, she does. Doreen told her. I don't think it upset her too much. She was never all that happy having Doreen as a mother, and there were times when she didn't think that much of me, either."

Gus felt his pulse pounding. He'd been afraid Larry would see him as an adversary, someone who might take Samantha from him.

Larry said, "She's happy with me as her father, but—"

"I'm certain she is."

"—but Doreen, to be honest, and I hope you won't think it's wrong of me to say this, but being honest, Doreen's—I don't know how much you know about Doreen?"

"Almost nothing."

Gus felt Carl's eyes on him.

"Not that I've been a great father. I haven't even really *been* a father. I've been away so much and we've always had a relationship that was more, sort of—sort of buddies, if you know what I mean. And to tell you the truth, I used to have a pretty bad drinking problem and I think if I'd been more of a father I'd have got that under control sooner than I did."

He stopped and gave Gus and Carl a long, steady look.

"I don't drink now. And I try to keep Sam away from places where I work. Saint-Tropez is hard. London, I could leave work and it was just a city, lots of things we could do together. But Saint-Tropez's not a city or a town or anything, it's just a big playground full of people who want to drink and do drugs and have sex. I go for a walk with Sam and you should see the looks she gets. She's very mature for her age. People think she's my girlfriend. Everyone wants to meet her, rich guys, guys with yachts with helicopters on the back. Sooner or later one of them's gonna get through to her, and then what? I see her staring at guys, really good-looking guys, and you can see it in her eyes, it's natural, she's attracted. I'm afraid what could happen. Maybe I should send her away to school, but I looked into that in London and that's not so great either, a thirteen-year-old with her parents on the other side of an ocean. I've seen what happens. So I don't know. I'm sorry. I'm just going on. You didn't come to hear all this."

He stopped. No one said anything. Finally, Gus broke the silence.

"There's something else, Larry, and this may be more difficult for you. We've had information that for the past few days an investigator working for a group of people who oppose my nomination has been in and around Saint-Tropez—"

"Saint-Tropez?"

"Yes. We don't know what he's there for. We don't know if he knows about you and Samantha or if for some reason he just followed Carl there. But it's troubling having him around you and Samantha. So—well, I'd like to suggest that you and Samantha come back to the States with us. We'll put you up someplace comfortable, just until the confirmation procedure is over."

It was a toss-up who looked more surprised, Larry or Carl.

Larry said, "I can't do that. I've got a contract. If I just took off—I can't do that. When? When do you want to leave?"

"The next flight. Tomorrow morning."

"I can't. Even if everything else was right—I mean, I haven't had a chance to think about it, but even if—no, I can't. I've got another six weeks on my contract. Is it that important? I mean, this guy—why's he here? What can he do? So we're here and he's here. What's he gonna do?"

"We don't know."

Carl said, "And we don't want to find out."

Gus said, "Larry, what if for a few weeks, Samantha just took a vacation, went away on a trip for a while. Would that upset you? Is that a possibility?"

"Well, I—"

"And then we'd bring her back, or you could come over and get her."

"If—this is coming at me pretty fast. I'm not sure why this is all so important. That she leave here. What's the problem? Really."

Carl said, "Larry, maybe this is just what you're looking for, get Samantha out of the Saint-Tropez atmosphere for a while. Maybe—"

Gus interrupted. "The people who oppose this nomination will want to make as much as they can out of my suggestion to Michelle that she end the pregnancy. To get maximum mileage out of that, they'll want to publish pictures of Samantha, probably try to talk to her. They'll search for her, want to televise her. They will be very, very persistent. Having seen one of their investigators in Saint-Tropez, it's likely they already know she's here. If she comes to the States with us we can put her up someplace safe where none of these people will be able to get to her. I would just feel very nervous about getting on a plane out of here and leaving Samantha—well, I don't want to sound alarming, but leaving her unprotected."

"You think she's in danger?"

"I don't think she's in physical danger, but—"

Carl made an abrupt movement in his chair and let out an animal-like snort that said, *Oh yeah?*

Gus said, "You can be on the phone with Samantha as much as you like. And we'll be in touch with you by phone, as well."

Larry said, "Will Doreen know where she is?"

"No one will know where she is. Except us."

Samantha and Michelle came through the door of the bar and headed for the table.

Gus said, "Why don't you talk it over with Samantha—and Michelle, too, if you want."

Five minutes later, when Samantha heard from Larry the suggestion that she go to Washington, she almost dropped her Coke glass. Suddenly she was once again the Samantha who'd banged on the car window in Saint-Tropez.

"Go to Washington? Without you? With *them*? I don't even *know* them."

Gus and Michelle tried to be invisible. Larry said, "They're your parents, Samantha."

"My *parents*! I never *saw* them before. *You're* my parent, you and—you're my father." She cocked her head at Gus. "*He's* not my father. I'm not going anywhere with him."

Larry said, "Don't talk like that, Samantha. It's best if you go to Washington."

She looked at Gus. "I'm sorry." Back to Larry. "It's *not* best. How can it be best? If it's so good, *you* come. You come, too. You come with me, and I'll go."

"I can't come. I explained that. I've got a contract."

"You've got a *contract*. So what am I, chopped liver?"

"Don't be rude, Samantha."

He looked down at his coffee.

Samantha's fists were clenched.

Larry said, "It's just for a few weeks, Samantha, maybe a couple of months. It's not forever. It'd be good to get to know your real parents. Someday you'll be glad you got to know them."

"They're not my real parents. You're my father. They're not like you. They scare me."

"They don't scare you, Samantha. Don't say that. We can speak on the phone."

Samantha put her hands to her face, then clasped them in her lap and remained silent. In a moment, tears replaced words. Samantha looked at Larry and said softly, "Daddy, I don't want to go."

It was a final plea, made to anything and everything that might be touchable in his heart.

"I'm sorry, honey. I don't want you to go. But . . ."

She smiled miserably through her tears. "Yeah. But . . ."

Michelle wondered how many times Samantha had had conversations like this. And how many times they had ended like that. "Yeah. But . . ."

15

Samantha's face was alive in the brilliance of sunlight reflected from banks of clouds beneath them. Alive but troubled. Michelle, sitting on the aisle, slipped over into the center seat beside Samantha. She put her head next to Samantha's and looked with her through the narrow window.

"Beautiful." Maybe she could cheer her up.

Samantha smiled and nodded, but did not speak.

The night before, Michelle and Gus had asked Samantha to call them by their first names. They wanted her to know they did not expect her suddenly to stop thinking of Doreen and Larry as Mom and Dad. Samantha had only shrugged.

Michelle looked with Samantha through the window at the clouds and sunshine. Referring to the difficulty of leaving Larry, she said, "Is it better now?"

"Hmmmm." Like a cat purring, but without the contentment. "It's okay. It's okay." Far away. Michelle could barely catch the words. And Samantha's eyes—a child's eyes in a woman's body. Michelle studied her, gazing out the window.

Michelle said, "I'm really sorry Larry couldn't come."

"He has to work. It's okay. Don't worry about it."

Samantha was too practical to carry the fight beyond defeat. It was done now. Accept it. It was hard to know how much Samantha would really miss Larry. They seemed more like brother and sister than father and daughter. Larry had telephoned the hotel in Saint-Tropez, and Carl drove back and picked up Samantha's things. He packed his own bag, and the next morning met the others at a Holiday Inn near the airport, where they had spent the night. That morning Larry had kissed Samantha goodbye, watched the three of them disappear into the departure lounge, and headed back to Saint-Tropez.

Samantha slept most of the trip. Gus and Michelle watched her, like parents staring proudly into the crib of a newborn.

The plane landed, stopped rolling, and a male voice on the PA system said, "Will Miss Samantha Young please call herself to the attention of a flight attendant?"

When Gus had called Rothman from Nice to tell him what was happening, Rothman had said not to leave the plane with Samantha. "If reporters find out you're on the plane we don't want them to see you with Samantha and start wondering who she is. I'll send some people to pick her up. We'll get you back with her later."

Samantha disembarked with two White House Secret Service agents, and five minutes later the other passengers got off. Just past the Customs and Immigration area, a dozen men and women with TV cameras, microphones, and lights, plus a crowd of print reporters and photographers, confronted passengers. At first Gus thought there'd been a movie star on board. Then they spotted him and Michelle.

Someone yelled, "What about the abortion?"

A young man wearing face makeup stuck a microphone in Gus's face.

"There've been reports you arranged for the abortion of your wife's child. Can you comment on that?"

Gus looked at Michelle, trying to keep her balance in the crush of reporters jostling them with microphones, pocket recorders, and notepads.

A woman waved a newspaper at him. A headline said PARHAM URGED ABORTION FOR WIFE. She yelled, "Did you see this?"

Michelle struggled to remain upright, her face a picture of fury.

A man yelled, "What about the rape case?"

Rape case?

Another voice: "Have you seen the TV ads? What's your reaction to them?"

A man pushed Michelle roughly aside to get closer to Gus. She glared for a moment at the back of his jacket, then kicked him behind his left kneecap. The knee buckled, and he dropped. Her face clouded with horror at what she had done.

Gus grabbed her arm. Through the mob he spotted

Rothman with two large young men in unbuttoned blazers. The men shot into the crowd, and twenty seconds later Gus and Michelle were in the back of a State Department limousine with tinted windows. Michelle's hair was mussed, and a button had been torn from Gus's jacket.

Rothman said, "Welcome to Washington. You still wanna be a Supreme Court justice?"

"More than ever." Gus touched Michelle's arm. "You okay?"

"I'm fine. What a battle." Dredging a comb from her handbag, she said to Rothman, "Where's Samantha?"

"In another car ahead of us."

Gus said, "I hope she didn't go through anything like that."

"No one even knew who she was."

Michelle stuffed the comb back into her purse. "What I want to know is, where'd they get that arranged-for-an-abortion stuff?"

"Someone suggested to the media that you ended a pregnancy."

"Who did that?"

"Harrington, probably. It was on the news last night. He must have leaked the documents about your interest in abortion but withheld the documents showing that in the end you rejected abortion and had the child. This gets the pro-life people down on you for supporting abortion. If we want to reveal that you did not have an abortion after all, it forces us to come out on the issue, giving it more life and energy, after which the opposition will suggest that we faked the adoption documents and you really *did* have an abortion. The more we fight over it, the more attention it gets. Whatever happens, we lose."

"But can't we do something? I never—"

"There is no way we can win an abortion battle, Michelle. If Gus appears to support abortion, the pro-life people will attack him. If he opposes abortion, the pro-choice people will go for him. In either case, he'll lose enough votes to kill his confirmation in the Senate."

Rothman glanced at Gus and smiled. "But don't be impatient. We have weapons too. It's just beginning."

Gus said, "What was all that about a rape case, and TV ads? We leave town for a day and it's like the world changed."

"A day can be a very long time in this town. We'll talk about it later."

"Where're we going?"

"We've got a house. State uses it for visitors. Very secure. No one will bother you." He looked at Michelle. "Samantha will be there when you arrive. How is she, by the way?"

"Wonderful."

"And Larry Young?"

"A very nice man."

No one mentioned Doreen.

The house was three stories, red brick, surrounded by a black, spiked iron fence, squeezed between the Brazilian and Norwegian embassies on a tree-shaded street of large homes and grassy lawns. A cook and a white-aproned maid lived on the top floor, and a team of round-the-clock State Department security agents, with jackets, ties, and nine-millimeter automatics, occupied a cramped office off the entrance vestibule, monitoring TV screens, motion sensors, and sound detectors arrayed around the building and on the roof. A locked steel cabinet contained stun grenades and Uzi automatic rifles. Six rosebushes along the south border had given the house its nickname and official security code: Blossom.

The limousine eased through metal gates into a narrow driveway separating the house from the brick-walled Brazilian embassy. At the rear of the house, the limousine maneuvered in a turning space and backed down into a partially underground garage. Before the driver could get around to open the passenger doors, Gus and Michelle were already out, nodding hello to a dark-haired, twenty-one-year-old Portuguese maid named Louisa.

The first thing Gus did was take a bath. He was up to his neck in steaming water when the door opened and Samantha walked in, carrying a toothbrush.

She said, "Oh, excuse me. I'll just be a minute."

She finished with her teeth, turned off the water, put the toothbrush back in its plastic case, screwed the top on the toothpaste tube, said, "See you later," and walked out.

As Gus lay there naked, stunned and silent, it dawned on him that he and Michelle may have been taking a lot for granted. Neither of them knew Samantha. They knew she was pretty and clever, and that she was their daughter. But they didn't *know* her. In the day and a half since Gus had met her in the Nice airport, she had managed to leave him charmed, frightened, and bewildered. Solidly in the grasp of adolescence, she was childishly helpless one minute, stubbornly independent the next. You accepted her as a cute, innocent Shirley Temple and the next thing you knew she was coming at you like a rottweiler. It was hard to know who she was. She probably didn't know herself. Growing up surrounded by more adults than children—as she appeared to have done—had left her bright but lonely.

Samantha wasn't sure about Louisa, the Portuguese maid. Louisa had been in Washington only two weeks and it seemed the only friend she'd made was a twenty-two-year-old unmarried State Department guard named Todd Naeder. Louisa was so eager for feminine companionship that the evening Samantha arrived they sat in Louisa's tiny third-floor bedroom while the maid poured out what appeared to be two weeks of stockpiled intimacies, most of which involved trysts with Todd Naeder in the back seat of the garaged Cadillac limousine.

"In the limousine?" Samantha asked, wondering if there was some polite way she could just say good night and go to bed.

"Todd says it's the safest place. The guards are the only ones with keys to the garage. It's armored."

"The garage is armored?"

"No, the limousine. Todd says the things we get up to in there it's a good thing."

There must have been something wrong with Samantha's smile. Louisa said, "How old are you?"

"Guess."

"Seventeen."

Samantha shook her head.

"Sixteen?"

Another shake of the head.

"Tell me."

"Thirteen."

"*Thirteen!* Oh, wow."

"It's okay. Everybody thinks I'm a lot older."

"I don't believe it. *Thirteen.* Are you . . ."

"What?"

"Have you ever . . ."

"Am I a virgin? Yes."

"Todd'll never believe it. That you're thirteen, I mean. You stay away from him."

Samantha shrugged. Louisa was okay, she guessed, but she didn't seem like the sort of person you really shared your memories with, not the kind of memories Samantha had.

Samantha went to bed that night thinking about her father and about the Steinway she'd seen downstairs in the living room. She closed her eyes and imagined that she could hear the faint notes of Dvořák's Concerto in G Minor. Dvořák was her father's favorite composer, the G Minor Concerto his favorite piece. She imagined that she could get out of bed, go downstairs, barefoot in her pajamas, and stand in the doorway watching his back as he played the Steinway. Then she'd walk over to him and put her hands on his shoulders. Without looking around, knowing it was her, he'd lay his cheek on her hand. After a moment, she'd move around him to the other side of the piano and lean against it, elbows on the polished mahogany, and watch him play. His eyes would be closed. She'd close hers. Together they would soak in the music.

She missed him a lot. Why had he let her go? He shouldn't have done that. She'd already lost her real parents, and then she lost her second mother, and now she'd lost her second father. What was wrong? Why didn't anyone want to hang on to her? Her second mother, Doreen, hadn't made any bones about it. Once, when Samantha was seven, she'd gone to bed early, nine o'clock, and her mother had dragged her out of bed. Her mother'd been fighting with her dad all day. As far as Samantha knew, she'd been fighting with him all her life. She just seemed to get angrier and angrier, nastier and nastier. Samantha had gone to her room to get away from the screams and threats. If they hit each other she didn't want to see it.

Her mother had yelled at her. "What did I tell you to do?" It was as if she'd come into the room dragging all her anger with her, couldn't move without it.

Samantha said, "I'm tired."

"What did I tell you to do?"

"Serve drinks."

Samantha was scared. Her mother had never hit her, but she'd hit her father, chased him with a knife into the bathroom. Lately she'd been mad all the time, never cooled down, never lost the lines of rage that marked her face like scars.

"So get dressed and do what you're told."

She was shouting. Samantha'd been up at six to finish homework she couldn't do the night before because she'd been serving drinks to all the people who came to the house. She was tired of being scared of her mother. She felt like giving up.

"I'm tired. I got up early this morning."

"Don't talk back to me, Samantha."

Samantha was silent. She didn't care.

"Did you hear me?"

Samantha turned toward the closet.

"I'm talking to you!"

She opened the closet door.

"Don't you ignore me, you little bitch."

Samantha turned and looked at her mother. Her

mother's hand struck Samantha's cheek. Face burning, tears blurring her vision, not caring what happened, Samantha said, "I hate you!"

She said it again, softly, not even minding if her mother heard. "I hate you."

"Don't you—how dare you talk to me like that! You think I care if you hate me?"

Her mother laughed, the nasty little laugh she used with her father. "Who cares if you hate me, a miserable little monster like you?"

"I'm not a monster."

They were still in front of the closet, Samantha streaming tears, her mother's eyes dark with fury, searching for ways to hurt.

"Your mother thought you were. You're lucky she didn't kill you before you even got born."

What did that mean?

"Oh, you don't know what to say to that? Nothing smart to say to that?"

Her mother nodded her head, staring at Samantha. Samantha knew that what her mother had said was something terrible, supposed to hurt her, and that her mother was waiting to see the pain.

"So, you know so much, but you didn't know that. Something you didn't know. Not so smart after all, are you?"

"What do you mean?"

Her mother crossed her arms. A man called from the living room, but her mother wasn't listening.

"You want me to tell you what I mean? You think it's so awful here? Have to stay up till eleven o'clock serving drinks? You are *so* abused, you poor little thing. You know how lucky you are? You never should've even been *born.*

And all you can say is 'I hate you.' You ought to be ashamed. If it wasn't for what you've got here you'd be in an orphanage. Probably you'd be dead. You oughta be thanking me every day. Without me you'd be dead, your mother'd've killed you, and all you can say is 'I hate you.' "

"You're my mother."

"Oh, really? You know so much. Well, you're old enough to know the truth. I never had a kid. Neither did your drunken father."

"I don't believe you."

"So now I'm a liar. Well if that's the way you feel, maybe it'd've been better if your mother *had* killed you. A lot easier for everyone."

"You can't kill a kid."

"You can if they're not born yet."

Samantha remembered that conversation at least once every day, usually at night. She promised herself that someday she would meet someone who would love her so much that his love, even if it didn't take away the memory, would take away the pain. She began to wonder who she really was. Most kids knew who they were. Why'd her real parents give her away? Why didn't they want her? What would it have been like with them? Who would she have been with them? *Was* she lucky to be alive?

As long as she could remember, she had felt like someone in hiding. In Milwaukee, with all the stuff that went on there, she'd go to bed at night, pull the sheets over her head, and hide. Traveling with her father, she'd still felt like someone hiding. And now, in this beautiful house with her *real* parents, she was still in hiding. What did you have to do to get out?

She saw her life as books, like the Nancy Drew adventures her father bought her in London. She knew that today her life had started a new book. The first eight years she had titled *Horror Story.* That was the part in Milwaukee. The next one, after Larry took her away, she called *On the Run.* Now, as she stretched on the soft sheets, letting her half-opened eyes roam among the unfamiliar shadows, she tried to think of a title for the new book. She was in a beautiful big house with a limousine, a maid, and embassies next door. Maybe *High Society.*

She thought about her father and looked at her watch. In Saint-Tropez it was five in the morning. Her father would have just finished work, walking to the hotel, thinking of her. Aloud she whispered, "I miss you, Dad."

The next morning, her father called.

"How are you? How was the flight?"

"It was fine. How are you?"

Gus had answered the phone, called her to his office, then quietly left her to talk in private.

Her father said, "I'm okay. I miss you."

"I miss you, too, Daddy. But it's great here. Don't worry. It's a big house and they've even got guards, like bodyguards? So don't worry. They won't even let me out without a guard. I'm real safe. But I miss you."

She could hear voices in the background and knew he was at work.

"I've got to get back, honey. I love you. I'll call again tomorrow."

He hung up.

She was happy to hear his voice, but after she put the phone down she felt an emptiness, as if she hadn't talked to him at all. It had been over so fast.

She waited for his call the next afternoon, but it didn't come. He called the day after that, and they talked for half an hour.

The reporters at the airport had been nothing. Over the next few weeks, Michelle scanned the newspapers, radio, and TV reports, and every day it got worse.

She said to Gus. "Isn't there anything—isn't there anything at *all* these people won't stoop to? Why do they hate you so much?"

"The White House nominated me. For some, that's enough. Others, they look at my record—I've ruled against what they like and for what they hate."

"But you've ruled the other way, too."

"They don't see it like that. They want someone who will rule the way they want every time. Politics is about dependability, Michelle. Justice is about impartiality. The two don't always mix."

"But this isn't politics. You're not running for anything. It's the Supreme Court. That's not politics."

"Not *supposed* to be politics."

The rape case. Years earlier, Gus had prosecuted a truck driver for the shotgun killing of two other men trying to rape a young woman in a parking lot. Women's rights groups demonstrated for the killer's acquittal. Gus argued that the truck driver's desire to defend the woman, while honorable, had not produced the right or the need to blow the would-be rapists away with a shotgun. Since Gus's nomination, opposition TV and newspaper ads (coordinated by Helen Bondell's Freedom Federation) had screamed that "support for rape" made Gus unfit for the Supreme Court.

Another series of ads claimed Gus had used his position

as a federal prosecutor to release a friend's teenage son, arrested with four other boys after a fatal car crash. In fact, the charges were not federal and the case did not involve Gus. The boy, a schizophrenic, had been sent to a state mental hospital.

More ads accused Gus, in ten years as a public official, of never having hired a black or Hispanic. In fact 42 percent of his staff had been minority.

Two reporters, stopped by police while trying to remove a bag of garbage from the sidewalk in front of Gus and Michelle's unoccupied Montgomery home, later wrote a story saying they had been "pursuing information from an informant" who said they would find "large quantities of empty barbiturate and tranquilizer bottles." They said they had also been seeking "incriminating" bank and brokerage-house statements. In fact they had found nothing. They never identified their source, who actually had been a staffer from Senator Eric Taeger's office.

Some writers denounced Gus for supporting capital punishment, others for condemning it. (He had done both, in different cases.) He had also, in different cases and for different reasons, ruled for and against homosexual rights, for and against affirmative action, for and against school prayer—for and against just about everything. There appeared to be no issue concerning which he had not ruled on both sides, taking each case as it came, judging according to the law, ignoring his personal convictions. Even outside the court, he declined to discuss controversial issues publicly and welcomed as unintended compliments opponents' charges that he was faceless, a man without opinions.

The burglar who had fled the Vienna, Virginia, garage at the sight of Michelle's kitchen knife had found in the one carton he got away with a photocopy of a lurid, handwritten, unsigned love letter to, judging from the context, a married woman with children. The Freedom Federation planted the letter with a supermarket tabloid, and to defend himself Gus was forced to provide handwriting samples. (An attorney had submitted the photocopy to Gus in connection with a bail hearing in a mail-fraud case.)

In the weeks since he had returned from France, ads vilifying Gus had shrieked from newspapers, magazines, billboards, even from the sky, where smoke-trailing airplanes over the beaches of southern California scrawled out *No Gus.*

Celebrities from film stars to prize fighters hit the talk shows to attack Gus and his views, real or imagined. Opponents demonized him as the thin edge of a wedge, the start of a movement to roll back judicial positions established over decades. He was feared and hated for views he had never supported but had not condemned.

Direct-mail campaigns put anti-Gus flyers in half the mailboxes of America. Recorded voices, connected by computerized dialing machines to hundreds of thousands of telephones, urged all who answered to "protest to your senator." Ads in professional law journals sought information from anyone who had ever heard Gus speak for or against controversial issues. Hoping to uncover quirky tastes, investigators visited every book and video store in Montgomery. Canvassers telephoned federal judges, Alabama state judges, politicians, prosecutors, prominent defense attorneys, journalists, and businessmen from coast to coast, asking for "questionable statements" they might have heard from or concerning Gus. Similar calls went to Gus's colleagues, friends, former professors, and Harvard classmates. Opposing senators on the Judiciary Committee demanded that Gus produce more than 47,000 documents relating to his official duties in Montgomery.

One day, a few weeks after they'd arrived at Blossom, Todd Naeder took Michelle to pick up Gus outside the Judiciary Committee hearing room. Waiting for Gus, she stepped into the back of the room through a door from the public hallway. A woman was testifying, questioned by a tall, elderly man Michelle took to be Eric Taeger, the committee chairman. Michelle was struck by how much everything resembled a courtroom.

The witness said, "Because I was there."

"You were there when he said Judge Parham had called him a nigger?"

"Yes, I was."

A senator next to Taeger said, "Mr. Chairman . . ."

Michelle felt her face turn red. She said to Todd, "My husband never used that word in his life. It's a lie. How can they—"

Todd touched her arm. "The judge is outside. He's waiting for us."

"But what does she think—"

Todd practically had to drag her from the room.

"Your name?"

"Carl Falco."

He looked her in the eyes, smiling. The eyes acknowledged his smile, but the face was brittle. She knew he wasn't bringing flowers.

"And you're with?"

Carl showed her the badge. Special Agent. Drug Enforcement Administration. Department of Justice. The White

House had arranged Carl's temporary assignment to Gus's security detail, providing an office for him in the Executive Office Building.

"Excuse me."

She disappeared through an unmarked door. In a minute she was back, holding the door open. "This way, please?"

Helen Bondell didn't look like the activist shrew Carl had expected. She was blonde, attractive, warm, relaxed. Carl was impressed. Not many people can do that—look relaxed when the feds walk in.

He said, "Sorry I didn't make an appointment. I thought maybe I could just catch you with some free time."

"Well, you did. I have all the time you need. What can I do for you?"

White silk blouse, gold bracelets, slender tanned face that looked as if it'd just come back from two weeks in the Caribbean.

"Nothing, really. I thought maybe I could do something for you."

"That's a nice change." She laughed, and the laugh had a tan too. "I don't often hear that."

She raised a hand to her hair. The bracelets tinkled down a long, slender forearm to her elbow.

Carl said, "Do you know a man named John Harrington?"

"I know an attorney by that name."

"Has a client called Ernesto Vicaro."

She looked blank.

"Does business as TransInter."

Still blank, giving nothing away.

"It's a South American holding company. Banks, hotels, airlines. Also cocaine."

"Oh, *that* Ernesto Vicaro."

She smiled.

"Right. *That* Ernesto Vicaro."

"I've read about him. I think CBS had a special, maybe six months ago?"

"Possibly."

"Harrington represents him?"

"Well, he represents TransInter. And when you peel the onion you find Ernesto."

"I see."

She leaned forward, intensely curious, eager to become more informed.

Lady, you are beginning to insult me.

"So there's cocaine, and then TransInter, and then Vicaro, and then Harrington."

"Fascinating."

"It is, isn't it?" He grinned, kicking a little cynicism into it. "Harrington does more than provide legal representation for Vicaro in his difficulties with the federal government. He also lobbies for TransInter."

She leaned back slowly in her chair, adding about two feet to her distance from Carl.

Carl said, "Recently that involved an attempt to bribe a federal agent."

She drew in her chin. Carl thought the slight tremble around her mouth might be genuine.

She said, "John Harrington tried to bribe a federal agent?"

"Of course not. Don't be silly. But someone who works for Harrington, or for his firm, took a shot at it."

Don't give her more than that. If she asks Harrington, he can tell her about the nice young attorney with an ankle problem.

Carl said, "I believe Harrington works for the Freedom Federation?"

"I wouldn't say he works for us. He has clients—other than Vicaro or . . ."

"TransInter."

"Yes, or TransInter, and sometimes our interests and the interests of one of his clients coincide."

"The nomination of Gus Parham." Out of the blue.

"Yes? What about it?"

"Ernesto Vicaro has reasons for wanting to influence that process. You want to influence it too. Mr. Harrington—"

"There's nothing wrong with—"

Carl waited. Patient. Hopeful. But she caught herself.

"Excuse me for interrupting. Please go on."

"I just thought you might like to know that when someone speaks to you in the voice of TransInter, they're speaking to you in the voice of Ernesto Vicaro, who at the moment is busy doing twenty years in a federal penitentiary. That may not be the kind of help the Freedom Federation wants or needs."

She said, "I'll keep that in mind."

Icy. Doesn't like being told what she needs.

"No offense. Just thought the information might be helpful."

"You've been very helpful."

"Want more?"

"If you've got it."

"TransInter controls about sixty percent of all the cocaine entering the United States. They would love to have that business become legal—make things a lot easier, safer, and more profitable. Their chief executive officer would also love to be out of the slammer. Neither of those objectives would be furthered by the presence of Gus Parham on the Supreme Court. Follow me?"

"Crystal clear."

"Ernesto Vicaro would do anything to keep Judge Parham off the Supreme Court."

"I understand."

"Anything."

Carl stared at her. She was frozen.

He repeated it. "Anything."

"You've made your point."

"Thanks for your time."

"Thanks for yours."

Going down in the elevator, Carl felt it'd been worth the effort. The interview had been Rothman's idea. It had two objectives. First, slow Helen Bondell down. There might be one or two things even the Freedom Federation wouldn't do. Maybe Bondell would draw the line at cooperating with a man like Ernesto Vicaro. And second, if she did accept Vicaro's help—money, contacts, something worse—she'd never be able to say she hadn't known who he was, who TransInter was, who Harrington was representing. Carl had told her, and she'd heard it. It was all on the recorder in his pocket.

In her first few weeks at Blossom, the State Department house, while Gus was working and testifying, Samantha spent her time with Michelle. They did a little shopping and sight-seeing, but mostly they stayed home and talked. Every time Samantha related some thought or recollection, she seemed to be holding back. She had a lot on her mind, thirteen years of memories, and Michelle was willing to wait for the right moment to hear them.

In the moments she wasn't with Michelle or Gus, Samantha spent a lot of time in the Box, the guards' name for their cramped office. The house itself seemed cold and sterile, filled with gloomy antiques, but the Box was friendly, warm and cozy. She felt safe there. She talked often to Todd Naeder, and one of the things she'd learned was that everything Louisa had told her was a lie. There had been no love affair, no backseat sex in the limousine. And there was no more friendship between Samantha and Louisa. Samantha hadn't broken it off, Louisa had.

"Don't worry about it," Todd told Samantha, "it's not your fault. She doesn't speak to me either."

"But she's so lonely."

"I tried to be her friend and look what happened. If my boss believed what she said, I'd be out of a job now. Leave her alone."

The last thing Louisa had said about Todd, a parting shot before she stopped speaking at all, had been that he was lazy, stuck-up, and "unaware." Samantha thought the unaware business was something Louisa had heard on a TV soap, and Todd was certainly neither lazy nor conceited. He spent more time in the Box than anyone else, and was always ready to fill in for other guards who wanted time off. He was hardworking, friendly, and not at all pushy, like most of the other young men she'd met, especially the rich ones. When she was with him she felt relaxed, taken at face value. She didn't have to spend a lot of time trying to figure out what he was really thinking.

Returning from a small shopping center near the corner, Michelle was on Blossom's front porch, digging in her bag for the key, when the door burst open and Samantha almost knocked her down.

She headed across the lawn, toward the street, moving with determination.

"Samantha!"

Todd Naeder came through the door and started after her.

Michelle grabbed his arm.

"Wait. I'll get her."

She dropped her packages and ran after Samantha.

"Samantha, stop. What's wrong?"

Samantha quickened her step. She was crying.

Reaching her on the sidewalk, Michelle put an arm around her.

"Samantha, wait a minute. Tell me what's wrong."

Samantha stopped, chin thrust forward in defiance and pain.

Michelle said, "Come back inside and tell me what's wrong."

"I'm going back."

"Good."

Michelle took a step toward the house, but Samantha pulled away.

"Not there. I'm never going back there. I'm going back to France."

"Samantha, you can't go back to France. I don't understand. What's wrong?"

"I'm going back to my—" She began to sob. "Where is he? I want to go back to my father. Where is . . ."

She put her head against Michelle's shoulder. Michelle

led her back into the house and climbed the stairs to a small sitting room next to her and Gus's bedroom.

Michelle sat next to her on a sofa. "What is it, Samantha? What happened?"

"Nothing happened. I just want to go back."

"Why do you want to go back?"

"I don't like it here."

She looked at Michelle. "I'm sorry. It's not you or Gus. I'm just—I'm scared here. I don't know where I am. I don't know what's happening. Everyone's always talking about nominations and confirmations. Everything's so serious and important. My dad's just a kid like me—nothing was ever very important except staying together, not getting caught by my mom. I don't know what's happening here. I don't know anyone. You're my mother, but I don't even know you. Gus—who is he? He scares me."

"Why does he scare you?"

"He's just . . . so important. I don't know. I just want to go back."

"He doesn't want to be scary."

"He tried to have me aborted. That's what the TV says."

"He loves you, Samantha."

"Why'd you have me adopted? Why didn't you keep me?"

"Samantha . . ." Michelle and Gus had talked about what to tell her about the adoption. How can you explain that to a thirteen-year-old? "It's a long story. We thought it would be better, we . . ."

"It doesn't matter anyway."

Michelle didn't know what to say.

Samantha was silent. She looked lost, filled with despair.

"I'm always losing people, aren't I?"

She looked up, searching Michelle's eyes.

"I lost you and Gus, and then I lost my other mother, and now I've lost my other father, and what next? What next, right? I'm going to lose you and Gus *again*. I'm tired of—"

She started to sob. Michelle reached out for her, but she pulled away.

"What's going to happen to me? What am I doing wrong? Other kids don't lose their parents. They just get born and that's that. I don't know who I am, or where I'm supposed to be, or anything. What's going to happen to me?"

"Nothing bad's going to happen, Samantha. You're with us now, with Gus and me, and you're our daughter, and we're going to see to it that you're happy."

They went downstairs and had lunch. Samantha's distress did nothing to diminish her appetite. An hour later, the pain locked away, back in its place, she chatted with the cook as if nothing had happened.

16

John Harrington was waiting for Vicaro. Lawyers *never* wait for jailed clients. But he was waiting for Vicaro. Who ran this prison, anyway? Vicaro should have been deposited in the interview room long before Harrington arrived.

Anyway, he had good news, placate the obese bastard. Vicaro's money had been well spent. Millions contributed toward the most massive political lobbying campaign Harrington had ever seen. And now the polls had begun to swing. That morning the CNN–*USA Today* poll had shown Parham's popularity down two points, the first time it'd ever been below 50 percent.

Harrington smelled the sweat before he heard the iron gate unlock. He got to his feet, put out his hand.

"Ernie, good to see you."

Vicaro ignored the hand, oozed into the metal chair, and grunted, open-mouthed, saliva spraying.

"Good to see me? You shouldn't think good to see me. You should think terrible to see me. Maybe someday you'll be here, be in a worse place than this, and I'll say good to see you."

He was carrying a folded newspaper.

"Ernie, you know I didn't—"

"All I read is this guy Parham. Parham, Parham, Parham."

He stopped, staring at Harrington, expecting a response. What response?

Harrington said, "But all you read is bad, right? You don't read nothing—anything—good, right?"

What the hell, he was even starting to talk like the guy. Vicaro spoke four languages—Spanish, English, Italian, and French. Unfortunately, his English sounded as if he'd picked it up on the street.

"Nothin' says he's dead. *That* would be good."

"Well, I have some good news for you, Ernie. The media campaign's starting to pay off. There's a new poll, out yesterday, says more than half the people in the country don't want Parham on the Supreme Court. That's going to have an enormous effect on—"

A forearm the size of a pig carcass slammed down on the metal table, sweat flying.

Harrington shot back in his chair, bushy eyebrows up around the hairline.

The room was windowed but soundproof. The guard outside sat placidly absorbed in a magazine.

While Harrington's shocked eyes remained fixed on the arm that had struck the table, Vicaro's other hand swung out of nowhere and slapped him across the face with the newspaper.

Harrington, swatted like a puppy who'd just wee-weed on the carpet, felt tears of humiliation and fury fill his eyes. Before he could speak, Vicaro reached across the table and put a hand on his sleeve. In a voice suddenly as calm as the eye of a cyclone, he said, "You don't understand, Johnny. What do I have to do to make you understand? I don't care about media campaigns and the polls look good. I care about Parham can't win. You understand? *Can't* win. You understand *can't*? You know what *can't* means?"

He took his hand back.

"I know what *can't* means."

Harrington, breathing hard, struggled for control.

Vicaro lifted his arm from the table and rested it on his knee. "So she never had the abortion."

"It seems that way."

"*Seems* that way? Why do we have so much trouble understanding each other? Five hundred an hour, I'd think you'd make more of an effort."

"What I meant," Harrington said with caution, "was that I agree that she never had the abortion."

"So you guys blew it. You said she had it. Now they parade out the kid, 'Here's the abortion.' You look pretty stupid."

Harrington was too frightened to speak. It was true that the previous night Helen Bondell had told Larry King on CNN that the supposedly aborted child, "a thirteen-year-old named Samantha," had been put up for adoption by the eventually-to-be Mrs. Parham. "The girl's in Washington now," Helen had said, "under lock and key."

Harrington had seen the broadcast in his living room, having a Chivas Regal with his wife, and if the word *betrayal* had still been part of his vocabulary he'd have used it. When he'd told Helen about Samantha, that Warren Gier had seen her in Saint-Tropez and that she was now in Washington, she had promised to keep it to herself.

"This is big news," King had exclaimed. "How do you know this?"

Helen smiled sweetly. "Sources."

King said, "You sure it's true?"

"Oh, it's true. Everyone's been saying Parham encouraged his wife to have an abortion, and now here's this beautiful, innocent, decidedly unaborted child—I assume she's beautiful and innocent, I haven't seen her."

"Egg on your face?"

"*My* face? I didn't have anything to do with any of this. I'm just a bystander. Like you, Larry."

This morning, every paper Harrington could find had the story on page one, expanded with speculations, exaggerations. "No Abortion—She's a Beauty." "Mystery Girl Is No Abortion." "Gus's Abortion Comes Alive."

Harrington finally had to admit it—it was a clever move. Not only had Helen isolated the Freedom Federation from any White House wrath the disclosure might provoke, she had destroyed the White House's ability to choose for itself when to reveal Samantha's existence.

"Ernie," Harrington said, "they have not paraded out the kid, and probably never will. If there's one thing they do not want, it's to pour fuel on the abortion issue. What they'd like most is to have everyone forget all about this girl. So far, no one's even seen her. The White House'll do everything they can to make the whole issue go away. Including the girl."

"I'd like to see Papa go away."

"I beg your pardon?"

Vicaro shouted. "Papa! Papa Parham! Go away!"

Harrington felt as if he'd spent an hour locked in a sauna with an angry lion. Did Vicaro expect Harrington to make Parham "go away"? To have him killed? Did he intend to do it himself? How far was Vicaro really willing to go to keep Parham off the Supreme Court? Well, certainly he'd love to see Parham dead. Parham was the one who'd locked him up.

Harrington waited to catch the eye of the guard, then cautiously pushed back his chair until he was safely out of range of Vicaro's hands. He didn't want to say anything—even in a soundproof room—that might suggest he had a suspicion of the mayhem that was on Vicaro's mind. But for his own sake he did want to discourage Vicaro from doing anything terminally stupid.

He stood and said, "Gus Parham cannot win. Even if his nomination gets to the Senate, the Senate will never confirm him. Never."

He looked at Vicaro and tried to bore a hole into the black eyes.

"You pay a lot of money for my opinion and advice. So please believe this. Gus Parham will never be confirmed."

And don't try to kill the guy, okay?

Vicaro's silent gaze was more foul and evil-filled than the hot, stinking room.

The guard came in.

Harrington said, "I'll be in touch."

* * *

Candles, dim lights, red velvet chairs, a dining room filled with young women and middle-aged men. Helen thought, We're the only ones here not committing adultery.

She said, "How do you like it? A friend told me the food's great, and so's the privacy."

She meant Warren Gier, and when it came to darkness and deceit, he should know. Helen needed a long talk with Harrington, and she did not want to worry about the ears of waiters and neighboring diners.

Harrington said, "I'm always happy to meet with you anywhere, Helen."

They were in rural Virginia, a forty-minute drive from the capital.

"Don't get smooth, Harrington. There's too much of that here already."

They ordered roast duck. Helen didn't like duck, but Harrington wanted it, and it was available only for two. So she ordered the duck. She had more important things on her mind than what to eat for dinner.

She said, "A cop visited me the other day."

Harrington, bent over his duck, gave her an up-from-under look through the eyebrows.

"What'd he want?"

"Who knows? What he said he wanted was to let me know that an attorney named John Harrington represents something called TransInter, which is controlled by an evil cocaine dealer named Ernesto Vicaro, who does not want Gus Parham on the Supreme Court."

"He used my name?"

"Actually spoke the sacred words."

"He's trying to intimidate you, throw you off your stride."

"He said you tried to bribe a federal agent."

"Tried to . . ."

". . . bribe a federal agent."

"When?"

"How many times have you done it?"

"Very funny. What did he say, exactly?"

"He said it was part of your lobbying duties for TransInter."

Helen studied him. She wished she could see his eyes.

Harrington nodded, took a bite of duck. "Did you lie to him?"

"Why would I lie?"

"We don't have time. But don't lie to him. Lying to a federal agent's a felony."

"What's happening with Ernesto Vicaro?"

"Saw him yesterday. I've had six baths since and I still feel dirty. He really hates Parham."

"He told you that?"

"Parham's the one who put him where he is. And everything he wants, Parham hates. He said he wants him out of the picture."

"Well, so do we. That's not—"

"Helen, he doesn't mean what you mean. When Ernesto Vicaro says he wants someone out of the picture, he means he wants him out of the *picture.*"

Helen didn't feel well. The restaurant was too warm. And too dim. She could hardly see her duck. The slices were rare, bloody. This was just the kind of place Warren Gier would like. Creepy. Gloomy. Why'd she come here?

She said, "How's your duck?"

"Fine. You can't imagine the evil that radiates from that guy."

She hated the sound of Harrington's voice.

"Then why do you talk about him?" Harrington was giving off a little radiation himself. "If he's so awful, makes you feel dirty, why do you even think about him?"

"I get paid five hundred dollars an hour to think about him."

"It's not enough."

"I agree. What should I charge, in your opinion?"

Helen wanted to get out. When she'd asked Harrington to have dinner, she'd wanted to know what Vicaro was telling him, but now she didn't. Better not to know anything. Harrington talking to Vicaro, plotting with Vicaro—how responsible was she for that? Harrington helped the Freedom Federation, he was on their side, but he *worked* for Vicaro. How responsible was she for encouragement Harrington gave Vicaro, and for what Vicaro did as a result?

She said, "Does Vicaro scare you, John?"

"Yeah, he scares me."

"What if he threatened you?"

He glanced up from his plate. "Threatened me—what do you mean threatened me?"

"Threatened you. Like to do something illegal."

He put his fork down and stared at her. Then he picked up the fork and went on eating.

She said, "The question makes you uncomfortable?"

"What question?"

Helen liked what she did at the Freedom Federation, she liked the political pushing and shoving, good guys versus bad guys. She liked the trenches, hated the boardroom, hated being with guys like Harrington. And she didn't even want to be on the same *planet* with Ernesto Vicaro. She'd worked with dirty people—Warren Gier came quickly to mind—but never before had she felt unclean.

She said, "Let's talk about something else."

"Fine with me."

After a minute of silence Harrington said, "You okay? You look funny."

"I'm fine. But I've spent all day dealing with all this crap, and I'd like just to have a nice, normal conversation, if you don't mind."

"Hey, all right. What is this, a date? You said you wanted to talk about Parham. I don't care. If you want to hold hands, I'm ready."

The head was raised, eyes gazing out warmly beneath the eyebrows, giving her a wonderfully sincere, Warren Gier grin. Oh, help.

She looked into her plate, fixed on the slices of bloody duck, and felt like throwing up. She wished she were home in bed. And suddenly the bottom line hit. Forget Harrington. Forget Vicaro. How far was *she* willing to go? How badly did *she* want Parham's nomination defeated? If everything she and all the others had been saying about Parham was true—if he was anti-abortion, anti–women's rights, anti–affirmative action, pro–capital punishment, pro–judicial restraint—where was the balance between all that and what Ernesto Vicaro wanted? Did she agree with Vicaro? Did Harrington? Better Gus Parham "out of the picture" than Gus Parham on the Supreme Court? Was that what she thought? Of course not. So what was she doing talking to Harrington, talking through Harrington to Vicaro? This is hardball, honey. What's it worth? Make up your *mind.*

They finished dinner and she drove home, but the

thoughts wouldn't leave her. How important was it, keeping Parham off the Supreme Court? What was it *worth*?

Ten days after meeting Helen, Carl was on the way out of his office when the phone rang. He took another step, then something made him go back. He picked it up.

"Falco."

"Is this Carl Falco?"

He recognized the voice.

"Yes, it is."

He sat down.

"It's Helen Bondell. Could we meet, just for a second? I know you're busy, but—"

"I'm not busy at all. I'd be happy to. Where and when?"

"Right now? My office?"

Carl didn't want a prearranged meeting in a room she controlled. Last time she hadn't known he was coming.

"I think there's a coffee shop across the street from you, right? I haven't had breakfast."

"Twenty minutes?"

He was there in ten, ahead of her, looking over the other customers, picking a booth in the back.

All she wanted to do was just say the name Ernesto Vicaro, just let Falco know that since they'd met, something had happened to increase her concern. Then it'd be up to him. She'd be off the hook. She'd have let him know. Why did she feel so nervous? She wasn't doing anything wrong, not breaking a law, not betraying anyone, just mentioning a name.

Carl was in one of the red plastic booths drinking coffee. She slid in across from him, ordered tea, and said, "I'm terribly sorry for asking you to do this."

"No problem at all. I was headed in this direction anyway."

He sat there, quiet, looking at her, waiting. She wasn't quite so relaxed this time. Must be feeling a little pressure.

He said, "What's up?"

For a moment she almost forgot why she'd come. Nothing about Carl resembled her late husband—different tone of voice, different face, different body, background, education, personality—but when he spoke, *What's up?*, she had the most vivid recollection of her husband she'd had since he died. Something in Carl, something coming from him across the table, a detachment from the immediate environment, from the things of this world, was just like her husband.

"I wanted to ask you something. Okay?"

"Sure."

It was as if she'd been injected with something. Her breathing accelerated. She felt faint.

Carl said, "You okay?"

"Yes. I'm just a little tired. I was up late."

"A woman's work is never done."

He sipped his coffee, but the eyes never left her face.

She took a drink of her tea, swallowed, and said, "Last time we met, you said Ernesto Vicaro would do anything to keep Parham off the Supreme Court."

"Right."

"What exactly did you mean?"

"I meant Ernesto Vicaro would do anything to keep Parham off the Supreme Court."

She forced a grin. "I know. But what—exactly—did you mean by anything?"

"Mrs. Bondell—"

"Helen, please."

"Helen, with people like Vicaro, when you say they'd do anything, what you mean is—anything. If you want a sharper point on it than that, let's just say that if Vicaro thought Parham was a sure thing for confirmation, and if Parham was sitting where you are, Vicaro would consider it a piece of routine business to send someone in here now and just blow him away."

Her hands gripped the teacup. She saw an image of a café in Algiers—flames, smoke, sirens, a man's torn body.

Carl said, "And, in fact, he'd actually be *delighted* to do it, because Parham's the guy who sent him to prison. Parham is the *only* person who ever got in Vicaro's way and kept on breathing."

Helen felt a chill.

Carl said, "You sure you're okay?"

"Yes. I'm sorry. I must have eaten something. But you've answered my question. Thanks."

He nodded—a repetitive, gentle, steady nod, as if he understood perfectly what was on her mind.

She'd done enough, hadn't she? He could read between the lines. She'd let him know she knew something, that Vicaro was an immediate threat, enough of a threat to get her to make a phone call, get her into this coffee shop, publicly face-to-face with a federal agent.

Carl said, "Is there something else you wanted to tell me?"

She wanted to tell him every word she'd ever heard from Harrington about Vicaro. But she couldn't. Carl was the enemy. And anyway, he probably knew more than she did about what Vicaro might be up to. That was his job, after all.

She looked into his eyes. "I don't think I have to."

"Might be helpful." Holding her gaze.

She didn't trust herself. Get *out* of here, before you say another *word.*

She stood, glancing at his empty cup. "Not much of a breakfast."

"Good talking to you."

"Same here."

He gave her a big smile. "Get what you wanted?"

"I don't know."

"Yeah, you did."

Why did she have the feeling he was reading her mind?

He wrote something on a scrap of notepaper and handed it to her.

"Here's the number of a cellular phone I use sometimes. In case I'm not at the office."

She took it. "Thanks."

"Cheer up." He was still smiling. "Don't look so glum. Everything's gonna be okay."

It was 3 A.M., and Senator Eric Taeger had just said goodbye to Warren Gier. In a few minutes Isaac Jasper would arrive. Then John Harrington. He'd wanted the meetings late, when the building, parking lot, and street were empty. The meetings weren't exactly secret, but the Parham struggle was getting as distasteful as politics usually got, and the fewer people who saw his visitors the better. He'd also summoned Helen Bondell of the Freedom Federation, but she had failed to return his call. Perhaps the conflict was growing too heated for Helen, though he would not have thought that possible.

When Isaac Jasper finally arrived, Taeger asked immediately what he thought was going to happen.

"Where's this heading, Isaac? Are we going to win?"

Isaac pushed back his chair. "That depends. How far will you go? How hard will you push?"

Taeger never really knew what to make of Jasper. He was a great strategist but a disturbing thinker, and he talked in parables. You could never be sure exactly what was on his mind.

"Meaning?"

"I don't have to tell you, Senator. Politics is like weather. Some days it's sunny, everyone's happy. Other times it's a light drizzle, not unpleasant, waters the flowers. And sometimes it's a tornado, rips up the countryside."

"You think we're facing bad weather?"

He shrugged. "This is not going to be a light drizzle. It's gone past that."

"What would you advise?"

"It's not an ordinary, conventional struggle, is it? There's a very high psychological element here. You've got an emotionally appealing nominee. I don't care what his position is on all the political issues—the public likes him, and if they start leaning on their senators, the senators are gonna do what gets votes. But mostly I'm worried about that thirteen-year-old girl. She is dynamite, Senator. She's just a bomb waiting to go off. If I were on the other side, I'd maneuver that girl right into the center of this whole fight, and I'd just leave her there, let her sit there. And I'd get her major exposure—TV, papers, magazines, every day all day—and I'd just blow you away."

"Maybe not. She could find herself under a lot of pressure. She'd have to be a very strong thirteen-year-old."

"In my opinion, Senator, the way this is shaping up, you will not win this, at least not by any orthodox means. If the decision were mine, I'd pack it in now, cut losses, accept Parham, and live with it. If not, you'll end up spending large amounts of money, time, and political resources, and you'll lose. So dump it."

"Orthodox means?"

"Any fight can be won if you're prepared to do whatever it takes to win."

Taeger stared at him. Isaac stared back.

After Isaac left, Taeger spent several minutes leaning back in his chair, reflecting on the meeting. Then he heard a car, looked out the window, and saw headlights flash across the parking lot. Five minutes later Harrington was seated at the desk.

Taeger said, "Bring me up to date, John."

"It's not looking good, Senator. Since Helen let it out on Larry King that Samantha's been found, the polls have been swinging fast and hard to Parham. A CNN producer tells me he could renegotiate his contract if he had an interview acceptance from Samantha. A picture someone stole from the video we had will be in the *Post* tomorrow morning. After that, look out."

Taeger swiveled his chair around to look out the window at the glistening asphalt. He was hearing from Harrington the same things he'd heard from Isaac. "You've had it. Give up. Cut your losses." Taeger'd been hearing those words since he first ran for office fifty-one years ago. When people said you'd had it, it meant the handshaking was over and you were down to business. If there was anything

Taeger loved, it was bare-knuckled politics. He'd never been in a fight so tough he couldn't enjoy it.

He could hear Harrington behind him, breathing hard, unhappy to be awake and out of his home at this hour. Taeger had nothing to go home for. Last night he slept in the office, and he'd sleep here again tonight, trying not to think about his wife, about Parkinson's disease, what it would do to him. He was glad the Parham thing was turning into a good vicious brawl. He was seventy-six years old, dying of Parkinson's disease, and would not run for reelection. He liked the idea of leaving the Senate after one final bruising fight, and if it was the most savage fight of his career, so much the better. Parham was—well, it wouldn't be too strong to say Taeger hated his guts. That did not put Parham in exclusive company; Taeger hated most people. He'd never met Parham, but he'd studied every case he'd ever prosecuted or judged. As a legislator who wrote laws but had never been a lawyer, Taeger had contempt for the judges who applied those laws, or in his view misapplied them. He admired men you could count on, men who did the right thing from their guts and didn't have to spend five days with a law book to find out what they believed. Men like Parham, you didn't know what they were going to think or do from one day to the next.

Harrington, addressing Taeger's back, said, "So, what do you think?"

Taeger ignored him. He was thinking now about *Hacker v. Colorado* and *Javez v. Rench*, two Supreme Court cases that had to be won. From the start, he'd made no bones about his support for both. Since they entered the appeal process five years ago, he'd been even more outspoken. Lose them now, Taeger thought, and I'll leave the

Senate as a loser, it'll almost be as if I was never here. And Parham—well, you could be sure how he'd stand on the partial decriminalization of cannabis, not to mention the law that helped put Ernesto Vicaro away for twenty years. On either of those cases, Parham's vote could swing the Court. Well, Parham's vote would *not* swing the Court. It would not have a *chance* to swing the Court. Taeger'd been in tougher fights than this one. And this was his last. This was his exit. He would *not* lose.

He said, "How much do we have left?"

"Money? Not enough. Isaac says it's no longer a matter of money, and I agree. It's psychology, public emotion. Attack Parham, you attack the girl. And that makes you look like a heartless bastard."

"What's Helen think?"

"I had dinner with her last week. I'm sure she thinks the same."

"So it's over. That's what you're saying?"

Harrington hesitated. "I'm out of ideas. I'm out of people who might have ideas."

"How's your friend Vicaro?"

"A lion in a cage."

Taeger slowly swiveled the chair around and faced Harrington.

"Why's that?"

"He's counting on *Javez v. Rench* to get him out."

"He's crazy."

"Of course. But the thought of Parham, who put him in prison, casting the Supreme Court vote that'll keep him there is too much for Vicaro. Right now he's just made of hatred. He's also got some crazy idea that *Hacker v. Colorado* will make him rich."

"Rich?"

"Richer."

Taeger thought carefully about what he was about to say. He reached under his desk and flipped a switch disconnecting the office telephone system. He glanced warily at Harrington's attaché case. He went through a mental checklist of everything they had done so far, of every anti-Parham initiative taken by the Freedom Federation, by Harrington independently, and by himself. He ran through everything Isaac had told him. He thought about everything he'd heard and read in the past twenty-four hours about Ernesto Vicaro. A lot had happened to that young man since Taeger first met him as a political officer and soon-to-be legislator. A 132-page DEA intelligence profile and an eighty-seven-page CIA profile made it clear—if there was anything Vicaro understood it was intimidation. He was a virtuoso of intimidation. When Vicaro wanted you to see things his way, you saw things his way. He had a genius for exploiting soft spots—find one, squeeze it, don't let go until you have what you want. An NSA annex to the CIA document mentioned intercepts of telephone communications between Vicaro and a man named Jonathan, followed by calls from Jonathan to a Who's Who of traffickers, law enforcement and intelligence officers, and politicians in Central and South America. Vicaro knew what he wanted, and he knew people who could help him get it. He was ruthless, treacherous, and well connected.

Taeger said, "What do you think would happen if he got out?"

"Got out?"

"You said something about a cage."

"Oh. If he were encouraged, I . . ."

"What might encourage a man like that, do you suppose?"

Harrington thought for a moment, picking his words. He knew he had an opportunity in the next half minute to do for Vicaro something that would command any fee he wished to attach to it.

"Well, Eric"—a sudden warmth in Taeger's manner seemed to invite the first name—"he's certainly a man with an experience of political power, both in his country and in others. I know he realizes the power resident in—well, in certain bodies of government, certain key people . . . your own power, for example. So that if he felt he had the . . . the friendship . . . the support . . . of people who would be able to help him in areas where he feels deserving—he believes, for example, and I feel he has some justification here, that his sentence was arbitrary and unjust—then he might have the confidence to attempt remedies that otherwise he would normally—"

Taeger raised a hand and stood. He'd said and heard as much as he dared to or needed to. "It's an interesting thought, isn't it? Perhaps we should pursue it."

"I think—"

"Yes, of course, think about it. I know you'll come to an effective decision. Politics is a fascinating science, isn't it. Soft one moment, less soft the next. And now, as unlikely as it might seem at this hour, I do have another appointment."

Taeger watched Harrington rise from the chair and reach for his attaché case. At the door Harrington said, "I'll call."

"Better not." Taeger looked at his watch. "It's late. You've got a lot to do. Come back at noon."

"At noon?"

Harrington looked shocked. But Taeger figured eight hours would be enough. A short nap, one or two phone calls. More than enough. All Harrington had to do was talk to Vicaro. Harrington himself had used the word—*encouragement.* Taeger was sure it wouldn't take much. Vicaro was on a hair trigger, and hair triggers don't require a lot of pressure.

Taeger didn't know precisely what Vicaro would do, and he didn't want to know. Whatever could be done to stop Parham, the only one left to do it was surely Vicaro. In politics it was often best to put things in the hands of the most capable people and not worry too much about their methods. He had never wanted to know how Warren Gier did what he did, or how Isaac Jasper did what he did, or how Helen Bondell did what she did, and right now he didn't want to know how Vicaro would do whatever he would do. Ignorance was insulation. If something went wrong, it'd be Vicaro's fault. Maybe, just possibly, it'd be Harrington's fault. But certainly not Taeger's. All Taeger had done was remind Harrington that he'd said something about a cage. But Harrington had understood, and Harrington would do whatever had to be done to unleash Vicaro.

As Taeger watched Harrington disappear through the office door, he reflected on the old adage that two things you never want to see being made are sausages and legislation. To those Taeger would now have added Supreme Court confirmations.

17

Phil, how are you?"

"Fine, Pete. What can you tell me?"

Peter Rexroth, the White House intelligence coordinator, had telephoned Rothman in his office.

"I just had a chat with a couple of our providers." CIA and NSA.

"Yes?"

"Something I think you need to know, maybe the President."

"Go ahead."

"Two Pen hits, one from a federally incarcerated, profiled Colombian trafficker, politician, and intelligence officer named Ernesto Vicaro-Garza to an active but undocumented contact called Jonathan." A Pen Register was a device secretly but legally attached to a telephone to record the numbers called but not the calls themselves. "The other was from Jonathan to a D.C. public phone. We don't yet have a hard identification on the male who picked up the phone, but the number's had three previous accesses by a Colombian intel cutout with special action clients. We've also had three documented Colombian special action agents passing separately through Dulles and Miami International over the past four days. That's highly unusual."

"And it all means?"

"Providers give a level four probability of a terrorist action in the capital within ten days."

"Just from that—two Pen numbers?" Level four was only three levels below certainty.

"Plus what they know about Vicaro, the cutout, his clients, the four agents at the airports. Analysts in the past have made bull's-eye predictions with less than that."

"Send all the hard stuff, Pete. Analysis, documentation, profiles." He looked at his watch. He had a meeting with the President in two hours and twenty minutes. "Call back in two hours. What makes them think ten days? Best guess for an objective and target."

"Yes, sir."

On a Thursday afternoon more than a month after they'd moved into Blossom, with the Judiciary Committee confirmation vote finally set for the following Monday and the win-or-lose Senate floor vote for Wednesday, Samantha was in the Box with Todd Naeder and Fred Knight, a balding, fatherly agent who was chief of the Blossom security unit.

Michelle had gone out and Gus was upstairs working in his office.

Todd rose from the desk and told Knight he was going to the bathroom.

He'd been gone a couple of minutes when Knight, lifting his eyes from a month-old copy of *Time* to a TV monitor covering the intersection at the west end of the block, said, "Well now, who's this?"

A Mercedes station wagon had just stopped at a temporary security kiosk in the middle of the street. The kiosk had been installed the previous evening to monitor vehicles entering the block in preparation for a reception that evening at the Norwegian embassy next door.

Knight waited until the Mercedes, cleared into the block, had pulled away from the kiosk, then picked up a white telephone handset and punched a button.

"Blossom Three. So what can you tell me?"

Blossom Three was code for the Box. He was talking to the kiosk.

"Plates and passport, Norwegian diplomatic."

"Registered to?"

"Plates to the embassy. Passport matches DL. You guys worry too much."

"Nobody worries too much."

Knight put the phone down and shifted his attention to a neighboring monitor, which picked up the Mercedes as it slowed in front of Blossom and maneuvered into a parking place between the house and the Norwegian embassy, across the street from a residence owned by the Colombian Trade Commission. The driver climbed out and disappeared from the screen, walking east toward the embassy's side entrance.

Knight returned to *Time.*

Samantha, looking fresh and cool in cut-off jeans and a white T-shirt, said, "It's so exciting."

Knight kept reading.

"Don't you think so?"

Knight grunted. He really liked Samantha, but privately he called her Cinderella. She'd really been bugging him about the reception. Would there be presidents, kings and queens, could you see them going in and out, what would they wear, what would they eat, would they dance?

Knight had worked security on about seven zillion diplomatic receptions, and what the guests ate was never a matter of interest, as long as it wasn't poison.

The phone buzzed. Knight picked it up.

"Yeah. Okay. But listen, last time it dumped all over the sidewalk. Keep it clean, okay?"

Todd walked in and Knight said, "The dog's here."

"I saw." He lowered himself into a chair. "Take a break?"

Knight put the magazine down. "Why not?"

Knight was just out the door when Samantha heard barking in the street. She had never heard barking so fierce. She darted to the window. A cute little black spaniel was going absolutely insane at the back of the Mercedes.

Todd yelled, "Hang on!"

Knight was back in the Box, a hand moving Samantha out of the window while he took a look.

Ten seconds later he was in the street.

"Can I go?" Samantha asked Todd. She was not allowed out of the house without permission.

"No way. Get away from the window."

The spaniel trembled and growled on the end of its leash.

Knight was back, picking up a phone.

"He alerted all over the back end of that thing. Man, he is just *crazy*."

"Yeah, this is Blossom Three. We've got an explosives dog just alerted on the rear end of a Mercedes station wagon with blacked-out windows, DPL plates have—"

He stopped talking, listened.

"Right. Be quick." Waiting, he said to Todd, "They just got it from the van. They can tell from the way the dog— Yeah, right, how long'll that take? I need it in three minutes, latest. Right."

He hung up.

"They're getting another dog and an RF locator. Who've we got?"

Todd looked at a chart on the wall.

"Us and the judge."

"Where's Mrs. Parham?"

"Out."

"Beggie?" The cook.

"Shopping. Something. I don't know. Not in the house."

"Louisa?"

"With Beggie. Who's that?"

Two men in dark suits had arrived at the Mercedes, talking to a tall man in a green windbreaker. Another man jogged over from the Norwegian embassy.

Knight was out the door.

Samantha watched him talk to the other men. Together they walked around the Mercedes.

Knight turned and ran back to the house. He came in yelling.

"Get the judge and Samantha in the limousine and *out.*"

"Where did—"

"The Norwegians say the plates and the driver's documents are all phony. Nothing matches. No one's seen the driver since he parked."

Todd grabbed a set of keys off a hook on a wall board and started for the door.

Knight, punching numbers on the phone, yelled "Run!" Then, into the mouthpiece, "This is Knight at Blossom Three. We have a confirmed explosives alert. We're gonna need ATF and an EOD unit. Feebs, military, PD. Fast as you can. Right. And get Falco."

He slammed the phone down and ran back to the street.

When Todd and Samantha reached the living room hallway they almost bumped into Gus coming down the stairs.

Gus said, "What's up?" He seemed solemn and distracted. Taeger had had him in the witness chair for three hours that morning.

"Please come with me, sir. There's a major security problem outside, and I've been ordered to take you and Miss Young out in the limousine."

"What's the difficulty?"

Gus looked ready to go to the Box and find out for himself.

"An explosives vehicle, sir. We have to get out right now. Please."

Gus said, "Let's go. Where's Mrs. Parham?"

"Still out, sir."

"Carl?"

"He's been called, sir."

Gus followed Todd and Samantha to the garage. Todd

opened the back door of the limo for them, climbed into the front, put the keys in the ignition, but before he could close his door he heard Knight's voice calling to him from the door to the kitchen.

"They in the limo?"

Knight would not be able to see them through the tinted glass.

Todd yelled, "Yes."

Knight said, "Leave them there."

Carl, out of breath, appeared beside Knight. "Leave them where they are."

Todd turned. "Do what?"

Knight said, "Leave them."

"But—"

Carl said, "Leave them." He turned and ran back to the street.

Another explosives dog, a brown-and-white beagle that arrived about two minutes after the first one alerted, walked its handler directly to the back of the Mercedes and sat down, panting and wagging its tail. Pulled away on its leash, it immediately returned and sat down.

"That's it," the handler told Carl. "Definitely."

"All he did was sit down," Carl said, trying to talk the handler out of it.

"That's what he does. Smells explosives, he sits down. It's there, believe me. Snoopy's our best dog. Never misses."

An ATF agent who'd come with the dog handler walked slowly around the Mercedes, examining the front, back, top, bottom. His name was Rolf Zaeder, and he was older than Carl, well into his fifties, short and fat, a roly-poly little man with a ruddy, jolly Santa Claus face. A small RF locator in his hand had already detected radio frequency emissions, consistent with a remote control receiver, coming from the Mercedes. Now Zaeder got down on his knees, breathing hard, and peered underneath. He waved a hand at Carl.

"See that?"

Carl took a look. A thin, stiff, gray-colored wire protruded six inches along the bottom of the left side of the Mercedes, disappearing into a hole the size of a pinhead.

"Antenna," Zaeder said. "Only you don't normally see antennas under the bottom of vehicles, do you? So something's not exactly kosher."

Carl said, "Talk to me."

"Probably comes from a remote detonator. Could be a garage-door opener, model-car radio control, cellular phone. Press the button, flip the switch, dial the number, current goes into a blasting cap, *Va-voom.*"

Zaeder struggled to his feet, brushed dirt off his knees, but seemed in no rush to put distance between himself and the Mercedes.

Carl said, "So it's a remote detonator. Not a timer."

"Both."

"You said—"

"If it's a remote, there's a timer too."

"How do you know that?"

"They've got a remote, they're waiting to see their target, waiting for something to happen, right? If it never happens, they never see the target, what do they do? Get in the Mercedes and drive back where they came from? No way. People who use remotes always—*always*—have a time limit. Usually a few hours. Rarely more than a day. Longest I ever saw was Cairo in 'eighty-nine, car bomb at the Jordanian embassy sat there two days, then *Boom!* Who wants to recover a car bomb? Real professionals, take pride in their work, the device never gets taken, enemy never gets a chance to examine it."

"So the Mercedes will sit there, and if nothing happens, eventually it'll blow up all on its own."

"Right. Eventually. Hours, days, who knows?"

"So what are you recommending?"

Zaeder took a deep breath and let it out in a long sigh. "If whoever has the remote hasn't blown it yet, he hasn't seen what he wants to see. They're waiting for something, an arrival or departure, maybe someone coming to the reception, or someone at Blossom. If they know there's fortification, they'll want to get their target outside."

Knight walked up, shook hands with Zaeder. "The PD's evacuating neighboring buildings. I told them at least a square block, maybe more."

Carl said, "Is Blossom fortified?"

Knight said, "Up to five hundred pounds per square inch on the facade."

Zaeder said, "The limo's probably another three hundred."

"If all the numbers are right," Knight said, "the judge and Samantha have a chance inside the limo inside Blossom. Inside the limo *outside* Blossom—in the driveway, on the street—it's another story."

Carl looked at Zaeder. He shook his head. "Outside, forget it. Zero."

Carl said to Knight, "Let's keep them where they are, at least for the moment. Till we work something out."

Knight left. Zaeder kept his eyes on the station wagon. "I'd like to know what's in that thing."

"Guess."

Zaeder made a face, eyebrows arched. "You could get

a thousand pounds into that vehicle, maybe closer to two thousand if you reinforced the shocks—half what they had in Oklahoma. Ampho, dynamite kicker, do a lot of damage. High explosive, say Syntex or RDX, and it'd be a lot worse. The whole block'll go."

"How much damage would it do to the house?"

"That house? There?" He pointed at Blossom. "Oh, it won't damage that house at all. It'll just totally mush that house right down into the ground, squash it so flat you won't even know there was ever a house there."

"And someone inside?"

"Turn 'em into slop."

"Two people, inside an armored limousine in the garage."

"Front of the house?"

"Back."

"That's good. Underground?"

"About halfway down. The house's built on a hill, so part of the back of the first floor is underground."

He shook his head. "Maybe. I don't know. They might make it."

"Odds?"

"Wouldn't want to say. We don't even know what's in the thing. Won't know till it blows up."

"We'd prefer not to wait that long."

Zaeder shot him a glance. He didn't like the sarcasm.

Carl said, "No way to find out?"

"Oh, there's a way."

"And that is?"

"EOD. Explosive Ordnance Division."

"What'd they do?"

"Start with a probe. Take a Customs probe, what they

use at the airport, find out is that cake you brought back from Paris filled with cocaine or diamonds. Drill a tiny hole in the top of the Mercedes, stick in a probe, couple of feet long, little barb on the end, come out with a speck of ammonium nitrate, you got an ampho bomb. Comes out with RDX, a whole different problem. Probe hits, say, six inches in from the top and sides, the vehicle's packed. Big, big problem. Not packed, not so bad. We might even cut a hole in through the top, get a man in there, take a look at the detonator, see something familiar, easy disconnect, no problem. Hook up the Mercedes, tow it way, everyone goes home safe and sound."

He smiled, widely, ear to ear.

Carl said, "Put a *man* in there?"

"Yeah. Or a woman. Someone little. Squirm around. Depends is the Mercedes filled or not."

"You've got people who do that?"

"EOD does. Oh, sure."

"What kind of person would do that?"

"Someone not too tightly wrapped."

18

Samantha and Gus had been alone in the limousine for three minutes, and Gus's eyes were in a hard stare. She didn't want to interrupt his thoughts. After another minute he looked at her.

"I'm sorry, Samantha."

"Sorry for what?"

"That you're . . . in this predicament." He smiled, trying to encourage her. "But don't worry, it'll be okay. A lot of action, right?"

"Yeah, really. At least if we're stuck in a car it's a limo. I never knew politics was this exciting."

"It's not politics. It's a judicial process."

She stretched her legs. Her feet didn't even touch the back of the front seat. She had a lot of questions, but Gus didn't look like he needed questions. The limo had a TV. Maybe something would be on the news. Too soon for that. Also a fax machine and a bar. Gus looked like he could use a drink.

With what she hoped was an encouraging smile, she waved a hand at the row of glasses in a door recess, and said, "Have a drink?"

Gus said, "What? I didn't—Oh, no, thanks Samantha, I don't think so right now. Thanks, anyway."

It was twenty minutes since Gus and Samantha had been rushed into the limousine, and Carl stood with Knight in a growing crowd of agents and police near the intersection of Blossom's street with a traffic circle three blocks away.

Knight said, "I don't like leaving them there. We ought to drive them out."

His boss, chief of security for State Department domestic dwellings, had just arrived and was agreeing with Carl. "If there's a remote and they're waiting for sight of Parham, he's better where he is. We need to talk to the fortification people."

Carl, standing on a patch of grass by the curb, said, "On their way. Along with everyone else."

Knight, looking up the street, said, "Speak of the devil."

A dark blue tractor-trailer made its way around the traffic circle. An FBI command truck, it had a yellow Justice Department seal and the letters FBI emblazoned on the side. It pulled to the curb, and a man in the passenger seat jumped down.

An agent in a windbreaker with ATF on the back said, "I wouldn't."

The FBI man looked at him with a half-grin, uncertain.

The ATF agent said, "Move it or lose it."

"Where would you put it?" The FBI man, understanding, had lost the smile.

"Up there. Out of sight. Get some buildings in the way."

Ten minutes later the command truck was parked 200 yards up a side street at right angles to Blossom. Inside, counters running the length of each side were covered with computer consoles, TV monitors, radios, telephones, and fax machines.

Knight, sitting in a wheeled swivel chair at the console nearest the entrance, said to Carl, "You have any opinion when that thing might go off?"

"Any second. Or next week. Or when someone sees the judge come out, or Samantha. The device has a remote detonator, but it also has a timer." He repeated what Zaeder had said about remotes always having timers. "I'd love to know when the timer's set for. But right now we have to be more concerned about the remote."

Knight said, "Who's holding it, would you guess?"

"Who's close enough to see? Norwegians? Brazilians?"

"Not too likely."

Carl said, "Across the street?"

When Knight took over the Blossom security job, he'd read classified background reports on the neighbors. The Colombian Trade Commission, which had moved in a year earlier across the street from Blossom, was run by the Colombian security service, tightly linked to the cocaine traffic, and if there was nastiness in the area the Trade Commission would bear watching. He had also seen a top-secret

White House "alert memo" mentioning Colombian agents and predicting a terrorist action in the capital.

Carl, who had also seen the memo as well as the hard data supporting it, had his own suspicions. The head of the Freedom Federation, with a reputation like Helen Bondell's for tooth-and-nail combat, had to have had something solid in mind, something that scared her, when she took the time, trouble, and risk to meet a federal agent in a coffee shop to warn him about Vicaro.

Carl sat in the swivel chair next to Knight, picked up a phone, and called the limousine.

"Gus, it's Carl."

"What's happening? Where's Michelle?"

"Michelle's fine. I'm not exactly sure where she is, but she's not in the house. She went out someplace. She's okay."

"Tell me about the Mercedes, Carl."

He told Gus about the explosives, the remote detonator. "We're going to have to ask you to stay put for a while. We've got about a million security folks out here, and more arriving. Samantha okay?"

"She's fine. Find Michelle, Carl."

"Don't worry. I'll call back. Are the keys still in the ignition? Todd said he left them there."

"Yeah, they're there."

"Okay. Talk to you soon."

Samantha asked, "What'd he say?"

"Well . . ."

He looked at her.

"You don't want to scare me, right?"

"Samantha . . ."

He'd have given anything to have her somewhere else, somewhere safe.

"Don't worry. I won't get hysterical or anything. Are we going to get blown up?"

"I don't think it's that bad."

His thoughts shot back to a meeting that morning with his father. It'd been the first time in two years he'd seen the man, and their conversation had been a disaster. They'd always seemed unable to meet each other halfway on anything, and this time—well, his father had really handed him a bombshell. And now he had another bomb to think about, a real one, in the street. What was going on?

Samantha said, "I could die. My mother used to tell me all the time, 'Do this you die, do that you die.' What'd Carl say?"

"Not much more than we already know. There's a Mercedes parked outside the house, and they think there might be a bomb in it. But there's armor on the front of the house and on this car, so if we stay here we'll be okay. And when they get the bomb disconnected we'll come out."

"How long does he think it'll be?"

"He doesn't know yet. He'll find out."

"Can we turn on the air-conditioning? It's really hot."

"I think we'd better save the power, Samantha. If we run down the battery, we won't be able to use the phone."

"What about the TV? Maybe we're on TV. Then Carl won't have to tell us stuff, we'll already know."

"Maybe later."

"You think we're going to be here a long time, don't you?"

"Not necessarily. But it's good to be prepared, right?"

Gus thought about the White House alert memo he'd

seen two days ago. The complete version, with attachments, was far more informative than the preliminary phone call the White House intelligence coordinator had made to Rothman. An investigator employed by a law firm friendly to the White House (Dutweiler had once been a senior partner) had "just happened" to be driving past Taeger's business office early one morning when he noticed the lights on. He parked and watched. A visitor went in, stayed twenty-eight minutes, came out, drove away. When the investigator checked the visitor's plate number, it turned out to be registered to John Harrington.

Forty-two minutes later, about the time it would have taken Harrington to drive home from Taeger's office, a Pen Register on his home phone showed a forty-seven-minute call to the Federal Correction Institute near Chicago, where Ernesto Vicaro was incarcerated. Twelve minutes after the conclusion of that call, prison telephone records showed a call from Vicaro to a "cousin" named Jonathan Tander. Four minutes after that call, Jonathan Tander's phone was used to call a New York apartment rented six months previously by a commercial trading company owned by TransInter, with links to the Colombian foreign intelligence service. A federal tap on that phone recorded coded conversation between two males discussing what CIA analysts believed were meetings and travel plans. Two days later three special action agents entered the country through Dulles and Miami International. Subsequent record checks identified one of the agents as an explosives and vehicle-bomb expert named Rubi Aguilera. And now, hardly more than a week later, there was the Mercedes station wagon, loaded with explosives, parked outside Blossom.

Gus thought about Vicaro, the fifteen-year-old bully trying to pull other kids off the wall of his father's bullring, and his father letting him do it. Four years later he'd been an intelligence agent in the Colombian embassy, then a Colombian legislator elected with his father's money, and finally, the obese young man under arrest in the back seat of a DEA car in Montgomery.

He thought about Harrington's offer of a bribe, and the bullets in the luggage locker.

He thought about the political treachery of men like Senator Eric Taeger, of other men with out-of-control ambition for whom Washington had been the final stop before suicide or prison.

He thought about the man Michelle had discovered in their garage, and the millions of dollars already spent in a media smear against him.

He thought about the stakes: the approaching Supreme Court decisions that over the next few decades could reshape the nation's social, moral, and spiritual assumptions.

He thought about physical violence and moral violence and the fundamental difference, if any, between the two.

He was certain of two things: First, the Mercedes out there was proof enough of Vicaro's determination to kill him. Keeping Gus off the Supreme Court wasn't the only thing motivating Vicaro—Gus had put Vicaro in prison, the only man ever to have denied him anything. Pride, reputation, and ambition demanded Gus's death. Gus knew, as certainly as he had ever known anything, that if he left the limousine and walked out of Blossom, he would die. John Harrington might be interested only in Gus's withdrawal from the nomination, and so might people like Helen Bondell and Senator Taeger, but Vicaro wanted him dead—whether he withdrew or not. The second thing Gus knew was that he was ready. He would not withdraw. If he died, he died. But he would not withdraw.

An FBI agent named Max Iverson, just arrived in the command truck from the Washington terrorist unit, said, "I say, tell 'em to drive out."

Skinny as a skeleton, Iverson had a bow tie, short-sleeved shirt, and he'd been told by his boss that the lead agent would be DEA's Carl Falco, on loan to the White House. The FBI wasn't happy surrendering leadership to another agency, particularly since Falco, a GS–15, ranked lower than Iverson. But Rothman, speaking for the White House, had told the attorney general twenty minutes after the bomb alert, "Falco's who we know, someone the judge knows, and Falco's who we want."

Another late arrival, a white-haired man sweating in a gray seersucker suit, unbuttoned his collar and said, "I wouldn't." He looked about five years past retirement age and had the mischievous eyes of a rocking-chair geezer in an old people's home.

"Garry Hardy," Knight said. "State Department Security. Our golden oldie. Fortification and armor expert, used to build castles in the Middle Ages."

Knight grinned. Hardy prided himself on knowing everything there was to know about fortification and armor—buildings, vehicles, boats, aircraft, people, even animals. Years ago he'd designed an armored garment for a German shepherd.

"So?" Knight said. "What can you tell us about Blossom?"

Hardy crossed his arms and stuck out a potbelly the size of a basketball.

"Four years ago, we put in two-inch Plexiglas windows, an inch of Kevlar between the brick facade and the interior plaster. It'll take twenty thousand pounds per square inch. That's about one ton of RDX in an unfocused detonation at fifty feet. After that . . ."

Carl said, "And if it's more than that?"

"Blast'll ride right up the front, like a mountain of water going a hundred miles an hour. Will the house stand up to that? I don't know. Explosives are like people. Fickle. They surprise you. Could be the whole block'll go and that house'll be left standing all by itself. But I wouldn't wanta bet on it. Now, if it's *not* high explosive, say it's an ampho bomb, a lot slower, more of a pusher than cutter, things might not be so bad."

Carl said, "The limo?"

Hardy thought for a moment. "Another hundred and eighty thousand psi, the limo's gonna fly. Weighs close to a ton, and anything over a hundred thousand psi will move it. Over two hundred thousand psi, you've got a projectile. I saw the Mercedes coming in, an E290 Turbodiesel. Take out the seats, strip it, you can pack in over a hundred cubic feet of the double-F mix they used in Oklahoma. That blows, the limo's gonna fly. I'd say, unobstructed, it'd do thirty feet easy. Hits the garage wall, it'll make a nice hole. That's a side wall. No Kevlar. I wanted to fortify the sides and back, but all they'd spring for was the street. They kept saying—"

"Double-F?"

"Fuel and fertilizer, ammonium nitrate."

Knight said, "If you've got all the numbers right, what are the injuries to the passengers?"

Hardy had the strangeness Carl had found in other men

obsessed with things that explode. He screwed up his face and gazed at the ceiling, his brain shuffling numbers.

"An armored limo blast in Beirut eleven years ago, the car flew forty feet, attained an *altitude* of six feet, and the four men inside climbed out with cuts, contusions, cracked ribs."

He smiled, geezer eyes flashing. "Some ride."

Iverson glanced uneasily at Knight.

"But they could live," Hardy said quickly, evidently seeing a need for encouragement.

Carl said, "If they drive out, and the Mercedes explodes while they're in the driveway or on the street, what are their chances?"

"Outside?" Hardy's eyes went wide with shock. "Driveway? Street?"

Carl said, "Yeah."

"Parts, my friend. Take us three days pick up the mess."

Carl nodded and looked at Iverson. "Still want them to drive out?"

Iverson unbuttoned his collar and loosened the bow tie. They were going to be here a while. "And where we are now. What'll happen here?"

Hardy grinned. "How far are we? Three blocks? Four hundred yards? A rumble. Shake, rattle, 'n' roll. Broken windows. I intend to stay away from the windows."

The truck was getting crowded. Through the open door, on the street, Carl spotted a familiar face. Familiar not because he'd seen it before, but because he recognized the air of furtive detachment. Its owner lived among secrets, as the other agents did, but his secrets, intended for a sharply limited official clientele, never had to endure exposure in a court of law.

Carl excused himself and went out to the street. The man, carrying a set of car keys, held the door of a blue Ford, and they got in.

Selecting the ignition key, the man said, "We believe it's a remote. Unless it's very old, which would be a surprise, it transmits not merely a signal but a code. So the transmitter can be anywhere. Could even be on a satellite. It's passive, gives no indication of its presence until it's activated, and then it's too late. So we're not wasting time looking for it, and you shouldn't either. Approaching the problem from the other end—people rather than technology—has been more promising. The driver of the Mercedes was a Colombian DAS agent, working under the cover of a private Miami security company owned by TransInter, which of course is Ernesto Vicaro. There've also been intercepts and other data pointing to Vicaro and a bag of mixed objectives—politics, drugs, vengeance. Not uncommon. And the Supreme Court nomination, of course. I have to admit, that's a first."

"How do you know who—"

"Videotapes of the vehicle's driver at the security booth. The phony documents and plates can be taken to have been a product of Colombian intelligence, to whom Vicaro, as you know, is not exactly a stranger."

The man stuck the key into the ignition.

Carl said, "The transmitter may be on a satellite, but someone with a view of the house has to press a button."

"And that button device could be disguised as almost anything. Cigarette pack. Belt buckle. Don't even think of trying to find it. Find Vicaro's people instead. Squeeze them. The right guy will scream. They always do. Anyway, that's our advice. Maybe it'll work in time, maybe not. Do as you like. I'm glad it's not me." He grinned. "I was never here."

"Why'd you tell me? Why not the FBI or ATF?"

"Someone said, 'Tell Carl.' So I told Carl. And one other thing. An intercept an hour ago, Bogotá to a phone in the Trade Commission—'Have you seen the girl?' They're watching for someone, the girl or the judge. So bringing them out would not be a good idea, in my view."

The man turned the key, the engine started, and Carl got out.

The car drove off, slowly.

Samantha said, "How're we gonna go to the bathroom?"

"Well, I don't know. Do you have to go now?"

"No. TV, bar, telephone—they should have a toilet in this thing." Her voice had an edge to it, enough to remind him of the young girl pounding on the car window in Saint-Tropez. "I was on a bus once that had a toilet. And that was in *Germany.* You'd think—can't we go back in the house to use the bathroom?"

"I don't think so, Samantha. We'll have to make some kind of arrangement out here."

"In this *limousine?*"

"Or maybe the garage. I don't see any other alternative."

"If you think—"

She caught herself, and took a breath.

"I'm sorry. You don't need that, right? Like you said, we'll make other arrangements, when the time comes."

The phone rang.

"Can Samantha hear me?"

It was Carl.

"No. Tell me what's happening. Where's Michelle?"

Gus's voice had a confident, cheerful lilt, certainly for Samantha's benefit.

"She's not back yet. We know she went out, but we don't know where. Soon as we find her, I'll call."

"Find her, Carl."

"I will. Listen, the limo people out here say if we want to have power to keep the telephone up you'll have to stay off everything else, including the air-conditioning."

"It's really hot in here, Carl."

"I can guess. I'm also told to ask you to keep the windows closed. They're bulletproof and they'll protect against flying debris. And from now on we'll have to use the scrambler." The limousine telephone was equipped with an optional scrambling device. "We don't want anyone copying our conversations. And we wouldn't like to hear them on TV and radio."

"How good is the encryption?"

"Most devices can break it in forty-five hours, but state of the art's more like ten minutes, and NSA does it simultaneously. So even with the scrambling, we're advised to talk with care."

"What's the estimate, Carl—how long are we going to be here?"

"I guess until we can find the remote, or some other way to neutralize the Mercedes. There're about a million people out here trying to figure how to do that. We've got people on the way from Mercedes, from the armor manufacturer, the architect who designed Blossom is coming over, also the builder, and a mob of people from FBI, ATF, State Department Security, a lot of people who investigated Oklahoma and the World Trade Center. Even Israeli intelligence is sending someone, and no one knows more about car bombs than they do."

"Don't worry. Samantha and I've been wanting to have some time together, and now we've got it. Right, Samantha? Okay, Carl. Call back when you know something."

"Someone says it'd help if we had an inventory of the food and drink in the bar in there."

"We'll count the drinks and cocktail biscuits."

"So there really is a bomb? That's not a mistake?"

Samantha thought maybe *High Society* wasn't the right name for the new book after all—maybe she should call this part of her life *Blown to Bits.* But she didn't really think anything bad would happen. This wasn't the kind of house where bad things happened.

"I'm afraid it's not a mistake," Gus said. "But they've got a lot of experts out there trying to disconnect it, and when they do we'll be able to go out. Anyway, we'll have some time together. We don't need to worry about getting interrupted."

"Yeah, except maybe *Boom!* Sorry, just trying to be funny." The child again.

For five minutes they were silent. Then Samantha said, "I'm glad we're alone. There've been things I've sort of wanted to tell you. And Michelle."

"What things?"

"Well . . . How much did my father tell you about me?"

"Almost nothing."

"Did you talk to my mom?"

"I've never met her."

"So you don't know anything?"

"Not really."

Gus felt a curious sense of anxiety. He wasn't comfortable cooped up in the back seat of a limousine with a thirteen-year-old girl. He knew nothing at all about thirteen-year-old girls.

She'd been facing him, but now she turned toward the front of the car, put her back against the seat, and clasped her hands in her lap. The lights were off in the garage, and the only illumination came through two small windows next to the metal roll-up garage door. The sun had started to set.

She said, "There's a lot maybe I should tell you."

"Then I hope you will."

"The thing is, once I tell, I don't know what will happen."

"I don't think anything bad will happen, Samantha. You'll still be my daughter and Michelle's daughter and we'll still love you. Nothing will change that."

"How do you know? You haven't heard yet. Sometimes parents say that and then something happens and *Wham!*, there it goes. I had a friend that happened to."

"It won't happen, Samantha. You can tell me or not. That's your decision. But whatever it is, I'm going to keep on loving you, and so is Michelle. That's our decision."

"You don't know how my mom and dad met, I mean Larry and Doreen, anything about that?"

"Nothing at all."

"That he's from Albania?"

"No."

"He's from the royal family, I mean before the, you know, the communists came. He changed his name because he said nobody in Milwaukee could pronounce Albanian names."

"Really?"

"It's true. You don't believe me."

"I don't know any reason why that can't be true, Samantha."

"He used to be a concert piano player. Even when he was like seventeen or eighteen. He has posters of himself, all dressed up, when he played at concert halls. And then he was in East Berlin and he escaped through the Wall and he started playing in nightclubs and hotels. And this group of hotels gave him a job and he was playing in a hotel in Florida, in Palm Beach, and he met my mom. He said she was the most beautiful person he'd ever seen. She was a teacher in Milwaukee on vacation. So he went to Milwaukee and they got married."

She had let it all out at once, and now she leaned back and stared at him through the half-light, assessing his reaction.

He was silent, taking it in. He'd heard a lot of odd stories as a judge, and sometimes it was hard to know what was true. Odd didn't always mean it was a lie.

Finally she said, "Do you believe that?"

She seemed not particularly accustomed to being believed.

"Yes, I believe that. Shouldn't I believe it?"

"Of course you should. You're a judge, and judges believe the truth."

What a statement. Judges believe the truth.

Gus said, "What happened next? They got married, and—they stayed in Milwaukee?"

"They stayed in Milwaukee. My dad played in hotels and my mom taught. The earliest thing I remember is my mom and me going to school together and my dad was still in bed because he'd been working late. And then when we got back home my dad would have something to eat all fixed for us on the kitchen table."

"That was nice."

"Yeah, and then my dad started drinking a lot."

"He told you that?"

"No. My mom told me. She told me plenty. And some of it, later my dad told me. I ask him stuff and he can't lie, he's a terrible liar. Not like my mom. She lies all the time. A friend of hers told me if her lips are moving she's lying, that's how you tell. I knew something was wrong because there weren't any more little snacks on the table when we got home, he was still in bed. And he started losing jobs, and my mom said he had to play in little bars and not the big hotels. And then my mom got into astrology, did you know about that?"

"No."

"It was something she did with friends and other teachers, and she was really good at it, you know, getting all these people to believe she could tell their future from the stars. Teachers, and they're supposed to be smart. Anyway, she started charging people for this and she branched out into reading tarot cards and Ouija boards and spiritism and talking to dead people, and all this stuff. And I guess eventually she was making more money at that than she was at teaching, so she quit teaching. And now my mom and dad weren't what they used to be anymore. They really changed. He was playing in dirty little bars, that's what my mom called them, and she was at home talking to people's dead relatives."

"What did you think of all that?"

She shrugged. "To me it was just—well, it's what she did. I didn't think anything. What would I think? I was just a little kid. Like, maybe everybody's mom and dad did stuff like that. Except that they sort of became different. I remember they just—mostly my mom, she started getting hard, she wasn't fun anymore. I remember trying to stay out of her way. And then Janine came to stay with us. I guess you don't know about that either?"

"Janine? No."

"That's when I *really* started to wonder about things. Because I was six then and I could see from the way things were at my friends' homes that things were definitely a little *different* where I lived."

"Who was Janine?"

Samantha hesitated. This was something she wasn't sure she should tell. If she did, she'd end up telling everything. Would he believe her? Would he jump out of the limousine and run for it? Things would change. But—she couldn't *not* tell him.

"Well, Janine was about eighteen, and she was someone who used to come over for all the horoscope, Ouija board mumbo jumbo, that's what my friends and I called it. Then my dad started losing his job more often, from the drinking, and I guess now he was running out of bars that would give him jobs, and we needed money and Janine didn't have a place to live because her parents had kicked her out for some reason, but she had a job as I don't know what and so she moved in with us—you sure you want to hear all this?"

"Very sure."

"She moved in and started paying rent. And then she had a friend named Dorothy, and Dorothy moved in too. And now we've got Janine and Dorothy around the house and all their *boyfriends.* And there were a *lot* of boyfriends.

And one of my friends, my best friend, who used to come over to the house a lot, told her sister about Janine and Dorothy and all their boyfriends and how they always had lots of money for clothes and things, and her sister, who was seventeen, said well maybe they're *prostitutes.* What's a prostitute? I was seven then. So she explained what prostitutes were. Wow! And then she said that if Janine and Dorothy lived in our house and they were prostitutes, then our house was a whorehouse. She said I was living in a whorehouse and my mother was a *madam.* And I got real mad at her because I didn't know anything about what a whorehouse was or what a madam was, but it certainly *sounded* like a whorehouse and a madam were insults."

Gus was stunned. How much of this was true?

Samantha said, "You're shocked, right?"

Gus said, "Well, I'd be lying if I didn't admit that it's a rather surprising story. I—"

"It's not a *story.* It's true."

"I don't doubt you, Samantha. I believe it. I'm just—you were seven?"

"Yeah, seven. Your little girl, living in a whorehouse. What if you'd known, right? But it wasn't that bad. Janine and Dorothy were nice. I liked them. Only it did get worse, though. You want to hear? Maybe I should stop. Would you like a drink?"

Would he like a drink!

"I want to hear it all, Samantha. If you don't mind. Maybe you'd rather—"

"No, I *want* to tell you. I've been wanting to do this for years, tell someone."

"Then go ahead." He would have given anything to have Michelle here.

"Men started coming over who weren't Janine and Dorothy's friends, I mean who they didn't bring. My mom would meet them and invite them over."

"Where was Larry?"

"He never had anything to do with it. He was just living there. Living there and drinking and sometimes playing in a bar someplace."

"He didn't know—"

"Of course he knew. How could he not know? But whenever he said something, Mom just yelled at him or ignored him. They needed the money and he wasn't making any. Not much, anyway, and what he made he mostly drank."

"I see."

"So these men are coming over, and pretty soon Janine and Dorothy and my mom get other girls to come over, because there were so many men and they wanted other girls. The girls didn't live there like Janine and Dorothy, but they came over. And some of the girls were younger. To me they looked old, because I was only seven, but they were younger than Janine and Dorothy, like maybe thirteen, fourteen. And they would go in the bedrooms with these old guys."

"You were around for all this?"

"I lived there. I helped."

"You helped?"

"Opened the door, said hello, hung up coats."

"What did you think?"

"Sometimes they'd want something to drink and I'd give them drinks. I thought it was kind of fun. Like a party. Everyone was nice to me. And then when I was eight it seemed like the girls were getting younger, or maybe I was just getting older, but they were almost like my age. And some of the guys would try to play around with me. Just like playing around, you know, slapping me on the butt and stuff like that, but then they got a little more—it wasn't just kidding around anymore. And I told my mom about it and she said it was just my imagination, that they were all nice people.

"And then one of the guys—a young guy, a nice guy, I liked him—we were sort of playing around, he was chasing me, and I'd chase him, just playing, and the next thing I knew we were in my mom's bedroom and the door was closed and he was on the bed and he wanted me to come on the bed with him, and boy I just turned around got *out* of there. And I told my mom. I thought she'd be really mad and kick him out, but all she said was—like it was nothing, like the whole thing was just nothing—she said, 'Well, why'd you run away? He wasn't going to hurt you. He just wanted to play a little.' And I knew what she meant by that because that was what the girls would say to the men, like, 'You wanna play a little?' And I knew what that meant."

She stopped. Gus waited for her to continue, but she turned toward the window in silence. Finally he said, "Then what happened?"

"I don't want to talk about it anymore."

"Okay."

Her mood had changed. What had happened? She swiveled her head toward him, and he could see she was crying. She said, "I really hate to tell you this."

"Then don't tell me."

"Even my mother, Doreen, she never talked about it to me, it's the only thing she never used to hurt me. She mentioned it once and I threw the TV through the window. It was just a little TV, a portable. There's a lot of stuff and after a while there's just too much. Do you know what I mean?"

"I know very well what you mean, Samantha. You don't have to tell me."

"I want you to know."

"It's up to you."

"One day early in the morning there was only this one guy in the house, maybe he'd spent the night, or he'd come over real early, I don't know, but he was an older guy I didn't know very well, a fat guy, with a big belly, not one of the guys who would always talk to me and kid around with me, and the house was like empty, Dorothy and Janine were still sleeping because they were always up real late, and I think my mom was out shopping, so it was really just me and this fat guy, who I didn't really know that well, he'd only been around a few times.

"And he was sitting in the kitchen, at this kitchen table we had, and I just walked by, I was still in my pajamas, like on my way to get some milk from the refrigerator for my corn flakes, and out of the blue, he didn't say anything, just like that, *Bam!*, real suddenly, this arm came out and grabbed me. And the next thing I knew I was on his lap and I didn't realize till then but he had his pants open, I hadn't noticed that, maybe because he was sitting at the table, but his pants were open and his, you know, his thing was out, and he had me on his lap and he was tearing at my pajamas and he had my pajama bottoms like in shreds where it was like I didn't have anything on at all, and I was—I knew what he was going to do, and I was terrified, and I screamed, and he put his hand over my mouth.

"And the kitchen table—the kitchen table was always a real mess, because there were always so many people in the house, and Dorothy and Janine never cleaned up anything, so there were always plates and pots and glasses and knives and forks and stuff all over the table. And there was this knife, about a foot long, with a serrated edge, for cutting bread but we used it for everything, meat, vegetables, wood, wires, anything, it was sort of the all-purpose knife. And it was on the table, with all the other mess, and I grabbed it and I just stuck him with it. I didn't even think. I just had the handle in my hand and I stuck it in his stomach, and it went in real easy, he was so fat, I didn't even feel it going in, it was like he was made of butter.

"I didn't even know that it had gone all the way in, because he just kind of jerked and slouched, but I thought that was just him going on trying to get his thing in me, because he'd been squirming and fighting even before I had the knife, and then I felt something really wet and sticky on my hand and I looked and everything was covered with blood. I don't think he'd even felt anything or seen anything, he was so busy trying to do what he wanted to do, but about the time I saw the blood he saw it too and his hand came off my mouth and he grabbed his belly and he screamed like I never heard anyone scream before, and then I screamed, and he let go of me and fell on the floor, and there was all this blood, I mean it was just gushing out, and then I heard the door, and my mom came in and she screamed, and the next I knew the ambulance was there and Dorothy had me in the bathroom cleaning the blood off me.

"And the guy died. They said he died on the operating table."

She stopped.

Gus wished she couldn't see his face. Shock and grief

and horror were all over it. Six years old, living in a brothel. Eight years old, attempted rape. Killed a man. As a judge, he'd heard a lot of horrifying stories, but this was his *daughter.*

She turned away.

"Samantha . . ."

Silent, perfectly still.

"Samantha . . ."

She tilted her head, just enough to get an eye on him.

"Samantha . . ."

She looked so fragile, an ash ready to crumble at the sound of his voice.

"Michelle and I love you, Samantha."

Her eyes filled with tears, and in a sudden lurch she fell against him and pressed her face into his shoulder.

Gus hugged her. It was almost three months since he had first seen the video of Samantha, and there were times when he still had trouble believing that she was really alive, that she had been given back. Years ago, as a prosecutor, he had often been reminded of how easy it was to deal with other people's crimes. He had tried to convince himself that the death of his own child hadn't really been a crime, but he knew deep in his heart that that was just a ploy, an ideological or political hoax. He also knew that he could be forgiven, but he was less sure about theological procedures for obtaining pardon than he was about the judicial procedures in the Middle District of Alabama. It was even more difficult to accept—as Michelle's family would have told him—that forgiveness could be his for free, that he need not, could not, do anything to earn or deserve it.

19

The phone call had come after lunch, an hour before the explosives dog alerted on the Mercedes.

Louisa said, "Mrs. Parham, it's for you. A Mrs. Young."

"Mrs. Young—I'll take it."

She was in the bedroom. She waited for Louisa to leave, then took a deep breath. "Hello."

"Is this Mrs. Parham?"

The voice was fresh and friendly.

"Yes, it is."

"This is Mrs. Young. Larry's wife?"

"Yes, of course." *How did she get this number?* "How are you?"

"I'm fine, thanks. I'm calling because I thought it might be a good idea if we met each other."

"I think that would be a wonderful idea."

"Can you meet me at the Four Seasons Hotel?"

"When?"

"Whenever you like. I'm free right now, if that's convenient."

"That's fine."

"I'm wearing a white suit, I have blonde hair, and I'll be near the reception desk. In about an hour?"

Cordial. Warm even.

"That's fine. See you then."

Michelle changed her clothes and wrote a quick note for Gus (*Gone to meet Doreen Young at the Four Seasons! See you later.*). She signed it with a happy face, left it on the dresser, and told Louisa, "I'm going out. I'll be back in a couple of hours."

Todd saw her leaving and asked if she wanted a ride. It was his way of finding out where she was going.

"No, thanks. I need the exercise. I'll catch a cab if I get tired."

"Mr. Rothman said—"

Mr. Rothman had said she shouldn't go anywhere alone, but Mr. Rothman said a lot of things. She was getting a little tired of Mr. Rothman. She'd been in this house since the beginning of the summer, and about every ten minutes someone was telling her what to do "just for the security."

She left the house, turned right at the corner, walked briskly to the shopping center at the end of the block, and waved down a taxi.

The lobby of the Four Seasons was blissfully cool. She saw Doreen immediately. White suit, blonde, late thirties, attractive, working at it, a little *too* attractive, in a way Michelle's mother would not have approved of.

Their eyes met, and Michelle immediately went on red alert. In high school, all the girls her brothers didn't have the nerve to bring home had eyes like that, filled with calculated charm, pouring out promises too bad to be true. This was the woman who had raised Samantha?

"Mrs. Parham?"

"Please call me Michelle. It's nice to meet you."

They shook hands. Doreen was so warm and radiant you could get a tan just standing next to her. She said, "Would you like a drink?"

"I'd love one. It's sweltering."

Walking across the lobby, Michelle realized her clothes were sweaty and her hair a mess. Doreen looked as if she'd never sweated in her life.

In the bar, Michelle ordered orange juice. Doreen said, "I'll have the same, please."

When they were settled, Michelle said, "There's so much I want to ask you."

"Me too. You can't imagine how much I miss Samantha. It's been almost four years since I saw her. I'm so happy you've brought her back."

Michelle wasn't exactly sure what that meant. She sensed peril, an awareness of a jungle beast showing up for the kill.

The orange juice arrived.

Michelle, feeling the need to speak, said, "She's a wonderful girl."

"When can I see her?"

The eyes hadn't changed, and the charm hadn't diminished, but inhabiting those words was a clear, deliberate threat.

Michelle said, “May I ask you something?”

“Of course.”

“How did you know where to call me?”

“I just—well, I don’t want to betray a confidence. I’m sure you understand.”

“I was just curious. I was told no one had the number.”

“I guess in Washington everyone has everyone’s number.”

“You can say that again.”

They laughed.

Doreen said, “You didn’t answer my question.”

“I beg your pardon?”

Michelle didn’t know how to deal with this. What should she say?

Doreen repeated the question. “When can I see Samantha?”

“I don’t know.”

She could practically smell the beast’s breath. She wished Gus were here.

“I really want to see her.”

“I can understand that.”

“So?”

“I just don’t know.”

“I’m the child’s mother. Speaking legally. And a few other ways, too.”

“I’m afraid I can’t answer your question, Doreen. I just don’t know.”

“I’m afraid someone’s going to have to answer it. I’m Samantha’s legal mother. I have a right to see her. I’ve come to Washington to see her, and—putting my cards on the table—I'm going to take her back to Milwaukee where she belongs, where she lived before her father kidnapped her."

From the top of her bleached hair down to her spike-heeled shoes, this woman was giving Michelle a lot not to like. The knife-blade tone of her voice, the phony-friendly eyes, the arrogant get-out-of-my-way attitude—Samantha had grown up with this, survived this. Right at that moment, over the orange juice, staring hard into those nasty, phony eyes, Michelle made a vow. Samantha would never, *never* go back to this woman.

"Well, I—"

"I know you want me to be frank." She paused for Michelle to agree, but Michelle was silent. "I saw an attorney before I came here and he told me that if you don't return Samantha to me immediately I can have you all charged with kidnapping. My husband kidnapped Samantha four years ago and now you and your husband and possibly others, as well as the government, are conspiring to assist that kidnapping and to deprive me and Samantha of each other's company. I'm sure no one wants to go to court over this, and *certainly* no one would want to see it all dragged out on television, so let me give you this"—she fished in her handbag for a small sheet of notepaper—"this is a phone number where you can reach me. Please let me hear from you by tomorrow morning. I'm sure we can work this all out."

Through none of this had her expression lost any of its warmth and cordiality. It was as if she threatened people every day and never failed to find the experience refreshing.

She went back into her purse for a ten-dollar bill, left it on the table, and stood.

"I hope you'll excuse me, but I have another appointment. It was wonderful meeting you."

Michelle got up, and took the hand that was offered to her. It was cold and damp.

Doreen said, "I look forward to seeing you again. Please give my love to Samantha and tell her I can't wait to have her back."

She left the bar, taking her smile with her.

Samantha sat up straight and wiped her tears with her sleeve. "Don't you want a drink? You look like maybe you need something to drink. It's really hot in here."

She turned to Gus in the half-light.

He said, "What happened next?"

"You still sure you want to hear?"

"Still sure. More than ever."

"Well, the police came, and they took me to this place for kids who do things, commit crimes. And I saw this judge, and after two days they put me in another home—like a regular house with a man and woman who look after kids who're in trouble. And then a lawyer my mom hired got me put back with her. And I saw a lot of lawyers and judges, and finally they let me stay with my mom, but I had to go to these juvenile probation people every day, and it seemed like I was always going places.

"The guy who died, it turned out no one really knew him, he didn't have a wife or family or anything. One of the girls just met him in some bar and invited him over. He was from Wyoming someplace, and it was really like, you know, nobody really cared that much, that he had died. I mean, the police and the district attorney cared, but I was only eight, and he'd been trying to rape me, and one of the cops even said I'd done everybody a favor.

"No one knew anything about how I was living in this whorehouse. None of that came out. No one suspected that. No one was going to say anything, right? It was just like here's this little eight-year-old and some guy no one really knows who's just invited over for a drink and he tries to rape her and she sticks him with a knife and he dies. I don't think anyone cared that much about him, except me. No one knew him, no one cared about him. I mean, he tried to rape me, but he's a human being, right? *Was* a human being until—I'm telling too much. I don't want to talk about it anymore."

He took her hand. "Samantha."

She said, "I told you it'd change everything."

"It hasn't."

Had she seen doctors? The court must have had her evaluated. What had happened? What was Michelle going to say?

"Nothing has changed, Samantha. I told you, nothing is going to change my feeling for you, or Michelle's."

He wanted to tell everything to Michelle, be alone with her and Samantha, let Samantha tell it all to Michelle.

He said, "Do you believe that?"

"That nothing has changed? I killed someone. I don't know how that can't change things."

She was right, of course.

"I'll tell you what it's changed, Samantha. It's made me . . . I just took for granted that you were . . . well, I guess I thought all thirteen-year-old girls were pretty much alike. I've never really known one before."

"I don't think many of them have killed people."

"Not many have had the experiences you've had. The important thing, Samantha, is to know, really believe, that Michelle and I love you. We are your parents. We've found you, and every day our love for you grows. And nothing that happened is going to change that. Do you understand?"

"Even if I killed someone else?"

"That's not going to happen, Samantha. But yes, even if you killed someone else."

"Well, I didn't."

She opened a little cabinet under the fax machine and took out a bottle opener, an unopened deck of cards, a lemon, a paring knife, and a shot glass.

"Are you sure you don't want a drink?"

"I'm sure, thank you."

She held up the cards. "Poker?"

"No, thanks."

"You want to hear the rest of the story?"

There's more? "Of course. I want to hear it all, Samantha. We should have had this conversation when we first got to Washington, and I'm sorry we didn't."

She put the things back in the cabinet and snapped it closed.

"My dad took me away. When all this happened with killing the man and the court and all that I guess he decided he'd better stop drinking so much. You know, start paying attention. And he and my mom had big arguments about what was happening in the house, all the girls and men. He wanted all that to stop. And my mom said it couldn't stop because he didn't make enough money to support the family. So he stopped drinking and got a job in a nightclub. But my mom still wouldn't get rid of the girls, and he wasn't strong enough to make her get rid of them.

"So one day he took me out and had my picture taken, and I didn't know why. And a few weeks later, one morning when my mom was out shopping, he gave me a suitcase and told me to put my clothes in it. I was really excited. Taking a trip! So we got a taxi to the airport and flew to New York and then got on another plane and went to London. He left a note behind for my mom, but I don't know what it said."

"How old were you?"

"I was still eight. He worked out some deal with this hotel chain—Intercontinental Hotels?"

"I've heard of them."

"So we were in London for a while, and I went to school there, but we were only there about four months. We were never anywhere more than about four months. They wanted new pianists all the time so the customers didn't get bored. And we went to Paris, and Milan, and then back to London."

"Sounds exciting."

"Yeah, and my dad, sometimes he'd let me come into the hotel where he was playing and listen to him. And that was the greatest, all these people around the piano and at the tables and the bar and they're all listening to him play, like *my* dad, and everyone's listening to him play. I loved it. But then he stopped letting me come to listen to him because I was getting older and I wasn't looking like a kid anymore. And once a customer asked me for a date, and boy, that was the end of *that*."

She stopped.

"Then what happened?"

"That's about it, until you showed up, or Carl did. My dad came back to the hotel and I heard him in the hallway, and I knew something was wrong, just from the sounds he made, his steps outside the door. I thought maybe my mom had found us and we had to run. He came in the room and sat on the bed and said there was this man who'd come to the club, and he showed me a card the man had written. It said something like, 'You really need to talk to me and it's okay because I'm a friend.' My dad showed it to me and he said, 'What do you think?' And I said, 'See him. Why not?' And two days later I met you and Michelle and the day after that, here I was."

Gus said, "That's a remarkable story."

He wanted to tell Michelle. What about Rothman?

"It's true."

"I know it's true. Samantha, I believe every word you've told me."

After a minute she said, "I'm glad I told you. At first I thought maybe I was making a big mistake. But now I'm glad."

"It wasn't a mistake, Samantha. The truth is never a mistake."

"Yeah. That's what my dad says."

They were silent.

Samantha said, "You know what else?"

"What?"

"I thought lots of kids lived like that. I mean, it never occurred to me that living in a whorehouse was that unusual. Then I killed the guy, and there were all the cops and judges and everything, and I realized that most kids don't live in places where this stuff happens, that not all fathers are drunks and not all mothers are madams and not all homes are whorehouses."

"And then?"

"I wanted to know how it would have been if I wasn't living how I was, who my real parents were, why they gave me away, why they didn't want me, why they didn't just get rid of me, was I lucky to be alive? All that stuff. I really wanted to know. Then I saw Michelle in the airport, and she looked just like me, and I knew, I couldn't believe it, I was so—I wasn't even happy. I was too shocked to be happy. In the ladies' room when I talked to her, *then* I was happy. Yeah, really happy, like now I'm gonna get some *answers*."

It was late now, near midnight, dark and silent. The car was sweltering. Gus didn't dare use the air conditioner more than a couple of minutes every few hours. He'd rolled up his shirtsleeves and now in the dark he unbuttoned his shirt to the waist. He couldn't stop thinking about what Samantha had told him. He wondered how it would affect Rothman's view of the nomination—and Michelle's.

He heard the cabinet snap open, snap closed, snap open—Samantha playing.

She had *really* lived in a brothel? What does it do to an eight-year-old to stick a knife in the belly of a rapist? How disturbed was Samantha, really? How disturbed was *he*?

The cabinet snapped again. Open, close, open, close. He wished she'd stop playing with it. A lemon, a lime, a bottle opener, gin, vodka, a knife.

He fell asleep.

20

Have you heard?"

Helen Bondell was in her office late Thursday afternoon, Warren Gier on the phone.

"Tell me, Warren. I'm busy."

"Gus Parham's about to be blown up by a bomb. You still busy?"

"What are you talking about?"

"They just interrupted CNN. There's a car bomb parked outside a State Department residence. It's where they've had the Parhams and their daughter holed up."

"Are they in the house?"

This wasn't happening. A bomb? Gus Parham? She

thought of the Oklahoma carnage, the World Trade Center. Madmen did these things.

"As far as I know. I'll find out more. I've got some good friends in that street."

"Tell me as soon as you know anything, Warren."

"Bet on it."

She called Harrington. Punching the numbers, her trembling fingers kept hitting the wrong buttons.

She said, "You hear about the bomb?"

"I'm afraid so."

He sounded scared.

"Any ideas?"

"None whatsoever."

"Dinner?"

"I already have an appointment."

She put the phone down. A man that worried about what he says on the phone is a man who knows things.

She walked across her office to the TV and switched on CNN. If she hadn't heard back from Gier by the end of the day, she'd track him down. By then he'd know everything there was to know.

She was sick and frightened. So, she imagined, was Harrington. But Warren had sounded thrilled, a pit bull off the chain.

She returned from the TV to her desk, hands sweating, Vicaro's name echoing in her brain.

Michelle sat in the Four Seasons lounge, finishing her orange juice and thinking. She'd had a letter that morning from her mother and father in Montgomery. They'd been reading newspaper stories about the nomination, all the lies the so-called Freedom Federation had been spreading about Gus.

And now comes this Doreen butter-wouldn't-melt-in-her-mouth Young. The only good thing—something unbelievably wonderful—to come out of the whole nasty nomination was Samantha. If they'd stayed in Montgomery, they would never have known her. Gus would not even have known she existed. Getting rid of that lie—it was like the breaking of chains—was worth the pain of this whole evil mess.

Did she want to go back to Montgomery? She squeezed the orange juice glass so hard it almost broke in her hand. The thought of giving in, surrendering, running back home, made her angry. It would all be over soon. Gus would be confirmed, the lies would stop, the people who were tormenting them would go away and torment others, and she and Gus and Samantha would have a normal life.

She left the hotel and despite the heat decided to walk. After a half hour she tired and hailed a taxi. When she gave the driver her address, he glanced at her in the rear-view mirror.

"You didn't hear?"

"Hear what?"

"They've got a bomb threat in that street. You won't be able to get near it. They've got the whole area sealed off."

Two blocks from her street several hundred spectators had gathered around police cars barricading the intersection.

Michelle's stomach tightened. She knew something was wrong at Blossom.

She paid the taxi and got out. She saw photographers and hid her face. If they recognized her and started asking questions about the nomination—about Samantha!—she'd come apart.

She pushed through the mob, found a cop, and asked what had happened.

"Bomb scare. You'll have to move, ma'am. You can't stand here."

If she told him she lived there, he might recognize her and tell reporters.

She joined the line at a public telephone in the drugstore at the shopping center. She dialed Blossom. No answer. If even the security people had left, it must be serious.

Where were Gus and Samantha?

She searched in her bag and found Rothman's phone number.

"Rothman residence."

"This is Mrs. Parham. May I speak with him please?"

"I'm sorry, I can't hear you."

She didn't want to raise her voice.

"May I speak with Mr. Rothman, please?"

"May I ask who's calling?"

"It's Mrs. Parham."

"Oh, Mrs. Parham, I didn't understand before. I can hardly hear you. I'm sorry. No, I'm afraid he's not here right now. I think he's over at Blossom."

"How can I reach him?"

"I don't know. Have you tried calling Blossom?"

"Yes, but thanks anyway."

She hung up.

Carl was in the command truck late Thursday night, on the phone with a State Department engineer who'd helped fortify Blossom, when he saw two new people, a man and a woman dressed in orange coveralls, step through the narrow door. They were with Rolf Zaeder, the fat, jolly ATF agent who'd shown him the antenna under the Mercedes.

"Can I call you back? Ten minutes. Thanks."

Zaeder said, "Hi, these are the folks I told you about. Just flew in from Dallas."

"Oh?"

"EOD. Explosive Ordnance Division."

"Oh, right, sure." The people who weren't too tightly wrapped.

They exchanged names, shook hands. One of them, a curly-haired young woman not much more than four feet tall, gave his hand a hard shake but didn't speak. She looked about as tightly wrapped as they get.

Carl said, "So what's up?"

The man said, "We need to identify the explosive, and see how much there is. Then we can think about ways to deal with it."

The woman, whose name was Terry, smiled. It was pushing midnight, but she seemed fresh and rested.

"Like what ways?"

The man said, "Hard to say right now. If we can put a probe in, we can go from there."

Carl said, "There may be people in the Colombian Trade Commission, very near where the vehicle's parked. We don't want to worry them."

"Take one person five minutes. Put out those floodlights, give us five minutes' darkness, nobody'll be the wiser."

FBI technicians had erected elevated lights illuminating the approaches to Blossom.

"Okay," Carl said, "you've got it. But take it easy." He smiled. "No loud noises."

"Never missed yet."

The woman, still smiling, small and shy, hadn't spoken.

* * *

Michelle left the drugstore and, keeping her face down, walked back through the growing crowd to the police barricade. Up the block she could see the flashing red lights of emergency vehicles.

How was Gus? How was Samantha?

She thought again of telling a cop who she was. She glanced around. Photographers, reporters. Two TV vans with satellite dishes. She saw a TV man, sweating in a suit, holding a microphone. The memory of the airport reporters, the thought of that microphone suddenly thrust into her face and the questions that might be asked ("Where is your daughter?" "Why did you decide not to have the abortion?") put to death any thought of telling anyone who she was.

But what could she do?

She thought, Eventually I'll see someone I know. They'll be looking for me. They'll come out. I'll see them.

So she spent Thursday night standing in the street, mixing with the crowd. Who were these people—up all night, abandoning TV sets to linger barely within the fringes of live action? What did they hope to see?

Every few minutes a car drove out through the police line and disappeared up the street. Sometimes men on foot came out. Others entered, showing credentials to the cops. Past the police barricades she could see the dim glow of floodlights illuminating the danger area.

She sat on a curb a few yards from a trio of other spectators and told herself that by midnight if she hadn't seen anyone she knew she'd approach a cop and say whatever she had to say to get past him to the house.

When midnight came, she picked out a nice-looking young cop and, hoping he wouldn't recognize her face from all the news photos, walked up and said, "Excuse me?"

He turned to her but didn't speak. Up close, she could see how tired he was.

She said, "I live in the second block up there. My family will be wondering where I am. Can't I please go in for just a minute? I promise I'll come right back out."

"I'm sorry, ma'am. There won't be anyone there anyway. The whole area's been evacuated. No one's in there now but emergency personnel, and they're not any further than right there." He pointed at flashing red lights fifty yards into the block. "Past those vehicles there, you won't find a cat."

"Well, where is everyone? Where did they go?"

"I don't know. Maybe you should call some relatives."

She thanked him and went back to the curb and sat down.

She knew that a lot of spectators had gone to the shopping area to get drinks and sandwiches at a store that was staying open for the night. But she was afraid if she left she'd miss seeing someone she knew. Sooner or later, someone would come looking for her.

Two yards of grass ran between the curb and the sidewalk. With her feet still in the gutter, she lay back, stared up at the stars, and thought about what Gus would want her to do. She fell asleep.

A sound next to her head brought her suddenly upright, dazed but awake.

"Mrs. Parham? Are you all right?"

It was Todd.

"Oh, Todd, where did you come from? What time is it?"

"It's five A.M. What are you doing here?"

"Well, where would I be, Todd? I live up there, remember? Didn't anyone think of that?"

"We didn't know where you were. We've been searching for you."

"I left a note. No one saw the note?" Why was she arguing with Todd? It wasn't his fault. "Where are my husband and daughter?"

"I think you should come with me."

"Where are they?"

"Carl can explain it better than I can."

"Are they all right? Are they hurt?"

"No, they're okay. Can you walk?"

"Of course I can walk."

He helped her up.

"I'm sorry, Todd. Excuse me. I'm not angry at you. I'm just tired. Where is everyone?"

"Come with me."

Todd led her past the barricades to a huge tractor-trailer truck with FBI written on the sides.

Carl was inside, sitting with a half-dozen other men and women at one of two counters running along the sides of the truck.

When he saw her, he shouted, "Michelle!" and slammed down a telephone. "Where the hell—let's go next door."

He took her hand, none too gently, and hurried her into a neighboring Winnebago camper ATF was using as an office and conference room. They sat in a small sitting room with chairs, a sofa, and a coffee table.

"Where've you been?"

"Where are Gus and Samantha?"

Carl told her everything he knew—the Mercedes station wagon, the explosives dogs, the opinions of all the experts.

"So that's where they are now. In the limousine."

Michelle said, "But they're safe?"

"Safe as anyone can make them. If the Mercedes has the maximum explosives it could possibly have, and if those explosives are the most powerful they could be, and if it goes off with the maximum effect, Gus and Samantha will experience a very rocky ride inside the limousine, and they may suffer cuts and bruises, but they'll be okay. That's why they're still there. It's safer than running the risk of trying to bring them out."

During the night, Gus allowed Samantha out of the car once to go to the bathroom in the garage. He turned on the ignition to activate the electrical system, and lowered the windows. He left them down for one minute, then closed them and turned off the ignition. It failed to make anything cooler, and the odor of urine and feces in the garage was worse than the odor of sweat in the car. He decided not to lower the windows again.

When Gus awoke Friday morning, the phone was buzzing.

"Gus, it's Carl. How was your night?"

Gus looked at his watch. Five-thirty. A few rays of light penetrated the garage windows. Samantha was curled into a corner of the seat, still asleep.

"The night was hot, is how the night was. Carl, where is—"

"Before you say anything, you might like to know that CNN is broadcasting pieces of our telephone conversations, even—"

"They broke the scrambling?"

"Not yet. They're broadcasting the scrambled signals, just to show what they sound like. But NSA says the networks have approached foreign intelligence sources, offering high prices for decryption devices, and may have them at any time. When the people behind this operation will have a device—or if they have one now—is less clear. To answer the question you were about to ask, there's nothing to worry about."

"What does that mean, exactly?"

"What was lost has been found. No damage, no problems. Don't worry. We've also heard from someone else. You remember L.Y.?"

Larry Young.

"Of course. What's happened?"

"He's back in London, called Carl, said he'd heard something on a radio station, not much. I guess the foreign media isn't that interested in our courts, but he wants to know is it true there's a threat, what's going on, is Samantha safe."

"What'd you tell him?"

"I didn't want to alarm him. I told him she's fine, don't worry about a thing, I'll keep him advised. He seemed relieved."

Even if Larry knew everything, how could he help? Gus wanted to tell Rothman about Samantha.

"Concerning what you just said about this phone, what if I had something critical to say?"

"How critical?"

My daughter's a killer. Is that critical enough?

"Immediately, not very. But overall, extremely."

"Don't say any more. Let me talk to the technicians."

Carl hung up, and Gus put the phone back between the armrests.

Half an hour later, when Samantha awoke, they each had a swallow from a half-bottle of Evian mineral water they'd found in the bar. Five minutes later they were thirsty again. He should have saved all the water for Samantha, taken whiskey for himself. He wondered how much alcohol he could handle in this heat. He didn't want to face a choice of drunkenness or dehydration.

Perspiration poured from him. He had tremendous admiration for Samantha's courage. She appeared to have made a vow not to complain.

He said, "How are you?"

"Okay."

"Thirsty?"

"Just a little. It's okay."

She had the cards out, laying them down on the seat between them for a game of solitaire.

The phone buzzed.

"Gus, it's Phil."

Rothman. "Give us some good news."

"I'm afraid I can't, Gus. In fact . . ."

Rothman's voice broke.

"What is it, Phil? Is Michelle all right? What's happened?"

"I'm sorry, Gus. It's your father. I'm sorry."

What Rothman had to say was obviously worth the risk of someone unscrambling the conversation.

"The maid found him in his bedroom this morning. He's dead. I'm sorry, Gus."

Samantha's eyes were on him. She knew it was bad news.

"How did it happen?" He tried to hide his shock. He didn't want to upset Samantha. He'd been with his father yesterday morning, listening to an incredible tale of disastrous judgment and attempted blackmail. He should have guessed, he should have done something.

"We just received a copy of a two-sentence note the police found with the body. You want me to read it to you?"

"Please." The limo seemed even hotter now. The poor man. What a life—all that money and nothing else, just lies and misery.

"Here it is. 'Please forgive me for the trouble I am causing. I saw Gus this morning and he will be able to explain.' "

"Who's it addressed to?"

"No one. It was handwritten on a piece of notepaper lying on the bed next to the body."

"How did he do it?"

"The coroner thinks pills. There were four empty prescription containers in the bathroom sink. Barbiturates. They'll do an autopsy."

There was a long silence while Rothman waited for Gus to say something. Finally, Rothman asked, "What do you think happened?"

"I know what happened." Gus held the phone, not speaking, then he said, "Give me a minute, Phil. I'm going to put the phone down, but don't hang up."

Gus lowered the instrument to his lap and put his head back and closed his eyes.

Samantha didn't say a word. She had picked up the cards, held them in her hand. After a couple of minutes Gus said, "It's about my father, Samantha. He killed himself last night."

He heard her breathe, a tiny gasp, a little girl's shock, disbelief dissolving into sadness. She knew about sudden death, and she was wise enough to say nothing. He felt her hand touch his forearm. Her grip made him want to cry. He opened his eyes and put the phone to his lips.

"You'd better prepare yourself, Phil. This is going to be a big one."

"Can you tell me what happened?"

"Are you worried about decryption?"

"Screw decryption. We'll risk it."

"You want it all now? It'll take a few minutes."

"Let's do it now."

"Two days ago my father called and said he had to see me immediately. Wouldn't tell me what it was about, but he had to see me. So yesterday morning I flew up to Connecticut, and we had coffee in his study. He said he had something to tell me that was shameful and humiliating and that he hoped I might somehow be able to forgive him for."

Gus glanced at Samantha. She had released his arm, and her eyes were filled with fear and curiosity.

"He told me that when he was serving on the board of directors of a tobacco company nineteen years ago—I don't know how much you know about my father, Phil."

"Not much."

"He's an attorney, *was* an attorney, worked eleven years for an investment bank on Wall Street, had lots of friends in that world and lots of money. He was always terrified of losing his money, of somehow not having enough money. He called it security. He never had a minute's peace in his life, Phil. He never talked about anything but money, business, and security. I couldn't've cared less. I should have tried harder to understand. He was on a lot of boards over the years and I wasn't surprised when he told me that one of them had been this tobacco company, Briggs & Paulman.

"He said nineteen years ago, when he was associated with Briggs & Paulman, a Colombian businessman he knew came to him with an idea. The guy was talking about all the bad press the tobacco industry was getting over what he called the cancer business, and that none of it had really been proved, and it was basically a lot of lies. So they talked about that, and then the guy said something like, 'Yeah, just like all the lies people tell about marijuana and cocaine,' how natives in the Andes have been using coke for centuries and it's just a cultural thing, never did any of them any harm. And it turns out this guy is an expert because he's in the timber business and his forests are in Peru, Bolivia, and Colombia and he knows all about the coca trade.

"My father told me that back then he didn't know much about the subject at all, didn't care much either, and then the guy started talking about how much money there was in the marijuana and coke business and someday when it's not illegal anymore how someone's going to make a killing. The guy tells him that when those drugs are legal and you don't have to pay millions in bribes and commissions, all that money will be profit. The guy said it would be a hundred times what tobacco produces.

"I was sitting there in my father's study, drinking coffee with him, and I couldn't believe what I was hearing. My father told me he started asking questions and the guy answered them and they decided to meet again. They met three or four more times and finally some lawyers brokered an agreement between my father, Briggs & Paulman, and this guy's forestry company. I asked my father, 'What kind of agreement,' and he squirmed and looked into his cup and the next time he looked up, where I could see his eyes, he was crying.

"I'd never seen my father cry before. It embarrassed the hell out of me. He said they signed an agreement that if someday marijuana or cocaine was no longer illegal, Briggs

& Paulman and my father and this timber guy would become partners in the growing, production, marketing, and distribution of the legal drug. He said he knew that today it sounded crazy that anyone would sign an agreement like that, but that back then cocaine wasn't the big thing it is now, and no one knew much about it, and he thought tobacco and alcohol were a lot worse and nobody cared about them, so he didn't think that much about it.

"I asked him who this guy was, and he said his name was Roberto Vicaro-Garza. Roberto is the father of Ernesto, and the forestry company is now a wholly owned subsidiary of TransInter. My father had been talking to the biggest coke dealer in the world—I mean Roberto Vicaro *was* in the forestry business, but he was in lots of other businesses besides, including drugs—and I guess my father must have known who he was. But it was money, it was business, and they were talking about if and when it ever became legal. And I met this guy, Phil. I took a trip to Colombia with my father the summer before law school, and I actually *met* the guy.

"So what happened, three days ago John Harrington came to see my father. He told him he knew about the agreement—Ernesto Vicaro was a client of his and had a copy of it. It was clear that if marijuana or cocaine were decriminalized, Briggs & Paulman and my father would be in a position to make a fortune. Harrington said he was concerned that people would think the reason I wanted to be on the Supreme Court was so I could speed the repeal of anti-drug laws and make a lot of money from the legalization. Harrington said the best way to avoid that scandal, of course, would be for me to withdraw, and if I did that Harrington could assure my father that the existence of that agreement would remain secret.

"So my father wanted me to withdraw. He begged me. He was in tears."

Gus stopped talking, and Rothman had the good sense not to interrupt the silence. Samantha was staring at the seat back.

In a minute Gus said, "There was no way I could tell my father what he wanted to hear. He kept saying, 'But the family, the family, think of the scandal.' He said, 'They'll call me a dope dealer. The newspapers will say I'm a drug trafficker. There'll be investigations, the police will get into it, I might be indicted.'

"I tried to convince him that he hadn't done anything even remotely criminal, but he wouldn't listen. 'Think of the family, think of the scandal.' I'd never seen him like that. He was sobbing, really, just coming apart.

"Then I guess it got through to him that I was not going to let this make me withdraw, and he stopped crying and said he understood, of course I couldn't withdraw, he was sorry to make such a scene, please forgive him, forget the whole thing, he hoped I wouldn't find it necessary to talk about the conversation with anyone else. I really thought he'd come to his senses and everything was more or less all right. I was going to talk to you and Dutweiler about it, what he'd said, Harrington's threat. Then I ended up in this limo and I never had the chance."

Gus felt he'd said enough—too much maybe.

Rothman said, "A call from Harrington came in a few minutes before the cops telephoned about your father. I haven't returned it yet. What do you think I should tell him?"

Gus took a couple of deep breaths.

"Phil, I do not want to withdraw, and neither will Michelle. The nastier they get, the more I want to stay. And frankly they can say whatever they want about my motives, that I want the job to legalize drugs and make money, or I want it to uphold abortion and murder babies, or I want it to repeal abortion and subjugate women, or anything else they want to say. Right now, Phil, the way I see it now, we're fighting a bunch of thugs, and I don't care if they're wearing three-piece suits or what schools they went to. They're thugs, Phil, and I will not submit to them. Period. Car bombs, blackmail, suicides—this is not the way this country needs to pick Supreme Court justices. If they get away with this, Phil, there'll be no end."

Gus stopped, inhaled deeply, and his lungs filled with the hot, foul air in the limo. Samantha was on the edge of her seat now, hands balled into fists. Why are children so ready for a fight?

Phil said, "When I've spoken to Harrington I should have a better picture of what the options are."

Gus hung up.

Almost immediately, the phone buzzed, and it was Michelle.

"Gus, how are you? How is Samantha? It's just—I'm so sorry, Gus. I don't know what to say."

He didn't want to talk about his father now. They'd have to wait until they were alone.

She said, "Is Samantha all right?"

"She's fine, taking everything better than I am, I think." Samantha was tugging on his arm. "She wants to talk to you. Here she is."

He handed the phone to Samantha. "Hi." Her voice was soft, almost shy, not matching the excitement on her face.

She listened to Michelle, then smiled widely. "He's okay. I'm trying to take care of him." More silence. "Yeah, it's really hot in here. But we'll be out soon. Don't worry about us. We're fine. We just miss you a lot. Okay. Right. Me too. Here he is."

She handed the phone back.

"Gus?" Carl's voice.

"We've gotta cut this short, Gus. The technicians are on us to save power on your phone. We'll call later."

They hung up, and in two hours Rothman called back. He'd picked Harrington up in his car and they'd driven around Washington and talked. Harrington, looking tired, bags under his eyes, had offered to suppress the agreement between Gus's father, the tobacco company, and Vicaro's father if Gus's name were withdrawn from the confirmation process. He said he had to have an answer by four that afternoon. Rothman said he'd see what reaction there was "from the others."

Gus said, "What are you going to tell him?"

The limo clock was at ten past one.

Rothman said, "What do you want me to tell him?"

"No go. No withdrawal."

"Are you sure, Gus? You don't have to do this, you know. You never signed up for car bombs."

"Phil, you know as well as I do that withdrawing would not change anything with this bomb. If we said I was withdrawing they'd just say, 'Oh, fine, we believe you, we'll disconnect the bomb right now.' And we come out, and they blow us up. They know the minute they let us out of here I'd un-withdraw myself. They want me dead, Phil, withdrawal or no withdrawal. Bargain with these guys, get an agreement, walk us out of here, and we're dead, Phil. These are *Colombians.* Ask Carl. He'll tell you."

"I understand what you're saying, Gus."

"Let me know what the President says, Phil. Let me know what happens with Harrington."

They hung up, and Samantha said, "Game of cards?"

"No, thanks, Samantha. I've got a lot on my mind."

"It'll help. My dad taught me. Whenever we had problems, we got out the cards. Play and talk."

"What do you want to play?"

"Five-card stud."

She took a sheet of notepaper from a side pocket in the door and tore it into pieces.

"These are postage stamps. I always play for stamps."

She dealt.

Carl left Michelle in the FBI command truck and walked outside.

Max Iverson, who'd asked to talk to him, was waiting. Carl said, "Take a walk?"

They strolled past a barrier and continued about thirty feet up the deserted, tree-lined sidewalk toward Blossom and the Mercedes.

When they were well out of earshot of other agents and police, Iverson said, "Interesting development."

"Tell me."

"Some of our tech people were over the Trade Commission in a chopper last night with infrared thermal imagers. They can see bodies inside the building. It's occupied."

"Can they tell how many?"

"They say two. There was warm body radiation concentrated at the front of the building, a sitting room."

"How do they know it's a sitting room?"

"Architects' drawings from the city records office. Inside the back door, there's a stairway to the second floor. At the top of the stairs, there's a corridor to a sitting room at the front of the building. That's where the tech people say the personnel are gathered."

"Keep going."

"We're developing a contingency plan for an intrusion. Just in case."

Carl led Iverson a couple of steps farther up the block away from the command truck. "What's State think about that?"

The State Department had sent over a deputy assistant to keep an eye on the enforcement people. State had already let it be known that if anyone was even thinking of requesting permission to enter the Colombian Trade Commission, they could save their breath. The Trade Commission was viewed as an extension of the Colombian embassy and therefore sovereign Colombian property, inviolable. Of course State *had* been known to change its mind. Changing your mind was what diplomats did for a living.

"I haven't yet seen a need to discuss it with them."

Carl said, "What's the plan?"

"First step, put someone inside, up the stairs, down the hall, insert voice sensors. We'll hear everything said in the front sitting room. Cover the rear door with a TV, tell us if anyone comes or goes."

"Put someone inside. Just like that."

"The spooks do it all the time. Stick a black box in the alarm line, read the current, duplicate it, feed it in, cut the line, the system can't tell the difference. In and out, no one's the wiser."

"Happy little band of burglars, you guys are."

"Not burglars. Burglars take things. We leave things behind."

"So you get in, leave your stuff. Then what?"

"We have the option of picking our moment, enter an intrusion team, take everyone out."

"Before they could set off the bomb?"

"The intrusion people say yes. They've got—they call them incentive inhibitors. Special ordnance. Grenades. Blast, light, sound. Flatten those guys, blind them, deafen them, scare them out of their minds, totally immobilize their will. It's thirty seconds before they even begin to think about thinking. No problem."

"No problem? Come on, Iverson. Nothing's that easy."

"These guys aren't amateurs, Carl. They went into a Delta Airbus in Italy, hit it through two doors, knocked out six terrorists, released a hundred and thirty-seven passengers and crew—elapsed time, six and a half minutes, casualties zero. The guys in that Trade Commission they could do before breakfast, not even get real awake."

"How long would they be out?"

"Recovery from the entry ordnance—blast, gas—about ten minutes. If they behave themselves."

"We need them cooperating."

"Oh, they'll cooperate. The entry operation leaves targets in a highly cooperative frame of mind. A whole personality change. Please and thank you all the way."

"I want to know about the device, Max. It's on a remote detonator, but there's a timer, too. I want to know when the timer's set for."

"If they know, they'll tell us."

Carl took a few more steps toward Blossom. He stood thinking, turned, and walked back.

"If we don't confront the occupants, just do a surreptitious entry, put in voice sensors and a TV camera, nice and quiet, what's the risk, total?"

"Virtually zero. Do it all the time. We've got specialists never do anything else."

"Okay. Camera and voice sensors. The rest, I'll think about it."

Carl left Iverson and went back to the command truck.

A young man in white shirtsleeves appeared in the doorway of the command truck. "The EOD guys are here."

Carl wheeled back the swivel chair and stood.

He said to Michelle, sitting next to him. "Come with me."

Two men and a woman waited for them in the sitting room of the ATF Winnebago camper. One of the men wore a suit, the other man and the woman were in bright orange hooded coveralls. Michelle's eyes were drawn immediately to the woman. She was young, early twenties, hardly more than four feet tall (her coveralls baggy, rolled up at the cuffs), with short curly brown hair and eyes that sparkled. A cheerleader, baton twirler. Baton twirling was a big thing in Alabama high schools. Was she from the South?

Carl said, "This is Mrs. Parham." He mentioned the men's names, but Michelle didn't get them. Her attention was fixed on this tiny, bright-eyed girl, called Terry.

Terry said, "Hi. Nice to meet you."

She was so perky she bounced on the balls of her feet. Definitely not the South. More like New York.

The man in the suit unfolded a side-view diagram of a Mercedes station wagon and smoothed it out on the coffee table.

He put a laptop computer next to the Mercedes diagram, opened the lid, and touched some keys. The screen showed a profile of the Mercedes, white lines on a blue background.

"We put in a probe and it came out with RDX, encountered ten inches below the vehicle's ceiling."

Carl thought, Well . . . and we're all still alive.

"We've made very close measurements of the height of the vehicle off the pavement. Working with our explosives people and Mercedes engineers, extrapolating the volume of the RDX from the distance between the Mercedes ceiling and the top of the RDX, computing from the weight of the RDX, and the capacity of the vehicle's shock absorbers, we get a very reliable estimate of 1,980 pounds of RDX. That gives a profile like this."

He pressed a key on the laptop. The white outline of the Mercedes profile filled quickly with yellow.

"The yellow shows the volume in the Mercedes of the RDX. You'll notice it's not completely full."

He ran a pencil point along a narrow area between the top of the yellow and the upper outline of the top of the Mercedes.

"There's a space."

Carl glanced at Terry.

"You like the look of that?"

Terry grinned. "Very much."

Carl said, "Forget it."

"Carl"—it was the man in coveralls—"this is our job. This is what we do. It's not the first time."

"You don't have to tell me again."

"People who use RDX in vehicle bombs are sophisticated. They know what they're doing. They use highly reliable detonators. No surprises."

Carl was silent, looking at the laptop.

Michelle said, "Excuse me?"

Eyes turned to Michelle.

"Can you tell me what this is all about?"

They looked at Carl, who took a step back from the laptop.

"They're from ATF's Explosive Ordnance Division. They deactivate explosive devices."

Michelle could not keep herself from flashing a look at Terry.

Carl said, "They want to try to deactivate the device in the Mercedes."

"How can they"—she looked at Terry—"how can they . . . are you . . ."

Terry looked at Carl. Carl said, "Go ahead."

Terry said to Michelle, "I can go in, locate the detonator, and deactivate it."

"What do you mean—go in? What if . . . I mean . . . I'm sorry."

The man in coveralls said, "We'll cut an opening in the roof. As you can see from the computer, there's not much room there, but there's a little, about ten inches between the RDX and the ceiling. That's about—"

Terry interrupted. "There's enough. I'm not very big."

Michelle didn't want to believe it. Gus and Samantha were a few yards from that explosives-packed station wagon. Not to mention Terry herself.

The man said, "It's not the first time we've done this,

Mrs. Parham. Mercedes people say the roof metal is one-point-seven millimeters thick. We use a circular saw we got from the Emergency Service cops in New York. No flame, no heat, no sparks. Two-foot hole takes thirty seconds. Lift it right out."

Terry said, "I squeeze inside, squirm back to the detonator, deactivate it, and come out. Then they hook up a truck to the Mercedes, tow it away someplace safe, and blow it up. End of problem."

Michelle shook her head. Then she said, "If this goes wrong . . . my husband and daughter . . . I'm sorry, Terry. This is very brave of you, and I appreciate the risk you're ready to take, but if something goes wrong . . ."

"It won't go wrong, Mrs. Parham."

Carl took a step to the diagram on the table. "You seem very confident."

Terry said, "We don't do this stuff unless we're confident."

Carl said, "And the more you get away with, the more confident you get."

"We're not reckless."

Michelle thought, Not reckless? Of *course* you're reckless. If squeezing yourself inside a vehicle filled with explosives isn't reckless, what in the world . . .

Michelle looked at Terry's hands. She was not wearing a wedding ring. She was not wearing any rings at all, or a watch or a bracelet. Maybe when you worked with bombs you didn't wear jewelry. She said, "Are you married?"

"No."

"Boyfriend?"

Terry grinned and looked at the man in the coveralls, who smiled. Both of them? What if they got married? Did they work together? What if one got blown up? What if they *both* got blown up? What if they had children and got blown up?

Carl said, "Any more questions?"

The man in coveralls said, "There's not that many alternatives."

Carl sighed and bent over the Mercedes diagram, staring at it.

In the silence, Michelle said, "Excuse me. Terry . . ."

"Yes?"

Michelle drew a breath and tried to keep her voice steady. "I just want to say to you that—" She stopped, waited. "I just want to say that—" She stopped again. She wasn't going to be able to do this. "I want to say, I know you're very concerned about the safety of my husband and daughter—that's why you're doing this—but I want to say . . ."

Terry put a hand on her arm. "It's okay, Mrs. Parham. Thank you. It's okay. I understand. They'll be all right."

Michelle nodded, left the Winnebago, and walked back to the command truck. She didn't want to be with all those people. They were so cool, so professional. And if they failed to save Gus and Samantha, they'd be cool and professional about that, too. They'd write their reports, study what went wrong, make procedural corrections for next time, and go on about their cool, professional lives. But she wanted Gus and Samantha *back*. It wasn't her *job* to want them back.

When Carl returned, Michelle said, "Are you going to let her do that?"

"Do what?"

"Go into the *Mercedes*! What do you think, what?"

Carl looked at her, his eyes searching. After a moment, so softly she could hardly hear, he said, "Yes, I think so."

"Dear God. Dear, dear God. What are you doing?"

"I'm trying to save Gus and Samantha."

"I meant what is *God* doing."

"He knows what he's doing, Michelle. Try not to think about it."

"Can't we have something else to drink?"

Samantha hung her tongue out of the side of her mouth, like a dog dying of thirst. It was Friday afternoon, outside the sun was high in a cloudless sky, and they were both sweat-soaked and stinking. The air was still and heavy.

Gus said, "Just a swallow."

She screwed the top off the Evian bottle, raised it to her lips, and he watched her throat tighten and relax. One swallow. She refastened the top. No argument, no pleas for more.

"We'll be out of this soon, Samantha."

She licked her lips. "I know."

The phone buzzed.

"How's it going?"

"We're getting pretty thirsty in here, Phil. And hot. And hungry. And I don't think either Samantha or I have words to tell you about the smell. What's the temperature out there?"

"High eighties. Where you are, we estimate over a hundred. The medical people recommend you increase your fluid intake. We know you don't have much, but dehydration's becoming a concern out here. Anyway, we hope to have you out soon. I spoke with Harrington."

"And he said . . ."

"He's trying to swing a deal. We withdraw and he suppresses your father's agreement. I told him to forget it—even if we took his offer, we'd still have the car bomb to deal with. He can't do anything about that."

"You sure?"

"That's a joke, right?"

"I hope so. Where's it stand now?"

"I've got something else we all think you ought to know, but we don't want to alarm you."

"What is it, Phil? Let me have it."

"Gus? This is Carl."

"What's up, my friend?"

"We've got some expert, competent people out here who say they've got a good chance of deactivating the device."

"How?"

"They've calculated there's a space about a foot high between the top of the explosives and the roof of the Mercedes."

"Go ahead."

"They want to cut a hole in the top of the Mercedes and have someone go in and locate the detonator and disarm it."

"Are you kidding?"

"Definitely not. I know it sounds crazy, but they say they do this stuff a lot. There's a very high confidence level."

"What does Michelle think?"

"She's—frankly, Gus, she's a little emotional about it. I'm not sure she's in a position to make a reliable decision."

"She's against it."

"Yeah, I guess."

"Let me talk to her."

"Here she is."

"Gus, how are you?"

"Hot, thirsty, hungry, and tired. Other than that, Samantha and I have been having a wonderful time. How are you? You're probably a lot more disturbed by this than we are."

"I don't know about that, Gus."

She sounded shaken. Exhausted, really.

"What do you think about this scheme Carl just told me about?"

"It scares me to death."

"You're already scared. Does this make it worse?"

"It's a girl, Gus. A very young woman."

"Who's a woman?"

"The agent who's going to do it. I know that shouldn't make any difference. It's just that—I can't explain it."

"Do you think she knows what she's talking about? Do you think she can do it?"

"Yes. It's just—"

"Honey, if you think she can do it, and she thinks she can do it, and everyone else thinks she can do it, and it can get us out of here—maybe she should do it. I mean, we're already in a pretty hazardous spot. Is it going to make things any worse?"

"If it blows up it'll be worse."

"That could happen anytime anyway."

"Carl wants to talk to you. I love you."

Carl said, "What do you think?"

"Carl, is Michelle okay?"

"Under the circumstances, she's doing fine."

"She sounds pretty stressed."

"She's doing fine."

"What about this thing, Carl? Are you in favor of it?"

"I think it's the lowest risk. Every minute you and

Samantha are in there, there's a risk. You're sitting forty-five yards from 1,980 pounds of RDX, with nothing between you and it except a quarter-inch of armor plate on the limo and three inches of Kevlar on the front of the house. You've gotta get out of there, Gus. And the EOD people—"

"EOD?"

"Explosive Ordnance Division. They say they wouldn't do it, she wouldn't do it, if the risk weren't minimal. She's been in EOD four years, done eleven real, live deactivations."

"And she's still got all her body parts?"

"Very much so."

"Okay. I'm agreeable if everyone else is. Hang on a minute."

Gus lowered the phone. "Samantha, they've got someone out there, a young woman, who's an expert at deactivating explosive devices like the one in the Mercedes."

"Yeah?"

"They're going to cut a hole in the top of the Mercedes, let her go inside and deactivate the bomb. What do you think of that?"

"Will it work?"

"They think so. They say it's better than just sitting here and waiting."

"So go for it."

Why is everything so easy for children?

"With us, we agree. If you guys think it's a good idea, let's do it. When will it happen?"

Carl said, "Couple of hours. I'll keep you advised."

Gus hung up the phone and looked at Samantha. She was thinking it over. Watching her, the deep look in her eyes, the wheels turning, Gus thought, Oh, Samantha, what's going to become of you? Where will you be in ten years?

Michelle left the FBI command truck and walked out alone into the abandoned street, looking up the block in the direction of Blossom. Behind her she could hear the confusion of voices, cars coming and going, reporters, police, and crowds. Ahead was nothing but emptiness and silence. It was hard to believe that just a few hundred yards away Gus and Samantha were in a limousine across Blossom's front lawn from a bomb. Struggling against a sense of helplessness, and against tears that made her feel ashamed and intimidated in the presence of people like Carl and Terry, she walked back to the Winnebago, expecting to find it empty.

Terry was there, sitting quietly and alone at the coffee table, reading a copy of *Good Housekeeping* magazine.

Looking up, Terry said, "Oh, hi."

"I'm sorry to bother you."

"You're not bothering me." She put the magazine down. "Most of this job is waiting, like firemen."

"I'm doing a lot of that myself."

"Yeah, it must be hard."

She looked as if she meant it, wasn't just making conversation.

Michelle smiled and tried to look pleasant.

Terry rose to leave. "I know you want to be alone."

"I think maybe alone is the last thing I want to be, Terry. Please stay, unless you—"

"No, I'm just kind of hanging around."

Terry sat back down, and Michelle took the chair across from her. When Michelle had first walked in, Terry had seemed shy, deferential, but now, as she began to speak, it was as if a wind had blown through the room, and Michelle realized that the timidity had been something learned, a way to act.

Michelle said, "What you do, it's really—"

She stopped herself. She wasn't this girl's mother.

"Everyone says that. But it's not as dangerous as it looks."

"Not dangerous?"

"Flying airplanes is dangerous if you don't know what you're doing."

"Well, yes, but—"

"Mrs. Parham, you must have something that's just the most exciting thing you do, that makes you feel really alive?"

She looked barely twenty. Her face was a portrait of eagerness, excitement.

Michelle's first thought was, Yes I do, and it's being with Gus and Samantha. She was afraid if she said that, she'd cry. All these brave people. Looking for something safer to say, she asked, "Why does it make you feel alive?"

Terry said, "I never feel more alive than I do when I'm working."

She was so enthusiastic, so sincere. She talked in exclamation marks. *I never! Feel more alive! Than I do! When I'm working!*

"You're one of these people we see in the movies, taking bombs apart while everyone waits at a safe distance."

Terry laughed. "You sound like my mother. It must be hard to understand."

She stared at Michelle for a moment, and then, her smile gone, she said, "When I'm with a device, all alone, everything's silent, it's like the world has stopped, it's just me and the device, and I know it's been put there for something evil. And I'm going to stop it. That's a wonderful feeling. It's exciting. People complain their lives don't have meaning. They should do what I do. It gets real quiet—even when there's a lot of noise around, you don't hear anything. It's just me looking at that ugly thing. And they are *always* ugly. Some machines are beautiful to look at, but explosive devices are *always* ugly. You *know* you're with an enemy. And alone, just by yourself, you say, 'Oh, no you don't. You've had it, fella.' You study the ugly thing, and you disable it. But it's really the people who designed it and built it and put it there that you're beating. You have to match wits with them. It's like I'm a doctor, fighting a virus, trying to figure out how this virus works, how can I destroy it. It's wonderful. I feel like that's what I've been put on earth to do, and when I'm doing it, I'm alive. That sounds crazy, right?"

Michelle looked into those smiling, excited eyes and felt as if she'd entered another world. She didn't like it. She wanted her own world back, the one with Gus and Samantha.

Rothman called.

Gus said, "Phil, what's the latest with Harrington?"

"I haven't talked to him. I called his office, and he wasn't there. His secretary said she didn't know where he was. She thought he might be out of town."

"Out of *town.* What the hell does that mean? Where would he be, out of town?"

"I haven't a clue."

21

Where's Harrington?"

"Not here, Ernie. Too late for John. Never comes out after dark."

Carl had taken a two-hour flight to O'Hare, drove another half hour to the prison. He could see Vicaro, be back in the command truck by midnight.

Vicaro oozed around the edges of the visiting room chair, his prison shirt straining the buttons over his belly.

"He told me he'd be here."

"He lied." Carl smiled. "I brought Mr. Brodski instead."

"I don't wanna see Brodski."

Brodski, a squat, heavy man, black mustache but no

hair on top, was sitting right there in front of him. He said, "You're hurting my feelings, Ernie. Damn, it stinks in here. They take away your shower privileges?"

Brodski was warden of the federal maximum-security prison in Bradley, Montana, the toughest in the country, and Vicaro had almost died there. He blamed Brodski for the attacks against him.

Vicaro said, "I don't wanna talk to you."

"You really gave me a bad rap, you know, Ernie." Brodski aimed a finger at Vicaro's stomach and made a plunging, slicing motion. "I never had anything to do with what happened to you."

Vicaro had been virtually disemboweled by another prisoner during an afternoon exercise period. He had a reputation for betraying enemies to the government, and found prison an unhealthy environment.

Vicaro's jaw muscles tightened, and he fixed his eyes on Carl, struggling not to respond to Brodski's taunts. When Vicaro had emerged from the prison hospital with thirty-seven stitches in his belly, Brodski refused his request for administrative isolation and put him straight back into population. Two days later he was in the hospital again, with groin wounds inflicted by a screwdriver in the hands of an angry tier mate named Tulio Huega.

Carl said, "Now, what's all this we hear about an agreement between your father and some tobacco company and Judge Parham's father? You ought not to be telling lies like that, Ernie."

"It's not a lie, and you know it. I've got a signed document."

"A phony signed document. You made the whole thing up."

Vicaro's black eyes darted from Carl to Brodski and back. "What're you guys up to?"

"To tell the truth," Brodski said, "we're not really here to talk about the agreement or Judge Parham or any of that stuff. We're just here to let you know about the transfer."

"What transfer?"

"You're comin' back."

"Screw you, Brodski."

"Now don't you talk to me like that, Ernie. You know I wouldn't lie to you. This institution's too crowded, and the director decided to move some of the more difficult prisoners back to Bradley."

"You're just—"

"Frankly, I'm glad to get you. I've missed you. We've all missed you."

"You're—"

"A lot of your old friends, Ernie. 'Where's Ernie? What's become of Ernie? We miss him. We want him back.' We're all so glad to get you back, let me tell you what I'm gonna do. I'm movin' everyone outta Tier Three on D Block, and I'm gonna fill it with all your friends. Tulio Huega, remember him? Asked *especially* could he cell with you. Already moved in, got the place spruced up, waitin' for Ernie. What? You got somethin' you wanna say? Don't thank me, Ernie. I'm happy to do whatever I can, you know that—make people happy."

Vicaro tried to twist in his chair, turning his body toward Carl. "What's all this about?"

Carl said, "You heard the man."

"You're tellin' me if I don't take back that agreement you'll send me back to Bradley?"

"I didn't say that. You hear me say that?"

"I go back to Bradley, I'm dead. I almost got killed there last time. Twice."

"So don't go. Why go? Tell Mr. Brodski here you don't wanna go. Simple as that."

Vicaro looked at Carl and nodded, his tiny chin bone bobbing on top of the cascading layers of flesh.

Brodski said, "You heard the man. Simple as that."

Vicaro said, "You don't have the authority to do this. You can't just send me anywhere you want, send me someplace where I was taken out to keep from gettin' killed."

Carl said, "You're right, Ernie. We can't do that. The only one who can do that is the director of the Federal Bureau of Prisons."

"Right. The director of prisons. My lawyer told me that when I was brought here. There's a note on my record, in the computer, says do not move without the authority of the director of prisons."

"That right?" Carl said to Brodski. "His package have a note like that?"

"Seems to know what he's talkin' about. Knows more than I do."

"Ernie," Carl said, "how'd the director of prisons get his job?"

"I don't know. Same way all you bastards got your jobs."

"Now don't be unpleasant, Ernie. He got it from the President. The President appoints the director of the Federal Bureau of Prisons."

"That true?"

"Well-known fact."

Carl waited, staring at Vicaro. Vicaro didn't move.

"Ernie, who nominated Judge Parham to the Supreme Court?"

Vicaro's body started to slide forward out of the chair. He grabbed the armrests.

"You're tellin' me the President's gonna move me back to Bradley?"

"I didn't tell you that. Stop jumping to conclusions. We're just talking politics here. Friendly conversation."

"If I don't back off and forget about the agreement, the President's gonna tell the director to send me back to Bradley? You're tellin' me that?"

"Not telling you anything, Ernie. Talking politics. Friendly conversation. Just stopped around to say hello."

No one spoke. Vicaro tried to twist in the chair. He sighed, exhaling droplets of saliva.

Brodski said, "You're a smart man, Ernie."

A bead of sweat ran down Vicaro's left cheek, dropped into a fold of neck flesh, and disappeared. He said, "I'm gonna tell Harrington, forget the whole thing, I made a mistake? He'd never believe that."

Carl said, "Oh, I think he might. You could persuade him. You're a major client, big bucks, he's done a lot for you, right, Ernie? Some of it maybe a little—" Carl cocked his head and made a back-and-forth tilting gesture with his flattened hand.

"Anyway," Carl said, "he doesn't come around, you need a little help, I'll be happy see what I can do."

The confirmation fight was getting nasty, and if it got any nastier, Harrington would be happy to disengage, get the hell out. No one wants to be on the receiving end of a car-bomb investigation.

Vicaro said, "He's already seen the agreement."

"Agreements get forged. Just tell him you made it, had some friends forge it 'cause you don't like the judge. Everyone already knows you don't like the judge. No surprise there."

"What if Harrington uses it before I see him?"

"I don't think that'll happen. He's got an appointment with you for"—Carl looked at his watch—"thirty minutes from now. Probably waiting outside already."

"Waiting outside, my ass. You said yourself he don't work this late."

"For you, Ernie, a top client, he'd come out anytime."

"I don't have an appointment with Harrington."

"Yeah, you do. It's in the book. Saw it myself."

"Made it yourself, too. You're really a cocky kind of bastard, aren't you?"

"Not really, Ernie. I just have confidence in your intelligence. You see what has to be done, you do it. You're not one of these guys has to be shown something over and over. You get it right the first time. You understand how the world works. Am I right?"

Vicaro sat there, breathing hard.

Carl said, "Mr. Brodski and I'll just hang around for a while, see how it all comes out. Anyone needs to say anything to John, we'll be here."

Vicaro was silent.

"So we have an understanding?" Carl stood and signaled through the window for the guard. "Don't disappoint us, Ernie."

Standing, Brodski said, "How's the belly? Give you any trouble?"

"Screw you."

* * *

Outside it was getting dark, diminishing even the few rays of light that made it through the garage windows and the limousine's tinted glass. Gus allowed Samantha and himself a thirst-quencher. He had an ounce of gin and Samantha had a Coke. Samantha said he should have tonic water with the gin.

"No, thanks. I'll have it straight."

"I could make it for you. I know how."

"You can still make it for me. Just leave out the tonic."

She took the shot glass out of the cabinet, filled it with gin, emptied it into a glass. "Lemon?"

"Thanks."

She found a lemon and the knife, cut off a slice, squeezed it into the glass, dropped in the peel, set the glass in the center of her hand, like a tray, and handed it to him.

"Thank you very much."

"You're welcome."

"You do that very well, Samantha."

"It's been a long time since I've mixed drinks, but I never forgot."

What other memories of Doreen's brothel would she never forget?

Gus searched through the cabinet. The hunger was almost as bad as the thirst and the heat. "Nuts and crackers."

Samantha said, "Go for it."

"They're salted, make us even more thirsty."

"I couldn't be more thirsty."

"Let's wait. Can you wait?"

"If you can wait, I can wait."

"You're brave, Samantha."

She had a swallow of tonic water. "Just one swallow,"

she said, and kept to her word, pressing the metal cap back onto the little bottle.

They sat silently, sweating, dozing. They'd stopped asking each other when it would end. They talked about Larry, where he might be, what he would think of all this. They both tried to keep it light, struggling to encourage each other. Gus thought, She's young, she's only thirteen, she should be crying, moaning, demanding to leave. But she seemed almost to be enjoying it. An adventure.

They played poker. She divided out the "postage stamps," two little stacks of torn bits of paper on the leather seat.

She said, "You know, this isn't much fun if you don't try. Last time you folded with three kings. My dad let me win, but at least I had to struggle a little."

"I'm sorry. I'll try harder."

She dealt.

Gus said, "Did you and your dad play cards a lot?"

"Yeah, mostly at night when I couldn't sleep. I had trouble sleeping. We'd play and talk. It was neat."

She won again, and they decided to put the cards away and just sit and talk. After half an hour, Samantha said, "Gus?"

"Yes."

"You know all that business about living with my mother and the girls and I killed that guy?"

"Yes."

"That was pretty bad, right?"

"Not too good."

"But it wasn't my fault."

"I know that. You didn't have a choice."

"That's what I mean."

Silence, the loudest silence Gus had ever heard. He said, "So?"

"You said you'd always love me. No matter what?"

"That's right." He held his breath. Fatigued and defiant, challenging any intention to make their lives even more complicated, he said doggedly, "No matter what."

"It's just that I feel so—I mean, killing someone. That's really bad, and I want to be sure you understand. I don't want you to think your daughter's a murderer. Even the police and the judge, they said it was self-defense, that I had to do it."

He held her hand. "I know you did, Samantha. It wasn't your fault. Don't worry about it, okay?"

"Okay."

They were silent.

Then Samantha sighed and said, "I don't want to spend another night in this thing."

It was her first complaint since the outburst about a toilet.

"I don't either, Samantha. Maybe we won't have to."

She gave him a look. "You think so?" Full of a child's hope.

"Who knows? There're a lot of people out there trying to get us out."

"When do you think they'll go into the Mercedes?"

"I don't know. I'm sure it takes time to set something like that up. But it should be soon."

"Boy. Go *inside.* I sure wouldn't want—"

The phone buzzed. Gus picked it up. "Phil?"

"Is this Judge Parham?"

An unfamiliar voice. A man. Young.

Resisting an impulse to hang up, Gus said, "Who is this, please?"

"Is this Judge Parham?"

"Who's calling?"

"This is Roy Jenkins of the Associated Press. Is this Judge Parham?"

"How'd you get this number?"

Coming in from a conventional instrument, the call would not be scrambled.

"Excuse me, but could I know if this is Judge Parham?"

"Yes, this is Judge Parham. I can't—"

"Judge Parham, we've just had a report concerning your daughter, Samantha, and I would like your reaction, whether you can confirm it?"

"What's the report?"

He knew he shouldn't be talking to this guy, but—well, a day and a half locked in a limousine does things to you. And the reporter was smart enough to play on his curiosity.

"We've been told that when she was about seven or eight she was living in a brothel in Milwaukee."

Gus felt his hand tremble. The Associated Press. Every word he spoke would be on the lips of every TV and radio news broadcaster within minutes after this conversation ended. And the words would stay with Samantha for the rest of her life.

"I'm sorry. I have no comment. I'm going to hang up now."

"Judge Parham. There was more. We—"

Gus hesitated. He had to hear it.

"We were told that there had been statements by her adoptive mother that she was actually a participant in the functioning of the brothel. That she in a sense worked there. Can you confirm any of this? Do you—"

"Who told you that?"

"Do you know what she actually did there, if she—"

Gus hung up.

Samantha said, "What's wrong? Who was it? You look really mad."

Gus tried to get the rage off his face, out of his voice. Calm down. Think. Once in court a female murder defendant had come at him with a knife, leaving him mentally paralyzed for half a minute while bailiffs wrestled her to the floor. This was worse.

"It's okay, Samantha. It's okay."

"Who was it? What did he say?"

He had to tell her.

"It was a reporter. He said he'd heard about how you used to live . . ."

"With the prostitutes?"

"Yes."

"Is that all?"

"Well, it's . . ."

"That's okay. I don't care. It doesn't make any difference to me."

"I just didn't like hearing it."

She said, "Forget it."

She put a hand on his knee, gave him a consoling little pat. "Have another gin. I'll make it for you."

He called Rothman.

"Would you be surprised to hear that I just had a call from a reporter for the Associated Press?"

A pause. "Not really. Some people have ways of getting

phone numbers. It had to happen eventually. What'd he say?"

"He said they had a report that Samantha was raised in a brothel."

"A brothel! What made—"

"It's true, Phil. It's a long story, but it's true."

"What did you tell him?"

"Nothing, of course."

"It's probably on the news already. I'd better get it to the boss. I'll call back."

Gus hung up, and Samantha said, "Is he mad?"

"I don't guess he's too happy. But he's calm. That's his job. Stay calm."

He smiled at her.

She nodded her head. "Good thinking. Stay calm. Keep cool."

Rothman called back.

"It's everywhere, Gus. You can't turn on a radio or TV without hearing about how Samantha lived in a brothel when she was eight. You wanna change places? It may be hot and smelly where you are, but it's plenty hot and smelly out here, too."

"What'd the President say?"

"Enraged doesn't begin to cover it. He wouldn't withdraw you now if they had nuclear missiles."

They hung up, and after twenty minutes the phone rang again.

"It's Lyle Dutweiler, Gus. I have someone with me who wants to talk to you."

In a second Gus heard the voice of the President.

"Gus? It's Dave. How are you?"

"Fine, Dave. How's it going?"

"I wanted to tell you personally, Gus, that I appreciate what you and Samantha are going through. I admire your courage, and I want to say something."

Gus waited. Silence. Then he said, "Yes?"

"We are going to win this, Gus. I want you both to know, you and Samantha, sitting in that limousine, that the country is going to have you on the Supreme Court. We are going to find out who put that Mercedes where it is, who's behind this, and we're going to get it out of there, whatever it takes. Period. That's it."

"I appreciate that, Dave. I'll pass it on to Samantha."

"May I talk to her?"

"Of course. Here she is."

Gus handed the phone to Samantha. Taking it, she asked him, "Who is it?"

"The President."

"The President! Are you sure?"

"I'm sure. Say hello. Talk to him."

"Hello?"

She listened.

"Yes. Yes, sir. Thank you. Me too. Yes, sir. I will. Thank you. Goodbye."

She hung up.

Gus said, "What'd he say?"

"Wow! I spoke to the *President.* I actually spoke to the President of the United States."

"What did he say?"

"I can't remember."

"You can't remember?"

"I was so excited I forgot to listen." Then she looked at him. "Yeah. He told me to keep my chin up."

* * *

Two hours later, Eric Taeger, watching CNN alone in his darkened office at the car center, was interrupted by a White House messenger delivering a package. Taeger tore the package open and found Phil Rothman's card clipped to a hot-off-the-press copy of the early edition of the *Washington Post.* A front-page story, quoting an anonymous source at the White House, carried a three-column headline:

DAVE TO SAM: 'CHIN UP!'

Taeger read it, grunted, and dumped it in the wastebasket.

In the limousine, Rothman was back on the phone.

"I've got news."

Gus said, "I can't stand the suspense."

"There was never an agreement between your father and any tobacco company."

"What the hell does that mean?" His voice was raised, angry. "Forgive me, Phil. I'm a little on edge. What is it exactly you're trying to tell me."

"I just got back from another drive-around with Harrington. He looked like he'd been fighting with lions. He tried to bargain again, would we give them a time-out, cooling-off period, would we do this, do that, and when I kept saying no, no, no, all of a sudden he said, 'Well, what the hell, it was all a phony anyway.' I said, 'Phony, whaddya mean phony?' He said he'd just spoken with Vicaro, who told him the whole agreement story was a hoax. The document itself is a forgery. The whole thing never happened. Vicaro made it all up because he hates you. Nothing better to do in prison than think up schemes to hurt Gus Parham."

"That's a lie, Phil."

"Right. It's all a lie."

"I mean, it's a lie that the agreement never happened. My father told me about it the day before he died."

"You're the only one who says that, Gus. As far as Harrington and Vicaro and everyone else is concerned—including the President—the matter's over, ended, never happened. All a big mistake. Mistake's been corrected. Period."

Samantha was watching him with a troubled what's-he-saying look.

"I'll have to think about all this, Phil. Let me call you back in half an hour."

"What's to think about? It's over. We won."

"I'll call you back."

Gus put the phone down, and looked at Samantha. She gazed back, worried, but didn't speak.

"Samantha, I don't know what to do."

Go along with the lie? Say the agreement never happened? He was a judge. Get on the Supreme Court with a lie? The last time he could remember lying, he was in high school.

Gus sweated in the heat and the darkness, and he thought, I know it happened. I *know* it's true.

He sighed. The odor filling his nostrils made his eyes water.

So far the charges against him had been lies and distortions. But this was true. Would he deny it? He'd never been a politician, and the thought of becoming one now—a political judge, a political justice of the Supreme Court—angered him. He'd known a corrupt state court judge once. Did a small favor for a friend, not much more than a handshake, and five years later he was the biggest whore in Alabama.

But what could Gus do? His father had placed the family in a position of potential enrichment if marijuana or cocaine was decriminalized. So if he was on the Supreme Court, and the time came—*Hacker v. Colorado*, limited legalization of cannabis, the thin edge of the wedge—would he vote against it and look honorable? Or vote for it and maybe get rich? Whatever he did, would anyone who'd heard about the agreement—Harrington, Vicaro, Chapman, Samantha, Michelle—believe he'd ruled impartially? Would even *he* believe it? Could he trust his heart?

Would he go along with Rothman? Easy to do that. Rothman's an attorney, White House chief counsel. He knows best. Don't be one of those moralistic prigs who ruin everything just to prove how principled they are.

Gus looked at Samantha. Her face was set in an expression of resolute silence. A thirteen-year-old who knows when to keep her mouth shut. Imagine that.

"Are you reading my mind, Samantha?"

She shook her head.

What was Rothman wanting him to do, expecting him to do, *certain* he would do? Why, nothing at all. Simply refrain from laying his head on the block. Forget what his father had told him. Forget why his father killed himself. Conceal, deceive, mislead. Which would be worse, disclosure of the agreement or concealment? Give the victory to Vicaro and Harrington or protect the lie, let everyone believe no agreement had ever been made?

Could he do that? Live with that lie, hide it for the sake of something he thought was more important? Well—more important than truth? More important than honor? What old-fashioned words. His father had tried to live that lie and ended up a suicide.

Had Vicaro won? Was he going to let Vicaro win?

Maybe the senators who would vote for or against Gus's confirmation had a right to know about his father's agreement with Vicaro and the tobacco company. But Phil would never agree to let Gus disclose the agreement. All the White House people, Justice Department people, *everyone* slaving away for his confirmation would think Gus was an ungrateful, self-righteous lunatic. Was this just some kind of false piety? All the good he knew he could do on the Supreme Court—throw that away for some nineteen-year-old agreement he hadn't even heard about until yesterday? Throw it way for the sake of *appearances*? That would be crazy. Of *course* it'd be crazy.

And yet . . .

"What do you think, Samantha?"

"I don't know what the problem is."

"I have to decide between something that's a lie and something that's wrong."

"Can't you just do what's right?"

"That doesn't seem to be one of the options."

"Why not?"

"It's complicated."

"I can understand."

Her face was dirty and her hair matted, but her eyes glinted in the limousine's half-light. Maybe what this needed was an application of thirteen-year-old innocence—thirteen-year-old innocence tempered with the hard reality of murder and attempted rape.

He said, "I have to decide whether to allow a lie, and

maybe get confirmed, or bring out the truth, and probably not get confirmed."

She waited, expecting more.

He said, "That's it."

"Everything?"

"Yeah."

"So tell the truth."

Easy. She hadn't even had to make a decision.

He thought about it, and then said, "Let me explain a little more, see what you think."

"Okay."

Looking at her—that sweat-soiled T-shirt, stringy hair. And the eyes. Intense. So *serious.*

"The agreement my father made with the tobacco company—you heard me talking about that."

"Yeah."

"Did you understand it?"

"I think so. If you were on this court there might be some decision you could make and because of that deal with the company you'd get a lot of money."

"And that'd be bad, wouldn't it? If making money for myself influenced how I voted on a case."

"Yes." She nodded.

"So these senators who are going to vote for whether or not I should be on the Court, do they have a right to know about that agreement and decide for themselves whether they think it might influence me?"

"I don't know."

"No opinion?"

"Well, it would be *good* if they didn't know, because then it couldn't make them vote against you. But if they *should* know, I'm not sure." She hesitated. "It's too complicated. I don't know enough. What do you think?"

"I'm not sure either. I think maybe I know, but I don't like what I know."

"You know what my dad, what Larry, used to say?"

"What's that?"

"He said if you can't make up your mind about something, just imagine you made a certain decision and then see how you feel about it. If it makes you feel peaceful, it was the right thing. Like imagine you tell everyone about the agreement, okay? Everyone knows. You told them. How does that make you feel?"

"I'm not sure."

"Yes you are. You're smiling."

22

Gus called the command truck and got Michelle on the line.

He said, "You've heard the news."

"That there wasn't an agreement."

"There was an agreement, Michelle. My father told me about it. It's just that for some reason Vicaro and Harrington have decided to suppress it."

"If it's true, Gus—"

"It's true. There *was* an agreement."

"I believe you."

"This isn't like telling someone you feel well when you don't. It's not saying you're busy for dinner when you're not. This is—"

"Don't lie, Gus. If someone asks you, tell them, yes, there was an agreement."

"And if no one asks? Because it never comes up? No one even knows enough to ask?"

He heard her sigh. He wondered how much sleep she'd had. How long would it take them to get over all this—assuming they got out alive in the first place? Would he and Michelle and Samantha ever be normal people again?

"Gus . . ."

"Yes."

"You have to tell the truth. I mean, any way it has to be done. If you have to tell people, then you have to tell people. You're not sitting in that car for a lie, Gus. Neither is Samantha."

"It means losing the confirmation."

"It doesn't matter what it means."

"It means letting Vicaro and Harrington win."

"You have to tell the truth, Gus. God will do what he wants."

"I'll call later."

He hung up, and Samantha said, "What'd she say? You know, what you should do?"

"She said the same as you."

She beamed. "So that's what you're going to do, then."

Twenty minutes later, Gus called Rothman.

"What's up?"

"You're not going to like this, Phil."

"What is it?"

"Hear me out. Try to withhold judgment until you've had a chance to consider what I've said."

"Just tell me. What is it?"

"The agreement my father signed with Briggs & Paulman and Vicaro's father . . ."

"Yes?"

"If really happened. You know that. The agreement really exists."

"Okay, so I know it. Now what?"

"I'm not going to lie about it."

"Of course not. You don't have to lie about it. I told you that. Harrington's forgotten all about it."

"If I know it's true, and I know it's important and relevant, and I conceal it, that's a lie, Phil."

"Oh, Gus, come on. You've been in that limo too long. Don't do this to me."

"This limo has nothing to do with it. It's very simple. The agreement is true, I know it's true, it's an important, relevant piece of information for the committee, and it ought to be part of the discovery package."

"Discovery package? This isn't a trial, Gus, this is a confirmation hearing. You are under no obligation to disclose anything. The committee asks questions and you answer them. If they don't ask, you have no obligation to disclose."

"I have a moral obligation, Phil. If they knew about the agreement they'd ask about it for sure. I can't capitalize on their ignorance."

"Gus, you're very tired and stressed, you admit that?"

"I admit it, but that has nothing to do with what I'm saying. I'm talking about truth and responsibility. Fatigue and stress don't change that."

"Gus, no one's asking you to lie. Why do you feel so compelled to answer a question no one's even going to ask?"

"Because if they knew enough to ask, they'd ask."

"Oh, Gus, that's just . . . It's just crap."

"Phil, listen to me. You're not getting it. This isn't a legal issue. It's a—"

"Moral issue. Gus . . ."

Gus waited. When Phil didn't continue, he said, "Phil, what seems like a million years ago, although I guess it was more like a couple of months, you said the President wanted to nominate me because I was a slave to the law. That was your phrase."

"I remember. You're not letting me forget it."

"Well—"

"This isn't the law, Gus. That's my point. The law doesn't require you to disclose that agreement."

"I've got a law on my heart that does."

"No offense, Gus, but could we just stick to the written law, and not get into subjective interpretations of what is or is not inscribed on your heart?"

"I'm sorry this is upsetting you, Phil."

"Well, of *course* it's upsetting me. We nominate you, you end up in a limousine with your daughter and a car bomb and the whole world looking down the President's throat—we can't withdraw you, we can't get you out of the mess you're in, we're about half a millimeter from having our nominee vaporized, looking like a pack of fools, and—"

"Phil, why don't you call me back."

"I'm sorry, Gus, I didn't mean that. But this is really stupid. Disclosing something that can kill your confirmation stone dead when you don't have to, no one even wants you to. That's just stupid."

"Maybe there's a practical aspect to this that can appeal to you, Phil."

"What would that be?"

"What if we don't disclose this, and—"

"*We?*"

"What if *I* don't disclose this, and then Harrington changes his mind and *he* discloses it, and says that I—and you, Phil, and the President—knew about it all along and concealed it. He says he knows we knew about it because he told us, and he is just shocked to death that we didn't disclose it ourselves and that he has to do it. Headlines, Phil. 'President involved in Supreme Court cover-up.' That could happen."

"And the sky could fall in. The earth could swallow us up. Lots of things could happen. It's called politics. You don't commit suicide just because you're afraid someone might murder you. It's stupid, Gus. Think about it."

"I will if you will. Call me back in half an hour."

"Gus, what if I talk to the President and we come up with a compromise? There's gotta be a way out of this. Keep an open mind, Gus. I'll call back."

Gus hung up, turned his head, and stared at the tinted window. He knew Samantha was watching him, and he didn't want to see her face. Compromise—was that the most we could ever expect? His father had been the first in Gus's life to preach compromise as a standard, a way of life, a maximum expectation, an excuse for not holding out for what was right.

Thirty-five minutes later, Phil called.

"The President can't believe it, Gus. He just can*not* believe it. He's wondering if the stress has got to you. He thinks maybe you're coming unglued. I think he might be right."

"Is this constructive?"

"Is your mind absolutely set on this, Gus?"

"Absolutely. More now than ever. But I have to tell you—well, you know that you do have a kind of solution."

"Solution? Oh, really? Please, please tell me."

"Withdraw my name from the nomination. Wash your hands of me. Then it won't matter what happens. If I disclose the agreement, so what? Who cares? I'm not a nominee anymore. At worst, I'm just some conniving district court judge who thought he could make a lot of money out of a Supreme Court nomination. Even if the bomb goes off, who cares? Nothing to do with the White House."

"Don't tempt me, Gus."

"So do it."

"Gus, you know damned well we can't drop you now. This whole country's practically worshiping at your feet. There you are, some damned hero with your newfound, unaborted daughter about to be blown up by drug traffickers, and the White House abandons you? Get real."

"So you're stuck with me."

"And when I hang up, your next call's to CNN. That's right, isn't it?"

"I'm sorry, Phil."

Gus's next call was not to CNN. It was to Roy Jenkins at the Associated Press, the reporter who'd called him earlier. He left his number, and Jenkins called back in thirty seconds.

"I can't believe it," Jenkins said when Gus had told him about the tobacco company agreement.

"It was a stupid thing for my father to do, but we all do stupid things from time to time."

"That's not what I meant. I meant I can't believe you told me. Why'd you tell me?"

"Because it's true, and relevant to the decision the Senate will have to make."

Jenkins laughed. "Because it's *true?* Well, that's an interesting twist."

Carl returned from his visit to Ernie Vicaro just in time to join agents in the command truck watching Terry's body on a night-vision TV monitor disappear through a hole cut in the roof of the Mercedes.

Her voice came in muffled grunts over the truck's speakers as her body squirmed toward the back of the station wagon.

"Another four feet. It looks like there's about a foot of open space in the back. I should be able to reach over. Hang on. I'm looking over with the light. The edge doesn't go all the way down. It fills out. It goes down about ten inches and then it fills out to where there's only about a half inch between the RDX and the hatchback. The detonator's gotta be underneath. If we're gonna get to the detonator we've gotta move out some of the RDX, or go in through the back door. I'm coming out."

In three minutes her head and shoulders appeared above the roof of the Mercedes. She climbed out, jumped down, and disappeared from sight.

"So what now?" It was Terry's boyfriend.

An FBI man said, "Like she said, go in the back door."

The ATF men were silent. Carl said, "Historically, how often are car-bomb doors booby-trapped?"

Rolf Zaeder, the agent with the Santa Claus face, said, "Forget it. Better than sixty percent, depending on the makers. What we've seen of this one—the RDX, way it's packed, remote antenna—we're looking at experts. If they haven't booby-trapped the doors I'm just ashamed of them."

Terry walked in and unzipped the front of her baggy orange coveralls, revealing a yellow T-shirt and khaki shorts. "Sorry, guys."

Someone said, "Man here wants to go through the hatchback."

Terry laughed. "Gimme a head start, okay? I'll be in Ohio."

Carl said, "So what now?"

Terry said, "Listen, I saw something."

Heads turned, waiting.

"When I came up through the top. I was twisting around to get my body out of the hole and I happened to look at the Trade Commission. There was a guy there in the window, silhouetted. I got a good look. Then he moved to his left, out of the window."

Carl said, "How many?"

"One."

"Sure?"

"That's what I saw. I only saw one."

So the thermal imaging people were right. The Trade Commission was occupied.

Carl walked outside with Max Iverson, away from the trucks and other agents.

"So what do you think?"

Iverson said, "Terry confirmed what the imaging people saw."

"What do you want to do with it?"

"I don't know. Tough call."

Carl said, "How sure are they there's two? Terry only saw one."

"Positive. They can measure it. They know how much heat the average body radiates under different conditions. They say there's no way there could be more or less than two bodies where they're seeing the radiation. And they're seeing it in the front room. Right where Terry saw the guy in the window."

"So all this tells you—what?"

"Go in. End it."

"And if they blow up the judge and his daughter?"

"It's gotta end sometime, Carl."

Carl raised his head, appeared to be studying the stars. Then he said, "What about your intrusion team—the voice sensors and TV camera?"

"They're ready."

Four minutes after the AP bulletin, CNN's "Breaking News" logo interrupted a science show, and the picture switched to a story about the agreement between Gus's father, Ernesto Vicaro's father, and the Briggs & Paulman tobacco company. An anchorman in Washington said, "Legalization of marijuana and cocaine could produce a sixty-billion-dollar-a-year legitimate industry. What this means personally for Judge Parham, should marijuana or cocaine ever become legal, is a fortune whose dimensions are virtually immeasurable."

The image had hardly faded from the screen when the opposition's pundits and spin doctors weighed in with demands for Gus's withdrawal. A special late edition of a Chicago tabloid was typical:

PARHAM A PUSHER?
DEAL SAYS YES!

There were three of them, wearing black sneakers, black cotton pants, black T-shirts, and black face paint. It was late Friday night.

Carl thought, Commandos. Give me a break. He said to Max Iverson, "So where's Arnold?"

"Arnold?"

"Forget it." Schwarzenegger. Iverson probably never heard of him.

The blacked-up team slipped out of the command truck toward the Trade Commission. In the silence around the consoles, someone said, "So should we listen for a loud bang, or what?"

Thirty-five minutes later they were back. A Puerto Rican FBI agent, in the command truck to translate Spanish-speaking voices from the newly inserted sensors, said, "We're getting the carrier and that's it. Either no one's there or they've got nothing to say."

A monitor for the night-vision TV camera installed outside the rear of the Trade Commission showed a green image of the back door.

The men in black disappeared.

The Puerto Rican agent switched the sound from the speakers to his headset, lit a cigarette, and picked up a copy of *Newsweek*.

Carl walked outside. It had been exactly thirty-five hours since the Mercedes arrived at Blossom. For the past eighteen hours, Rolf Zaeder had been wandering around outside the command truck telling everyone he expected a timer to set the bomb off "any second now . . . any second

. . . annnnny second." Carl would have given anything to know what time the timer was set for.

Max Iverson appeared beside him.

"Carl, tell me what you think of this."

"What is it?"

"Those people in the Trade Commission aren't going to stay there when the bomb goes off."

Carl said, "I know what you're thinking."

"When they come out, we'll see them on the TV. They'll give themselves some running time—ten, fifteen minutes at least. However long they figure it'll take them to get to safety will be long enough for the judge and his daughter to drive to safety."

"So you'd want them to drive out."

"Why not? If they've got the time. It's a lot better than just sitting there and hoping to survive the explosion."

"Let me think about it."

Rothman called.

Gus said, "Phil, I'm sorry about all the media—"

"Don't be. It may be turning."

"What do you mean?"

"Some preliminary polling indicates that your integrity in disclosing the agreement is hitting harder than the agreement itself."

"Well, well, well."

"But I've got something else you need to know."

"What is it?"

"The experts out here have a new idea. If they could find out when the device is set to detonate, you might have time to drive the limousine to safety. They don't know that they *can* find out, or how much of a window that will give you, but if they get some forewarning, they want you to be prepared to drive out. So what they want, they want to make sure you've shut down everything—air-conditioning, radio, minimize phone use to near zero—because you'll need power to start the limo. The engineers are afraid that very soon now you'll lack starting power."

"Phil, we've hardly used anything. The air-conditioning—"

"No more air-conditioning, Gus."

"We've got to have some air in here. You can't imagine. It's not survivable without the AC, Phil."

"If may not be survivable with it. That's what they're saying out here. I'd believe them."

"Then let's get off the phone. We'll do our best. There's not much left to cut."

23

Since late Friday morning, Phil Rothman had been struggling with a question that excited his political heart. How could the threat of the car bomb be turned around, used to the advantage of the White House? The bomb contained tremendous political power waiting to be harnessed to a good idea. And now Rothman thought he had that idea.

What if Samantha came out of this alive and were herself to testify before the Judiciary Committee? You would have a thirteen-year-old girl, innocent, beautiful, survivor of a car-bomb threat, responding to sordid revelations of prostitution brought by evil forces attacking her while she was down. She tells the world her side of the story and declares her love and respect for her newfound father. On television. Senators of both parties would be buried beneath an avalanche of letters, faxes, E-mail, and phone messages demanding Gus's confirmation.

Of course, you'd have to get the chairman of the Judiciary Committee to allow it—old Eric Taeger. But there were weapons. Taeger wasn't too old to have libidinous desires that occasionally drove him to embarrassing indiscretions. If the need were sufficiently pressing, there were cards to be played.

It looked good. Rothman took the idea to Dutweiler, who liked it. They decided not to trouble Gus with it now. Better to wait until the bomb threat had been resolved and he and Samantha were out of the limousine.

Friday morning Helen called Gier's mobile phone. No answer. She waited an hour. Still no answer. She called Gier hourly all day. She called Harrington. Harrington hadn't heard from him either. Gier was either dead or he'd dropped off the face of the earth. CNN said the Judiciary Committee had postponed, "until this difficult situation is resolved," the confirmation vote that had been scheduled for Monday. The Senate floor vote set for Wednesday had also been put off.

Friday night, her phone rang.

"How ya doin'?"

Cheerful, relaxed, not a problem in the world.

"Fine, Warren. What's happening?"

"Not for the phone. You wanna meet?"

Oh, no, Warren, of course not. Why would I 'wanna meet'? "In the office? Right now?"

"I could come over. Save you the trouble opening up."

Warren Gier in her home? That'll be the day.

"The office is easy. Thirty minutes?"

"You got it."

Warren came in slowly, taking his time, strolled around the white conference table, picked a chair, leaned back, and sighed. A man at the end of a productive mission, lots to say, no need to rush, savoring the impatience of his audience.

"So, Mr. Warren Gier, is there anything you can't do?"

She hated sucking up to that revolting ego, but it was the price he put on his wares.

"It does not look good for the judge. The car-bomb operation is controlled by Colombian security agents inside the Colombian Trade Commission across the street from the house Parham's in. The chief of the operation drove the Mercedes into the block, parked it, went into the Trade Commission, changed from his chauffeur's uniform to civilian clothes, and even now, as we speak, is watching the operation from the end of the street, right in among the cops and reporters."

"Warren . . ."

"Yes?"

"How do you know all this?"

"Everyone knows it. Almost everyone. The only thing the cops don't know yet, I think, is that the agent's at the end of the street."

"So how do you know?"

"You don't believe me?"

"I believe you, Warren. How do you know?"

"A Filipino girl who works in a building behind the Trade Commission saw him come out—a cook, undocumented, not supposed to be here, but can't keep from telling friends, who tell other friends. I'm always amazed how much trouble people have keeping their mouths shut. Sometimes you just can't turn them off."

He smirked. If Helen believed in the devil, she'd say Warren had his help.

She said, "So what do you know about him, the guy on the street?"

"Tall, dark hair, blue polo shirt, jeans, white running shoes. I saw him this morning, standing around, chatting with cops and reporters. He wandered off a couple of blocks and talked on a mobile phone, briefly."

"Have you told the police any of this?"

He let his jaw drop in mock surprise.

"I work for the cops? I work for you, Helen."

"We don't pay you, Warren."

"Don't I know. But Taeger pays me, and he says, 'You're not working for me, you're working for the Freedom Federation.' He pays, so I'm working for whoever he says I'm working for. Why is it no one wants to claim me but everyone wants to know what I know?"

"Don't you think you should tell the police?"

"Most of it they already know."

"And the rest? The part about the agent on the street?"

"I can find out, they can find out. I don't have to worry about the police."

"Have you told Harrington?"

"Of course. He—"

"—pays you. What did he say?"

"He was too scared to say anything." Warren's lips formed a contemptuous little smile. "Isn't it interesting? There's no end to what some people will do to destroy each other as long as it's not actually physical. Then a guy like Ernesto Vicaro comes along, couldn't care less, actually *prefers* if it's physical, and people go into absolute megashock. A *bomb*? A real *bomb*? Blow someone up? Couldn't we just ruin the guy, wreck his life, send him off into outer darkness, disgrace, contempt, poverty? Do we actually have to *hurt* him?"

"I guess they don't have your high moral values, Warren."

"Does anyone?"

She got rid of Warren and telephoned Carl. As the phone rang, she mentally thanked Warren for letting her know who she was—one of those blighted people who drew the line when things got physical. She might be an idealist, but she was not a terrorist.

No answer. She tried his mobile phone. Still no answer.

Warren had said the agent in the street was chief of the operation. So he could do something—call it off, make a deal, *something*.

She called both numbers again. At 10:40 Carl answered the mobile phone.

"It's Helen. I have to see you."

"What's the problem?"

"I have to see you."

"I'm really tied up now, Helen. What is it?"

"I can't tell you on the phone. I know something you have to know. You've got to see me."

"How important is it, Helen? I'm involved in something pretty critical right now."

"On a scale of one to ten, it's a hundred."

"Where are you?"

"In my office."

"Be out front in five minutes."

* * *

She jumped into Carl's car, closed the door, and as he pulled away from the curb he said, "What is it?"

"The car bomb's controlled by two Colombian agents inside the Colombian Trade Commission, and a third outside who's really running things. He's the same guy who drove the Mercedes in and parked it."

"Where is he, the guy outside?"

"Around the intersection someplace, with the cops and reporters."

"How d'you know this?"

"I can't tell you. A very reliable source."

"Warren Gier?"

"I can't tell you."

"What's the agent's name?"

"I don't know, but I know what he looks like."

"Tell me."

They had arrived at the intersection, Carl showing his DEA badge to uniformed cops blocking the street.

He said it again. "What's he look like?"

She didn't want to tell him. As soon as he knew everything, he'd drop her, send her away.

She said, "Let's take a look around. Maybe I'll see him."

"Tell me what he looks like."

"Just let me see if I can find him."

Carl took a pair of handcuffs from the glove compartment and put them in his jacket pocket.

They got out, and she led him on a wandering path through the crowd of onlookers. Gier had said the agent was tall and dark. Well, big help. There must have been about 2,000 people milling around the intersection, crowding the police barriers.

So she looked for a blue polo shirt, jeans, and white running shoes. She scanned the crowd for tall Latin males in blue polo shirts, then maneuvered until she could get a glimpse of their pants and shoes.

When she finally saw him, it was easy. He was outside the crush of spectators, standing alone. She wondered why Warren, with his taste for the bizarre, hadn't mentioned the man's face. It was fat and beefy, dark but not clearly Latin, the face of a German butcher, sitting on top of a frail, skinny body like a pumpkin on a stick. As she watched him, his gaze kept roaming. He wasn't smiling, talking to friends, having a good time. He was intent, purposeful, there on business.

"That's him."

Carl followed her gaze.

"How do you know?"

"I was told—tall, dark, blue polo shirt, white running shoes, Latin."

Carl was still and quiet, studying the man. The polo shirt hung loose outside the pants.

"Helen, how sure are you of whoever told you?"

"Very sure."

"You're going to have to tell me, Helen. Was it Warren Gier?"

She was silent.

"People could die, Helen."

"It was Warren."

"That's good."

"Why is it good?"

"Because Warren would know."

Carl didn't move. Finally he said, "Helen, will you help me? I don't want to take my eyes off this guy."

"What can I do?"

He handed her his car keys.

"Bring the car right over there." He pointed.

Helen said, "It's one-way. And there aren't any parking places."

"Doesn't matter. Put the car there, in the street. If there's a problem I'll come over and talk to the cops. Just put it there."

She got the car, parked it where she'd been told, left the emergency flashers on, and went back to Carl. He hadn't moved. Nor had the agent.

Carl said, "You know his name?"

"No."

"Rubi Aguilera. We got a profile on him, but we couldn't find him. Old buddy of Vicaro, when Vicaro was in the legislature mixing coke and politics. Did eleven months as an intelligence officer in the Colombian embassy right here in Washington, can you believe that? Let's take a walk. Just a casual couple, live nearby, out for a stroll, see what's going on."

He took her hand, walked toward Aguilera, angling to pass through a knot of onlookers on a plot of roadside grass. When they were three yards from Aguilera's back, Carl let go of her hand and took two quick, silent steps. Directly behind Aguilera, he put both arms around his belly in a bear hug, reached one hand under the polo shirt, withdrew a pistol from the waistband, and slipped the hand with the gun into the front of Aguilera's jeans.

Aguilera, not turning around, laughed. "Whoa, man! Whoa!"

From behind Aguilera's ear, Carl said softly, "I'm a friend, Rubi. Just relax. Everything's okay."

"Who are you, man? Get your hand outta my crotch!"

Carl said, "Settle down, Rubi. Let's not disturb all these nice people. You don't want someone calling a cop. Just relax."

"You're the boss. You got a gun down my pants, I'll do anything you want."

Carl relaxed his hug but kept one arm around Aguilera's waist in what looked like a friendly embrace. The hand holding the gun was still hidden under the polo shirt.

"Everything's cool, Rubi. We need to talk for a minute. What we're going to do, the lady's gonna drive a car over here and we're gonna get in the back seat. We'll sit there and talk for a couple minutes and then you'll get out and go on your way. No trouble for anyone. You understand that?"

"You're the boss, my friend."

"Helen, if you could bring the car over, please?"

Helen went to Carl's car, and sat for a second behind the wheel. She was shaking. She took a deep breath, closed her eyes, and for the first time since college, when she had come briefly under the influence of a Pentecostal football player, she prayed. "Dear Lord, make me do the right thing. Don't let me screw this up."

Then, driving slowly through the milling crowd, she pulled the car to the curb next to Carl and Aguilera.

They climbed into the back seat. To Helen it looked as if Carl's hand was halfway down the front of Aguilera's jeans.

"Just drive ahead a few yards, Helen, get out of the crowds. Maybe over there, away from the streetlights. Yeah, that's good. Right here. Fine."

She stopped the car and turned off the lights and ignition. In the rear-view mirror she could see their faces, professional and businesslike, as if none of this was new to either of them. But from Aguilera, no longer laughing, came a threat completely different from the toughness she saw in Carl. She was frightened to have him behind her.

Carl said, "Well, Rubi, what a day it's been, right?"

Aguilera chuckled, as if he and Carl were old friends and this entire encounter were some kind of prank.

"Some day, that's right."

Carl's arm moved.

Aguilera gave a painful grunt. "What do you want with me? Who are you?"

"The point, Rubi, is that you're a DAS agent and you're running this car bomb and you know when the bomb's going off. That's a given, okay? So we don't need to discuss that. What we—"

"You're crazy, my friend. I don't know what—"

Aguilera let out a low, sudden howl so charged with pain it made Helen sick.

"I said, we already *know* these things, Rubi. They're not open for discussion, okay? Don't waste time. I'm a nice guy, calm and considerate, but if I get angry you could get your balls shot away. What I started to say, all I want to know is when the bomb's going off."

Aguilera was quiet, and as the seconds ticked away Helen was terrified that Carl would do what he'd done before, and there'd be another howl of pain.

Aguilera said, "If I told you, how would you know I was telling the truth?"

His voice didn't match the face now, or the menace. Behind the Latin accent, the pretense of mirth abandoned, was the almost soft-spoken tone of a disciplined professional, a man who had never acted on impulse, who could always be counted on to do the reasonable thing.

"A very good question, Rubi. Been thinking about that myself. My feeling, I think you're an honest man. I think I can trust you. You're not some thug, are you Rubi? Not some cheap terrorist? You're an educated, trained intelligence agent. Isn't that right, Rubi?"

Aguilera didn't speak or move. His eyes were closed.

"And here's something else I think, Rubi. I think you've been standing in the street there, trying to figure out how to get back to your friends in the Trade Commission. So here's what we're going to do. You tell me when the bomb's going off, and I'll walk you right past the police line, through the barricades, and take you straight down that street to the Trade Commission and watch you walk inside. You'd like that, right? Tit for tat. You do something for me, I do something for you. How's that?"

Aguilera laughed. "You think I'm stupid. You'd take me back there? Get serious, my friend."

"Doesn't matter if you believe it or not. Truth's the truth. Anyway, I don't see any choice for you."

"You get me in there, take me behind one of the buildings, and do anything you want."

"You think I'd hurt you, Rubi, after you told me what I want to know? No chance. I did that, the word'd go out—Don't talk to Carl, he can't be trusted."

Aguilera was silent, thinking. Suddenly he grinned—his whole face, ear to ear—and he said, "She comes too."

"I beg your pardon?"

Aguilera laughed, as if this were the funniest thing that'd ever happened to him. Helen was beginning to wonder if the laughter was an act or if Aguilera was insane. He said, "She comes."

"Oh, now Rubi, I never dreamed you were—"

Helen heard herself speak. "It's okay, Carl. I—"

"Be quiet! Rubi, you don't trust me."

Carl's arm moved. The howl again. Helen wanted to throw up.

Carl said, "You don't trust me?"

Rubi, hoarse with pain, sweat glistening on his forehead, said, "I believe you. But I want her with us."

"You really think I'd get you in past the cops there and hurt you?"

"You already hurt me."

"Kill you?"

Silence.

"Well, that is a thought. Why not? You're trying to kill the judge and his daughter, right? Kill you. Good idea. Yeah. That's a chance you'll have to take. What time's the bomb going off?"

"She comes."

Another cry of pain. Aguilera's head jerked back against the seat.

"What time, Rubi?"

"You're crazy. You're gonna kill me. I'll tell you if she comes."

Carl's arm made a deep thrust forward and down.

Rubi let out a heavy, almost silent shriek, gasping for air. In a painful whisper, he said, "She comes."

"Helen?"

If Aguilera felt more secure with a witness, then let him have a witness.

Helen said, "It's okay. I'll go. I'd like to go."

"Okay, Rubi. She comes. What time's it going off?"

"You're gonna take me back? With her?"

"Right now. Straight back. With her."

"Three A.M."

Helen looked at the car clock. It was 10 P.M.

Carl said, "Three A.M.? Don't lie to me, Rubi."

"Three A.M."

"Fine. Thank you. You did the right thing. Helen?"

"Yes."

"Drive as close to the barricade as you can get. When a cop stops you, we'll all get out. Stay close. And Rubi, you so much as wiggle an eyelash and I'll blow your balls into your socks. Guaranteed. You understand?"

He nodded, painfully.

Carl showed his badge to a cop, who moved a wooden barricade and let them through. They got out of the car and walked up the sidewalk toward Blossom. When they reached the corner, turned, and crossed to the next block, they saw the Mercedes. They continued another half block and stopped on the sidewalk in front of the Trade Commission. Light from high-intensity lamps on the corners had at this distance diminished to a gloom not much brighter than moonlight.

Carl, his gun hand still down the front of Aguilera's jeans, looked around and said, "Over there. That's a good place."

Aguilera said, "This is the commission, right here. I go in here."

Carl gave him a shove and headed for a tree on the Trade Commission lawn, directly across the street from the Mercedes and Blossom.

Aguilera said, "You said you'd let me go inside."

"I didn't say when."

Carl stopped next to the tree.

"Put your arms around the trunk."

"What're you—"

Carl gave his arm another thrust downward. Aguilera embraced the tree.

Carl pulled the handcuffs from his jacket pocket and cuffed Aguilera's wrists around the tree. He wanted to be on the lawn between the Trade Commission and Blossom. If someone decided to cross the street, enter Blossom, and do something to Gus or Samantha, they'd have to get past Carl.

"You wanna sit down, sit down. Helen, thanks for coming. You can go back now."

"I'd like to stay."

Her words surprised her. The street was quiet, and even in the dim, long-shadowed light, the Mercedes looked as peaceful as any parked car had ever looked. Nothing she had ever done before had given her such a certain sense that she was exactly where she was supposed to be, doing exactly what she was supposed to be doing. Despite the nearness of the explosives-laden station wagon, she felt a tranquillity completely new to her.

Carl said, "In a minute you may change your mind. Rubi—"

Rubi was trying to slide his arms down the tree trunk and position his legs so he could sit on the grass.

"Rubi, I'm talking to you."

"Yeah. And I'm listening. I'm listening to every word you say."

He was smiling again, hiding behind the mirth.

Carl said, "We're going to sit here until you tell me the truth about when the bomb's set for. Then I'll know when it's safe to go in and bring out the judge and his daughter. Okay? You wanna keep it a big secret, that's fine. You'll get blown up and I'll go with you. You ready for that? I'm ready."

Aguilera let out a roar of laughter. "That's wonderful! We'll both get blown up sky high. You're crazy, my friend. Crazy, crazy, crazy."

Carl grinned, and to Helen he looked genuinely amused by Aguilera's laughter. For several minutes she'd felt the same sense she'd had in the coffee shop of a kinship between Carl and her late husband. They were part of a different world, and listening to Carl and Aguilera now, watching them, experiencing the atmosphere around them, she understood a large area of her husband's life that had been hidden to her when he was alive. So often she had felt a barrier between them, and she had blamed him for putting it there, for refusing to share his life with her. Now she knew what the barrier had been made of—it was not a barrier, it was a shield, and it had been made of love. She no longer blamed him. She loved him for protecting her from the place Carl and Aguilera were in now. She didn't want to be in that place, but watching Carl and Aguilera, confronting for the first time the world that had driven, and killed, her husband, she felt held. She couldn't move.

Carl said, "You're the crazy one if you let yourself get blown up. But you're not crazy. You're a vicious bastard, but you're not crazy, and you're gonna tell me as soon as we need to get outta here. And you'd better give me plenty of time, because the judge and his daughter are going with us. Get them out of the house, I figure about ten, fifteen minutes. Be really safe, say half an hour. So you tell me half an hour before the bomb's gonna go, and that'll give us plenty of time to clear out."

"I told you, three A.M."

"That was before you were hugging the tree. I figure now you've got a little more incentive to tell the truth. You don't wanta be here when it blows."

"You don't either."

"I won't be. Because you're going to tell me."

"I don't care if I get blown up."

"You care, Rubi. You're not some fifteen-year-old suicide car bomber wants to die for Allah. Not you, Rubi. You've got plans for the future—girls to screw, money to steal, people to hurt. Helen, it's time for you to go."

Helen, cross-legged on the grass, couldn't move. She tried to get up. Something held her to the grass.

She said, "Not yet, Carl. Please. A few more minutes."

Aguilera said, "I can't see my watch."

"You don't have to see your watch. You just tell me when you think we'd better move. But don't guess wrong, Rubi. Don't guess wrong."

Now Carl was smiling. Helen wondered if maybe, possibly, he was really prepared to get blown up. Maybe he wasn't bluffing. Maybe Aguilera wasn't bluffing.

And at that moment, Helen thought she saw movement in a second-floor window of the Trade Commission.

Late Friday night, Rothman was in the White House Situation Room with Dutweiler, two White House attorneys, a White House political polling expert, the DEA administrator and his counterparts from ATF and the FBI, deputy assistants from the State Department, CIA, and the National Security

Agency, a deputy attorney general, and an army general from the Pentagon.

They were listening to reports from the FBI command truck, as well as abstracts of decrypted intercepts of Colombian embassy telephone and cable traffic, when an army colonel leaned over Rothman's shoulder to whisper that he had a personal telephone call from Carl Falco.

"In the truck?"

"Yes, sir, but he said it's for you personally, doesn't want anyone else connected."

Rothman excused himself, left the room, and took the call in an outside office.

"What is it, Carl?"

"I just had another call from Larry Young in London."

"And?"

"He said there was something he thought we might like to know, maybe he should have told us earlier, thinks maybe it wouldn't be good if certain other people found out first. Samantha killed a man. When she was eight. Guy tried to rape her and she stabbed him with a knife."

"She *killed* a man?"

"Right. That's what he said."

"And he thought we *might* like to know?"

"Considered it a possibility."

"Oh, boy. Where?"

"Milwaukee. I'll get someone over to the courthouse, see are the records still there."

"Thanks, Carl."

The records would be there, but they'd better not stay there. The first place investigators would go to confirm a rumor of the killing would be court records.

Rothman left the White House and spent an hour and a

half driving around Washington, thinking. The more he drove, the more certain he became. He was holding a bomb. A very valuable bomb. How to place it, how and when to trigger it?

In the command truck, the Puerto Rican agent flipped a switch and yelled, "Listen!"

A Spanish voice boomed from the console speaker and filled the truck.

Iverson said, "What's he saying?"

"He says there's people on the lawn. He's talking to someone."

Four times during the night they had heard two men talking in the Trade Commission. Mostly they argued about what to watch on TV. One wanted game shows, the other wanted news. Neither said anything about the Mercedes or a bomb.

More Spanish.

The agent said, "He says there's three people on the lawn."

Iverson said, "Who the hell's on the lawn?"

A phone buzzed on another console. An agent in shirtsleeves grabbed it, listened, yelled at Iverson.

"Baker post says three subjects have arrived in front of the TC. Two men and a woman."

Baker post was a position in a doctor's office twenty-two floors up in an office building half a mile away, with an uninterrupted view of the Trade Commission and Blossom. Agents there had high-energy telescopic night scopes.

Carl said, "Put it on the speakers."

The agent flipped a switch and the Spanish voices in

the Trade Commission were replaced by a southern American accent from Baker post.

Carl said, "What've you got?"

"Two white males and a white female. Number one male is five-seven, one-eighty, stocky, polo shirt and pants, can't give you color, everything's green on this scope. At the moment it looks like he's cuffed to a tree. Number two male is six feet, one-ninety, T-shirt, pants. Female's five-six, one-thirty, blouse and pants. They just came walking up the block about three minutes ago and when they got in front of the Trade Commission, number one male walked over to a tree, put his arms around it, and number two appeared to cuff his hands so he was hugging the tree. Now all three are sitting by the tree. Just sitting there. Talking, I guess."

Iverson, straining to keep his voice from showing the anger evident on his face, said, "Where's Falco?"

No one answered.

"Where's Falco! When was the last time anyone saw Falco?"

An ATF agent said, "I saw him two hours ago outside the Winnebago."

Talking to Baker post on the speaker phone, Iverson said, "You ever meet a DEA agent named Carl Falco? You know what he looks like?"

"No, sir."

"What're they doing now?"

"Still sitting there. Looks like a picnic."

Iverson nodded his head. "Picnic."

Someone said, "Who's the woman?"

Iverson said, "Where's Terry?"

"Right here."

She was standing by the door.

The Puerto Rican agent, a headset over his ears, said, "Iverson?"

"Yes?"

"They're getting a little excited."

"Get it up."

Baker post was disconnected and the truck filled with Spanish voices.

Iverson said, "What're they saying?"

"They're arguing about what to do. They know one of the men on the lawn. They call him Rubi—"

Iverson looked at another agent—the only one wearing a tie—standing behind the translator. The agent nodded. "Aguilera."

Iverson said, "They say anything about the woman?"

"No. Just that there's a woman. I don't think they recognize anyone except what's-his-name, Rubi. They're really confused. They say there's a woman and another man, and Rubi's cuffed to a tree. One of them keeps saying, 'Shoot him, shoot him.'"

Iverson said, "Who're they talking about? Rubi or the other guy?"

"Can't tell. The other guy, I think. They were talking about the other guy, who is he, who could he be, and one of them said 'Shoot him.' Hang on." He strained to hear. "The other guy says, 'Rubi's in the way. He's behind Rubi.'"

Iverson picked up a telephone. "Put Baker post on this."

An agent, flipping switches, said, "You got it."

"Oster?"

"Yes, sir."

"What's the position of the people on the lawn?"

"Number two just got up and moved over where he's

between number one and the Trade Commission. Then he sat down again. The female's sort of over to the side, a little out of it."

"Would someone in the Trade Commission have a shot at number one?"

"Hard to tell from this angle, but I don't think it'd be a clear shot. Number two's pretty much between number one and the TC windows, from the best I can see."

Iverson put the phone down, looked at the agent in the tie. "Would they shoot Aguilera?"

"Aguilera knows the plan, knows the time."

Iverson picked up the phone again. "Oster, how good a shot would they have from the windows at number two?"

"Number two? Like I said, it's hard to tell from this angle, we're a half mile away, a lot of elevation, but I'd say pretty good, he'd have a pretty uninterrupted line of fire."

Aguilera said, "I need to see my watch."

"You worried, Rubi?"

"What time is it?"

Carl lifted his hand and held his own watch in front of his eyes.

"Guess. What time you think it is?"

Helen saw the movement again, certain this time. Someone was in the window.

Aguilera said, "Don't play games, my friend, this is serious."

Carl said, "Oh, really? Serious? *Now* it's serious? Let me tell you something, asshole—excuse me, Helen—this started getting serious the minute your nasty little ass was born. How many people you killed, Rubi? Don't tell me. How many women you tortured, you brave, macho load of crap?

Now it's serious. 'Cause it's your ass cuffed to the tree. You know what, Rubi? If it wasn't for the judge and his daughter, I might just walk off and leave you cuffed to that tree. See how macho you really are. Laugh your way outta that."

"You're trying to scare me. Forget it, friend, you don't scare me."

"Then stop asking what time it is."

"That thing goes off, it'll kill the judge."

"Well, that's the idea, right? Why you put it there? Now you're worried about the judge?"

"You're the one worried about the judge, not me."

"Not you, you don't care who gets blown up, just as long as your ass isn't around. Whaddya think your friends in there are thinking about this, Aguilera, watching from the windows? They're watching, aren't they?"

So Carl had seen it too.

Aguilera chuckled, enjoying the game.

Carl said, "Right, they're not any dumber than you are. You think they're worried, figure you might tell me when the bomb's going off?"

"They know I wouldn't—"

"Wouldn't what, Rubi? Wouldn't tell, right? So you do know, you little bastard, and it's not three A.M. You're not only vicious, you're stupid, you know that? Let a dumb old DEA agent trick you like that. Your friends in there knew how stupid you were, they'd put a bullet right through your head. Figure you're gonna tell me the time, let me get the judge and the girl out, they'll shoot you dead. That right?"

"Don't be stupid."

"If I were you, Rubi, I think I'd try to sort of just scoot around the other side of the tree there, put a little wood between me and the commission windows. What about that? You want me to give you a hand?"

"I don't need your help. No one's gonna shoot me."

"Suit yourself. They don't kill you, the bomb will."

"You talk too much."

"Tell me what time and I'll shut up."

"I wouldn't tell you even if I knew."

He laughed.

"I like your laugh, Rubi. You've got a really nice laugh."

"I like to laugh, I laugh. What can I tell you? Why not laugh? Life's a laugh, is that right?"

"I'm disappointed in you, Rubi. You said three A.M., and you lied. You don't know how to tell the truth. Been so long, you forgot."

"You never lie, right?"

"Talking to you, I wouldn't do anything else. Complete waste of time, telling you the truth. You know what a preacher said to me, Rubi? He said the devil's the father of lies, couldn't tell the truth if he wanted to. That's you, Rubi."

Aguilera let his mouth drop open. Then he laughed.

"A *preacher*. You're really funny, you know that? A preacher."

Helen saw something change in Carl. He'd found an opening, or thought he had—a knife he could twist, maybe provoke Aguilera into saying something useful. Carl hesitated, watching Aguilera's grinning face.

Then Carl said, "He was talking about the devil. I thought that'd interest you, Rubi."

Aguilera moved his crossed legs, nervous. His face was a blank.

"You don't believe in the devil?"

Aguilera was silent.

"You believe in God, Rubi?"

"God!"

"Your mother believes in God."

"My mother's dead."

Carl said he'd seen a profile of Aguilera. How much was in it?

"Believed in God. Didn't she?"

"What do you care about that?"

"Believed in all that stuff, right? God? The devil? Stuff like that?"

Aguilera didn't answer.

"Did she know you blow up children?"

"I never blew up children."

"Just put the bomb in the bus. She'd forgive you for that, right? A very forgiving person, your mother. You ever forgive anyone, Rubi? That wife you beat all the time, and your kids, you ever forgive them for anything? You catch your wife in bed with her boyfriend, you forgive that?"

"My wife never had a boyfriend."

"Oh, come on, Rubi. No boyfriend, just customers, is that it? She's probably screwing some guy right now. You run off to blow people up, do your job, away from home working hard, earn a living for your family, and that's all the thanks you get, that's how she repays you, sleeps with every young stud in town. How you gonna forgive her for that? I'll bet even God—"

"Shut up! I'm tired of listening to your stupid mouth."

"Take it easy, Rubi. Easy, easy. Don't get all upset. We're just having a few laughs, talking while we wait for you to tell me when the bomb's gonna go. You better tell me soon. Remember, I need half an hour to get everyone out. I might even leave you cuffed to that tree for another half hour while I walk the rest of us out of here. Come back and get you later. You wouldn't want something to happen before I got back."

"You wouldn't come back."

"Well, that'd be terrible. So be nice to me, Rubi. I'd never do that to a friend. Of course, if you really pissed me off, I'd be tempted."

Aguilera shifted his cramped body. He looked exhausted, his face less determined, almost out of smiles. Helen began to feel as if she were watching a wax man, the face slowly melting into expressions less and less contrived.

"What time, Rubi? We still got plenty of time?"

"Please show me your watch."

"Please. Now that's more like it. The magic word, I tell my kids."

Carl glanced at his watch.

"It's seven to midnight."

"Show it to me."

"Trust me. I say it's seven to midnight, it's seven to midnight. You're the liar, the devil's friend, right?"

The Puerto Rican agent said, "They're really steamed in there."

He didn't have to tell Iverson. You could hear it in the voices. They were back on the speakers. Baker post had been relegated to headsets.

The Puerto Rican agent said, "It sounds like a cockfight."

Iverson said, "Keep it coming, what're they saying?"

"They're debating his balls and his loyalty."

"His?"

"Rubi. Is he gonna sit there and get blown up."

"No mention of the explosion time?"

Iverson had been asking that about every ten seconds. And about the woman on the lawn. Who the hell was the woman?

"No. They just talk about the time, *el tiempo*, but they don't say what it is."

"What's their feeling—Rubi's gonna give it up or not?"

"They're not sure. But they're real nervous about it. One of 'em keeps saying, 'It's him or us,' like if he gives up the time something bad's gonna happen to them."

Iverson said, "That's for sure. Something bad's gonna happen to them no matter what he does. Who's in charge, would you guess, the guy who wants to shoot him or the one who doesn't?"

"Hard to tell. They're both yelling. But they can't shoot him 'cause they can't get a clear line on him."

"Unless they drop the other guy first."

"Well, yeah, take out him and the woman, and you don't have to worry about Rubi. He wouldn't have anyone to tell even if he wanted."

Samantha awoke to hear Gus snoring.

She straightened in the seat and listened. Snarl, whistle. Snarl, whistle. Snarl, whistle. Her father was more of a choke, snort, choke, snort. She'd never heard Doreen snore. Probably Doreen didn't snore. Probably Doreen didn't sleep.

She was so hot, so thirsty, so hungry, so dirty, so tired. She wanted to go to the bathroom, but couldn't bear the thought of leaving the limo for the even worse smell of the garage.

She waited as long as she could, then quietly, slowly, listening to Gus's snores, she cracked open the limousine door and stepped softly into the garage. She tiptoed a few steps, and stooped. She finished, stood, and started back to the limo.

She thought of water—cold water from the refrigerator. Ice. Clean air. Maybe the air conditioner was still on. Just for a minute—the bomb wouldn't go off in the next minute.

She walked over and turned the knob on the hallway door. In the darkness, she found her way to the kitchen. She took a half-filled bottle of milk from the refrigerator and tipped it up to her mouth.

A sudden sound made her jump. Milk ran over her chin onto her shirt. She was scared, frozen. Ringing in the dark, sharp and piercing. The telephone. Just the telephone. Calm down. Probably a wrong number. She let it ring.

She left the kitchen and went to a vertical row of jalousie windows along the side of the front door and looked out. The moon was bright. Long, eerie shadows caused by a gloomy kind of leftover light came from way down past the end of the block. The ringing had stopped. The Mercedes sat there at the curb. Everything looked so quiet and peaceful. She longed for just one deep breath of the fresh night air.

She walked to the front door and gave the handle a twist. Locked. She found the key on the metal key board in the Box, then walked back and opened the front door. She stepped out and stood for a moment on the front porch.

Then she saw them—three people sitting in the shadows on the grass across the street. Her heart jumped. The people frightened her more than the Mercedes.

She backed quickly into the house, returned to the garage, slipped into the limo, closed the door, and felt safe again.

She relaxed, reassured by Gus's steady snoring. Snarl, whistle. Snarl, whistle. Snarl, whistle.

24

Carl looked at his watch.

"Past midnight, Rubi. How much time we have? Lots, I hope. I got so much more to say, and I got a lot of questions to ask about your mother and your wife and kids. I read this profile someone gave me. Very thorough. They must've talked to your whole family, all your friends, colleagues, know all about you. That happens when you get sent to Washington. Big time. Everyone wants to know all about you. Wife's name's Maria. Three kids, Vincent, Gilberto, Ismelda. See, I know."

"That's a lotta crap."

"No, no it's not. You know it's true. You really interest

me, Rubi. I mean, your wife, Maria. Now, how'd she happen to marry you? No offense, but a guy who makes his living blowing up children, most women wouldn't think that was a first-rate career choice. What's she say about your job?"

Aguilera moved his legs and glanced at the Trade Commission's windows. Helen thought he might be hoping they'd shoot him and get this over with.

"Don't wanta talk about your wife. Don't blame you. Lots of painful stuff there, screwing all the neighbors. Okay, let's talk about your mother. Mrs. Aguilera. A good churchgoer, must've told you about God when you were growing up, right? So how come you've got it all wrong now? Excuse me? You say something?"

Aguilera had groaned. "These cuffs are hurting. They're too tight."

"That's your fault. The more you squirm the tighter they get. Sit still and it'll be all right. Tell me what time, and I'll take them off, walk you outta here."

"Forget it."

Carl said, "Where were we? Yeah, your mother, telling you about God and you getting it all wrong. Acts have consequences, she told you that, right? Something like that? That's why you're here, makin' love to a tree, listening to me, cuffs hurting. How're the legs? Cramped. Sorry about that. But look at it this way, it's all just the natural consequences of a rotten life, doing all the bad things you do. Take the judge in there. You know lots of judges, Rubi. They've got judges in Colombia. You've killed a few, for sure. They kill judges all the time in Colombia, right? No kids to blow up today, let's go out and kill a judge. Don't you have any respect at all, Rubi?"

"Am I supposed to answer that?"

"I'd love you to answer that."

"You don't know what respect is."

"Well, maybe you're right. Tell me. Educate me."

"Why should I? You don't want to know."

"Sure I do. Tell me. Don't make me do all the talking."

"I respect the man I work for."

"Loyalty."

"Yeah. Loyalty. You understand that?"

"Perfectly. Man says, 'Blow up that bus,' you blow it up."

"That's not loyalty."

"I agree. You like judges, Rubi?"

"Judges are scum."

"That's why you kill them."

"We kill the ones who're scum."

"The ones who won't do what you want them to do. That's why they're scum. You like justice, Rubi?"

"Judges don't know anything about justice."

"That's not what I asked. You like justice?"

"Yeah, of course, everyone likes justice."

"No, they don't. I don't like justice."

Aguilera turned his head to look at Carl.

Carl said, "Yeah, that's right. I get justice, I'm dead. If I was perfect, I'd want justice."

Aguilera laughed. It was a quiet laugh, just the voice, the face stayed the way it was, melting wax.

Carl said, "Funny, right? You like justice, Rubi?"

"It makes no difference. I'm not gonna get it anyway."

"Oh yeah you are. For sure you are. Probably you're gonna get it right here, cuffed to that tree."

"And who's gonna give me justice? You?"

"Blown up, or shot by your friends in the windows over there, you'll get justice."

"That's what you think. You're not gonna give me justice, no matter what you think."

"That's for sure. God's gonna give it to you. You are so *dumb,* you know that? You're gonna get stubborn and you're gonna show off how brave you are and how stupid I am and you're gonna just sit there and let yourself get blown up and then you're going to hell and stay there for the rest of forever. Didn't your mother ever tell you that, tell you about hell?"

"Don't talk about my mother."

"You don't like to hear what she said? You don't respect her? You think she was stupid? You think that, don't you, Rubi? Your mother was just some stupid old bag, right?"

"I don't think that."

"She was smarter than those guys in the window. They're over there arguing should they shoot you or not, and you've got more respect for them than for your mother. You're really stupid, Rubi."

"You're an idiot. You listened to that preacher too much. You're brainwashed."

"My brain's washed in better stuff than the filth you washed yours in."

"Get me outta these cuffs."

"You telling me it's time to go?"

"I'm not telling you anything. You want to die, sit there and die."

"We're going together, Rubi. Thing is, I know where I'm going and you don't."

"You think a lot of yourself, don't you?"

"I don't, but I know someone who does."

"Jesus."

"You swearing? Or you telling me you know what I'm talking about?"

"You sound like my mother."

"If I'd been your mother I'd've drowned you."

"Leave me alone."

"Tell me what time the bomb's going, I'll leave you alone. You think I like not leaving you alone? Rubi, as someone to leave alone, you're number one on my list. People who blow up judges—for you that's just a job, right? Same's putting bombs in school buses."

Aguilera sighed again and twisted his body to put his back to Carl.

Carl said, "That judge in there has spent his whole life protecting scumbags like you, make sure nobody hands you a wrong one. Heaven forbid you should do time for the wrong killing. That right, Rubi?"

Aguilera, his back to Carl, was silent.

Carl, sitting on the grass two feet behind Aguilera, shot out a foot, sudden as a snake's tongue, and kicked Aguilera in the back of the neck.

Aguilera winced and let out a cry.

"Answer me when I talk to you, asshole."

"Don't kick me."

"I'll kick you to *death* is what I'll do."

"Why are you asking all this?"

"I'm interested in you. I never met someone before likes to blow people up. After tonight I might never have another chance to talk to someone like you."

"After the Mercedes blows up you won't have a chance to talk to anyone."

"I'll be in heaven, talk all I want."

"Heaven!" Aguilera shook his head and snorted.

Carl said, "You believe in marriage, having kids, blowing people up, what else? What do you believe in, Rubi? Money, for sure. Career opportunities? Who's gonna get the big job? You really love your wife, or you just screw her and have kids?"

Helen couldn't see Aguilera's face, but she saw the muscles tighten on the sides of his cheeks.

Carl said, "You want another kick in the head?"

"I love my wife. And my children."

"Good start. You're not all bad. Maybe there's hope. You ever beat your wife, the kids?"

"Why are you asking me all these dumb questions?"

"Gotta talk about something. You tell me the time, we'll stop. You ever beat your wife?"

Aguilera took a deep breath. Helen knew he was weighing the indignity of answering Carl's questions against the pain of another kick in the head.

"I do not beat my wife."

"Tell me something, Rubi. I mean, seriously. I really want to know. No disrespect intended. How can a man with three kids of his own blow up a school bus?"

"I never blew up a school bus."

"September, nineteen ninety-two, Calle Bolivar, San Isidro, four kids died. An accomplice, worked over by FARC, gave your name. The bomb had the same characteristics—RDX, remote antenna, electronic detonator—as the one in that Mercedes."

"You know everything."

"Answer my question. How do you do it?"

"It's my job."

"Oh, it's gotta be more complicated than that, Rubi.

Who d'you hate? You gotta hate someone a lot to do that. Would you agree? Have I got it wrong?"

"Hate has nothing to do with it."

"You're just an evil bastard, and that's all there is to it, you telling me that?"

"What's evil?"

"You tell me. You're an expert. The devil's friend, remember?"

Aguilera sighed.

"You want another kick in the head?"

"I don't know what evil is."

"You know what good is?"

"I don't know that either. Why don't you stop asking questions? Marriage. Kids. Evil. Good. That's all idiots like you ever think about."

"What do geniuses like you think about?"

"How come you do all the talking? Your partner doesn't have anything to say?"

"Do you have anything you'd like to add to this, Helen?"

Before Helen could answer, Carl's eye caught a sudden movement on Blossom's darkened front porch.

Not wanting to alert Aguilera, Carl concealed his concern, but shifted his position on the grass to give him a better line of vision to the porch. In a moment, he saw the movement again, and this time he picked out the shape of someone in short pants and a white T-shirt. He was sure, beyond a doubt, that it was Samantha.

Why was Samantha on the porch? Had something gone wrong in the limousine? Where was Gus? If the bomb went off while she was on the porch she wouldn't have a chance.

As the questions rocketed through Carl's mind, he saw the figure move again—definitely Samantha. She opened the front door, reentered the house, and closed the door.

What should he do? What if someone in the Trade Commission had seen her? He studied the commission windows and saw movement. Someone was still there. How could they have missed seeing her? Would they go to the house, try to get in?

Helen and Aguilera stopped talking. The only sound was the distant hum of traffic beyond the security perimeter. From his position on the lawn, Carl could not keep both Blossom and the Trade Commission in his vision at the same time. He studied the commission for movement, ranged his eyes across the lawn and the street, and studied Blossom. Everything was still. He said, "Do you have something to tell me, Rubi?"

"If you mean the time, I couldn't tell you if I wanted to. I don't know."

"If you don't know, no one knows."

Rubi shrugged, but there was an uncertainty in the shrug that hadn't been there before. He said, "What time is it?"

Carl said, "Why do you care what time it is? If you don't know anything, why do you care?"

Rubi jerked his head and twisted his upper body.

"Just tell me the time. What's wrong with telling me the time?"

"It's getting close, isn't it, Rubi? You can feel it, right? Tell me, Rubi. It's not worth dying for."

Rubi took a deep breath, lifted his chin, and fixed his eyes on Carl.

Carl nodded at him, slowly. "If you tell me right now,

Rubi, I'll let the sentencing judge know how you saved all our lives. Maybe he'll give you a deal, knock off a few years."

From the corner of his eye, barely within his vision, Carl saw something move at the side of Blossom. Carl turned his head and glued his eyes to the spot. It moved again, toward the back of the house, then stopped, motionless.

Carl glanced quickly at the commission. Someone came halfway into the window and withdrew. He looked back at Blossom. The figure took slow steps toward the front of the house, staying close to the side of the building.

Which was the bigger threat—the bomb or the man creeping toward the front of Blossom?

Carl stood and said to Helen, "I'll be right back. You get outta here."

"Where are you going?"

Aguilera looked sharply from Carl to Helen, back to Carl. It was the first time Carl had seen on Aguilera's face anything resembling fear.

Carl said to Helen, "Get out. Go back."

Aguilera pulled at the cuffs and said, "Where're you going?"

"Tell me now, Aguilera. What time?"

"Where are you going?"

Carl thought, He's scared to death—it's going soon. He looked at his watch. "The time right now is five past one. What time is it going?"

Rubi's eyes were black balls of fear.

Carl gave him five seconds, and said to Helen, "Go back. Run."

Then he walked rapidly across the lawn to the street, crossed to the front of Blossom, and removed the Walther from his waistband. He heard Aguilera's panicked voice shouting, "Come back!"

Carl edged through the shadows at the side of Blossom, heading toward the back entrance, searching through the darkness for the man he'd seen from the lawn.

Gus awoke with a cramp in his back. He'd slept for an hour, knocked out by exhaustion, and was still too tired to think.

"Hi! Have a good nap?"

Samantha. Thirteen-year-olds were never tired.

"Well, a nap, anyway."

She said, "I have something to tell you."

Attempted rape and homicide—could there be more?

"Promise you won't be mad."

"I won't be mad." *No more, no more.*

"When you were sleeping I had to go to the bathroom, and while I was out of the car I took a walk—"

A walk. His head snapped around to look at her. Was she joking?

"—and I saw some people outside."

"People?"

"Yeah. Three people on the lawn."

"Where?"

"Across the street."

"Where were you?"

"On the porch."

The porch!

"What were you doing on the porch?"

"I just went out to get some air."

He couldn't believe it. To get some air. Just like that.

"Did they see you?"

"I don't think so."

"What were they doing?"

"Just sitting there."

"And then you came back inside, and they didn't see you?"

"Yeah, right. You're mad, aren't you?"

"No, Samantha, I'm not mad, but you shouldn't have done that. If the bomb had gone off while you were out there it would have been very, very bad."

"I saw the station wagon and—"

"You went up to the Mercedes?"

"Of *course* not. You think I'm crazy? I just looked at it from the porch."

Was this real? Who had she seen?

Gus said, "Wait here. Don't move."

"Where are you going?"

"Samantha, I mean it. Don't leave this car."

"I won't. Are you going outside?"

"Don't even open the door."

"I won't. I promise."

He left the garage and hurried to the back vestibule off the kitchen. He wanted to know who those people were on the lawn, but he did not want to show himself at the front of the house. If someone had seen Samantha, they might be watching the porch.

He cracked open the back door and slipped out into the darkness. Standing in the narrow corridor between the house and a row of hedges, he heard a distant siren. Through the hedges, across the street, he could see the outline of the Colombian Trade Commission's roof. He could not see the front lawn where Samantha had said the three people were sitting.

He moved slowly toward the front of the house. When

he could make out the lawn across the street, he saw the people, two dim figures crouching in the shadows next to a tree. Samantha had said three. Maybe she'd made a mistake. Or maybe the third was hidden behind the tree. It didn't matter. He decided to return to the limo and call Carl at the command truck.

He was halfway back to the kitchen door when he heard a noise ahead of him and dropped silently to the ground. He lay still, holding his breath, his face pushed to the dirt. When he raised his eyes, he saw the dark outline of a man pressed against the wall, inching his way toward the back of the house.

Gus had left the back door unlocked. All the man had to do was walk into the house, go to the garage, and that would be the end of Samantha.

He thought of the Uzis in the cabinet next to the board where he'd found the door key, and wished he'd had the sense to bring one with him. Certainly the man himself would be armed. Gus would have to tackle him and hope for the best. He had the advantage of surprise, and no matter what happened—even if he died doing it—he had to keep the man away from Samantha.

The man continued slowly along the wall toward the back corner by the kitchen. Gus bolted, sacrificing silence for speed. He'd try to hit the man hard from behind, grab his throat, drive his fingers into the windpipe, hang on as they fell, choke the breath out of him until there was no more struggle.

Gus was six feet away, moving with increasing speed and noise, when the man wheeled in the darkness and raised an arm. In the exploding flash from the muzzle of a pistol, Gus caught the image of Carl's face.

* * *

"Max!"

Iverson took a step toward the TV monitor showing the Trade Commission's rear door. "What is it?"

"Hang on."

The agent at the monitor rewound a tape, studying the monitor, fingers poised to hit the stop and replay buttons.

An image flashed backwards. The agent reversed tape. On the monitor, two men burst from the Trade Commission door, took two quick steps, and disappeared from the image.

"They came out running."

Iverson said, "So would you. They say anything?"

"They were screaming at each other, just before they hit the back door, when they were still upstairs. I heard 'ten minutes.' And then the other one said something I couldn't get."

Iverson glanced at a clock over the monitor.

One thirty-five. If they gave themselves ten minutes, that's one forty-five. Plenty of time.

Iverson called the limousine.

A girl answered. Wrong number. He said, "I'm sorry," and was about to hang up and call again. Then he said, "Excuse me. Is this the number for Judge Parham?"

That sounded stupid. Like Parham lives in a car.

"This is his daughter. May I help you?"

"Samantha?"

"Yes. Who's calling, please?"

"Where is Judge Parham?"

"Who is this, please?"

"It's Special Agent Iverson of the FBI. Where is the judge?"

"I don't know. He left for a moment. If you'd like to leave a number I'll have him call you when he returns."

About to get blown up, and she sounds like an answering machine.

"Where did he leave for?"

"I don't know. I think he just wanted to look around."

Parham gets bored and goes for a stroll in the garden? Car bombs don't hold his attention?

"Would you tell him to call me immediately? Would you do that?"

"Sure. Special Agent Iverson. How do you spell that?"

"I . . . V . . . Never mind. Just tell him to call the command truck. Carl's number."

"Okay. Thank you."

Iverson hung up and yelled, "Where's Falco?"

No one answered.

A voice boomed from a speaker: "In the truck!" An agent at Baker post.

Iverson yelled, "Go!"

"Two subjects exiting the area, a hundred yards from the Trade Commission, Daine Street, and they are *moving*, southwest, running like hell."

Iverson said, "Buckley?"

Three consoles down the row, an agent wearing a telephone headset talked into his mouthpiece. "Captain, this is Buckley in the truck. Two Latin males on Daine Street, running southwest, two blocks from the Trade Commission. Please detain?"

Iverson shouted, "Baker post! The three subjects on the lawn?"

"Still there. No activity."

"If you—"

"Now they're moving. Number two walking fast toward Blossom. Number one still at the tree. Female approaching number one."

Buckley, still on the phone, shouted, "PD has two Latin males in custody on Daine Street!"

"Come back! Come back!" Aguilera stopped screaming at Carl and turned angrily to Helen. "Get him!" He yanked desperately at the handcuffs. "Make him come back!"

Helen stood, taking care to stay out of kicking range of Aguilera's feet.

"Is it going to go off?"

"It's a bomb, you stupid bitch. Get him back here, get these cuffs off. Run! Go!"

Go was just what Helen wanted to do. If the wild behavior of Aguilera was any indication, the bomb was ready to explode in seconds. But Carl was still here—or at least headed for the house—and so were Gus and Samantha, not to mention Aguilera.

"Get these cuffs off!"

Aguilera was raving now.

"I can't. I don't have the key."

The soft, unhurried tone of her voice astonished her. With a steady authority that seemed not her own, she said, "I don't have the keys. All you can do is wait for Carl."

Aguilera screamed at the Trade Commission windows, shaking his cuffs, flailing his legs to get the attention of anyone inside.

But all movement on the other side of the windows had stopped.

"They've gone! The bastard cowards have gone! Come back! Bastards!"

He dropped to his knees beside the tree. His cheek pressing hard against the bark, he hugged the trunk as if fearful it would fly from the earth.

Helen heard an explosion. Aguilera looked up and froze.

She said, "What was that?"

"I hope he's dead."

"What was it?"

"You're friend's been shot."

Helen ran for the house.

Samantha heard an explosion, muffled by the thickness of the garage walls, and thought for sure the bomb had gone off. Obedient to the instructions of numerous flight attendants, she put her head between her knees and waited for something terrible to happen. The sound faded, silence returned, and in the continuing stillness she raised her head. She was still alive.

What had happened? Maybe the bomb had gone off, but it wasn't as powerful as everyone had thought. Or maybe the explosion was a gunshot. Maybe Gus had been shot.

She didn't know what to do. She had promised Gus not to leave the limo, and she knew she should stay where she was. If everything was okay someone would come to get her. If not—well, she'd still better stay where she was.

After five minutes, fear and curiosity were getting the best of her. How long should she sit here, waiting for she didn't know what? Where was Gus? What if he'd been killed? She didn't want to think about that. She picked up the telephone, but the only number she remembered was the hotel they'd stayed at in Saint-Tropez.

She opened the limo door and had one foot on the floor of the garage when she heard a voice scream her name.

"Samantha!"

The garage door flew open and before she could think, Carl had her by the hand, pushing her back into the limo. Gus, covered with dirt and mud, ran around the limo and jumped in behind the wheel.

Samantha said, "What happened? Did the bomb go off? I thought you'd been shot."

Carl yelled "Stay in the limo!", slammed Samantha's door, and ran from the garage.

Gus said, "It's okay, Samantha. No one's hurt."

Iverson, watching the clock, called the limo again. One thirty-seven. Eight minutes to go. Maybe the judge was back, hadn't called.

Parham answered, out of breath.

"Judge Parham? This is Special Agent Iverson in the command truck." He'd never spoken to Parham before.

"What is it?"

"We don't have much time, sir. Colombian agents in the Trade Commission have left the building. We figure you've got about seven minutes before the bomb goes. We'd like you to drive out. If you—"

"Drive out?"

The phone was losing power.

"Yes, sir. We'd like you to open the garage doors."

"Excuse me. You're breaking up. I can't hear you."

"The garage doors. We want you to open the doors and drive out. You should—Can you hear me?"

"Just barely."

"When you get to the street, make a left. We're removing all police barriers as far as the traffic circle. Drive as fast as possible. Can you hear me?"

"You're coming and going. It's very faint."

"Open the garage doors and drive out. You've got about six minutes. Do you hear me?"

Iverson waited. There was no answer.

"Do you hear me?"

He listened, shook his head, and hung up.

When Michelle, shoved against the wall of the command truck by the crush of agents, engineers, and technicians, heard Iverson tell Gus on the phone, "You've got about six minutes," she slipped quickly out into the night air.

Earlier that night she'd walked into the Winnebago and seen Terry's orange coveralls neatly folded on the conference table. She hurried back there now. The coveralls were still there. She put her hand on them, and the thoughts came faster and faster. Had Gus heard Iverson, did he know he was supposed to drive out? They had time to drive out, to get away—if they knew, if they'd heard Iverson, if someone told them.

By now there'd be five minutes left. Plenty of time, if she rushed. She could get to Blossom, running, in a minute. Get down to the garage, the limo, tell Gus to drive out, and come out with them.

She heard a noise and turned.

"Oh, hi, Mrs. Parham."

"Hi, Terry."

Their eyes met.

Terry said, "Those are my coveralls."

"I know."

"They wouldn't fit."

"Terry, I—I don't have very long."

"About four minutes would be my guess."

"Please."

Terry turned. "I wasn't here."

Michelle grabbed the coveralls, sat on the floor, and yanked until she had them on. The cuffs, unrolled, barely reached her ankles. But she was in them, and the ATF-EOD initials were flat and visible on her back.

She pulled up the hood, tucked in her hair, and jogged to the police barrier blocking the street to Blossom.

As she passed the cops, maneuvering around the barrier, she waved a hand and kept going, praying they wouldn't call her back.

Five steps past the barrier, she knew she'd made it.

She speeded up, running as fast as she could in the tight coveralls, sprinting for Blossom. She was still a block away, out of breath, when a woman came charging toward her. The woman—short blonde hair, gold bracelets jangling—stopped, struggling for air. "Come . . . Run . . ." She took Michelle's arm, fighting, not letting go, pulling her back toward the command truck.

Samantha said, "What did he say? He called before, while you were out. Where were you?"

"We're getting out of here, Samantha."

Gus hunted in the dark of the front seat for the garage door opener. He flipped on the dash light. A dim glow. He found the opener on top of the dash. He extinguished the dash light and pushed the red button.

Nothing happened.

Samantha leaned over from the back seat.

Gus pressed the button again.

The garage door lurched upward, then jolted to a stop three feet from the floor.

Gus pressed the button.

Another lurch, in the other direction. The door banged closed.

He pressed the button.

The door clanged open two feet—and stopped.

Samantha said, "Try it again."

This time the door jammed about three feet from the top. Gus wasn't sure the limo could make it under the door, and he didn't have time to get out and measure.

"Can we make it through there, Samantha?"

She stared out from the back seat, squinting.

"I don't know. What do you think?"

"I think we don't have a choice. Get down on the floor. Flat as you can."

Gus gripped the ignition key, still in the lock, and turned.

The starter groaned. Groaned again. Stopped.

He turned the key back to the off position.

Samantha lifted her head. "It's not starting."

Carl left Gus and Samantha in the garage and raced back to the street, looking for Helen. He almost knocked her down. "Where the hell are you going?"

"Looking for you."

He grabbed her arm. "Run!"

"Where are the judge and Samantha?"

"Leaving in the limo. Run!"

"What about Aguilera?"

"Run!"

Carl sprinted fifty feet with Helen, then slowed, dropped a step behind, and headed back for the lawn. Aguilera stood by the tree, still as a statue, looking at him, watching him approach.

Gus gripped the ignition key and, as if the determination in his fingers could make a difference, gave it a hard, decisive snap into the start position.

Groan. Grind.

He pumped the accelerator.

The engine roared.

He flipped on the headlights. The garage door was too low.

He yelled, "Get flat and brace yourself. We're gonna hit the door."

He put the shift in neutral, raced the engine, gripped the wheel, slid down in the seat belt until he could barely see over the dash, and slipped the shift into first.

He shot forward with the impact, felt the seat belt tighten across his body, and heard a metal-against-metal crash that sounded like the end of the world. A blast of glass pellets struck his face and chest.

The car had made it through the door and stopped in the turning circle. The windshield was gone, glass pellets like hailstones blanketed the hood, dash, and front seat. The chrome around the top of the windshield was bent back and the front half of the roof was crushed to the level of the window tops.

He yelled, "Are you okay?"

"Are we out? Can I get up?"

"Stay down!"

He pulled himself up straight, got the limo heading toward the driveway, and hit the accelerator. He skidded into a left turn and roared up the block, glass pellets flying at him across the hood.

Red police lights flashed three blocks ahead.

Gus tore through the intersection, gaining speed, made the next intersection, and headed for a wooden police barricade. Two cops dragged it out of his path and dived for the curb. Gus flashed by them, hit the brakes, spun the wheel, and tried to aim the limousine into the traffic circle at the end of the street.

The limo rammed the curb, lifted, rotated a quarter turn, hurtled over the grass, and came down on the hood of an empty police cruiser.

For a moment, suddenly silent and motionless in the flashing red glow of police lights, the limo perched on the cruiser. A cop aimed a flashlight into the front seat. All Gus could see was glass pellets and blood—on his lap, his hands, his arms, the steering wheel.

The cop holding the light screamed "Ambulance!" and put out his hand for the door handle.

Reaching into his pocket for a cuff key, Carl raced for the tree. Still ten yards away, with the key in his fingers, Carl saw Aguilera's face, the tree, the grass, the front of the Trade Commission, go suddenly white as burning phosphorus. Something hit him from behind and his body smashed facedown onto the earth, flattening beneath a rolling weight of wind and fire.

A blinding white flash filled the night sky. A giant fist punched the side of the limo. Something clutched the roof, lifted the car, shook it, and slammed it down. The roar of a thousand oceans filled Gus's ears.

"Samantha!"

25

Samantha arranged herself in the leather chair, clasped her hands in her lap, looked up at the fourteen senators facing her, and smiled. She was surrounded by a forest of TV cameras and still photographers.

It was eight days since the explosion. She and Gus and Michelle had moved back to the rented house in Virginia. Carl was dead. The man who'd put the bomb in the Mercedes—Samantha couldn't even pronounce his name, Ag-something—he was dead. Gus was bruises and cuts and scratches from head to foot. Michelle had been in the street, two blocks from the Mercedes, against a curb, pushed up next to another woman, Helen someone. It was a miracle, as if the blast had washed right over them. Emotionally, Michelle was a wreck. Once she found out Gus and Samantha were safe, she went hysterical over Carl. All she could talk about was Esther and their two children. As for Samantha herself, with bruises everywhere, she looked as if she'd spent an hour in a washing machine on spin-dry.

But she was here. Phil Rothman sat beside her at the witness table, and behind her the front row of spectators was filled with family and friends. Gus and Michelle were there, small bandages covering face cuts. They had agreed to let Samantha testify.

Michelle's father, Bob, who had flown to Washington with his wife and sons the first day of the car bomb, sat next to her—crew-cut, white-socks, friendly but powerful, a bear in a blazer. Her mother, next in line, tiny hand smothered in her husband's paw, was beautiful, the clear eyes and angled features whispering dignity. Beside her were Michelle's two younger brothers, in their late twenties now, ranchers, brown and weathered. Carl's widow, Esther, was there with the children, Paul and Ali. Next to them, an arm resting lightly along the back of Esther's chair, was Helen Bondell. Gus's mother, recovering from her husband's suicide (and making no bones about what she regarded as Gus's role in provoking it), was at a friend's home in Palm Beach. Gus had telephoned Larry Young in London and assured him that except for minor cuts and bruises Samantha was unharmed. Larry didn't say anything about a trip to the States to pick her up, and Gus didn't think it was a good time to raise the subject. From Doreen came nothing but silence, a blessing that seemed—correctly, as it turned out—too good to be true.

A man moved the microphone closer to Samantha's

lips. She touched it and it let out a loud hum. The man moved it back and asked her not to touch it. She said, "I'm sorry."

She wriggled in the chair, trying to avoid a lump that was sticking her in the back, and in the process leaned close to the microphone. She pulled back, as from a snake's head, and said, "Sorry."

She took a deep breath and smiled again. She felt she was making too much trouble.

Several of the senators looked at her and smiled. The chairman was Eric Taeger, old and white-haired, his harsh impatience already evident in the way he pushed the papers around on his desk. Mr. Rothman had told her, "Answer his questions, but don't be frightened. Two minutes after this starts, he's going to be more scared of you than you are of him."

Senator Taeger looked at her and said, "We're glad to have you with us, Miss Young, and we hope that despite everything you've been through you won't find this too difficult."

"Oh, that's okay," she said. "I'm fine."

He looked to the side. "Would you swear the witness, please?"

Taeger had not wanted Samantha to give sworn testimony ("She's too young to know what it means, and too young to be tried for perjury if she lies"), but Gus's supporters on the committee had insisted, knowing sworn testimony would have greater impact.

Someone offered her a Bible, and she put her hand on it.

"That's a nice Bible," she said.

"Do you solemnly swear . . ."

She said, "I do," and took her hand back. "I feel like I just got married."

"I beg your pardon?"

"Nothing. I'm sorry."

Taeger said, "Can we adjust the microphone, please? We're having trouble hearing the witness. Thank you."

Philip Rothman was exhausted. In the eight days since the bomb went off, he'd led a twenty-four-hour-a-day war to get the Judiciary Committee to resume the hearing quickly and allow Samantha's testimony. The White House and its congressional allies had pleaded fairness: Gus had been smeared by horrifying accusations made against his daughter—that she had been raised in a whorehouse, actually worked there. Surely Judge Parham and Samantha deserved the right to explain, to give the other side. The news media, foreseeing the drama, added its voice to demands that she be allowed to testify.

Rothman knew—and the ferocity of the opposition's resistance made it clear that they knew too—that if Samantha took the stand while public sympathy for her was still high, and if the committee vote and the floor vote came before the emotional response to her appearance had had time to cool, Gus's seat on the Supreme Court was assured. How could the opposition stand against the innocent candor of a bright, pretty thirteen-year-old girl who had just escaped from a drug trafficker's car bomb?

During the last two days, opposition to her testimony had abruptly declined, as Rothman had guessed it would. A week ago, the day after the explosion, Rothman had spoken with Samantha's doctor. She was not seriously injured, but she was exhausted. "Emotionally, she's been through a war.

She'll need a lot of rest. She's on the edge. Anything more, you could have a breakdown."

Four days after that conversation, Rothman had walked into the office of Peter Rexroth, the White House intelligence coordinator.

"Peter, I need a little favor. Confidential, to say the least."

"It all is." Rexroth was a former CIA officer.

"How long would it take to get me a voice distortion device and a non-pub phone number?"

Rexroth opened a drawer in his desk, withdrew a disk of transparent plastic resembling an orthodontic retainer, and handed it to Rothman. "The number will take about ten minutes. What's the listing?"

"Warren Gier. His home."

Senator Taeger put his forearms on the desk, leaned toward Samantha, and gave her the most unsuccessful smile she had ever seen, warm and sympathetic as a knife edge.

Then he dropped the smile—Samantha thought she could hear it hit the floor—and said, "Well, young lady, you've had quite a stressful adventure, and we don't want to add to your distress here. Some of us, however, do have one or two questions you could help us with."

"Okay." She nodded, smiling.

"Before we get to your recent relationship with Judge Parham—"

"He's my father."

"—we'd like to get a little of your background. You were born and brought up in Milwaukee by a Mrs. Doreen Young, is that correct?"

"I was adopted by the Youngs."

"Why were you adopted?"

"They wanted a child."

A tiny ripple of laughter rolled gently through the hearing room.

"I mean, how did you come to be adopted?"

"My mother couldn't keep me, so she put me up for adoption."

"And why couldn't she keep you?"

"I think . . . Well . . . You could ask my mother. She's right here. She'd know."

Another ripple. Along the row of committee members, half smiled and half did not.

"You never saw your real mother until—"

"My biological mother. My legal mother was Mrs. Young."

"Thank you for correcting me. You anticipated my question. You never saw your biological mother until a few weeks ago, is that correct?"

"I saw her for the first time nine weeks and two days ago, at eleven-thirty in the morning, at the airport in Nice, France."

"You have a good recollection of it."

"Yes, sir. It was the most important day of my life. My father was there too. Judge Parham."

Rothman had his elbows on the table, his chin in his hands, his eyes fixed on Taeger. Things were not going well for the chairman. Things rarely went well for seventy-six-year-old men jousting with thirteen-year-old girls. Guile is never a match for innocence.

* * *

Gus was glowing, literally. He could feel the blood warming his face. Samantha was so beautiful. Michelle and she had spent half of yesterday shopping, picking out a dress "suitable for the Judiciary Committee." They'd picked something dark blue with a white collar, simple but elegant, youthful but dignified. Gus had never seen anyone so beautiful as Samantha at this moment, so natural, so relaxed. Could you believe it? She was having *fun.*

Taeger said, "You've been following the various media reports about your situation?"

"Well, we weren't allowed to use the TV in the limousine, and then afterwards I was in the hospital for a couple of days."

"And they found that everything's okay?"

"Oh, yes. I'm very healthy."

"Good. Before you were in the limousine, did you follow the media reports?"

"A little. I'm not sure what you mean."

"Well, did you read or hear that when your mother told your father she was pregnant that he urged her to have an abortion?"

Rothman was on his feet.

"Mr. Chairman—"

"Please sit down, Mr. Rothman. These are necessary questions. I would remind you that it was not I who insisted that Miss Young testify. If you want her to testify, then you will have to allow us to ask questions."

"Appropriate questions."

"If I feel I need your assistance in determining what is appropriate, I will call on you. Meanwhile, please sit down."

* * *

Rothman sat. Nothing so far had surprised him. Taeger's questions had been anticipated. Rothman's job was to exploit the questions as best he could and let the simplicity of Samantha's answers win points for Gus. Later, when Taeger really got down to the dirt, Rothman's payoff would come.

"Miss Young, did you hear the question?"

"Yes, sir."

"Would you answer, please?"

"I heard that on the TV."

"That . . ."

"That my father had wanted my mother to end the pregnancy."

"How did that make you feel?"

Rothman was up.

"Mr. Chairman, may I remind you, sir, that you are talking to the thirteen-year-old daughter of a nominee for the Supreme Court? It's difficult to see how the intent of this hearing is furthered by humiliating, hurtful, and unnecessary questions."

"Sit down, Mr. Rothman."

Rothman lowered himself slowly into the chair.

"Can you answer the question please, Miss Young?"

"How did it make me feel? It didn't make me feel at all. I mean, I don't even know if it's true. I know my mother and father love me. I know that, for sure. And anyway, I wasn't aborted, was I? I mean—here I am."

That drew a couple of claps from the spectator section.

Taeger said, "I would ask the spectators to please remain silent. If there are further disturbances I will have the room cleared." Looking at Samantha, he said, "Do you think your father wanted to have you aborted, as appears to be the case from various documents that—"

"Mr. Chairman—" Rothman was up again, allowing his anger to appear suppressed beneath a tone of supplication. "We have had no testimony regarding these so-called documents. They are nothing but media hearsay and—"

"Mr. Rothman, I am trying to be as patient as possible, but you cannot be allowed to continue to disrupt this committee's questions. Please sit down."

Rothman did as he was told.

"Miss Young, do you think your father wanted to have you aborted, as appears to be the case from various documents that have been disclosed?"

"I don't know."

"Have you seen the documents?"

"No, sir."

"Have you heard of them?"

"Yes, sir."

Taeger shuffled some papers, found the one he was looking for, and adjusted his glasses.

Rothman stood. "Mr. Chairman, if you are going to read from documents produced by the news media, I have to—"

"Mr. Rothman, *please*—I have read from nothing."

"You are about to."

"Why don't you wait to launch your attack until I begin?"

Rothman lowered himself into his chair, slowly, his eyes not leaving Taeger.

"Miss Young, at the risk of driving your advisor into a cataleptic rage, I must ask you if you are aware of allegations that when your mother was pregnant—with you, I mean—she and your father met with a counselor, and that your mother told the counselor that your father had urged her to have an abortion?"

"Mr. Chair—"

"*Sit down!* Miss Young, are you aware of that?"

"No."

"Well, as you hear it now, what is your reaction?"

"I don't think it's a very nice question to ask someone."

"Thank you for your opinion of the question. I appreciate that, and I think I tend to agree with you. It's not a nice question. But it is, unfortunately, a necessary question. What is your answer?"

"That was my answer. You asked for my reaction. My reaction is that it's not a very nice question to ask."

"Do you think your father wanted your mother to have an abortion?"

"No."

"Why do you say that?"

"I'm here."

"I didn't ask if she had an abortion. We know, and we are delighted, that she did not. But I asked if you think your father wanted her to have one. That's what your mother told the counselor."

"I don't know that."

"You don't know that?"

"No."

"Why?"

"You said that's what a document said a counselor said that my mother said my father said. I don't really know who said what."

"Miss Young—"

"I wasn't there."

Rothman smiled and stayed in his chair.

"I understand that. But you have no opinion concerning your father's alleged statement to your mother that she should have an abortion?"

"I don't even know that my mother ever said he said that, or that anyone else ever said that my mother said that he said that."

"So if—"

Samantha's face went a shade pinker than it had been, and she shifted in her chair, sitting up straight and squaring her shoulders toward the row of senators. She seemed to have awakened to something.

"But I do know something else. I know that my father would never have had me aborted. My father loves me very much. He has always loved me. I may not have known him very long, but I know him real well now. When you spend two days with someone in the back seat of a car you think's going to blow up, you get to know them. My father is a wonderful man. He is brave and he loves me and he loves my mother. And about the abortion, or anything like that—well, here I am. So you make up your own mind."

She had tears in her eyes. The room was dead silent. Taeger remained motionless, didn't even blink.

Then the audience exploded into applause.

Had Taeger not had the good sense to forget his threat to clear the room, there would probably have been a riot. He waited for the applause to subside, allowed another five seconds to pass, and said, "Miss Young, perhaps you could tell us something about your youth. Can you fill us in a bit on your youth?"

"Well, I think I'm still in it."

The audience laughed.

"Let's start when you were living in Milwaukee."

"Well, I was born in Milwaukee. And then I was adopted, and I lived with my adoptive parents, who are named Mr. and Mrs. Young. You know that."

"Yes, and what was it like living with them?"

"I think you probably mean the part about the prostitution."

"Was there prostitution?"

Taeger tried to appear shocked, but didn't get far. The news media had had the story days ago.

"My adoptive mother had teenage girls living in the house, and they invited other girls over, and men came and had sex with them for money."

The tears were gone, and her voice, now solid and businesslike, let everyone know that she was not going to be shamed or intimidated by events she had had no control over.

"And you were living there?"

"I was living with my adoptive parents, and that's where they lived."

"Your father lived there too?"

"Sort of. He was out working a lot. He's a pianist, and he was working in hotels and bars. And he drank."

"He drank a lot, didn't he?"

"I think so."

The hearing room had returned to a hushed attention, the print reporters scribbling furiously. The only sounds were Samantha's and Taeger's voices and the *clunk clunk clunk* of motorized still cameras.

"And what did you do, when you were home and the girls were there?"

"I helped."

"You helped? How did you help?"

"Welcoming people and serving drinks. I thought they were all friends of my mother's, my adoptive mother's, that they were guests, so I took their coats and got them drinks."

"And that was all you did?"

"There wasn't anything else for me to do."

"How old were you?"

"About six to eight."

"And then you left home with your father?"

"Yes."

"It sounds, Samantha, as if up to this point, at least, you had not had a very happy time."

"It was okay."

"If Judge Parham, your father, had known about the life you were living, do you think he would have approved?"

"Of course not."

"He wouldn't have wanted you living in a place like that?"

"No."

"Any parent whose conduct was such that their child ended up in a place like that wouldn't be a very responsible person, would you say that?"

"You're trying to say that my father wasn't responsible."

"I didn't say that, Miss Young."

"My father had nothing to do with where I was living. He didn't want me to be adopted in the first place."

"How do you know that?"

"Because I know him. He loves me."

"Did your mother want you to be adopted?"

"Of course not."

"She loves you too?"

"Yes, she does."

"So how did you end up with the Youngs and living in a brothel with prostitutes?"

"I don't know, but it wasn't my mother or father who did it."

"Your father didn't want you adopted, you said that."

"Yes."

"And he didn't want you aborted."

"He loves me."

"So what happened? How did you get adopted? How did you end up living with prostitutes? Who did it?"

"Mr. Chairman—"

Rothman, on his feet, had stepped around the witness table and appeared ready to charge the dais.

"—there are limits, and they have been passed, as to what—"

Samantha ignored him. She said, "Bad people did it."

Taeger said, "But not your father."

"*Mr. Chairman*—"

"No! My father is not a bad person. My father is *great.*"

"Mr. Chairman—"

"This hearing is in recess until two o'clock this afternoon."

Taeger banged his gavel, rose, and walked out of the room.

Gus and Michelle flew at Samantha. Photographers and TV cameramen fought to get near them. Reporters, fingers stuck in their ears against the pandemonium, screamed into telephones.

In the midst of it, a smiling Rothman relaxed at the witness table, an island of sweet stillness in the storm. It was going better than he had hoped, and the best was yet to come.

* * *

At ten past two, they were back. During the two-hour recess, CNN, ABC, NBC, and CBS had canceled other programming and carried replays of Samantha's testimony. Rothman and Dutweiler raced from microphone to microphone arguing the White House position against opposition senators and pundits.

In almost every interview, Rothman was asked about a growing rumor that the opposition had a secret last-minute disclosure that would blow Gus and Samantha out of the water. He laughed. "Gus and Michelle and Samantha are what they are. There are no secrets. Totally transparent. The opposition's problem is that when they see Samantha testify they're seeing truth, and they're not used to it. It blinds them."

Taeger said, "Miss Young, good afternoon."

"Good afternoon."

"Senator Kostner?"

You could almost hear the groans. Everyone had been expecting round two of the Taeger-Samantha match, and now Taeger was passing the microphone to another senator, one friendly to Gus's nomination.

Kostner asked a few innocuous questions and passed to the next senator. As the turn moved from senator to senator it became clear that Gus's supporters wanted to say nothing that might distance attention from Samantha's morning display of love and loyalty to her father. And those opposing the confirmation were not about to climb into the ring with Samantha, to cast themselves as tormentors of a thirteen-year-old girl who that morning had won the nation's heart.

So in less than half an hour, the microphone was back with the chairman, Senator Taeger.

"I think we're about to wrap this up, Samantha," he said, using her first name for the first time since early in the morning's testimony.

She smiled.

"We heard your testimony this morning about prostitution in your house in Milwaukee."

Samantha nodded.

"I'm sorry. The stenographer can't hear your nod."

"Yes. I should have said yes."

"You said, if I remember correctly, that you helped, that you welcomed customers, took their coats, served them drinks."

"Yes."

Rothman wished she had said that she didn't know they were customers, thought they were guests. Much of her morning's feistiness was gone. She looked tired.

"And they were nice to you, for doing that?"

"Yes, sir."

"You found them likable?"

"Most of them."

The shark was circling the bait. Rothman struggled to keep his expression vacant. He was not a good poker player.

"You weren't frightened of them."

"No."

"They never harmed you."

She said nothing. A slight nervous movement in her shoulders made Rothman's breathing accelerate. It had been vital that she not be prepared. She had been told nothing of what would happen. Nor had Rothman told Gus.

Rothman rose from his chair. "Mr. Chairman . . ."

"Yes, Mr. Rothman?"

Taeger's voice was perfectly calm, unthreatened and unthreatening.

Rothman said, "I think . . ."

He had to play the part. Taeger was sniffing the bait, but he hadn't yet taken it.

"Yes, Mr. Rothman?"

So calm, the voice of a man holding four aces against a pair.

"Excuse me," Rothman said, and sat down.

Taeger said, "Samantha . . ."

A fine sheen of perspiration glistened on her forehead. She said, "Yes?"

"I'm afraid now, Samantha, that I have to do something very painful. I apologize in advance to you and to your father and to your mother, and indeed to all those who have taken such a heartfelt interest in your welfare. But there is a question I must ask."

He paused, timing it, letting the tension grow.

Take it, Rothman thought. *Take it, you bastard.*

Speaking slowly, word by word, Taeger said, "Samantha, did you kill a man—"

Rothman heard gasps behind him.

"—when you were eight years old? Didn't you plunge a kitchen knife with a five-inch serrated blade into his stomach?"

Photographers lunged closer, shoving for position. Gus and Michelle were on their feet.

"And isn't it true that he lost almost a pint of blood on your kitchen floor before anyone called an ambulance, and didn't—"

Rothman turned in time to see Samantha, hands flat on the table, try to push herself upright. She was half out of the chair when her face went pale, her knees buckled, and she fell. Her right shoulder hit the table on the way down, and she ended in a heap next to the chair. Motionless, she was immediately covered by photographers. Gus and Michelle fought their way to her side, and by the time she came to, a minute later, paramedics had arrived out of nowhere with a gurney.

It was more drama than Rothman had even hoped for. Gus was in. No one could stop the confirmation now.

26

It was Rothman, of course, who insisted she go to the hospital. Whether he did this for reasons of health or politics was a question Rothman refused to answer and cynics never had to ask. Certainly it helped to cast Taeger as a child abuser. And having the ambulance in which Samantha rode (and that Rothman had arranged to have waiting at the entrance nearest the hearing room, its paramedics on standby in the hall) appear on TV screens coast to coast, with flashing lights and wailing siren, less than forty-eight hours before the full Senate confirmation vote, was applauded all over town as a stroke of political genius. Within minutes, a flood of pro-Gus phone calls, faxes, and E-mail inundated Senate offices.

Rothman admitted nothing, never told anyone that he had known nine days before Samantha's testimony that she had killed a man, and that he had spoken anonymously by phone with Warren Gier and had sent him court documents, knowing Gier would pass everything to Taeger, who would use it to try to discredit Samantha and shift public sentiment away from Gus. Certainly Taeger would think he could attack Samantha's appealing innocence—and the support that gave Gus's confirmation—by a surprise revelation that she had killed a man. And whatever Samantha's reaction might be (even if she had not collapsed in a dead faint), Rothman had intended to rush to her side, hand her over to the paramedics for a dramatic, lights-and-sirens dash to the hospital. As it happened, everything had worked even better than Rothman had dreamed it might.

In the ambulance with Gus and Michelle, Samantha could not stop crying. As they raced through traffic, the ambulance pursued by reporters and TV vans, she sobbed, "You're going to lose now. After everything. Carl's dead and—" Her head fell back onto the gurney.

Michelle held her hand and looked at Gus, who was squatting beside the gurney, holding on.

Gus said, "It's all right, Samantha. It's all right. Everything's all right."

Samantha lifted her head, eyes red, face soaked with tears.

"It's *not* all right. What's going to happen now? What's going to happen?"

"Samantha, nothing's going to happen. Everything's—"

The ambulance stopped, the back doors swung open, hands reached in for the gurney.

The George Washington University Hospital emergency room—not since the shooting of President Reagan had it achieved such notoriety—filled with correspondents and cameras, and every politician in the city marveled at the stroke of luck, or genius, that had handed this prize to the White House.

Warren Gier, in John Harrington's office watching the televised pandemonium as Samantha was wheeled into the hospital on a gurney, almost wept. "She's even better sick than she was healthy."

Freedom Federation staffers gathered with him sank deeper into sorrow as they saw their cause collapse beneath the weight of this live television drama.

Helen wasn't with them. Out of the hospital two days after the explosion, she had introduced herself to Esther Falco, who had arrived from Montgomery with her two children. Helen installed them in her apartment, trying to do what she could to relieve their grief. She told Esther about her own husband, killed in a café in Algiers, and about the similarities she had seen between him and Carl. Together, they mourned them both.

Gier said, "To lose like this. Television's supposed to be *our* thing. And the little bitch isn't even hurt. What's she doing in an ambulance? They did this on *purpose.* This whole thing is *orchestrated.*"

He watched the screen, riveted, obsessed. The gurney disappeared through a double door marked EMERGENCY.

"These guys are really milking it."

Photographers pushed toward the door, blocked by men in white coats.

Gier could hardly speak.

"Brilliant."

He breathed the word, shaking his head.

"Brilliant. Just brilliant."

Across the room, as far as he could get from Gier, sat a rumpled Isaac Jasper, obscured behind a newspaper. When the action became interesting, he raised his eyes, observed over the top of the page, then dropped his eyes back to the paper. He was reading the comics.

Larry Young took a break in the piano bar of London's Renaissance Park Hotel and walked into the lobby. He was sweltering, and he wanted a beer. He seldom drank, usually spent his breaks in his room, but tonight he had a craving for a beer. He went to the Cock and Crown Pub, a small, smoky bar at the far end of the lobby, sat at a table near the cash register, and told the waitress he'd like a Heineken.

As she walked away, he glanced at the TV over the cash register. The screen showed an ambulance and police cars with flashing red lights. He hated TV, rarely watched it, and was glad the sound was off. He had other things to think about. For the past six weeks he'd been practicing every day with a professional chamber orchestra. His hotel contract was up at the end of the month, and the orchestra had asked him to join them on a world tour. It was his first opportunity in years to return full time to the serious music that had once been his life.

He loosened his tie and watched the ambulance pull up to a hospital emergency entrance. The picture shifted to another camera, a close-up of the ambulance's back door.

Someone jostled the cameraman, and the image shook. The ambulance doors swung open. Cameramen and reporters pushed and shoved. A gurney with an IV bottle swept past. A face, eyes closed, flashed across the screen.

Larry leaped to the cash register. "Turn it up!"

The bartender, ringing up a sale, spun toward him.

"Turn it up! Turn it up!"

Men in white coats blocked the camera at a door marked EMERGENCY.

The bartender picked up a remote, touched a button.

". . . since collapsing in the hearing room, but we cannot be certain at this moment exactly what—Robert do you have something for us? Let's go to Robert Allman at the Senate hearing room."

The picture remained the same, but the voice changed.

"Yes, John, we've just been told that the moment Samantha was asked if she had killed a man, the paramedics were already positioned outside a side door of the hearing room. Whether this means that there was some expectation of her reaction, we can't—"

Larry was out the door, headed for his room and a telephone.

In the hospital they gave her an injection, took blood and urine samples.

She slept.

At 7:30 that night the phone by the bed rang and Gus picked it up.

"Judge Parham?"

"Yes."

"This is Fred Knight at Blossom, sir." Knight and a small security detail were camping out in the rubble of Blossom, which had lost half its roof and most of the front wall. "We have a phone call for you from Larry Young in London. I wasn't sure you'd want to take it right now, but he's very insistent. Should I patch it over, or—"

"Yes, definitely. I'll take it."

"Just a second, please."

"Hello?"

"Larry? This is Gus."

"What's happening? How is Samantha? What's going on?"

He was talking fast, distressed, angry. Gus glanced at Michelle.

"Samantha's fine, Larry. We—"

"I saw her on TV, in an ambulance. It said something about she killed a man. I told Carl, but I didn't think you guys would give it to people to ask her on TV. What's happening? Why isn't—"

"Larry, calm down. Let me explain. I thought Phil Rothman had been talking to you."

"What happened?"

"She was testifying at the hearing and someone asked her if she had killed someone. She—"

"Why did they ask her that? How did they know? Who told them? What—"

"Larry, let me finish. The chairman of the committee asked her if she had killed a man and—well, obviously it was very upsetting. She fainted. People thought that for her welfare, to be sure she was okay, she ought to go to the hospital and get checked. So that's where she is, and she's sleeping and all the tests say she's fine."

A long pause. Gus could hear Larry breathing.

"Larry—"

"I want to talk to Samantha."

"She's asleep. She's been sedated. I don't think the doctors would want us to wake her up."

"No, I don't want you to do that. Don't wake her."

"Michelle's here. Do you want to talk to Michelle?"

"I don't want to talk to anyone. I want to talk to Samantha. When will Samantha be awake?"

"I don't know. Probably not before the morning."

Gus could almost hear the turmoil in Larry's brain. He said, "What are you going to do? Are you coming over?"

"I don't know. I have to think. I don't know what I'm going to do. I want to talk to her. I'll call back."

He hung up.

Michelle said, "What did he say?"

Gus told her. "He's very upset. Maybe he'll call back. If not, I'll call him, see what—I don't know. See what his plans are."

Gus and Michelle stayed with Samantha overnight, and through Tuesday and Tuesday night, resting on cots beside the bed. Tuesday morning, the day after Samantha's testimony, the Judiciary Committee voted 9–5 to confirm Gus's nomination.

At seven o'clock Wednesday morning Samantha awoke. In a few hours the full Senate would vote. There had been no further word from Larry.

Michelle said, "How'd you sleep?"

"Wow. I feel really strange." Heavily sedated, she had done almost nothing but sleep since Monday night.

Michelle sat on the edge of Samantha's bed and held her hand.

Samantha glanced around, her eyes watery and dazed.

"Where are we, anyway?"

"We're in the hospital," Gus said, standing by the bed, "but you're okay."

"Oh, yeah, I remember."

She looked at Gus, her eyes clearing. "Did they vote yet?"

"The Senate votes today."

"I guess it doesn't matter. They don't even have to vote now, right?"

Gus said, "Oh, they'll vote. And we'll win."

Samantha looked at Michelle.

"I want to go home."

"We'll leave soon, honey. They just want you to rest."

"I've *been* resting. I just woke up."

The phone rang.

Gus picked it up.

He glanced uneasily at Michelle, then at Samantha.

"Samantha, it's Larry."

She beamed and reached for the phone. Then she pulled her hand back.

"What can I tell him?"

Michelle said, "Tell him the truth."

Gus gave her the phone, and he and Michelle left the room.

Twenty minutes later, when they cracked the door and looked in, she was off the phone. Her eyes were red and tears streaked her cheeks.

Michelle said, "What happened, honey?"

"Nothing. He said he's worried about me, how am I, how long will I be in the hospital. He asked me if I still like it here being with you."

"What did you tell him?"

"I said I loved it with you. I do love it with you."

She wiped her eyes and didn't speak. Michelle said, "How is he?"

"Oh, great. He's really excited. He's got a new job. He's going to stop playing in bars and nightclubs."

"What's he going to do?"

"He's playing with a chamber orchestra. They're going on a tour around the world. It's like a new life."

Michelle glanced at Gus. "What did you say?"

"I said I thought it was great."

"Will he be coming here?"

"He said if I wanted he'd come and get me. But how can he do that? He's in this orchestra and they're going around the world. I don't want him to get me. I want to stay here."

"What else did he say?"

"He said Doreen got the name of his hotel from a reporter. She called him and said she wanted us both back, me and him, and if he agreed, the court would have to give me back to them."

Michelle's eyes filled with anger.

"She told him she had a deal with a newspaper and to write a book and maybe a movie, but it'd look better if we were all back together, so if he came back she'd give him some of the money."

Michelle's mouth was open.

Gus said, "What did Larry tell her?"

"He told her to forget it, she wasn't going to get me or him. He said what did I want to do. If I wanted, he'd find someplace I could stay and go to school while he was on tour, or he could quit the orchestra, not travel all the time, change jobs. But I know he can't do that. And anyway . . ."

They waited. After a minute, Michelle said, "And anyway?"

"And anyway, I don't want—I just want to stay here."

An hour later breakfast arrived. When she had finished eating, Samantha said, "When are they going to vote?"

Gus said, "Mr. Rothman will call us."

Someone had put a TV at the nurses' station. Gus could hear it faintly. Rothman had urged him to watch the vote at the White House. "The President will be there. Watch it with him. Or I'll come to the hospital and watch it there with you and Michelle."

Gus didn't want to watch it with anyone, didn't want any White House people hanging around the hospital.

"Just call me, Phil. Tell me how it all comes out."

Phil didn't have to. Gus heard a cheer from the hallway. He glanced at Michelle. She said, "Go see."

By the time he got there, it was all but over. The Vice President looked down at a paper, looked up, leaned into his microphone, and said, "Yeas, fifty-six. Nays, forty-four. The nomination of Augustus Parham of Alabama to be an associate justice of the U.S. Supreme Court is hereby confirmed."

Nurses, doctors, orderlies turned toward Gus, smiling and laughing, and began to applaud.

He said, "Thank you. Thank you very much. Thank you for taking such good care of Samantha."

He walked back toward the room. Something, perhaps the doctors and nurses, the medical surroundings, drew him suddenly into a distant memory. He was driving past the clinic on Bakersfield Boulevard, caught in the violence of a demonstration and despairing at the loss of his child. If someone had told him then that the day would come, in this life, when he would be with that child, he would not have believed it. And yet here he was, with Samantha. He felt a sudden warmth, gripped the hand rail along the wall, and closed his eyes. His body filled with an intense, luxurious heat, the heat of the love of a Father for his Son. He wanted it never to stop. It was a joy so overwhelmingly intense that—

"Judge Parham? Are you all right?"

He opened his eyes. It was a young nurse, pretty, grinning.

"Yes, thank you, I'm fine."

"You're red."

"Really?"

"You look sunburned."

"I'm fine."

He knew what it was like to have lost a child, and to have that child handed back. And he knew that it was not just the child who had been restored. For the first time in thirteen years, Gus felt forgiven, cleansed, and free.

"Yes, thanks. I'm fine."

"Well, anyway, congratulations."

He smiled at her. "Thanks."

He felt hands on his back, turned, and saw Michelle and Samantha. For two minutes the three of them stood there, hugging, eyes closed, an island in the stream of doctors and nurses hurrying past them in the hall.